Marius' Mules X

Fields of Mars

by S. J. A. Turney

1st Edition

"Marius' Mules: nickname acquired by the legions after the general Marius made it standard practice for the soldier to carry all of his kit about his person."

For Liz and Mark.

I would like to thank Jenny for her help in making Marius' Mules ten legible. Thanks also to my beautiful wife Tracey for her support, and my two children Marcus and Callie for keeping me smiling during my busiest times.

Thanks also to Garry and Dave for the cover work.

Cover photos by Hannah Haynes, courtesy of Paul and Garry of the Deva Victrix Legio XX. Visit http://www.romantoursuk.com/ to see their excellent work.

Cover design by Dave Slaney.

Many thanks to the above for their skill and generosity.

All internal maps are copyright the author of this work.

Also by S. J. A. Turney:

Continuing the Marius' Mules Series

Marius' Mules I: The Invasion of Gaul (2009)
Marius' Mules II: The Belgae (2010)
Marius' Mules III: Gallia Invicta (2011)
Marius' Mules IV: Conspiracy of Eagles (2012)
Marius' Mules V: Hades' Gate (2013)
Marius' Mules VI: Caesar's Vow (2014)
Marius' Mules: Prelude to War (2014)
Marius' Mules VII: The Great Revolt (2014)
Marius' Mules VIII: Sons of Taranis (2015)
Marius' Mules IX: Pax Gallica (2016)

The Praetorian Series

The Great Game (2015)
The Price of Treason (2015)
Eagles of Dacia (Autumn 2017)

The Ottoman Cycle

The Thief's Tale (2013)
The Priest's Tale (2013)
The Assassin's Tale (2014)
The Pasha's Tale (2015)

Tales of the Empire

Interregnum (2009)
Ironroot (2010)
Dark Empress (2011)
Insurgency (2016)
Invasion (2017)

Roman Adventures (Children's Roman fiction with Dave Slaney)

Crocodile Legion (2016)
Pirate Legion (Summer 2017)

Short story compilations & contributions:

Tales of Ancient Rome vol. 1 - S.J.A. Turney (2011)
Tortured Hearts vol 1 - Various (2012)
Tortured Hearts vol 2 - Various (2012)
Temporal Tales - Various (2013)
A Year of Ravens - Various (2015)
A Song of War – Various (Oct 2016)

For more information visit http://www.sjaturney.co.uk/
or http://www.facebook.com/SJATurney
or follow Simon on Twitter @SJATurney

Maps

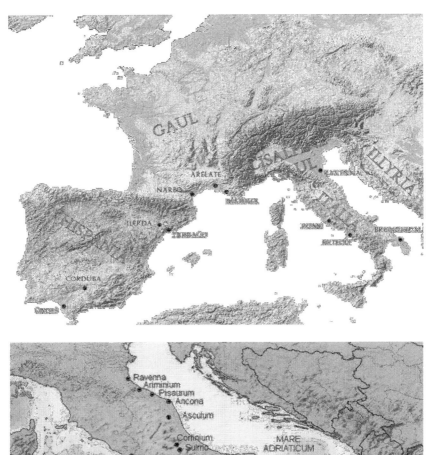

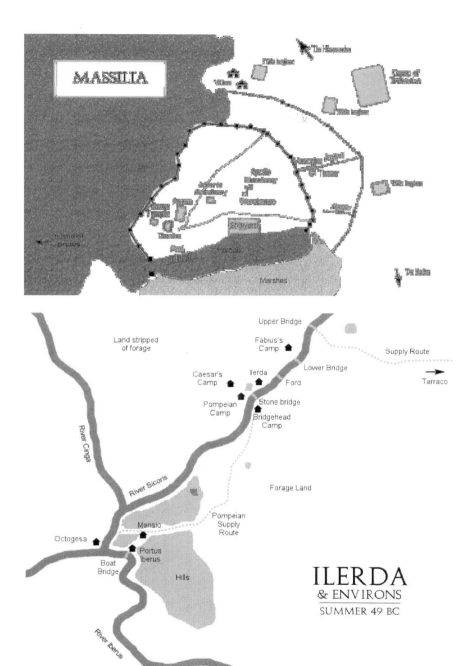

MASSILIA

To Hispania

Villa legion

Camp of Trebonius

Villa

Villa legion

Villa legion

Island of Druids

Shipyard

Harbour

Marshes

To Italia

Upper Bridge

Land stripped
of forage

Fabius's
Camp

Supply Route

Caesar's
Camp

Ilerda

Lower Bridge

Ford

Tarraco

Pompeian
Camp

Stone bridge

Bridgehead
Camp

River Cinga

River Sicoris

Forage Land

Pompeian
Supply
Route

Mansio

Octogesa

Portus
Iberus

Boat
Bridge

Hills

River Iberus

ILERDA
& ENVIRONS
SUMMER 49 BC

Prologue

FRONTO kicked irritably at an errant stone, which skittered along the wooden boards of the walkway and disappeared into the azure water with a plop. The motion of the kick momentarily sent him off-balance on the slippery timbers and he had to grab one of the waist-high wooden piles to prevent himself following the guilty pebble into the water.

Why Caesar would choose such a place was beyond him. Almost a decade ago, when he had first marched north with the general to chastise the Helvetii on the first leg of a campaign that had taken nearly a quarter of his life now, he and the Tenth had been camped close to Cremona in their winter training quarters. Cremona was sensible. It was a walled, thriving little town deep in the flat arable lands of northern Italia. Food and goods were abundant. It was on a river with good fishing. It was on a trade route – two actually – which meant there was always access to whatever you needed.

And Caesar had traditionally held his court in Aquileia during his time as Proconsul of Cisalpine Gaul. Aquileia. Flat and abundant. Arable land and farmers. Trade from east and west and every amenity.

What *Ravenna* had to offer was beyond him. Ravenna, which he'd never had cause to visit during his long life, was on no great trade route, save the long coast road which ran close by. It had plenty of flat land. It was just that a great deal of it was several feet below the water, either in the form of troublesome marshes that provided endless insects or small lagoons that came up by surprise. There was plenty of fish, mind. Too *much*, if you asked Fronto.

And no walls. You couldn't wall Ravenna. The whole place sprawled across the lagoons in two equally ill-conceived forms, to Fronto's mind. Each small island in the lagoon was packed with houses and shops, almost like a self-contained village, usually close enough to the next occupied island that a man could throw a stone from one to another. But in recent years, what passed for the town's council had engaged on a project of drainage, draining some areas of marsh and filling others in, all in an attempt to marshal these various population centres together into one great whole.

The place already was one great hole, Fronto grunted to himself as he peered across at the other ridiculous form of housing. There was not enough room on the islands for the entire population – hence partially the drainage and consolidation scheme – but that had led to numerous families building their houses on wooden piles sunk into the shallow water and raised above the lapping surface on timber platforms. As was almost always the case with constructing something in a swamp, most of these had acquired a lean over the years. Some almost critically, such that it must be hard walking about inside without falling over. These houses were connected with the land by wooden walkways that resembled jetties.

The whole place stank of salt and of decaying fish. The place either leaned, was slowly sinking, or was slippery and dangerous. Fronto hated a lot of things. He was free and unabashed with his hatred. He had to admit that Ravenna was coming close to the top of his list, along with the red, itching insect bites he had acquired from the place.

But, he had to admit, there were three advantages for Caesar in Ravenna.

One: it was in his safe territory, Cisalpine Gaul, a longstanding supporter of his.

Two: it was very close to the coast road and to the border with Italia proper, and so very handy for communication.

Three: no one in their right mind would seek to attack him there.

And given the vast swathe of enemies the general had picked up in his time, this last was always worthy of consideration. And as for communication? Well, that had certainly come into play over the winter. Endless to-ing and fro-ing of messengers to Rome, to friends, enemies and those neutral folk playing their dangerous game.

Actually, it was much the same conversation going on over and over again, and just over a week ago Caesar had sent his latest proposal. His latest 'last chance'. That both he and Pompey lay down their commands and put their fate in the hands of the Roman people. Of course, Caesar was the darling of the population, while Pompey could call on the senate's backing, so there was little chance the fat, knob-nosed old psychopath would allow those terms to be agreed.

Behind Fronto, Hortensius snorted.

'Need a hand there, Marcus?'

'No thank you,' he snapped back as he skittered on along the damp timbers toward their destination. The new year had begun only days ago, and winter still gripped Cisalpine Gaul in her glittering, chilly hand. Nothing was safe to walk on, sit on, or stand on.

Ahead stood the only part of Ravenna that could be considered any sort of hub, where a tiny forum square was surrounded by important-looking buildings, which meant that they didn't lean too much. The largest of these buildings – a basilica of sorts – had been taken on by Caesar as his headquarters while in the city. The nobles and mercantile class of the place had fawned around their proconsul, granting his every wish. And so most of this central island was temporarily under his command.

Of course, they fawned after the general largely because he was here and with a legion close enough to smell the boot oil and the late night farting contests. Fronto had no doubt that had Caesar been away for a while, their vocal opinions would change a great deal. They would be less respectful about a man who was these days often seen as opposed to the authority of the Roman senate. Fronto wondered what was said behind closed doors, and how many of them kept a knife by the bed just in case.

The smoke pouring from the flues around the large building's roof at least suggested that the place would be warm, which was more than could be said for the house that Fronto, Galronus and Masgava shared. Galronus would be there already, as would most of them. Fronto would be late, of course, but there was a level of tradition to keep up here, after all. If he were to be on time for Caesar's meetings the old man would expect it on *every* occasion. Besides, he could blame Hortensius this time.

He *was* intrigued, though. It would be nice to see Brutus again.

Decimus Junius Brutus Albinus was one of the few men on Caesar's staff throughout most of the past decade who Fronto felt he could trust implicitly and liked unreservedly. He'd missed Brutus' company since the younger man had been off in Rome conveying messages and carrying out duties both official, and less than official, on behalf of the general. News of Brutus' arrival at Ravenna had set tongues wagging in the past hour.

The small square was largely empty at this early hour and the air clear and crisp, since the sun was yet to climb high enough to warm the lagoons and marshes and release the clouds of mist that would envelop Ravenna for most of the morning. Two of Caesar's Praetorian guardsmen stood at the door of the large building, though they did not move to stop Fronto and Hortensius. Normally, Fronto would challenge them on their lack of care in letting *anyone* past without a password, but they were late and he knew Caesar well enough to know that the man had likely given the guards specific orders to chivvy him on.

Sure enough, as he entered the large hall with its twin rows of pillars and its statue at the far end that supposedly represented Jupiter, but looked to Fronto suspiciously like many of the statues he had seen in Gaul, the staff of Caesar's province and army were all gathered.

'Good of you to join us, Fronto,' the general said, looking up from a table spread with a map and tokens. 'I trust we did not interrupt your beauty sleep too much? We know how much you need it.'

There was a ripple of chuckles around the room, some genuine, some dutiful. Caesar had aged since the day he had led the legions north against the Helvetii. Those who saw him regularly probably did not notice so much, but when you really looked at him and dredged your memory, you could see the difference. The skin had become like parchment, the lines more pronounced, with worry rather than humour. The eyes were more deep-set and the form slightly more aquiline. And the hair? Well, it was now a flecked white-grey and began somewhere around the top of his ears, receding by the year. Still, there was a power and an energy about the man, and no dullness of the wit in those sunken eyes. Only a fool would think Caesar less of a power because he had aged. If anything, Fronto would take *more* care around him.

'My apologies, Caesar. Hortensius' rather dull slave has lost his belt and so he came to borrow one from me. We assumed we would be better a few moments late than on time but with his tunic flapping around his ankles.'

The challenge in his eyes met Caesar's and held them for a moment, before the general waved the matter aside with his palm. He tapped the table a couple of times and straightened. Fronto peered at the great chart. The tokens on the map had moved for the first time in weeks.

The Seventh, Eleventh and Fourteenth legions were still scattered around central Gaul in the Aedui and Arverni region, the Sixth, Ninth and his own beloved Tenth were near Narbo in the west of the province, close to Hispania, and the Thirteenth where they had been all winter: half a mile from Ravenna, camped close to the road. But the Fifth, Eighth and Twelfth had been moved. They were no longer in the north and east of Gaul – Vesontio, Samarobriva and Durocortorum. Names that evoked memories of slaughter and trial for Fronto. No, now those three veteran legions were in the valley of the Rhodanus, close to the Alps. Close enough to march into Italia in days if called. Had news of *that* reached the senate yet? A provocation, for sure. Fronto tore his gaze from the map as Decimus Brutus stepped into the open space. He looked tired, and not just from travel.

'Now that we're all listening,' Caesar gestured to the younger man, 'what news of Rome?'

Brutus sighed. 'Little has changed, and that little not for the better, sadly, General. Your former legates Galba and Rufus were considerably less receptive to your overtures than we had hoped. Galba had stood for the consulate this year, but he feels that his connection to you cost him his chance and will likely forever deny him high office. And Rufus, while he does not believe you should be prosecuted and has spoken against that, refuses to countenance any move against what he calls 'the legitimate senate'. They have closed their doors to us.'

'What of Marcus Calidius?' Caesar prompted.

'He does speak against trouble, but will not speak directly for you, General. Though he did try to persuade for a bill to send

Pompey from Rome to his province and remove all the growing military presence in Italia. He believes that if that happened, a general solution could be achieved. He might be correct, but we will never know. He was shouted down by so many senators I went deaf for hours. The consul Marcellus – the *elder* Marcellus, now – was as vocal as his cousin and brother in opposing you, and the senators fawn to him just as they did to them. I bear a message from the senate, General. I do not know its contents, but they will not be favourable.'

'Read it.'

Brutus shuffled uncomfortably. 'That is not my place, General. And this may be something for private consumption.'

Caesar shook his head. 'Every man here has seen the pains to which I have gone to try and reconcile with the senate, and that I am blocked at every move by the spiteful and the short-sighted. There will be nothing the senate has to say to me that I need to hide. Read it.'

The younger officer cracked the seal on the scroll and unfurled it, drawing breath.

'To the Proconsul of Cisalpine Gaul, Gaius Julius Caesar, greetings. The senate has met in session under the Consuls Claudius Marcellus Major and Cornelius Lentulus to consider the troublesome matter of your replacement and the military situation in the north. It is the decision of this senate of Rome that you are required to disband all your legions before the Kalends of Februarius, when your place will be taken in Cisalpine Gaul by the Praetor Marcus Considius Nonianus, and the new province of Transalpine Gaul will be governed by Lucius Domitius Ahenobarbus.'

'*Domitius Ahenobarbus?*' coughed solid Trebonius, leaning against one of the columns, interrupting in surprise. 'The man is a dangerous one to put in command of a province. Headstrong and unpredictable. He will probably cause a new Gallic revolt within the year.'

There were nods from the knowledgeable few in the room.

'But he is favoured by the senate, a friend of Marcellus and his lips are almost stuck to Pompey's arse,' Fronto muttered, earning a few humourless chuckles.

6

'The senate goes on,' Brutus said loudly, over the murmur. 'If you do not accede to the will of the senate in disbanding your army and returning to Rome, this august body will consider you an enemy of the Roman state, with all the disadvantages that implies. This order signed and sealed this day, one day after the Kalends of Januarius, by Furcus, secretary to Considius Nonianus on behalf of the Senate and the People of Rome.'

'It's official, then,' Fronto sighed. 'No more bandying of words. You have a month and then you're at war with the senate.'

'No longer a month,' Caesar replied. 'Three weeks now. They wasted no time. The consuls had been in power for less than a day before the senate produced their ultimatum. All aristocratic channels for me in Rome are cut. Pompey and the consuls have everyone cowed. The people will still support me, but *they* do not control Rome.'

Brutus shrugged. 'Marcus Antonius and Quintus Cassius tried to prevent it, as did I, but it was like three pebbles trying to dam the Tiber, Caesar. And as for the people, yes they do love you, but not even the lowliest beggar will support you at the moment, for Pompey has flooded Rome with his retired veterans and those on furlough. No one dare speak for you in case the man standing next to him is a veteran killer who owes Pompey his career. You simply would not believe the tension and discomfort in the city.'

Brutus gestured to the map. 'It may even be that word has reached the city of your army moving south from Gaul. Rumour in Rome places four of your legions in Cisalpine Gaul, not one. I refuted it whenever I heard such a thing, but now I see that they are close enough that they could piss on Cisalpine Gaul from their camp latrines. Pompey has been raising levies all around Latium, and his military power in Italia grows, even with his seven veteran legions far off in Hispania. And the tribunes have quit Rome in fear of their lives. Marcus Antonius is rumoured to be in Ostia, where he can take ship urgently if required. The situation is dire, Caesar. I can see no way forward that does not involve drawing a blade.'

Titus Labienus, long one of Caesar's most important lieutenants and a considered and cautious man shook his head. 'It cannot come to that. Drawing a sword on fellow Romans is a damnable idea. Besides, there is little chance you would manage to launch any campaign against the senate from this province. Ravenna may *seem* safe, but there are military ships along this coast loyal to the senate rather than you, and politicians here and across the province who have supported you, but will never do so against the senate. No noble or official of Cisalpine Gaul will follow you into a war against Rome.'

'I think you overestimate their loyalty to a senate who cares little for them,' Caesar replied quietly. 'Who was it who granted rights and citizenship to their towns? Me. Who arrested the deputation from Comum and stripped them of their citizenship? That same senate. Cisalpine Gaul is not Latium, Titus.'

'Regardless, there will be chaos here if you leave the province and march on Rome. And I for one will not cross that boundary with sword drawn and the names of senators on my killing lips.'

Caesar rounded on Labienus, and Fronto expected anger, but was surprised to see only sad acceptance. 'I would not ask you to betray your conscience, Titus. You have been one of the rocks upon which my campaigns have been built. But I would not have you stand in Rome against me, either. Report to the legions in Transalpine Gaul and take command of that force.'

Labienus nodded and stepped back.

'He's right about one thing, General,' Fronto said. 'If you march away from Ravenna on Rome, this city will be in chaos. Some will support you, but others will not. And for all your munificence, I think you are not seeing the province for what it is. They may have been loyal to you, but thus far, you have *been* Rome. If you turn on Rome, I would not give a denarius for their loyalty.'

'Then it will have to be done carefully,' Caesar murmured. 'But the fact remains that the senate have given me a month, and I cannot accede to their demands. By Februarius, we will be at war with the senate.'

Chapter One

10th of Januarius - Ravenna

FRONTO stood on one of the few points of Ravenna that was high enough to grant a view of anything but swamp and the roiling white blanket of marsh fog and watched the figures moving along the coast road like ghosts in the mist. Maybe thirty men in just tunics and boots, they could easily be fishmongers or wheelwrights or beggars, or even slaves. But if he could see them up close, he knew he would recognise the shape of gladius and pugio under padded linen or jutting from packs.

For these were no common citizens, but men of the Thirteenth Legion in civilian attire, and they were veterans of more than half a decade of brutal war. Each man was the hardest and strongest the republic could breed. They padded off south in small groups, chatting and separating as they moved, some filtering in among merchants with their wagons of vegetables, others stopping by the roadside for bread and cheese. By the time they were half a mile away from Ravenna they would be indistinguishable from the common citizenry on the road.

Just like the three hundred who had already departed in small, nondescript groups that morning. Their centurions and even the tribune assigned to that cohort would be there among them somewhere, making for Ariminium.

Ariminium! Ten miles inside the borders of Italia. *Senatorial territory*. The first major town south from the border of Cisalpine Gaul. Ariminium had a small garrison – a few military ships in port and a reasonable force of veterans who the town's ordo could call upon if it felt the need for defence. Certainly if Caesar sent the Thirteenth marching south they would find the place manned against them. But a cohort of veterans filtering into the town as ordinary citizens and then securing it quietly and subtly?

He shivered. Those last few departing men did not look to be much, but they were as good as a spear cast against the senate. They were a declaration of war.

'What of the rest of the legion?' Galronus asked quietly at his shoulder.

'They are armed and ready. They just await Caesar's order to march. This is it, my friend. What I've feared for so long. Despite everything I've said for a decade, I find myself solidly on the side of Caesar in defiance of my own republic. And while I should feel like a betrayer and full of guilt and self-loathing for what we're doing, I actually feel oddly proud.'

'You could be Remi, with that attitude,' Galronus chuckled.

'Where is Caesar?'

The Remi prince shrugged. 'He rose early and went to the baths as though nothing untoward was happening. He's held his morning meeting of clients and is going to attend the fights in honour of some local goddess this afternoon.'

'He's packing the day full,' Fronto muttered. 'What with the banquet tonight.'

Galronus nodded. 'I am surprised at the number of people who are attending, given the short notice.'

'The power of curiosity,' Fronto snorted. 'All the important folk of Ravenna will know of the senate's demands by now and will want to know Caesar's plans. And they will want to look supportive as long as the general remains in town. They will have discarded any other plans and rearranged to be here tonight.'

'Well,' Galronus stretched, 'what are our plans for the day?'

'Are you packed and ready?'

'Isn't everyone?'

Fronto nodded. 'Well if Caesar is indulging in mundanities to keep the populace unawares, then perhaps we should too. I could certainly do with a massage, and I haven't seen a good fight for weeks.'

* * *

The room hummed with conversation and the air quivered with strange tension, though that tautness had been gradually relaxing with every cup of wine consumed. Fronto had watched with appreciation as the general carried out the subtlest of manoeuvres, more cunning than any battlefield strategy he had ever carried out.

Incredibly subtle. In every fine detail.

The wine was Rhodian, from a vineyard that was hailed in some quarters and shunned in others, known for the intoxicating strength of their brew – a wine that Fronto's mother had called 'the choice of a vulgar drunkard', often in reference to his father. It was served in smaller jars than usual, so that the jugs of water with which to cut it appeared larger. The drinking vessels were not the best glassware as one might expect, but fine red ceramic, embossed with the forms of gods. Hard to see what proportions were mixed in such a cup. Fronto had watched Caesar's slaves at work throughout the evening and estimated even conservatively that each guest had already consumed twice the alcohol he believed he had. There was a vagueness to the expressions of the attendees, and many had begun to giggle at times, while others were starting to drool or fall asleep, their gentle, content snores adding to the background noise.

Then there was the seating. Rather than placing his officers at specific tables and separating the groups, Caesar had filtered them in here and there among the important figures of Ravenna, so that the whole was a good mix.

The entertainment, too. A wiry Thracian lyre player accompanied by a flautist at the far end, strumming and tootling in a constant stream of melody. Three Arabian dancers, lithe and sinuous, moving in time to the music before the only blank wall with no door, drawing the hungry gazes of the attendees. Two wrestlers throwing each other around before a third wall. The fourth side empty, drawing no gaze.

'And Cicero, standing atop a step, proclaimed "I was talking to the cow",' Caesar said loudly, drawing laughter from those around him, wine bursting from the nose of an unfortunate and rather intoxicated member of the city's council.

Fronto's gaze panned around the room. Almost half the seats were now empty, and the growing number of absences had thus far gone entirely unnoticed. Brutus was sitting between an enormously fat man who was already dozing off with his hands folded across his belly, and a strangely angular man who was arguing with his other neighbour, hammering his wine cup on the table repeatedly

11

in a staccato punctuation of the discourse. The younger officer caught Fronto's eye and gave a miniscule nod.

Unnoticed by the men beside him, Brutus rose from his seat and padded off to a door at the rear of the room, in that bare, unwatched wall. The buzz of social engagement went on. Fronto carefully poured himself another wine, not trusting the slaves who were busily drugging the locals. Despite his prodigious capacity for wine, even he was being relatively careful tonight. This was not a night to be drunk.

He sipped down that cup and the next at a careful, sedate pace, and the next, too, as the hours passed. He watched Hortensius leave quietly and unobserved. And Trebonius too. And Pollio. Galronus had been one of the first to go, and Labienus was not attending, since he was already well on his way back to Gaul and his distant posting. A quick count revealed only four of them left. Still, the guests paid little attention. In fairness, by this time most of them were either asleep or were so deep in their cups you could have driven a siege tower over them and they wouldn't notice.

Even as he wondered when someone would twig what was happening, he saw Curio, who had so loved this afternoon's games, rise, stretch, nod slightly and then slip out of the room. Surely someone would soon question this? Certainly when Caesar left, at least?

Just Hirtius, Caesar and himself now.

Another cup of wine.

Hirtius was struggling to lose the attention of an old local who was waffling drunkenly into his ear. Fronto had no such troubles. The men to either side of him had tried to engage him in conversation early in the evening, but Fronto was long practiced at offending people. He had called Cisalpine Gaul a 'career graveyard' in conversation with one, following which he'd seen only the man's back all night. The other had lauded the local fish – he seemed to be some sort of piscine magnate – and Fronto had replied that fish made him fart. To add substance to his argument he had done his best to engulf the man in a cloud of noxious gas numerous times during the night and now the man would not even look at him.

Finally, the noisome local next to Hirtius turned away at some salacious comment about the dancing girls, and as soon as his back was turned, Hirtius rose and slipped from the room unnoticed.

Caesar gave Fronto the merest of nods. With a grin, the former legate glanced at the men to either side, who had not looked at him in over an hour, rose, drained his cup and sauntered from the room. He reached the side door and slipped through into the dim room beyond, where he paused and, his curiosity piqued, glanced back within. Caesar was now the only one of them left in the room, and still the locals revelled drunkenly on, barely conscious, unaware that over a score of men had left the room over the last two hours.

'Friends,' Caesar said with a smile, rising from his seat. 'I have a treat for you, specially to mark the occasion and to give thanks for the hospitality the ordo of Ravenna has shown for my staff and I. Fresh from Tusculum and, before that, Rome, where they have gained an unsurpassed reputation, I give you the "Naked melody of Antioch".'

A grin slid slowly across Fronto's face as his attention turned to five stunningly attractive Syrian beauties wearing only jewellery and flimsy netting who wafted into the room gracefully, bending and whirling in a manner that must require a great deal of stretching beforehand. As though attached by strings, every eye in the room moved with those figures. Caesar paused only long enough to make sure the remaining wakeful audience was captivated, then straightened and spoke to the man beside him – something about using the latrines.

A moment later the general passed through the doorway and was suddenly all activity.

'Marcus, good. Time to move. Come, now.'

Fronto found himself all-but swept along in the general's wake as the older man hurried through the room and along the short corridor that led to a rear door which opened onto a narrow street that led off the small forum square. They paused briefly there to gather up their cloaks from the table beside the door. The night air was more than a little chilly as the general pulled the door open to admit a blast of winter.

'All very masterful, General,' Fronto said as they emerged into the darkness and turned toward the archway next to a bakery across the road, 'but even dulled as they are, it will buy you only moments. An hour at most.'

Caesar gave him an infuriating knowing grin as they passed beneath the arch to where Pollio and Brutus awaited with the carriage, horses nickering and ready to leave, breath pluming in the cold night air. There was no crowd of a score of officers lurking in the archway. Most of the others must already be on the way. He glanced this way and that, something unseen making his spine tingle.

His heart jumped as he realised they were not alone. Shadowy figures were emerged from the alleyways nearby. Two of them – career criminals, Fronto decided from the look of them – bowed. Neither looked trustworthy, like the worst resident of the Subura, and Fronto's hand automatically went to his pouch at the sight of them.

'All is ready?' Caesar asked the two men.

'It is.'

'Then look to your tasks. For Rome. For the future. And, of course, for the money.'

Teeth flashed in grins in the gloom as the men melted away.

'Insurance?' Fronto asked quietly.

'I think the local ordo will be disorganised and confused until the morning anyway,' Caesar replied. 'Then they will find none of the ships in port ready to sail and no sign of the city's usual couriers. Any message sent by road is extremely unlikely to make it past the first milestone. Effectively, no news will travel faster than us.'

'This is why I don't like to play you at Latrunculi, General.'

'Unprepared men lose wars, Fronto, and that is what this now is. Since the First Cohort of the Thirteenth wandered south this morning dressed as farmers, this became a war. And the moment *we* cross into Italia it becomes official. Now is the time to back out if you cannot countenance such a thing, for the Italian border is only twenty miles to the south.'

Fronto swallowed as he climbed into the carriage alongside the others and slid into the seat next to Brutus. 'I think the time for doubt has now passed, Caesar,' he declared, reaching down by his seat to where his military boots sat along with his belt and the sword with the beautiful embossed orichalcum hilt. Gripping the handle the truth sank into him that unless something unexpected happened, in the coming days he might be required to push that point into the soft flesh of a fellow Roman.

'Agreed,' Caesar nodded. 'Now let us hope that when faced with our advance, the senate sees sense and offers terms. I have no wish to march into Rome like Sulla, though I will do so if pushed into it.'

The driver geed the horses and the carriage creaked forward, emerging from the archway into the street. Fronto could see already dark figures at work destroying one of the wooden walkways that connected the islands. If the general's hired criminals were working like this everywhere, within the hour Ravenna would be a mess, unable to function. Caesar would be able to amble slowly across the border like a man out for a stroll and still stay ahead of the tidings of his advance.

He had burned his bridges – figuratively speaking, and almost literally too – with Ravenna. The ordo would be unlikely to support him now, but that was immaterial. In the coming days either Pompey would crush any advance and their little insurrection would be over, or Caesar would stand triumphant in Rome, at which point Ravenna would hurriedly backtrack and claim they had always supported him.

The game had begun.

* * *

'Are we not going the wrong way?'

Caesar turned his infuriating expression on Fronto in reply – that expression the former legate knew all too well and which seemed to say "Really, Fronto, have you not figured it out yet?" It was an expression Fronto had seen often enough in his life that he was able these days to resist rising to the bait. He waited, and Caesar rolled his eyes.

'Misdirection and misinformation, Marcus. If you learn anything from daily dealings with the senate and men like Pompey, Cato and Crassus it is never to meet their expectations. Always misinform and surprise. This morning, while the cohort was moving off slowly to the south, I sent messages via the couriers to Aquileia to prepare my villa. No one would admit to infiltrating the courier system, of course, but I will give you your body weight in denarii if the information in my letters wasn't known to the council of Ravenna by noon at the latest.'

'How do you play more than one game at a time without getting confused,' Fronto grumbled.

'Always have more than once dice, Marcus. The messages served three purposes. Firstly, they kept the ordo's spies busy looking at my correspondence and therefore away from the camp where the soldiers were leaving. Secondly, it gave context to tonight's social engagement. They believe it was intended as a fond farewell as I prepare to depart Ravenna...'

'Which it was.'

'Which it was, yes, though not in the way they suspected. And thirdly it adds to the confusion of the next twenty four hours. When they know we have slipped out of town, they will not immediately worry. Even Pompey's spies in the town – and it would be naïve of me indeed to presume that there were none – will simply think I tired of the party and returned to Aquileia, just as my missives suggested. Some suspicion will naturally fall on me when it transpires that no ship will be ready to sail for hours, their captains and helmsmen and musicians are all missing or drunk or both, and that the port records have vanished into the bargain.'

'Your lowlifes were clearly busy during our gathering.'

'I could not possibly comment,' Caesar smiled. 'When it becomes clear that the sea is of little use, my opposition will look to land exits and will discover that many bridges have collapsed during the night and that banditry is suddenly rife in the surrounding countryside. Again, suspicion will fall on me, but there is no concrete evidence. And word will be that the only coach to leave Ravenna at the appropriate time made off north along the Via Popilia in the direction of Aquileia.'

'Does your brain ever ache,' Fronto muttered.

Caesar smiled irritatingly. 'By the time anyone who opposes me in Ravenna has any idea what is happening and manages to mobilise, even if they do not immediately go the wrong way, we will be well and truly set on our course. I do not like to leave things to chance if I have the option to prepare.'

Fronto shook his head. He was a soldier, straightforward and blunt, if clever in his own way, but no twisted politician like

Caesar. As soon as it had been decided that they would move and that the time had come to stand against those bloody minded enemies in the senate, Fronto had expected Caesar to call the Thirteenth to order and march south with trumpets blaring, announcing his intention for all the world to hear. It was the soldier's way. And it was known to work. For a start, it displayed your determination and set any less-than-confident enemy to quaking in their boots.

Not so, Caesar. He had looked at things and decided that he would need to secure his route as he went. The most important – indeed, the *critical* – bastion would be Ariminium. That large coastal port town thirty miles south would be a necessary peg in the works. It marked a meeting point of roads, where the Via Aemilia, Via Popilia and Via Flaminia met. As such, it was a hub of communications. It was a garrisoned town at the edge of senatorial territory, and it often played host to a number of military ships.

If Caesar had marched south and Ariminium had taken against him, closing its gates, he would either have to march on, leaving a defended enemy strongpoint at his rear, or get bogged down in a probably lengthy siege. Neither would be a good way to start the campaign, just having crossed the border and declared war.

No. Caesar had decided that Ariminium had to fall swiftly and without a fight. That would give him a good supply base, and would present an example to the other towns on their route. Caesar could allow news to move ahead as to how easily the bastion of senatorial power on their northeast border simply fell into Caesar's hands. It would make many a councillor of other towns think twice about resisting.

The general was ever a dozen steps ahead of his opponents.

Fronto gazed out at the dark fields to their left and right. Low-lying farmland that periodically became too soggy to work. And the marshland only became more prevalent as you travelled north. Pollio began to hum a happy little tune, which seemed rather ill-fitting to Fronto in the circumstances and had a teeth-grindingly repetitive refrain. Fronto was almost reaching the point where he would have to ask the rodent-like officer to kindly shut up when the carriage suddenly veered off the main road and onto a rough track. The jerky, bouncing motion made it impossible for Pollio to carry his ditty, and the four men were silent as the vehicle lurched for a moment before reaching a gravelled section and settling down once more. Fronto caught sight of a sign marking the road as a route to a country estate, and a moment later the lake that lay just inland from Ravenna, a stagnant lagoon four miles long and two across, appeared on their left. They were turning now. Out of sight of Ravenna and two or three miles north of its extremities, they had now turned west. They would then veer south, following the lake on small roads, crossing another minor road, passing through the village of Sabis, and then making for Ariminium on a secondary route.

He watched from the carriage window as the view gradually changed, the position of the cold winter moon showing their rough orientation at all times. They gradually rounded the lake, Ravenna lying like a shadowy spider at the far end, reflected in the rather still surface of the water. They crossed several tracks and roads and, perhaps an hour after leaving the party, they passed through the village of Sabis, little more than a collection of a dozen houses surrounding a mansio, bath house and temple to Mercury, and then they were off on a good, paved road for a change, clattering toward Ariminium. It did not escape Fronto's notice that the village shared a name with the river where eight years ago he and Caesar had fought side by side with desperate legions against a Belgic ambush. They had won that day against all odds. Was that a sign, Fronto wondered?

He settled in with a sigh to welcome the onset of a headache as Pollio once again took up his jolly refrain, humming the same melody over and over again. Brutus was too busy peering out of the window to notice, and Caesar sat with arms folded and eyes closed. Anyone who didn't know him would think he was asleep. Fronto was under no such illusion.

They passed through another small community, which Brutus noted as Ad Novas, and a couple of miles further on Fronto was just working up to telling Pollio how irritating his humming was when Brutus suddenly sat upright, his face still at the window, and whistled through his teeth.

'Well now, there's a sight.'

Fronto, interested, leaned forward to look past Brutus out of that window. He blinked.

The men of the Thirteenth Legion, gleaming in the moonlight, all shadowy red and glinting silver, stood formed in a column across the fields to the side of the road. Behind them, their baggage train sat waiting, the artillery packed aboard for transport. The other officers who had been party guests were waiting here, too, including Galronus on his steed. A smattering of fog drifted among them from the frosted breath of four thousand men and half a thousand beasts. But the truly impressive and shiver-inducing thing was that they waited in absolute silence. Not even the jingling of a harness or the mutter of a cold soldier.

Fronto mentally mapped the area and realised that the legion must have set off not long before their own carriage, but the camp lay to the southwest of the town anyway. They could slip out of the far side and move off with little chance of observation, especially with Caesar's various lowlifes running interference for him.

'Where are we?' Fronto muttered, sitting up as the carriage rumbled to a halt.

'The place doesn't have a name,' Pollio replied. 'Just two farmhouses and a bridge. But unimpressive as it may be, it is somewhat auspicious.'

Fronto frowned, and Caesar nodded. His smile had gone and been replaced with a serious, even grave, expression.

'This, Fronto, is a small river – a stream, really – called the Rubicon.'

'We're at the Rubicon already?' Fronto said, his heart suddenly picking up pace. 'So soon?'

Caesar simply nodded again and opened the carriage door, slipping out and stepping down to the road. The others followed suit and peered at the bridge. Wide enough for a single cart and of old, pre-Roman stone, it was an ancient edifice, existing here long before some unnamed bureaucrat planned the road to cross it. And flowing beneath it, from right to left, a sluggish stream narrow enough that Fronto could comfortably plant a foot on either side and not stretch his groin. As a provincial border, it was unimpressive. As a declaration of war it was even less so.

The army waited on the north bank, a matter of paces from senatorial lands. The carriage sat eight horse-lengths from the crossing. And the gathering of four officers stopped short of the bridge, as though it might burn their feet.

A tribune walked his horse across from the lead elements of the Thirteenth and dismounted, approaching Caesar respectfully. The broad stripe on his sleeve marked him as the legion's senior tribune and, therefore, currently the de facto commander. The man had pale skin, made almost alabaster by the moonlight, dark, shining eyes, and severe, white-blond hair, which receded to either side, to leave an arrow of hair pointing down at his nose.

'Caesar,' the tribune greeted his proconsul.

'Salvius.' The general turned to the other three. 'Lucius Salvius Cursor, gentlemen, my adjutant and current commander of the Thirteenth. Salvius, this is Brutus, Pollio you know, and this is Fronto.'

The pale officer nodded, with not a hint of warmth about him, but then none of them were exactly grinning right now. There was a growing tension in the air you could almost chew. It was as though all the gods had stopped what they were doing and were watching this small bridge over an insignificant stream. Across the grass, and with some small relief, Fronto could see Galronus walking his horse toward them too.

'The men are ready to move on your command, General,' Salvius said. 'All wagons have been double-tethered for speed. Might I recommend your cavalry guard take the lead and the Thirteenth follow along behind your carriage? Your officer Ingenuus has been twitching at not being by your side.'

Caesar waved a hand as if to shush the man.

'General?'

'Patience, Salvius. We will move in due course. Give me a moment.'

'This is it, Caesar,' Fronto said quietly as Galronus arrived and slipped from his mount to stand beside them. The general simply nodded. 'Across that river,' Fronto went on, 'we are not only up against Pompey, but against the current senate, the consuls, and any nobiles and governors who choose to side with old knob-nose.'

Again, Caesar just nodded.

'Can we yet go back?' the general asked quietly.

'Sir?' Pollio frowned.

'I asked if we can yet go back,' the general repeated. 'Once we cross that little bridge, years of strife and conflict will come to a head, and it will only be settled with the sword. I know we all hope that the senate and the people will see sense and back down – capitulate and accede to my requests. And some might. It may even be that the consuls can be persuaded and the senate cowed. But as long as Pompey stands and breathes, he and I will be irreconcilable now. There will be no peace between us. So no matter who accedes, the decision will end on a blade. I ask one last time: Can we yet go back?'

Fronto bit his lip. He would love to have answered with a positive.

'Only by placing your neck in Pompey's hands,' Brutus said quietly.

'And subjecting yourself to prosecutions,' Pollio added.

Fronto sighed. 'That was not a real question, Gaius. If you believed there was even a chance this could be avoided, you would not have done what you've done. We are as committed to our course hovering here on the north bank as we will be when we stand on the far side.'

Caesar was nodding as Tribune Salvius coughed. 'The Thirteenth stand ready, Caesar. They thirst for action. Give them blood, General.'

Caesar's head snapped round.

'Blood? Not if it can be avoided, Salvius. Remember that the blood you advocate spilling is that of Romans, not some nameless hill tribe.' The fire went out in the general's eyes as quickly as it had kindled. 'But you are right. If we are to move, then we must move. The time has come.'

'The game proceeds, Caesar,' Fronto said quietly, his eyes raising momentarily to the sky where the gods watched.

'Then let the die be cast,' sighed Caesar. 'Bring me my horse. If I am to invade the republic, I will do it in honour and glory and at the head of my column, not skulking in a wagon any longer.'

An equisio hurried forward with the officers' horses. Pollio waved his away. 'I will stay in the carriage for the good of my rump,' he said with a half-smile. 'I'm not as young as I was and I appreciate every opportunity to not tan my arse to leather on the back of a horse.'

Brutus nodded. 'I too.'

Fronto reached for Bucephalus' reins. 'I for one am sick of the carriage and its endless melody.' He gestured to Caesar. 'I shall be at your back, sir, as always.'

'I can think of no one better to have there,' smiled Caesar. 'Very well then. Salvius? Look to the legion and send Aulus Ingenuus up front, but tell him no more than six riders. I do not want to be swamped by my own guard.'

They mounted as the others moved off. There was a long, pregnant pause during which Fronto, his breath pluming, rubbed Bucephalus' mane and neck lovingly, the ebony beast nickering quietly. He nodded to Galronus, wondering if the Remi noble felt the same ominous sense of fate as his Roman companions. The lead element of Ingenuus' Praetorian cavalry moved forward, half a dozen men following the young prefect as he approached and bowed to Caesar, expertly controlling his own horse with his knees and his three-fingered hand.

Fronto had to correct himself as he looked over the professional cavalry veteran. Ingenuus was no longer a young prefect. Almost a decade had passed since he had been blooded during the war against the Helvetii.

The Thirteenth began to move into position with a light jingling and a steady thump of feet on turf. Finally, they were all ready.

'The dubious honour is yours, Caesar,' Fronto said breathlessly.

The general nodded and, hesitantly, stepped his horse out onto the bridge. As they passed the narrow, snaking stream and moved on along the road from the south bank, making for the last ten mile stretch to Ariminium, Fronto felt the world shift subtly around him. He had spent his entire life serving Rome. In Hispania and in Gaul. He had upheld the republic's values and laws his whole life. Now, as an ageing officer, he was turning his back on all that in favour of a man he had more than once accused of megalomania. But whatever he might think of Caesar, the man was in the right here. He had been manoeuvred into a corner with only one path open to him. What man could do anything else?

Biting down on the feeling that a dozen generations of Falerii were glaring disapprovingly from their funerary urns, he walked his horse on into Italia at the head of their small army.

* * *

Ariminium was truly a fortress. Fronto had expected something powerful for he knew, as did every Roman who'd held a sword, that for two centuries Ariminium had been Rome's fortified north-eastern bastion against the Gauls. For much of that time it had been a city, and had been a powerful, walled one, too.

Ariminium was a stronghold. Positioned by the sea and in the crook of two rivers, it was entirely surrounded by water, reached by three bridges, facing north, west and south. The most impressive of these was the one that faced the travellers as they arrived – a huge long span of white arches marching across the blue torrent and leading them to a solid gatehouse in impressive heavy walls. Caesar's instincts had been correct. If they had to lay siege to this place it would be the work of months.

Fortunately, things seemed to be more welcoming than that.

The sun had begun to make an appearance, though as yet it was but a glow on the horizon, still the light was enough to show that the city gate lay open and that crowds thronged the walls. Not soldiers – evocati and garrison men armed with spears and catapults – but bakers and gardeners and scribes and slaves.

It was forced, clearly, and yet given the alternatives, the sight was as welcoming to Fronto as if it had been genuine.

'They seem happy,' Galronus noted, pointing at the waving figures on the battlements.

'*You* would wave with delight had you a sword point at your back. This is the work of the cohort Caesar sent here yesterday. The entire population of Ariminium on the walls to welcome us before dawn? Hardly. This is a show of loyalty from a populace who know their fate relies upon one man's goodwill.'

The column rode, trundled and stomped across the bridge slowly to the cheers and adulation of the crowd above. It could only logically have been happy accident that the sun chose that very moment to peek over the briny horizon just as Caesar was halfway across the bridge, catching his gleaming cuirass, white hair, red cloak and white horse and making him look like a hero straight out of legend. And yet Fronto could easily imagine the old bugger sitting in the carriage at midnight working out the time of the sunrise and planning his approach accordingly. Certainly the effect raised an 'ooooh' from the crowd.

Lucius Salvius Cursor had contrived to move ahead of the legion so that he was among the riders at the front with Caesar and his officers, which was fortunate as the general turned as they neared the walls and gestured to him. 'Have the Thirteenth form in cohorts in the forum.'

Salvius saluted, his glassy dark eyes playing across the defences as though working out how to breach or hold them as required. The vanguard passed through the gates to find several centuries of the Thirteenth in civilian dress but formed up on the sides of the street at attention. A junior tribune who had led the insurgents, along with the senior centurion commanding, were clearly such, even dressed the same as the others, and the tribune stepped forward as Caesar reined in his horse.

'This way, General.'

Quarter of an hour later, the new arrivals had passed through the packed streets of Ariminium, through a tense, cheering crowd, and to the forum. Fronto followed Caesar, along with the other officers, as they moved up the steps and into the basilica off one side of the square. Inside, more soldiers in just tunic and boots had clearly secured and emptied the grand edifice. Caesar was escorted to a large office, where he sank into a seat. The tribune cleared his throat.

'It is my pleasure to report that Ariminium is yours, General, and is secure.'

Caesar nodded. 'And what of its councillors and commanders? They are not here to greet us?'

A nervous look crossed the face of the tribune. He was young and inexperienced but he had clearly done well, heavily reliant no doubt upon that senior centurion.

'The centurion and I differed in opinion, General. I gave orders that the ordo, who were extremely resistant to our arrival and the imposition of military law in the city, be locked up in a secure location, along with the garrison prefect and the evocati commander who had been identified to us.'

Fronto rolled his eyes. Excellent!

'The centurion advocated freeing the civilians to follow their own course and quartering the officers pending your arrival.'

'And where is this secure location?' Salvius Cursor asked his junior tribune. Again the man swallowed nervously.

'I'm afraid I acceded to the will of the senior centurion, sir. He is a veteran of some standing, and I felt would more correctly anticipate the wishes of the proconsul through familiarity than I who have only served with the Thirteenth a few months.'

Salvius huffed and slapped his hands on the table. 'Unacceptable, Tribune. Now those civilians, frightened mice that they are, will be running straight to the forces of Pompey and the senate and telling them where we are and what we have done.'

'And that is as it should be,' Caesar interrupted, raising a silencing hand to Salvius. 'You have shown leniency, which is exactly what I would have done.' He caught the look of disbelief on the face of the senior tribune and nodded at the man's hands, still resting on his table. Salvius straightened and Caesar continued. 'We are pitted against Pompey, who is popular and strong, but whose ire forever rides in his veins. He marches and fights on the whim of his anger and it drives him. Many do not see that, but I have no doubt it will become abundantly clear in the coming days. And as Pompey is anger and violence, so we must be seen to be sense, forgiveness and honour.'

He sighed at the scepticism still on Salvius' face. 'News needed to be suppressed in Ravenna, so that Ariminium could fall the way it has without a fight. Now, however, let the news spread. Let the cities across Italia hear that towns open their gates to Caesar and that he respects and honours their leaders and their people. A reputation like that can save us a hundred sieges.'

Grudgingly, Salvius nodded. 'Fair enough, Caesar. What of the garrison?'

'The garrison hold Ariminium in the name of the senate and the people of Rome. When I have healed this rift, I will once more be a part of that senate and a part of that people, so these men are not my enemies. Only those who take up a sword and follow Pompey will be my chosen enemy and even then only if they will not throw off their yoke and join us. The garrison will stay, though they will be supplemented by three centuries of the Thirteenth, for the sake of security, and Tribune Portius here, who I saw something in early enough to make me assign him this critical duty, will take over command of the city's military. Well done,

Portius. You have earned yourself this role, and I am sure you will do well.'

A centurion appeared in the doorway and cleared his throat, saluting. 'Apologies for the interruption, General, but the legion is assembled awaiting your pleasure.'

'Good.' Caesar waved the man away. 'Now, gentlemen, I must clarify our position for the men, in just such a way that the people of Ariminium cannot help but overhear. In the meantime, Salvius, I want you to locate the mansio, find couriers and send to Vienna for the legions I have in the Rhodanus valley. The die is now cast and bringing in soldiers can no longer do any harm. We will be moving south along the Via Flaminia and then the Adriatic coast road for some time. We will leave messages at every official post we pass so that they can follow on. With luck at a forced march they can be with us swiftly.'

'The coast road?' Fronto asked in confusion. 'I thought we were bound for Rome?'

'I have no wish to enter Rome at the head of an army like Sulla the dictator. No. When we enter Rome it will be as peaceful citizens to settle matters. But to do that we need to remove Pompey from the board. Latest intelligence has it that Pompey has been raising levies across Latium. If he hopes to stand against me without calling his legions back from Hispania, there will not be enough men available in Latium to raise a large enough army. He will not call the legions back across the sea, because of my presence on the Hispanic border near Narbo. And he cannot move north of Rome to recruit his levies for that brings him closer to me and he needs time to raise, equip and train an army. So he will have moved south. He will be in Campania perhaps. But more likely in Samnium or Apulia, where there is more than adequate population to create his legions, and they are hardy hill folk rather than soft, wine-soaked farmers.'

Fronto tried hard not to be offended at the description of his native Campania, but when he looked up, he saw that Caesar was looking at him with a twinkle in his eye. Damn the man.

'So,' Caesar went on, 'Pompey will be in the south, raising legions, and it is there we must face him, preferably while his army is still small and poorly-formed. And so we move with speed and trust to the veteran legions, hardened by a decade of war against the Gauls, to catch up with us before their help is needed too desperately. In the meantime, we must look to the spirit of the Thirteenth upon whom we rely and see that our reputation is fine and spreads well and fast. Come.'

And the general was up, striding from the room, all business and waiting for nobody. The officers scurried off after him and emerged into the glow of a cold dawn, with an ice blue sky and frost hanging on everyone's breath. The Thirteenth were gathered before them, excluding two centuries who maintained control of the gates and walls.

As they stood atop the basilica steps, looking over the heads of the men, Fronto was interested to see a group of older men and a century or so of neat-looking men in blue tunics. The garrison and the evocati, clearly, despite the lack of armour and weapons. They stood neatly to attention just like the Thirteenth.

'Greetings, men of the Thirteenth Legion, veterans of Ariminium and men of the garrison. It is a sad day when a loyal son of Rome is forced to defy the rulings of the senate and bring himself under arms into the heart of the republic, and I realise that there will be many among you who disapprove of my actions. Let me explain myself, and attempt to put your hearts at ease.'

There was an expectant ripple across the crowd.

'Despite my loyalty to Rome, the money I have spent, the blood I have shed and the years of my life I have given to forever remove the threat of Gaul from our doorstep, that bane of all good men, Pompey Magnus, has turned the senate and the consuls against me. Me! Rome's most faithful servant! They deny me the right to serve her further and would *prosecute* me for strengthening the republic and conquering Gaul!'

There was a collective rumble of disapproval and Fronto could see the balance already tipping toward Caesar. He really was a master of the oratorical art.

'And so I am driven to the only course left open to me. To call out Pompey for his vile actions and to remove his tainted influence from the government of Rome. This I vow to do. I shall take arms against my enemy, Pompey Magnus, and cow him. Not, you note, against Rome. I do what I do to *save* the republic, not to destroy it. Not to control it. I would have the senate in control, but not doing

Pompey's will as they now do. I will free them from him, and they will make things right with me.'

He had them. Fronto could feel it in the air, even without their solemn nods.

'And any man who serves me faithfully will not find me ungenerous.'

Ah... loyalty, Rome, and a fat purse. Throw in looting, and they would march into the maw of Cerberus himself for the general.

'But I have no wish to come between a man and his conscience,' Caesar went on. 'The city's ordo has been allowed to depart to their country estates. It is my fervent hope that they will return in time, but that is their choice. I make the same offer to you all. If any man here owes his loyalty to Pompey and does not feel they can follow me, they may leave the city now. I will grant safe passage to any man wishing to do so.'

There was a strange, low murmur. A few of the garrison and the evocati were exchanging quiet words and looks, but no one moved as yet. Galronus frowned. 'Isn't that dangerous?' he whispered to Fronto. 'What happens if half the legion deserts? And certainly the locals have every reason to.'

Fronto smiled. 'You don't think that any man who might favour Pompey was weeded out of the Thirteenth long ago? And the garrison and evocati? They'll mostly have wives and family here. Maybe business interests, too. Property, very likely. Few if any are going to want to leave their home just because Caesar is now the one making the rules and not the senate.'

Sure enough, as the silence stretched out, not one figure left the throng in the forum. Caesar threw out his arms exultantly.

'Your loyalty and honour humbles me. I shall see an extra month's pay delivered to every man in Ariminium for their display of Romanitas. And now, centurions assign your camps and watches. Centuries are to be granted furlough in the city on rotation, on the condition that they comport themselves respectably.'

As the officer began shouting out orders and the columns and files of legionaries began to move out of the forum square in good order, Fronto watched and, more importantly, listened, to the crowd. Locals were drifting away alone or in pairs or small groups, their conversation hushed, excitable, urgent. He was not watching the dispersal of citizens. He was watching news of Caesar's munificence spreading.

Chapter Two

20th of Januarius - Ancona

'DID I not tell you?'

Caesar leaned on the balcony of the rather grand edifice formerly occupied by the local port master. Despite three days of rain and a temperature that would make a snowdrop shiver, the morning had dawned clear and blue and the world looked glorious and bright. Fronto pulled his cloak around him as he looked down at the seven ships they had impounded in the port when Ancona had rather ostentatiously thrown open its gates to them and strewn the general's route with rose petals. The port of Ancona was the most important naval station on the east coast, some sixty miles south of Ariminium and the closest they had yet come to Rome, even if they were still on the other side of the peninsula.

'You did,' Fronto mumbled, shivering.

Down below, Roscius, currently one of Rome's Praetors and formerly a legate of Caesar's army, hurried out to his carriage to return to the city. He was proof that Caesar still had friends in the capital. In fact, if his tidings were correct, then the number of Caesar's enemies in the city was diminishing all the time.

The meeting had been short, mere transfer of news, really, but it had improved Caesar's mood after a poor start to the day, recovering from 'one of his spells' during the night.

Roscius bore interesting tidings as well as confirmation that Caesar had been correct. Pompey was in the south – in Teanum, in fact, almost two hundred miles away in southern Campania. Whether he was planning to move east to collect the mountain folk for his military as Caesar had suspected, or south even further to the hunting grounds of the infamous Tarantine horsemen of old remained to be seen. But either way, they had been right to move south and not march on Rome. Had Caesar turned up at the city gates with a legion and Pompey not been there, he would have been seen as a new Sulla – something he seemed to wish to avoid with all his heart.

Moreover, Roscius had informed them that the consuls had quit Rome for their country estates, an action copied by many of the leading senators, for fear that Caesar might come against the city in his march. Rome was steadily emptying of Caesar's more vocal enemies, despite his unwillingness to march upon it.

Roscius climbed into his carriage and the driver urged the horses on along the well-paved and washed-clean street toward the south gate, where he would take the Nuceria road, joining the Via Flaminia in the mountains and making for Rome once more. And like blackbirds, startled in a field by some predator, the rest of the messengers emerged from the building, some on foot, making for the port or for carriages, some already on horses and heading for the various town gates. Missives sent everywhere.

To Marcus Antonius, who had now moved north to Arretium, telling him to wait there as five cohorts were on the way for him to command, forming a second prong to the advance south and making sure that Pompey did not somehow slip past them. To Ariminium, calling for those centuries who had been left there to bolster the garrison. Ariminium was now of reduced importance since Ancona's fall to Caesar, and those men were now required elsewhere. To Aquileia with orders to begin raising and arming new legions using all available manpower in Cisalpine Gaul, draining the provincial treasury if necessary. To Labienus to move his three legions as fast as possible if they were to be of any use against Pompey in the coming days. More. Messages to friends who might still owe Caesar both favours and loyalty. To those who might consider him an enemy, urging them to stay neutral in the affair. To governors and administrators and commanders and more.

And one critical one.

Clearly, despite his resolve and the success they had enjoyed since crossing the Rubicon, Caesar was still haunted by the shock of what he had done. He often carried that same look in his eyes as he had when they had stopped at the river. A desire to avoid the fate for which he seemed destined.

For one letter in particular was now leaving the building, heading southeast with an escort of a score of cavalry, such was the importance Caesar clearly attached to it.

Riding at pace for Teanum.

For Pompey.

There had been mixed feelings among the officers about Caesar's letter, but the general had overridden the nay-sayers and sent it anyway. A last attempt. *Another* last attempt. A request for Pompey to come to Rome and meet with Caesar in peace with a view to avoiding a clash that would cost a vast number of Roman lives on both sides. From his expression, Caesar did not believe his request would be taken up, but from the almost imploring tone of the letter, he desperately wished it would.

'A week, Caesar.'

'Hmm?' The general looked around at Fronto, pulled from some inner musing.

'Even at good courier speeds it will be a week before you receive a reply from him or from Cisalpine Gaul. Do we remain in Ancona or begin to move?'

Caesar shook his head. 'Let Antonius confirm he is moving with his cohorts first. Then, if Pompey refuses, we are ready to fall upon the south. And with luck Labienus will be here by then with three more legions. They will make a great deal of difference.'

* * *

The days rolled on, remaining cold and intermittently showering them with icy rain and drying out to a crystal blue. Daily, Caesar returned to his balcony, watching for the arrival of messengers. Typically, when the tidings finally came, they came unexpectedly, by night, and the troubles came home to roost all at once.

Fronto answered the summons blearily, rubbing the sleep from his eyes and hastily throwing on his tunic and cloak, belting the former and tightly wrapping the latter before hurrying from the hostel in which he had made his quarters. He met Brutus and Galronus in the street, similarly exhausted and hastily dressed. 'Must be urgent, then,' Fronto said through chattering teeth.

'Why?'

'Caesar might never sleep, but he knows his officers need to. If it wasn't urgent, he'd have waited for dawn.'

They hurried across the street and to the general's headquarters in the port authority offices. Aulus Ingenuus was standing with his men in the doorway, dark circles under his eyes suggesting that he had been the first man up in Caesar's wake.

'Fronto. Galronus. Brutus,' the prefect nodded as they arrived. He gestured for them to enter, and they did so, trotting up the stairs and into the large office where Caesar now held his briefings. A number of officers were already there, but there were yet empty seats. Fronto slid into a chair to one side, his friends joining him. Caesar was nowhere to be seen. Gradually other officers arrived and once Pollio and Curio had arrived, the arranged seats were full. They could hear Ingenuus' men closing up the entrance to the building, and a few moments later Caesar emerged through another door.

Fronto felt his heart rise into his throat in worry as soon as he saw the general's face. Caesar rarely looked nervous. Even when he was in direct danger, his brain was constantly working to produce a solution, leaving him little time for worry. Perhaps this enforced stay at Ancona had given him more opportunity than usual to consider any difficulties, but Fronto didn't think it was that. Caesar was actually shocked and shaken, and that was a rare sight.

'What is it, Caesar?' asked Brutus, clearly spotting the same worrying aura as Fronto.

The general sagged into the seat behind his table, which was strewn as always with maps, lists and documents.

'We have had three missives. One is of a faintly hopeful nature. The others are much more troubling. I wanted to share the tidings and discuss their implications with you before rumour begins to circulate.'

More worry.

'News has arrived from Rome, and it concerns the forces arrayed against us. While we were aware of Pompey raising troops in the vicinity of Teanum in southern Campania, it seems he has a lieutenant in my would-be replacement as proconsul. Domitius Ahenobarbus is also gathering legions against us in the name of the senate. He is south of us, in the east of the peninsula which is, I presume, why Pompey is not there as I expected. And while Pompey is too powerful to fawn to the will of others and might still be swayed, Ahenobarbus is an attack dog of the senate. He sees his future wealth and position as reliant upon them, on Pompey and on the consuls. And so unless Pompey agrees to peace, we can expect nothing from Ahenobarbus. Moreover, given the man's history of unrestrained recklessness, he might well continue to oppose us even if Pompey can be drawn in. Latest reports have Ahenobarbus with three new legions, partially-trained but well equipped, moving toward Corfinium, only a hundred miles from here.'

Fronto cleared his throat.

'You speak as though there is some hope of reconciliation with Pompey, General? I'm somewhat surprised to hear that?'

Caesar nodded. 'As I said, one piece of news is hopeful, and I am grateful for it considering the others. In addition to Ahenobarbus, the senate's terrier, joining Pompey, I have had word from the legions that were quartered in Vienna.'

Fronto felt his blood chill. They were reliant upon those men. With Pompey gathering forces and Ahenobarbus marshalling three legions, they would *need* the Fifth, Eighth and Twelfth from Vienna.

'They are delayed?' hazarded Pollio.

'No,' Caesar said quietly. 'The legions come still and are closing on our position. Their commander, however, is not.'

Something had happened to Labienus? Fronto's mind formed a picture of the calm, pleasant, self-assured and competent commander who had worked so hard to make the war in Gaul one of assimilation and control rather than extermination. He liked Labienus. What had happened to the man.

Caesar pinched the bridge of his nose.

'It seems that Titus Labienus has departed, resigning his command. He rode for Massilia where he took ship for Neapolis to join Pompey.'

Fronto blinked. *Labienus?*

There was a stunned drawing of breath around the room as the news sank in. Labienus had been Caesar's ablest lieutenant. His staunchest ally, and the only man who could rival Antonius or Fronto in the general's esteem. He had been so trusted by Caesar in fact that he had often been given whole swathes of legions and sent off to do the general's work as well as he could himself.

'Labienus, it seems, tried to persuade the legions to follow him into the enemy's service. Fortunately, they remain loyal to me and refused. But he did take almost four thousand cavalry with him, mostly of Gallic and Belgic origin, but including our dreaded German horsemen. Our enemies have had good cause to fear those cavalry over the years and now is seems that soon we might be facing them ourselves.'

Fronto remembered the vicious horsemen at work with a shudder. The very idea of Labienus facing him across a battlefield was worse in almost every way than Pompey. And the inclusion of the Gallic, Belgic and German cavalry was pulse-quickening. He glanced at Galronus and could see the conflicting emotions on his friend's face. This had suddenly become a civil war for him too. Rather than fighting with Romans against Romans, there was now every chance he might take the field and find himself facing cavalry drawn from his own Remi tribe.

'The good news, Caesar?' Fronto urged. 'You said there was some hope? Pompey I presume?'

Caesar nodded. 'It is slim hope, admittedly, but I am forced to consider it nonetheless.'

'Pompey will agree to meet me in Rome. His conditions are troubling. In fact, under normal circumstances I would consider them insulting and unacceptable, but the arrival of Domitius Ahenobarbus on the scene, and the defection of Labienus, mean I might have to consider this.'

'What are his conditions, General?' Curio asked, leaning forward.

'He requires that I come to Rome without a military presence. A small bodyguard of lictors appropriate to my former position as a proconsul at most.'

There was an explosive snarl of disbelief around the room.

'He cannot believe you will walk into a trap so easily, General,' Salvius Cursor barked.

'He believes just that, and more. He requires that all my forces retire back across the border of Cisalpine Gaul and out of senatorial lands before he will speak to me. The army would need to return once more to Ravenna.'

'Caesar,' Pollio said, rising from his seat, 'that would mean giving up everything we've gained. Ariminium. Ancona. Frightening the senate and the consuls out of Rome. '

'But while Pompey is a killer and a shrewd politician,' Caesar retorted, 'he has never, to my knowledge, reneged on a promise or broken his word. If he gives me his oath that I will remain unharmed when I come to Rome, I have no reason to suspect he will do me harm. The forces gathering against us are starting to become serious, gentlemen. When it was just Pompey with a few green legions in Italia, I planned to put him down quickly and secure peace in Rome. It would be a simple, incisive action and within a single campaigning season we would have everything we sought. We had ten veteran legions to Pompey's nine, and seven of those are trapped in Hispania. But now he raises men swiftly. There are at least five legions in Italia against us, two of them veterans, and even when the Vienna forces join us we will still only have four. And with Ahenobarbus and Labienus taking the field for him with my own cavalry... things are starting to look considerably less certain for us. I am seriously considering taking Pompey up on his offer.'

'You cannot do it,' Salvius Cursor spat, forgetting even title or honorific for his commander in his anger. '*You* might trust Pompey, General, but you are in the minority. I served the man years ago and I know him for the devious snake he is. He will set you a trap and you will walk blindly into it. Mark my words, Caesar, you will be dead within an hour of passing the first milestone on the Via Flaminia.'

Curio shook his head. 'There is too much at stake for Pompey to take so bold an action. It might turn the senate against him.'

'The senate would *drink his piss* if he asked them,' snapped Salvius Cursor. 'No one opposes Pompey but us. Do you not see that? I was once Pompey's man. I do not serve Caesar out of some ancient loyalty like most of you, or because I am his client or owe him in some way. I came voluntarily. I signed on with Caesar's command because he opposes Pompey. Because he is the only man in the whole republic who can both see what Pompey is, and is capable of doing something about it. If we treat with Pompey and Caesar does not emerge in control, then Caesar will either die there and then, or he will fade away to obscurity and Pompey will be left as the only power in the republic. A despot. A king like Tarquin the Proud.'

Salvius Cursor turned on the whole room, throwing out his arms imploringly. 'Did we not form the republic just to avoid such a thing? Did we not eject the kings from Rome? And now the senate would hand over their authority to Pompey and he would sit on a gilded throne and rule. No. I did not sign on for this. Caesar is the saviour of the republic. *That* is why I am with him. And that is why I counsel defiance *whatever* the cost.'

'But Labienus…' began Pollio.

'*Screw* Labienus. Piss on him. Piss on him and *any* man who turns his back on Caesar and on the republic for which he stands. Piss on any man who goes to shelter in Pompey's fat shadow. I personally will drive my blade through his black heart the first moment I ever get the opportunity, and I will do the same for any man who stands in my way, be he barbarian or Roman. And if any of you are so timid that you cannot stand proud and defiant, then run to Pompey now and prepare yourself, because I for one will come for you with my blade naked.'

Silence filled the room, a sense of shock settling across the officers. Fronto frowned as he peered at the shaking form of Tribune Salvius Cursor. In some ways, Fronto felt emboldened just by his presence. The man was right, at the core of the matter. He was seeing everything in a fairly simplistic manner, but it was a seductive idea, and Fronto could see it at work among his peers.

Salvius Cursor, he decided, was a zealot. And zealots could be both powerful and dangerous.

'I agree with Salvius,' he said finally. 'Caesar, the tribune might have been a little too forthright in his harangue, and I think there are subtleties that he has glossed over, but he is right in one thing: no good will come of you walking into Rome to meet Pompey. The man has invited you for one thing only – legitimacy. There are still those in Rome who oppose him, as we see in Roscius. By doing what he proposes, Pompey gets to look as though he has given you every opportunity to make peace. He will present you with impossible conditions, and you will have to leave again. And then those few nobles and senators who still back you will believe that you are unrepentant and bent on the destruction of their world. Pompey is being cunning, and while it will damage your reputation to refuse his offer, it will be nothing compared to refusing him face to face.'

The room fell silent again, but the officers were all nodding. Caesar sighed and rose.

'On balance, I can see the futility in any meeting. We must instead move on. But if we are to face greater odds in the coming days, we need to reduce their forces as fast as possible. We will therefore move on Domitius Ahenobarbus at first light. See to your commands and have a courier sent to me. I need to distribute a few letters.'

The officers, summarily dismissed, rose and began to filter from the room. Fronto and Galronus, tucked away to one side, were the last to leave, filing from the chamber as Caesar's secretary entered to take dictation. As Fronto emerged into the dark corridor, fingers closed on his upper arm. He turned sharply, ready to lash out, only to find Salvius Cursor standing in the passage, his glassy eyes fixed on Fronto.

'I am grateful for your support in the meeting Marcus Falerius Fronto, even though you made veiled snide comments about my oration. And I will march alongside you and fight alongside you across the breadth of the republic in the name of Caesar.'

Fronto pulled his arm free of the man's oddly icy grip.

'But,' Salvius went on, 'I know your history, Fronto. I know you for a man who has turned your back on Caesar more than once, and denounced him. I know that even though you came crawling back when you needed something, you once sought out Pompey's patronage and that you count some of Caesar's opponents among your friends. I will accept for now that you serve the general, but bear in mind that whatever I do in this campaign, I do not trust you any more than I do Labienus, and I will ever have one eye on you. The day you turn on Caesar, expect to meet the point of my blade swiftly and surely. Do you understand me.'

Fronto snarled. 'Don't think to lecture *me*, you madman. I can see the lunacy in your eyes. And you are a turncoat yourself with a Pompeian history. You have no idea. You'll be watching me? I don't trust your judgement or your temper, and *I'll* be watching *you* too.'

Salvius Cursor grabbed his arm once more, and Fronto raised a fist threateningly. There was a moment of almost unbearable tension, and suddenly Galronus pulled Fronto's arm out of Salvius' grasp, hauling him back. 'Come on Marcus. Have a cup of wine and settle down.'

'Oh yes. Wine,' snapped Salvius Cursor. 'I've heard about your wine-soaked history too. And your sot of a father. Go climb into an amphora with your Remi friend, but watch him closely too. His friends are now riding south with Labienus. As trustworthy as you, Fronto.'

For a brief moment, Galronus looked like he would react, but the Remi prince quickly got hold of himself and pulled Fronto away. 'Come on. Leave the little runt.'

* * *

Their path into Italia read like a catalogue of fortresses.

Ariminium had been first. Then Pisaurum and Fanum had opened their gates as they marched the coast road to find Ancona awaiting them with a warm welcome. Flowers and cheering at Potentia and Cupra. Then, finally, the end of the shoreline as the legion turned inland, heading up the wide valley to Asculum, where they would turn south once more and march on Ahenobarbus' fortified position at Corfinium. En route, each town capitulated with ease, though tellingly many had been garrisoned by Pompey's officers and those men had fled ahead of Caesar's advance, taking their men with them to support Ahenobarbus or Pompey.

Asculum had boosted the morale of the whole army, for it had provided the first good news in weeks, in the form of reinforcements. Marcus Antonius had re-joined the army with his five cohorts and on his travels south he had connected with the Twelfth Legion who were moving at a forced march to join the general. Their presence more than doubled the manpower of Caesar's army, and granted everyone a breath of relief, almost as much as the news that the other two legions, the Eighth and Fifth, were only days behind, having had to detour to secure extra provisions.

Februarius arrived, bringing warmer but wetter weather. When the army finally emerged from the narrow valley to see Corfinium three miles away on its spur of land, dominating the valley and guarding the plateau of farmland beyond, Caesar's army numbered almost ten thousand, with another ten less than half a week away. Fronto tried not to think too hard on the fact that the walls ahead sheltered half as many men again as marched along the valley behind him, even without any extras they had received from the garrisons fleeing south.

Caesar gestured to a low rise ahead to their left and the entire officer corps, along with Ingenuus and his riders, peeled off from the vanguard of the column and made for the hill while the army continued along the valley behind. Reaching the summit, Caesar reined in.

'It's going to be trouble, Caesar,' Pollio noted.

Corfinium had strong walls and was shaped like an elongated diamond along a ridge at the edge of a plateau formed by a 'V' of valleys. Well-fortified by both man and nature, it clearly had the space to hold Domitius Ahenobarbus' legions. And given what the scouts had said about the ample farmland on the plateau beyond, likely their supply situation was very healthy.

'I wonder what their artillery capability is?' Caesar mused.

'Why, General?' asked one of the tribunes.

'Because we're going to have to take the legions past the town, down this valley and then bring them back up onto the plateau. I wonder which side of the river would be more useful…'

Caesar's words tailed off as he frowned.

'Look, gentlemen. Down at the bridge!'

Perhaps half a mile from the hilltop the main valley road passed across a wide, solid bridge on its approach to Corfinium. Even as they watched, soldiers in chain armour burst from the undergrowth and swarmed the bridge, battering at it and pulling at the stones.

'Unbelievable,' Fronto breathed. 'There must be half a legion there.'

'If they take down that bridge it'll cause havoc for our supplies and artillery wagons,' Salvius noted. 'Your permission, Caesar?'

'Deal with them,' the general replied and, as Salvius raced off to his men, the officers sat astride their horses and watched the legionaries of Domitius Ahenobarbus trying to buy extra time by destroying the only wagon approach to the city. Moments later there were buccina calls back among the men and the lead elements of the Thirteenth broke into a run, armour clattering and jingling as they plunged on down the valley. Fronto's fingers went white as his grip on his reins tightened. Galronus leaned closer and patted his arm. 'Not your fight Marcus. Our time will come. Let the attack dog have his moment with a bridge.'

Fronto watched, tense, as the men of the Thirteenth ran at the bridge. Ahenobarbus' men were still green recruits, with a few quiet garrison troops among them, the only true veterans being the officers and a few soldiers and engineers amid the levies. An engineer down there spoke to an officer and half the men formed up in a shield wall before of the bridge, while the others continued to tear and hack at it.

'Got to give them credit for trying,' Pollio said quietly.

'They *need* to buy time,' Marcus Antonius said. 'Ahenobarbus is in a strong position, but knowing that he faces us he will be expecting Pompey to march to his aid. He will hold out for that day and so every hour bought counts.'

The lead elements of the Thirteenth hit the raw recruits at the bridge like a bull to a rotten gate. Even Fronto was surprised at the effect. The charging legionaries formed into a wedge at the last moment and as they hit the shieldwall they burst through it with ease, carving their way across the bridge in a bloody swathe. The enemy's initial stand hopelessly beaten, the attacking force began to break up into centuries, some pressing the two groups of legionaries who had so recently been a solid wall of shields, until they broke with panic and fled into the undergrowth and across the river, many dying before they could even leave pilum reach. Other centuries of the Thirteenth went to work on the men at the bridge, removing them with bloody ease and securing access for Caesar's army. Many of the new legionaries broke and fled quickly, while the veteran centurions fought on to the last man, holding their positions and dying on the bridge.

Fronto closed his eyes. He'd thought such days gone when the war against Sertorius ended, but it seemed there would be no end to the killing of Roman by Roman.

It was over swiftly and the victorious Thirteenth rather ignominiously tipped the bodies of the dead from the bridge into the torrent below. Even as the bloody clean up went on at the bridge and the rest of the army closed, Tribune Salvius Cursor came galloping up the hill once more. He had a cut above his eye and was liberally drenched with blood.

'If the defenders of Corfinium are of similar mettle, Caesar, this siege should not be too troublesome.'

Caesar turned a sour face on Salvius. 'Have some respect, man. Those are young Romans you're talking about. Some of them will have been involved in making pots you've eaten from, or wine you've drunk. Some might have fathers in Rome who have sought your family's patronage. We do what we must, but never let it be said that I took pleasure in robbing Rome of her sons.'

Salvius seemed unabashed, shrugging and causing droplets of blood to fly.

'They are the enemy, General. Roman they might be, but they chose to follow the enemy. I did not force them to do so, and so I will not shed a tear for a single corpse that no longer stands in our way.'

The general and his tribune stared at one another for a moment in silence, locked in some unseen battle of wills and it felt to Fronto as though he and the others were intruding on a very private moment. Finally Caesar nodded. 'Clean yourself up and look to your legion, Salvius. Once we pass Corfinium, we cannot be certain what we will find on the plateau.

'Uh oh,' Brutus muttered. 'What's this?'

They turned to follow his pointing finger. A party of riders was approaching along the valley on this side of the river.

'Deputation from Corfinium?' Antonius mused.

'Unlikely. They would come from the other side, across the bridge.'

They watched silently as the riders closed. A dozen men, all civilians by the look of it, and of varying ages. Despite the fact that they presented no obvious threat, Caesar's bodyguards spread out across the hilltop protectively, and Ingenuus took up a position ahead and to one side of the general.

'Don't you wish you had your bodyguard with you,' Galronus murmured and Fronto turned to find a smile on his friend's face. Truth be told, he did miss Masgava and Aurelius and Arcadios. He would have liked nothing more than to have them with him. But they served a better purpose in the current circumstances guarding the villa at Tarraco and looking after Lucilia and the family. He tried not to think about how, despite moving them as far from Caesar and the war as he could, he had placed them inadvertently between Pompey's provincial army and the three legions of Caesar's at Narbo.

'I'm happy they're where they are,' he replied.

The riders were closing now, and Fronto straightened in his saddle, trying not to look so aged and stooped. He examined them as they arrived. Two men were clearly well-to-do, and a third, older, man had even tried to ride here in a toga, though the result made him look more like a trainee medic's bandage practice than a noble Roman as he struggled to keep the weighty wool garment even remotely covering him. The rest were young men with the bearing of soldiers or at least men who had the leisure to spend plenty of time training at the bath house.

'Proconsul Caesar?' asked the lead of the three older nobles.

'I am he,' the general replied, bowing his head.

'We represent the ordo of Sulmo, Proconsul. Are you aware of our city?'

Caesar scratched his head, apparently dredging his memory. 'Sulmo. I do believe it is the next town south on this very road, is it not? Perhaps eight or nine miles from here?'

The old man, still struggling with his toga, one end of which was now trailing in the mud beside his horse, looked gratified that they had heard of his town. 'Excellent, Proconsul,' *Toga* answered in a hoarse voice that sounded like the crackling of parchment. 'Sulmo seeks your aid, sir. Our ordo voted to open our gates to you and add our garrison to your forces as well as any provisions we can provide, but our town currently languishes in the iron grip of two of Pompey's dogs: Quintus Lucretius and Lentius Attius.'

Fronto nodded. Attius he did not necessarily know, though there were plenty of people around of that name, but Quintus Lucretius had been a senator and one of Caesar's most vocal opponents during that endless to-ing and fro-ing of communications while at Ravenna. Many senators had fled Rome, but to find one of them here, holding a town against Caesar, was a surprise.

'They have troops?'

'Six cohorts, sir,' one of the younger men said. 'Green men, though, and recently raised locally. With the right pressure they could be perhaps persuaded to change their allegiance, along with the town's ordo. If only their two commanders' influence can be removed.'

Caesar tapped his lip in thought.

Marcus Antonius shook his head and drew Caesar aside, away from the riders. 'We need every man we have to take down Corfinium, Gaius. Corfinium is the prize. Corfinium and the fall of Ahenobarbus.'

'But this is a war of hearts and minds, Marcus, as much as of swords and shields. Think of the goodwill we can create among other cities when they hear about this. And it will not require the loss of men, with luck. If we have to fight that garrison then we have failed anyway. We need to win them over.'

'I think this is a waste of time and resources,' Antonius grumbled.

'I'm sorry you feel that way,' Caesar replied quietly. 'Since I'm sending you. This is a job for a silver tongue and you could charm the birds from the trees. Take your five cohorts again just in case. They won't make much difference when we invest Corfinium. But try not to use them. Win me Sulmo with words, Marcus.'

Fronto caught the expression Antonius threw back at his friend and almost laughed out loud, stifling it as Antonius turned. 'Terrentius?' he gestured to one of the junior tribunes. 'Have my five cohorts move out onto this bank away from the army. We're off to play word games with a senator and I want veterans at my back when it all goes wrong.'

Caesar grinned and trotted forward to the deputation once more. 'My good friend and lieutenant, Marcus Antonius, Tribune of the Plebs, will bring five cohorts and free you from your oppressors. Would that I could spare the time to ride there myself, but the notorious Domitius Ahenobarbus rules in Corfinium, and I must devote my energy to rooting him out. Antonius has all my confidence and wields my authority as all know.'

The old man blinked as he realised he'd been summarily dismissed from the conversation and that Caesar had all-but forgotten him already as he turned to Fronto, Brutus, Pollio and Curio.

'Let us make camp on the plateau and hope there is still adequate provision. The supplies will follow on, but it would ease matters to have plenty of free, locally-sourced grain. And have the engineers start looking around Corfinium. I am hoping we can get away without actually circumvallating the city, but should we need to do so in the coming days I want to know every aspect of the place. Ahenobarbus is impulsive, and possibly even mad, but he is not stupid, and he will be prepared for us.'

Fronto looked up ahead at the town on the hill. He had, over the past decade, besieged so many hill towns that they had begun to blur into one giant nightmare, but never before had those walls contained Romans. He shuddered at the idea of cutting off their water supply and starving his own people just because of a feud between two great men.

Angry at himself, he shook it off. Partially because it was thinking like that which led a man to follow Labienus' path. And partly because if there was one thing he was determined not to do it was to prove Lucius Salvius Cursor right.

He would arm. He would bite down on his conscience. And he would besiege Corfinium with the rest of them.

* * *

Corfinium was surrounded. For seven days now the legions had penned in Domitius Ahenobarbus and his defiant force – three of those with a solidly superior army – and though it had rained non-stop for all seven days and the ground was becoming boggy and mire-ridden, still an air of optimism reigned in the camps. After the departure of Antonius with his five cohorts, Caesar had settled the other half of the Thirteenth Legion close to the bridge that Ahenobarbus had tried to destroy, securing the route to the north and protecting said crossing. The rest of his men – the Twelfth Legion and various other units – he had encamped a short distance from the walls on the farmland plateau.

Three days later, the Eighth and Fifth legions had arrived to the great relief of all, bearing a cornucopia of supplies, right down to Spanish garum, Ligurian oysters and Campanian wine. They had been immediately positioned to the eastern and western ends of the city at the edge of the plateau, effectively sealing in Corfinium.

There was still talk, though, of whether a full circumvallation would be required – even Caesar seemed to be putting off the decision, perhaps in the hope that Corfinium would fall without such a requirement.

Certainly the pro-Pompeian garrison of the place seemed unwilling to open hostilities. A number of times now, Caesar's scouts and a few smaller units had come close to the walls, probing the defences. The enemy artillery atop the towers, which could so easily have drawn first blood, remained silent, and the few arrows that rained down from the walls had clearly been meant more as a warning not to come too close rather than a serious attempt at defence. The missiles had thudded into the ground just ahead of approaching units, and in seven days not one man had died, and injuries were minor and almost always the result of accident or misjudgement.

'What do we do, Caesar?' Pollio asked quietly, standing at the officers' usual vantage point and peering at the thick, heavy walls. The general remained as taciturn as ever and the other officers looked at one another, seeking a way to advance the discussion.

'We cannot afford to tarry here forever, General,' Curio said voicing the thoughts of every man present. Pompey remained at large, recruiting and training to the southwest, and he was the true prize, not the headstrong, troublesome Ahenobarbus.

'We need to storm the place,' Salvius said in a matter-of-fact tone.

'What?' Curio turned to him.

'A full push against Corfinium. The place will be ours by sunset.

'I don't know whether you noticed,' Pollio snapped, 'but it has huge walls, artillery, natural defences, and a garrison almost the size of our own army. It's no push-over.'

'On the contrary, that is exactly what it is,' Salvius replied in an acidic tone. 'The garrison are nervous about facing their own people and they are green and untried. Even their commander holds back, unwilling to commit to an act of civil war. That will be their undoing. You can call it as civil as you like, but it's still a war. And war is not honourable or just or glorious. It's purely about who's standing at the end of it. You take hold of, and use, every advantage you can get. If they are nervous about committing, then they are unprepared. We strike now, while they expect nothing, and we can flatten the whole place in hours. This is an opportunity we need to take advantage of.'

'That is deplorable,' Curio replied.

'Yet sensible.'

'Those men are *Romans*,' added Pollio.

'This is war against Pompey and his senate dogs,' snapped Salvius Cursor. 'Romans are going to die on both sides. Only the man who can look past that and identify his goal can win. No man who baulks at killing fellow Romans has a place in this campaign. How long do we have to faff about until you all realise that?'

Fronto glanced across at Caesar, then at Galronus, whose face was a picture of irritation. Caesar was still showing no sign he was even listening. His beak-like nose rose as though he were a hound, sniffing the air for a scent, his gaze twitching to the horizon back beyond the camps as much as to the town ahead. He *did* have the scent. What of? Victory?

'This, as the general said,' reminded Fronto, 'is a battle of hearts and minds as much as blades. Yes, Romans are going to die, and we cannot afford to meander about and get bogged down with lackeys when Pompey remains our focus. But there must be a way to take Corfinium without such civil bloodshed.'

'Weak, Fronto,' sneered Salvius Cursor.

'Sensible,' retorted Fronto.

'Come with me,' Caesar said, suddenly. The other officers exchanged a look as the general heeled his horse and started down the hill toward the walls of Corfinium.

'What in Hades is he doing?' Fronto sighed as they raced to keep up. The general rode within arrow shot of the walls as though impervious to all harm, and the officers trotted along behind, glancing up nervously at the parapet. Aulus Ingenuus and the general's bodyguard crowded around their master and did their best to protect him, yet nothing came from above.

Caesar reined in his horse just thirty paces from the gate, where if the enemy so wished it, they could very easily drop things on him. Still, nothing came.

There was an odd silence as the other officers reined in behind their commander, and Salvius Cursor cleared his throat to ask a question only to have Caesar put a silencing finger to his lips. They sat there, tense, for some time as Ingenuus and his men raised their shields ready to form a roof over the general should they be required to do so at a moment's notice.

Finally, the gate to the city opened. Fronto vaguely remembered Domitius Ahenobarbus from odd mutual occasions in Rome. The man put him in mind of a praying mantis, his hands usually clasped together beneath a face that looked thoughtfully predatory with hooded, unreadable eyes, stalking, long legs and an overall manner that suggested he liked to creep around rather than walk. He was, however, unarmed and dressed in an ordinary prefect's gear rather than some ostentatious general's cuirass, which endeared him to Fronto in some small way.

Behind Ahenobarbus came tribunes and centurions. They looked serious. Seriously unhappy, even.

'Gaius.'

'Lucius,' Caesar replied with a courteous nod.

'You wish to speak?'

Caesar nodded and straightened.

'We have known each other many years, Lucius. We might not see eye to eye very often, and neither of us would say we are friends.'

A nod from the mantis.

'But,' Caesar went on, 'neither do we want to waste Roman lives in a costly and stupid conflict.'

'I hear only your own fear, Gaius,' the man in the prefect's kit said in a hiss. 'Any siege here will cost you half a legion at the least for every century of my defenders who fall. I know they're boys and untried, but we have the advantage nonetheless.'

'Lucius,' Caesar said with apparent exaggerated patience, 'it's no good holding out for Pompey. He won't be coming.'

Ahenobarbus did not reply, simply tipping his head to one side quizzically.

'Pompey's legions are even less well trained than yours Lucius. He is not going to commit them against my Gallic veterans until he has plenty of chance to train and harden them. The only veterans he has – the First and the Fifteenth – spent three years among my forces in Gaul, and he will worry that in committing them against me, they will simply turn on him. I suspect that he would be right, too. My legions were ever faithful. You, Lucius, are alone in

Corfinium and alone you will stay. Pompey is using you as a delay. A road-block, while he strengthens the real force he is raising to face me.'

'Nevertheless, I will hold senate territory against any would-be despot such as yourself, Gaius.'

Fronto narrowed his eyes. The man was resisting staunchly even though he must recognise that Caesar's assessment was very likely true.

'I will make you an offer, Lucius Domitius Ahenobarbus,' Caesar said suddenly, loudly, his head rising in that hunting hound manner once more. 'You and every officer who surrenders to us will be given total amnesty and guaranteed safe passage away from Corfinium.'

'General, that is...' began Salvius Cursor, but fell silent at a look from the general.

'All officers,' Caesar repeated. 'The town will be unharmed and all its citizens and leaders will remain in their current positions. Effectively there will be no change for most, and you may run back to Rome or even to Pompey's side if you wish. Your newly-raised forces will, of course, take a new oath to me and join my legions.' This last was said with a steady look at the various enemy officers gathered behind Ahenobarbus.

'No one would be foolish enough to trust your word, Gaius,' the man in the prefect's uniform shrugged. 'Your offer is as ash on the wind to us.'

Fronto was less sure, from what he could read in the faces of the gathered officers. He wondered how long the town's populace would support the garrison when they knew they could be free with just a word.

'You wish a gesture of my goodwill?' Caesar asked quietly.

'It would be pointless,' Ahenobarbus snorted, though some of his officers were nodding behind him.

Caesar smiled and straightened in his saddle.

'Fronto, would you do me a favour? Just trot out toward the north and meet Antonius' column, would you. Ask him and his party to join us.'

Fronto blinked and opened his mouth to argue, but realised the general was playing a very tight game with the emotions of the men he faced. It would not be Fronto who spoiled that game. He nodded and turned his horse, riding back up the gentle slope.

Once he reached the high point from which they had earlier been observing the walls, he peered down the long, gentle incline to the plateau. The huge, sprawling legionary camp lay directly opposite the gate but, *damn the man*, Caesar must have had sharp eyes. While they had all been discussing the best way to proceed, the general had already made his decision as soon as he'd caught sight of Marcus Antonius' cohorts in the distance, returning from the south. And he knew Antonius had achieved his goal, for the man's army had swelled to twice its former size.

Now, Antonius' force, the equivalent of a full legion, was moving off into one of the gaps between the encamped legions, preparing to fortify its own position, though a small party of riders continued on toward the main camp and Caesar's headquarters. Fronto hooked two fingers into his mouth and issued a shrill whistle. Antonius turned as he rode, spotted the waving figure on the hill, and diverted his party toward Corfinium.

Fronto watched the approaching horsemen. A dozen cavalrymen from Antonius' cohorts – the man always did favour his cavalry – half a dozen senior officers, and the man himself

'Fronto, nice to see you. The general?'

'Sitting rather smugly outside the gate of Corfinium, talking to Ahenobarbus and waiting for you.'

Antonius snorted. 'He is an infuriating bugger. Come on, then.'

With the others in tow, Fronto led Caesar's cousin over the hill and down toward the small group at the gate. Caesar's head turned at the sound of approaching hooves.

'Just the one, Antonius?'

The curly haired commander shrugged with a carefree smile. 'The one they call Lentius Attius, who appears to be a jumped up local with delusions of grandeur, ran for the hills the moment his cohorts turned on him. It wasn't worth the time and effort of hunting him down. But the best news, Caesar? The six cohorts this man led in Sulmona are, in fact, the understrength remains of the Fifteenth. As soon as they realised what was happening, they all-but begged to join you again.'

Caesar nodded. 'Agreed. Send the good senator forward.'

As Antonius gestured to one of the officers with him, Fronto realised that the man was wearing a general's knot around his midriff. He had been a prisoner riding among the cavalry and not one of Antonius' officers after all. A grin broke out across Fronto's face as the rebel senator from Sulmona walked his horse forward to join Caesar.

'Lucius,' Caesar began once more, nodding to Ahenobarbus, 'you will understand that your route to Pompey at Teanum is the road that passes Sulmona. The garrison that held that town for Pompey has already seen sense and joined us, so now even if Pompey *did* intend to come to your aid, he no longer holds the strongpoints on the route. Pompey is not coming. You are alone and the only hope to avoid the horror of protracted siege is to accept my clearly very favourable terms.'

Ahenobarbus' lip curled in distaste, so the general once more directly addressed those behind him – the officers of the town and the army within. It did not escape Fronto's notice that the walls were lined with watching faces too.

'Your general here, who is rabid and would see the world burn in an all-consuming conflagration rather than admit that he is wrong, believes I do not keep my word and that I cannot be trusted to grant mercy.'

He paused, gesturing to the man on the horse next to him.

'You may know this man, or you may not. He is Quintus Lucretius, senator of Rome, my opponent and a supporter of Pompey. He has been the commander of Sulmona garrison until today and now he is our prisoner. But, you see, this is not what I desire. I do not wish to imprison Romans any more than I wish to kill them. We are one republic, strong and gods-driven, and it makes the Fates weep to see us turn on each other so. The Sulmona garrison – the *Fifteenth Legion*, in fact – are not harmed. They are now with me in my army. Sulmona itself lives on quiet and free, and, Lucretius, you are free to go.'

The senator in the general's kit on the next horse gave Caesar a disbelieving look, and Caesar smiled. 'Lucretius, the very sight of you offends me, given how many unpleasant lies you spread in Rome about me, but if I killed every man who lied about me I'd be able to climb to the gods themselves on the pile of bodies. Go away. To Rome or to one of your estates or even to Pompey's side if you wish. But go.'

Fronto caught sight of a hint of irritation on Antonius' face – the man who had spent days negotiating to take Sulmona and this man, only to watch Caesar immediately free him, but the expression quickly turned to an understanding nod. It was a politically astute move. Salvius Cursor's face could have withered the rind from a melon.

Lucretius did not wait to be told twice. Turning his horse without a word of gratitude, he rode off along the low ground, then up the slope, angling for the wide gap between legionary camps.

'See that the pickets don't stop him,' Antonius nodded to two of his cavalrymen, who rode off after the senator, calling to him.

'This offer is open to Corfinium just as it was to Sulmona,' Caesar announced. 'Think upon it while we begin our siege works. My quarrel is with a senate who refuse to grant me simple concessions, not with the army, the people, or even with Ahenobarbus here.'

Without another word, Caesar turned and rode away. Leaving the seething Ahenobarbus surrounded by officers who looked half-convinced. The rest of the staff officers fell in behind the general, his cavalry bodyguard bringing up the rear.

'What now, General?' Curio asked quietly.

'Now? Now we circumvallate. Throw up as solid a circuit of defences as we can. Every sod we pile up and every stake we drive in will shake their resolve and edge them toward accepting my generous offer.'

* * *

It took four days. Fronto was standing atop the newly-raised rampart that crossed the low ground to the east of Corfinium when the commotion began. By the time he had mounted and ridden toward the city gate, the staff and several centuries of steel-clad veterans were there too.

Corfinium opened like a punctured and upturned pomegranate. From the gate issued officers in red tunics and burnished steel and bronze, members of the town ordo in togas and even a priest with his head covered as though this were some kind of religious ceremony.

Caesar appeared on the observation point opposite in all his glory once the pomegranate had scattered its red seeds into the low ground. He looked magnificent on his white horse with red cloak and gleaming cuirass. Everything the man did was calculated, even his attire, and Fronto wondered if Caesar had dressed like this in the privacy of his tent every morning against the possibility that this might happen.

A notable absence among the scattered seeds, to Fronto's eye, was Ahenobarbus.

There was a brief confab among the emerging figures, and two set off forward together, one in a toga and the other in the uniform of a senior tribune. Behind them the priest started to follow, but was hauled back by one of the other officers. The two leaders approached the half-built defences and stopped fifty paces from the line of burnished steel atop it.

'Proconsul,' opened the tribune, 'I, Tiberius Ulpius Fullo, represent the combined officer corps of the garrison of Corfinium, and this man represents the town's ordo. We wish to enquire as to whether your terms stand, or whether our continued defiance has cost us the friendship of Rome's most famous son?'

Caesar walked his horse down toward the deputation and waved the shield wall of soldiers to the side. 'I do not think we need so fear two unarmed men, eh?' The centurion chuckled as he moved the men aside. Fronto and the other senior officers followed Caesar into the open.

'My quarrel,' Caesar announced, 'as I keep stating, is with the vicious, barbed tongues of certain corrupt senators, not with any of the Roman people. I do not desire war in any way. In fact, it is my chief goal to conclude matters without any conflict at all if possible. So in answer to your question, my terms most definitely stand. Corfinium may continue to live free and govern itself. Its garrison will be allowed to take a new oath to me and join my forces, who are heroes of the republic and the vanquishers of the Gauls, and the officers may do as they please. Stay, flee, or join me.'

The two men looked at one another and nodded and finally the tribune bowed his head to Caesar.

'Then we hereby deliver Corfinium into your hands, Proconsul. May her cohorts serve you well. And I, for one, will take your oath and continue to lead my men if that meets with your approval.'

Caesar nodded and straightened, raising his voice. 'The surrender of Corfinium is agreed. All officers are free to leave or to retake their oath as they so desire.'

'What of Ahenobarbus?' Curio murmured.

'He comes now, seething and slinking,' sneered Salvius Cursor, pointing down at the gate. Domitius Ahenobarbus had emerged from Corfinium in full armour on his horse and with an entourage of eleven lictors bearing their bundles of sticks and axes. Fronto held his breath. Eleven lictors denoted a proconsul. Ahenobarbus was goading Caesar? Bedecked as Caesar's successor to the proconsulship? He caught sight of the general's hand on his saddle horn and noted how the fingers dug into the leather, the knuckles whitening. Trailing his lictors – Caesar's lictors were only evident at appropriate times, and battles and sieges were not among them – Ahenobarbus rode through the sea of officers and councillors as though parting the waves, reining in not far from the general.

'Gaius.'

'Lucius. You are well? Command suits you.'

'It would appear the eel-like silver tongue of the Julii has worked its dark magic once again and torn my forces out from under me like some low, underhand trickster.'

Caesar shrugged. 'I offer clemency. Only a fool seeks death unceasingly, Lucius.'

'Your offer extends to me?'

There was an uncomfortable silence. Finally, Caesar rolled his shoulders. 'It does, with a single condition.'

'Go on.'

'You claim the authority and pomp of a position that I have not yet agreed to lay down.'

'The senate made me your successor.'

'A senate whose power over me I do not acknowledge. And who have fled Rome in panic, for justice is coming to the city of Romulus. Until the senate meets once more and a solution to this crisis can be found, then I remain proconsul, and therefore I cannot allow you to claim my rights. You are free to go, but your lictors will stay.'

Ahenobarbus' nose wrinkled. 'How petty. You would deprive me of honours for your own personal amusement.'

'That is the offer, Lucius.'

'Very well,' snapped Ahenobarbus, dismissing his lictors with a waved hand. 'But when the senate meets once more, I will see you stripped of every iota of power, honour and respect. Remember that, Gaius.'

Caesar smiled. 'Charmed, as always, Lucius.'

'General,' snapped Salvius Cursor, stepping his horse forward. Fronto's eyes swung to the tribune, whose face was white with suppressed rage. 'You *cannot* let this man go.'

'Mind your tone, Tribune,' Caesar said with a definite edge of steel.

'General, this man is a snake. He is your worst enemy, or at least one of them. He is strong and cunning, and he carries a deal of weight in certain areas of the republic. To release him is to sell your future for a day's peace now.'

Ahenobarbus turned to Salvius Cursor. 'Who is this runt, Gaius?'

Fronto started to reach out, fearing genuinely that Salvius might just go for the man despite any truce.

'General, listen to me,' Salvius hissed. 'If you let this man go you will live to regret the decision. I warn you and counsel you to deal with him now.'

'Can you stop your puppy yapping, Gaius, he's giving me a headache.' Ahenobarbus turned the most oily, smug look on Salvius Cursor and this time Fronto did grasp Salvius' reins just in case. The tribune turned and flashed a look of furious disbelief at Fronto. He tensed, as if prepared to fight, as Galronus' hand gripped his reins on the far side.

'See how popular you are, Lucius,' smiled Caesar. 'I strongly advise you to run while you can. I have given you my word, but if Salvius Cursor here catches you, I doubt even I could stop him tearing you to shreds.'

Ahenobarbus' smug smile faltered for only a moment, and then he nodded. 'Farewell, Gaius. Until the next time.' As he wheeled his horse, he glanced over his shoulder and smiled at Salvius Cursor. 'And *we* will meet again also, runt.'

As the opposition disbanded, some back to Corfinium, others gathering in preparation to lead out the Corfinium legions for their new general, Caesar turned to the small knot of men to his side. 'I appreciate your concerns, Salvius, and I hold your martial abilities and loyalty in high regard, but there are political niceties to observe at times, and you are no politician. Kindly restrain your temper during future negotiations. Fronto? Galronus? Release him.'

As the general rode forward to meet his gathering of new officers, Curio, Trebonius and the others riding close at heel, Salvius Cursor turned a look filled with the fires of Tartarus on Fronto. 'The next time you or your pet barbarian here lay a hand on me or my horse, I will put a blade through it.'

With a snarl, he rode off in the lee of Caesar's command party.

'Makes friends easily, doesn't he?' smiled Galronus.

'He'd better be as good a soldier as Caesar seems to think, else he's not worth the trouble,' Fronto sighed. 'Still, I dare say we'll find out soon enough. With Corfinium and Sulmona secured, there's nothing now that stands between us and Pompey. The *runt* will get his chance to bare his teeth soon enough.'

Chapter Three

9th of Martius - Brundisium

IN all his time serving Rome, Fronto had never travelled further south than Surrentum, across the bay from his home of Puteoli. The ancient lands of Magna Graecia to the south were mysterious. For all his homeland felt very different to the haughty land of Latium or the rougher, more direct charms of the north, the south of Italia was a different world. Still very Greek in its culture, clinging to memories of the war against Carthage that had so ravaged the region for lifetimes.

He'd not been prepared for how pleasant and rural the entire region had been. If it continued to change like this as you headed south, no wonder Africa was considered Rome's bread basket.

The army, bolstered by the forces gathered at Corfinium and now numbering the equivalent of perhaps eight legions, had moved on toward Pompey's recruitment centre at Teanum in southern Campania but news awaiting them at Aufidena some forty miles south immediately changed Caesar's plans.

Perhaps panicked, spurred on by Caesar's increasingly powerful army that was closing on his position, Pompey had uprooted his green, untrained legions, along with the First, his single veteran force, and had fled south and east into the heel of the peninsula deep into Magna Graecia.

Accordingly, Caesar had changed course at the town of Aesernia, following the mountainous Via Bovialis along the spine of the peninsula and making for the south. Two hundred and fifty more miles among the high, forested ridges, gradually descending through the rolling hills to the flat lands of the southeast. And as they passed, so the tide of Italian opinion rolled with them, town after town throwing open their gates and welcoming the proconsul and his army. The great towns of the highlands fell to Caesar without a blade drawn: Benaventum, Aeclanum, Aquilonia, Venusia – where they tarried for some days as Caesar gave thanks to the city's patron goddess who was his own family's progenitor – Silvium, and finally, Tarentum on the south coast, home of the feared cavalry who had fought across the Greek world for so many brutal victors.

Arriving at Tarentum, which lay within the arch of Italia's foot, they felt sure they had cut off Pompey somewhere in the peninsula's toe, toward Sicilia. News awaiting them there, though, confirmed that Pompey's army had passed by recently, bound for Brundisium on the east coast. Consequently, in order to secure the south, Caesar sent thither the cohorts from Corfinium, rapidly training up now into solid legions, and led the remaining six legions east, penning Pompey and his untrained horde in the heel of the peninsula with nowhere to run.

Or so they had thought.

Brundisium sat glowering at them over thick white walls from its near impervious position in the twin arms of a wide 'U' shaped harbour that protected three sides of it, the harbour itself connected to the sea by a single channel beyond. The city was large, but nowhere near large enough to hold the sizeable force that Pompey was said to have raised. Moreover, Brundisium was reputed to be one of the busiest ports on the peninsula and yet there were relatively few ships in view,

A little probing and interrogation produced exasperating answers. Pompey's entire force had, indeed, arrived here some days earlier, in the company of the consuls of Rome – which came as no surprise. But the consuls had commandeered every available ship, both military and civilian, and had begun to ship the cohorts away one by one at surprising speed. The number of men who had put to sea varied from account to account, but the one thing they held in common was the eye watering size of the number. The consuls, moreover, had gone with them.

A little more probing turned up a likely answer. Though several rumoured destinations for the enemy army cropped up, by far the most common was Dyrrachium, on the coast of Illyria, across the Adriaticum. What appeared to be perhaps two legions remained in garrison of Brundisium, though it was said that Pompey remained in personal command of them.

Fronto stood on the tiny hummock that was what passed for a hill in the region and peered at the well-protected city.

'Do you think he's controlling it because he thinks he can control southern Italia and the seas from it, or did we just catch up with him before he got out and he ran out of ships temporarily? If he does have two legions they'll never fit on the few ships left in port.'

Caesar clicked his tongue irritably. He'd been increasingly fidgety and acerbic since he had discovered that the consuls had escaped the peninsula with the lion's share of a powerful new army.

'Right now, Fronto, I do not much care why he remains. What I want to do is take him. How do we control the harbour?'

Pollio tapped his fingers on his arm. 'The mouth of the channel is narrow. Can we dam it?'

Brutus shook his head. 'Too deep. It would take months of work and the sea would constantly erode our work. We could narrow the mouth considerably, mind, building out on the shallower areas with a mole from each side. That would constrict shipping considerably.'

The others nodded sagely, taking the words as truth from the only one of them who had successfully commanded a fleet in recent years.

Galronus frowned. 'Do you have to fill the channel from the bottom to dam it?'

'Last time I heard,' chuckled Pollio, 'even if you drop earth from a great height, it still builds up at the bottom.'

Galronus rolled his eyes. 'What I mean is... well when we were children, my cousin couldn't swim. He hated water, but he was a thief. A real little shit. So we made ourselves a secure place to store whatever we didn't want him to have. We built a wicker raft and packed it with earth and turf, then put a little log hut on it – only a couple of feet square, but enough to keep our stuff dry and safe. Then we floated it out into the pond so he couldn't get to it.'

Caesar turned a thoughtful frown on the Remi prince. 'A novel idea. If these rafts were bigger, then the little wooden house could be more. Perhaps a small fence? Maybe even a tower?'

'The tide would move them,' Brutus pointed out.

'Not if you tethered them to the new moles. We could effectively seal even the deep water of the channel. Thank you, my Remi friend. We shall do just that and trap the shipping. Have two legions encamp here, blockading the city's landward wall, and send two around each side of the harbour to begin work on these plans.'

* * *

The days passed in a constant proliferation of forces.

Caesar's legions encamped and fortified outside the city, building out the moles that narrowed the harbour mouth. Pompey set masons to blocking the city's gates and rigged the few ships he had with siege weapons. Caesar's engineers constructed numerous fighting platforms and floated them out across the water, tethering them to the shore, but Pompey's ships made continual forays toward them, loosing artillery barrages and sinking platforms with ballista balls, smashing down towers and peppering the men with a barrage of arrows and bolts.

The first true casualties of the conflict began to make themselves manifest. A medical station was set up on either side of the harbour and bodies began to be incinerated on the pyres. The buoyant mood of the army, undampened even by the discovery that the bulk of the enemy had managed to slip away, was finally brought crashing down into deep unhappiness at the realisation that Roman legionaries and Roman sailors had unleashed the horrors that had killed their companions. The harsh truth of civil war suddenly found a home in each man's heart, tarnishing his soul.

But where righteous and confidence driven enthusiasm declined, an iron hard will to win began to take its place. Fronto could see it in every eye. All the way down Italia, the men had not truly thought on what it would mean to face Pompey's army. Such a thing hadn't happened for decades, since Marius and Sulla. But now blood had been shed, and that meant that war had truly begun. There were no more illusions.

In one last ditch attempt – though more for the look of it than out of any real intention in Fronto's opinion, Caesar sent Caninius to the gates of the city with a proposal that Pompey and Caesar meet and try to agree terms to save the republic from further fracture. Pompey's answer was short and sharp and not entirely unexpected. There could be no agreement without the consuls, and they were away overseas. So that was that.

Work on the floating platforms was slow at best, with the constant harassment of Pompey's hastily refitted ships, and it slowed even further as they had to move further out into the channel and away from the land, where Pompey's marine artillery could do the most damage, not having to fear the Caesarian weapons on the shores.

Nine days passed in such a state, the tension biting at the nerve ends of every man. Even those like Trebonius, usually so calm and studied in his approach to anything, began to become taut and angry, itching to do something about the enemy. It was as though the entire officer corps was beginning to emulate the blood-hungry Salvius Cursor, which made Fronto nervous.

The ninth day saw something new.

'Fronto, get up.'

Fronto's eyes shot open where he'd dozed off in the chair in the tent's corner following a larger than usual repast.

'What is it?'

'There's a fleet on the horizon.' Galronus looked somewhere between worried and excited as he gesticulated at the tent door.

'Surely not the consuls come back with their army? That would be idiotic with them untrained and green.' Fronto blinked away his grogginess as he rose, wondering what time it was. About sunset, he would guess.

A moment later the two of them were out of the tent into the last of the sun as it dipped below the western horizon, odd scudding clouds too few and far between to threaten rain. The ever-alert equisio had Bucephalus and Eonna, Galronus' bay mare, saddled and ready by the time they reached the shed, and the two mounted and rode off southeast. At the edge of the camp they could see in the gathering gloom Trebonius, Salvius and Curio also ahorse and making for the coast.

Riders from the regular cavalry under the command of an enterprising decurion caught up with them as they rode across the springy green turf, staying out of ballista shot of Brundisium's towers and off around the shorter, southernmost, of the harbour branches.

Fronto's heart sank as he glanced left and could see the silhouetted dark ships departing Brundisium's port, black shapes against wine dark water. A thought occurred to him and he narrowed his eyes, peering up at those ballista towers they had skirted around so carefully. They were distant, and it was almost dark, but he was fairly sure they were extremely undermanned, and could hardly hope to loose a shot. Indeed, there were precious few figures along the walls.

'If Pompey's left anyone at all guarding Brundisium, then it's a pitiful handful,' he shouted to the men riding alongside him.

'What?' Curio yelled back.

'Hardly anyone on the walls, and I'll bet they're sympathetic locals and not his own troops. Pompey's men are in those ships making a break-out.'

'Rubbish,' snorted Salvius. 'Pompey has two full legions in Brundisium. Even with the biggest warships he would need probably twenty five ships to carry two legions and their mounts. Even without artillery and supplies and everything. There are just *twelve* ships *there*.'

Fronto nodded. 'There are, but they're merchant ships, not military ones. Fat bottomed cargo ships built to transport huge amounts of goods. Yesterday those ships were covered in artillery and palisades to cause trouble for our engineers. Today that's all gone. Why? To make room for the men. Pompey's on the run.'

Salvius frowned, then glanced at the ships again and nodded. 'Minerva, but you're right. How can they hope to make it across the Adriaticum like that? One big wave or a strong wind and they'll lose thousands.'

Trebonius shook his head. 'They don't need to. They only need to get out to sea. The consuls have sent their fleet back for Pompey. He gets out to sea and he can diffuse his men across the whole fleet and sail east comfortably.'

'And leave us no ships with which to follow him' Curio sighed. 'I heard that no new traders had come in to Tarentum while we were there. Pompey's been snatching every ship on the coast of southern Italia for his fleet. He gets out and puts to sea it will take us half a year of scavenging and shipbuilding to follow him.'

'Shit, shit, shit,' grumbled Fronto as they raced on, closing on the narrow spithead where two legions maintained their fortification and were constantly attempting to close the gap. The camp was visible mostly as the twinkling of torches and campfires in the increasing gloom, the flickering orange reflecting on the surface of the harbour water. The riders outpaced the ships, though only by a narrow margin and, as they raced along the coast to where the channel narrowed, Fronto could see that the ships had all been fitted with new, outsized iron and bronze rams meant for much larger ships of war. Their purpose was painfully obvious.

As they closed on the channel, Fronto could see a small group of officers standing on the shoreline, black statues against a purple sky, directing matters frantically. He and his companions ran over to find, unsurprisingly, Caesar leading them.

'It's Pompey,' Fronto shouted as they ran in.

'I had guessed,' said Caesar. The fleet awaits him less than a mile out. We did not manage to seal the channel, so we cannot hope to stop them all. Brutus is doing what he can.'

Fronto could see the younger officer down on the newly built mole, shouting to men on the far side. Small rowing boats had been repeatedly used to connect the two sides, and now, hurriedly, they were being used to string long ropes across, attempting to create some kind of net using the cables and the floating platforms. It was an effort doomed to failure, which Fronto could see, and was sure Caesar could too, but there was in truth little else that could be done.

The officers stood on their observation point and watched with sinking spirits while Pompey's ships changed formation as they neared, moving into a narrow spearhead, with the largest and heaviest, affixed with the most powerful ram, to the fore.

The ship hit the feeble net.

The various towers and palisades on the floating platforms had been filled with archers, and a few of the smaller artillery pieces had been placed on the moles where they could reach their targets. These opened up on the vessels as they hit, tearing into timber and flesh with equal ease, occasionally catching one of the Caesarian legionary workers by mistake in the growing darkness.

The first ship's ram punched into a floating platform, shredding the timber frame and ploughing the earth and turf atop it like a Titanic farmer with giant oxen, shattering the defences built on it and sending those men loosing arrows from it into the dark cold water to drown. And then the ship was through, barging aside the next two platforms and toppling a third with its wake.

In its lee came the other vessels, swatting aside Caesar's unfinished works like towers of sticks and straw. There was a moment of excitement when one ship's helmsman misjudged his course and the vessel struck the mole instead of a floating platform in the darkness and confusion. The ship foundered and began to sink, its occupants screaming and desperately trying to climb up from the hold to jump to safety. The mole shook under the impact and one of the artillery pieces slipped into the water, men knocked from their feet. Another ship found itself unexpectedly snagged in ropes before slamming into the far mole and being boarded by the legionaries there.

But they were the minority. Two of the smaller ships stopped, while the other ten were even now racing out across the black water to rendezvous with the fleet awaiting them. And no one among the officers believed remotely the possibility that Pompey himself had been aboard one of the collisions.

Their great enemy had escaped with the bulk of his force to join the consuls and their army in Illyria. And with precious few ships available there was simply no hope of following. Any pursuit would require marching back along the length of Italia, around the top of the Adriaticum and back down the Illyrian coast.

Fronto sighed.

'We should have seen it coming. He was never going to stay and fight it out with you until he knew he stood a chance, and he was always going to have a sneaky plan to escape. You can guarantee also that he's left lots of unpleasant surprises for us in Brundisium.'

Caesar nodded, his expression unreadable, his eyes glinting in the dark.

'And he will strengthen and train his forces in the east,' Curio muttered. 'Then he will be ready to march on Rome in strength like Sulla did half a century ago.'

Fronto remembered the day the great dictator had stormed into Rome like the charge of gods. He'd been a boy at the time, but that kind of thing stuck in the memory. It had been that damned war that had started his father's decline. 'We have to stop him,' he said suddenly.

'What? How?' Trebonius said looking up.

'I don't know,' admitted Fronto, deflating a little.

'There *is* no stopping him for now,' Caesar announced finally, turning and folding his arms. 'For the time being we are done with Pompey.'

'You'll leave him to strengthen, General?' Pollio asked.

'We are left with little choice. We cannot follow him. And there is much to do elsewhere. Rome needs to be settled and calmed, the senate restored to position and authority, my own legitimacy to take care of, and thereby all of yours too. And we must secure what we can from those rebels who have gone east. For they may call themselves the consuls, but in abandoning Rome and fleeing east they forfeit that right in my eyes. Pompey, Lentulus and Marcellus are enemies of the Roman peace now, not us.'

'So what do *we* do, Caesar? March on Rome?' Trebonius looked sour at the thought.

'Hardly. I am no Sulla and I will not bring violence to the city. I will come to Rome in peace and not cross the pomerium as long as I remain proconsul. The fleet from Gaul and the west can be brought to give us access to Pompey, but not this summer. It will be too late. No. We must secure the lands against further influence from those enemies we have identified. The west is closed off to them by Cisalpine Gaul and Italia, where we shall raise new legions and post a smattering of veteran units to deter approach. Quintus Valerius Orca knows Sardinia. He has governed there. He can take a legion to Sardinia and wrest control from Cotta, the pro-Pompeian governor there, which will secure the west coast of the peninsula. Curio, you will take three legions to Sicilia where Cato sits strong and resistant. You will remove Cato from power, and when you have consolidated Sicilia you will cross to Africa and secure the grain supply for Rome.'

Fronto nodded. This was the Caesar he knew, taking charge with energy even when faced with potential disaster.

'But General,' Salvius breathed, 'can we afford to leave Pompey the east?'

Caesar shrugged. 'Focus west. Once Rome is at peace, we have another force to deal with. Pompey's province was Hispania, and he has seven legions there loyal to him. All veterans, remember. The last thing we can afford is for some enterprising officer or official over there to decide to impound the fleet and shipping and move those seven legions to Illyria to join Pompey and the consuls. That would sound the death knell for our entire campaign. We need to deal with Hispania before Pompey calls upon them. We go to Rome, and then on to Hispania. First we deal with an army without a general. Then we can deal with the general without an army.'

Fronto felt a faint lurch of nerves. His family were supposed to be safe in the villa at Tarraco. Even though it was Pompey's province, there had been little chance of trouble there, with Pompey and Caesar set to face off in Italia. Now they could be caught in the vice between Pompey's veterans and Caesar's Gallic legions.

'Give me a command,' Fronto said suddenly.

'Marcus?' Caesar turned to him.

'I'm a legatus and a good one, and you know that, Caesar. You'll need good men against Pompey's veterans. Give me a legion.'

Caesar appeared to be studying him curiously.

'I will think on it, Marcus. First, though, we have business in Rome. And I may have a task or two for you there. For you and our Remi friend, in fact.'

* * *

For three days Caesar sent out letters and messages, commands and requests. Legions departed with new commanders to consolidate Italia's territory. Marcus Antonius was dispatched with great haste for Rome where he would gather together as many senators as remained in the city and call for a meeting of the senate on the Kalends of the next month. Finally, with everything progressed as far as possible, the general rode for the capital with a cadre of officers and his ever faithful bodyguard under Aulus Ingenuus. The army was dispatched the same day and would make their slower way north, past Rome and on toward Cisalpine Gaul and then to Narbo where the legions would gather against Hispania.

Caesar's route was direct, up once more onto the great road that traversed the peninsula's spine, and passing into the fertile lands of eastern Campania, tantalisingly close to Fronto's home ground. Past Capua, faced with a choice of roads, Caesar unexpectedly chose the western, coastal one, and the reason became clear the next day when they arrived at the coastal town of Formiae and made a stop at a luxurious seaside villa. At first Cicero would not emerge to speak with them, but Caesar persisted and finally wore down the man's resolve.

Cicero, while vocally critical of Caesar and supportive of Pompey, had been one of the few leading lights in Rome who had not actively sought to destroy the proconsul, and had not run off in support of his enemy. In fact, he had stayed in the city as long as he dared, and then retired to his villa to avoid the inevitable conflict.

The orator had finally emerged from his house and confronted Caesar in a formal garden overlooking the sea. It had not been a comfortable exchange for any of them. Caesar was no mean speaker himself, and he seemed entirely genuine in his admiration for the villa's owner and his desire that Cicero join him and attend the meeting of the senate in a few days' time.

Cicero, however, was perhaps the most glib, silver-tongued orator of their age, and when he put forth his reasons for refusing, they were so well constructed it was almost embarrassing to be part of Caesar's retinue. Caesar began to sound imploring, noting that Cicero's constant refusal was as good as any condemnation from his enemies. If Cicero refused, many moderate men would not attend purely on that point. The debate had then swiftly devolved into argument, and then bile, into which spat Cicero:

'Well if you insist so and intend to force my presence in the senate, then I shall have no choice in my course of action other than to deplore what you have done to Pompey and to refuse you the right to take an army either to Hispania or Illyria against his legions. I cannot condone civil war, Gaius, and you will gain no words of support from me.'

Caesar had deflated, fixing the orator with his steely gaze one last time and exhorting him to think on it. Then they had mounted once more, and in gloomy silence ridden on up the coast for Rome. Caesar, true to his word, maintained the letter of the law and remained outside the sacred boundary of Rome itself, for Antonius had made every arrangement in advance. He had secured an estate belonging to his own family on the far bank of the Tiber for them all during their sojourn, and had arranged the senate meeting to take place two days hence at the temple of Janus atop the Janiculum hill close to the estate, outside the pomerium so that Caesar could legally attend and, curiously, the very spot where Caesar had met with Pompey and Crassus seven years ago.

The morning of the Kalends of Aprilis dawned chilly but cobalt blue, and Fronto awoke and dressed and wandered out into the atrium to stumble upon one of the more amusing scenes he had encountered in some time. Galronus was standing in the centre of the room, by the decorative impluvium pool, with a look of baffled fascination. A slave stood in front of him with a pile of white material.

'That?' Galronus said in disbelief.

'Yes, Domine.'

Fronto sauntered across, yawning and stretching, and looked from one to the other. Galronus was hardly identifiable as Remi these days. It had been years since his hair touched the nape of his neck, and he had likewise been clean shaven for a long time. His clothing was that of a Roman nobleman, and if any man caught an accent to his Latin, they would assume him to be a rural Italian.

The slave was of Greek extraction, or possibly Levantine. And in his arms he held a new and neatly folded toga. Fronto grinned. 'They're hard to wear the first time. I remember mine. Of course I was a few decades younger.'

'I do not want a toga,' Galronus said flatly.

'Senators wear togas, Domine,' the slave said patiently. 'Especially on the senate floor.'

'I am not a senator,' snapped Galronus.

'The proconsul said otherwise, master. He said that with the censors and the consuls all absent in foreign climes with Pompey, he had as much right as anyone else to appoint a senator.'

Galronus turned a frown on Fronto. 'Don't I have to consent or something? Isn't there a ceremony?'

Fronto chuckled. 'Right now, given the strikingly low number of senators in Rome, I wouldn't be surprised to see dogs and chickens in togas flooding the Janiculum. Just let the man put the toga on for you.'

Galronus narrowed his eyes, sending waves of resentment at Fronto as the slave began his work, draping and tucking, tweaking and pulling as Fronto grasped an apple from the bowl and watched while he chewed. Every now and then, Fronto would put down his apple, step in and interfere with a grin, much to the irritation of Galronus. Finally, the slave was satisfied with the results and Fronto stepped back, gesturing with his apple core.

'Mighty Jove, but you are the very embodiment of Coriolanus himself. A pillar of the Roman republic.'

'A pillock of the Roman republic,' muttered Galronus shrugging his shoulder blades to resettle the heavy, itchy garment.

'Ah, good,' Caesar smiled, striding into the atrium in a similar toga. 'You look every inch the senator, my fine Remi friend.'

'I feel like an idiot. Or an armour stand, under all this weight. I feel like both. An idiotic armour stand.'

'You need to become used to it,' Caesar said, quietly, but earnestly. 'This is no joke and no temporary measure. Those men who formerly filled the ranks of the senate but fled when we crossed the Rubicon are no longer viable senators. Many will now be marshalling with the consuls in Dyrrachium and others have retired to their country villas. In order to have a functioning senate to govern the republic, we need more than a handful of senators. Last year, when you and Fronto came to me, I told you I would make you one of the equites, and perhaps even a senator. Never let it be said I am not a man of my word. There is property across the river that will be in your name before the month is out, and you now have the right to raise your voice in the senate and help steer our republic. What man could have a better right to wed into the Falerii, eh?'

Galronus nodded, still unconvinced.

'Come. All that is required is your vote on certain matters, and as a senator of Rome, you should be above corruption, so I shall not ask you how you intend to vote on any issue. And Fronto? Get your toga on too. *Your* voice counts.'

'I'm not a senator,' Fronto snorted.

'Oh, but you are. Toga, Fronto.'

And leaving Fronto staring, Caesar departed, ushering Galronus on.

'Would you like a hand donning your toga, Domine,' the slave asked quietly.

'Oh shut up.'

* * *

The Janiculum temple was too small to host a true meeting of the senate, but with the vastly reduced number of senators in the city, it would be more than adequate. Fronto stumped up the hill irritably in his heavy toga, Galronus ambling along at his side with a thoughtful expression. Other figures in pristine white were converging on the temple, and Fronto caught as many faces as he could. There was not one he recognised. Of course, he'd spent little time in Rome in the last ten... *twenty* years? Was it that long? But he would know the *famous* faces. Those figures who had made the senate their home and driven the ship of state for years. And none of them were there. That in itself was telling. But there was something even more interesting to be observed if one looked closely and knew what one was looking at.

Almost half those senators he could see converging on the meeting looked exactly as any Roman senator should. But beneath their toga, the cut and material of their tunics, or the manufacture of their boots, betrayed them. They were not Italian. In fact, with Fronto's long experience of the region and given the general's clear connections, it was not much of a leap in logic to identify them as men of Cisalpine Gaul. Those men who belonged to towns that had only been granted citizenship in the past few years and only at Caesar's order.

This was *Caesar's* senate. It might look to the world like any other, but there was no doubt in Fronto's mind what this was. It was Caesar granting himself legitimacy. Half the senate had been installed by him and the other half were the ones who did not oppose him enough to flee the city, or perhaps were not influential enough to even worry about.

The interior of the temple had been expanded by the addition of bench seats raised on three sides in steps to allow more seating than would realistically be required. Despite the brightness of the day, the interior remained gloomy due to the height and size of the windows, and it took Fronto and Galronus time to let their sight adjust upon entry. The occupants had already polarised. Caesar's new senators from Gaul were seated along one wall, with the few remaining old senators glaring at them from across the room, as though they had stolen someone's seat. Which, in some respect, they had, of course. And along the end wall, as though a barrier between the two, sat those of Caesar's officers who could claim or had been granted senatorial status which, through Caesar's careful organisation, was all of them barring Ingenuus, who, with his armed horsemen, had formed a cordon around the summit and the temple upon it, to prevent 'interruptions to the meeting'.

Fronto and Galronus joined Brutus, Trebonius and the others on the end wall and took a seat. Caesar was, of course, one of the last few to enter. In a move perhaps designed to relieve some of the pressure in the room, he strode across and stood against the wall beside the old senators' seats. The last man to enter was Marcus Antonius, and Fronto smiled at the realisation that, with the consuls and censors absent, Antonius as tribune of the plebs had as much right as any city Praetor to preside over such a meeting.

Caesar's lictors had shuffled in barely noticed among the crowd and lined the fourth wall behind Antonius. Notably, because here they were outside the pomerium, each carried an axe inside his rod bundle, and that fact had not escaped the worried notice of more than one wavering senator. One of the lictors, at a nod from Caesar, rapped his rods with his palm several times until the low murmuring stopped.

'Thank you for your attendance,' Antonius said, his voice strong and rich in the high, echoing hall. 'I realise that this extraordinary session of the senate is unexpected and possibly unwelcome, and we all have much we should be doing. We have begun late and therefore I intend to move proceedings along as fast as possible. Firstly, I would like to invite Gaius Julius Caesar, Proconsul of both Gauls, to put to you the case he has been desirous of so doing for more than a year, while being blocked by those who have since fled our august presence.'

There was silence. Well, who was going to argue now?

Caesar stepped forward, and Fronto was in truth only half listening to what the man said. He'd heard the arguments and the rhetoric so often over the months he could almost have given the speech himself. He did not want war. The bitter moves of his political enemies had pushed him into it. All he wished for was the position and authority granted him by the tribunes but denied by the senators. And though in his opinion the consuls had effectively

71

resigned their position by their flight and abandonment of the city, he would not push for his wished for consulate. He would remain proconsul for the remainder of this year and stand for the consulate for the following. If the senate wished to find some practical solution, then he would willingly lay down his Proconsular powers. Of course, Fronto knew that Caesar was hoping the senate would declare the consuls enemies and vote him in as a replacement, but one look at the assembled faces of the old guard suggested this was unlikely. Still, the general's back up plan kept him safe and empowered until such time as he could legitimately stand for consul, and no one was going to try and take Gaul from him now.

There were various bits of miscellanea touched upon, and Fronto had almost dozed off when the first surprise came.

'And so I have two requests to put to the senate for debate today,' Caesar announced. 'Firstly the dispatch of senatorial envoys to Pompey and the consuls in Dyrrachium in a last attempt at reconciliation...'

Clever old bastard. Even with his new senate, the old-fashioned extant senators had been resistant, but this crumb of humility and the seeming desire for peace went to work on them instantly, and Fronto could see it glowing in their eyes.

'And I would ask the senate's blessing in drawing money from the public treasury to pay the legions of the Roman state who I have had cause to raise in the interest of the security of the Roman people.'

'You want our money for your legions?'

The speaker was Lucius Caecilius Metellus, the other tribune of the plebs along with Antonius. In the old days such tribunes would have been forbidden from the senate, but such days were long gone. Antonius gave his colleague a hard stare, but Metellus was defiant as he rose to his feet. Caesar simply shrugged.

'When I was considered a threat to the republic, which has been proved repeatedly to be false, did you not open your vaults to Pompey to raise legions against me? Am I to be afforded less honour and accommodation than the man who fled Rome and left you defenceless? Had I actually been a Sulla for our times, bent on bringing my army to Rome, what use would your money have done you in his hands. But now, as he begins to form a solid threat across the water, my new legions have been raised with the sole premise that men will be required to protect Italian soil from invasion. These are the units for which I seek financial support.'

'Never,' snapped Marcellus.

'One man's voice counts only as a note in the chorus of the senate,' said Antonius meaningfully. A vote must be taken on both matters.'

'I thank you for your time and consideration,' Caesar said, with a bow, stepping aside.

Fronto watched proceedings with interest for the next hour as senator after senator spoke on the merits and flaws of both questions, each man who cared to speak having his opportunity in descending order of importance. It did not escape Fronto's impressed notice once more that with the most senior senators absent and Caesar's new additions being clearly the most junior, those older senators who had always been at the bottom of the heap suddenly found themselves being the first to address, and their pomp and self-importance blossomed, clearly boosting Caesar's chances with even them.

The vote to send envoys to Pompey was a close thing. Despite the motion being Caesar's own, the officers of his corps were split in how they voted, as were the old guard, who felt as much betrayed by Pompey's flight as they were worried by Caesar's presence. In the end his new Gallic senators carried the vote by an acceptable margin, which kicked off a second discussion about who would be sent. It would have to be a high official. And now the only high officials in Rome were in this very room, given that the others were with Pompey already. But no matter how many times the question was asked, no names were put forward. No one wanted to go to Pompey. The debate finally fizzled out. Everyone wanted a deputation sent, but no one wanted to *be* a deputation.

The second debate was considerably less close. While undoubtedly few of the senators truly liked the idea of Caesar digging into the city treasury, many of them owed not only their sudden new prosperity but perhaps even their ongoing existence to the proconsul, and failing to pay his armies might be an utterly self-defeating move. And with those eleven hard-looking lictors and their shiny axes at the rear of the room, the incentive to do right by the general was higher than ever. The vote was carried with only six against.

Fronto watched as the senate's business was allowed to run fully through its traditional cycle. It reaffirmed Fronto's opinion of the institution. It needed to exist, and it needed to be free, but it would never be for him. His mother would have had him on this bench much of his life. Of course he might have ended up consul? Proconsul? Might right now have been skulking in Illyria worrying about what Caesar was doing with his city? He shook his head in irritation and felt Galronus watching him.

'What?'

'Are you ill? You look ill.'

'Politics. It does that. Do you think we can leave yet?'

But Caesar was now strolling around the edge of the room, leaving the discussions to the white-clad pilots of government and making quietly for their bench.

'Fronto?'

'Yes, Caesar.'

'In the morning, I would like you to go to the *aerarium* treasury at the temple of Saturn and empty it.'

Fronto blinked. '*Empty* it?'

'Yes. Pompey will already have taken the lion's share for his army. We will require what is left. If the city runs short, the senate will have to start declaring some of the absent antagonists enemies of the republic and impounding all their estates and money. They'll soon fill it up again. They could fund the city for a year on Cicero's estate alone.'

'You devious bas...' began Fronto, then caught the general's expression. 'Yes, General.'

Galronus punched Fronto on the arm and called him something unkind in his own language.

* * *

The next morning dawned grey and overcast, a good deal colder than the previous one, and Fronto shivered as he stumped through the Velabrum on his way to the forum, cloak wrapped tightly around himself. Galronus traipsed along next to him, his expression blank and unreadable. The steady, rhythmic tromp of military boots echoed behind them, as well as the creaking of cart wheels. The idea of bringing soldiers into the forum to essentially rob the state for the military did not sit well with him, and images of the city running red following Sulla's march on Rome filled his head repeatedly. At least none of them were armed on this occasion, other than the centurion with his vine stick and the optio with his staff.

The populace of Rome, while used to being wary in the streets due to the modern prevalence of violent criminals and political disturbances, were not used to seeing armour and uniforms, even if those men had left their weapons behind. People pushed back into doorways and alleys, keeping well out of the way of the small military column as it crunched and rumbled along the Vicus Tuscus.

The slope of the Palatine rose to their right and the heights of the Capitoline, towering above the Tarpeian Rock from which traitors were traditionally thrown, lay to the left. *That* rather bleak reminder did little to quiet his conscience over his current mission. Ahead: basilicas, temples, the curia, columns and shrines. The political and spiritual heart of the Roman world.

Fronto felt less and less happy with what he was doing as they reached the Basilica Sempronia and turned, making for the great rectangular shape of the Temple of Saturn which sat at the head of the forum beneath the Capitol. A white fortress of piety and wealth with a frontage of six grand columns atop a lofty staircase. Fronto glanced back at the soldiers as they moved swiftly across the forum toward the place.

'Centurion? Line the carts at the foot of the staircase. Half your century will have to stand guard with them while the others do the hard work, I'm afraid.'

The centurion nodded his head in acknowledgement and, as they reached the base of that flight of steps, the legionaries secured the carts and wedged the wheels, affixed feedbags to the horses' bridles and prepared everything.

'Is that a door?' Galronus murmured, pointing at a man-sized rectangular aperture in the base, facing the forum.

'It was, once. Now it's barred off thickly. Access only through the temple these days.'

'Will there be a priest?' the Remi asked quietly as he looked up at the temple steps. It struck Fronto that while his friend had become Roman in so many ways, he had never seen Galronus go to a temple without him. Did he acknowledge the Roman gods? Fronto hadn't truly noticed.

'Actually, probably not,' he replied conversationally. 'Saturn doesn't have a priest of his own. His temple is served by the Rex Sacrorum, who's sort of the head of the whole Roman priesthood. No one else has enough authority. And the current Rex Sacrorum is one of so many who have fled the city. Where he is no one seems to know, but my money is on Dyrrachium with the consuls. There are staff who maintain the temple, of course, but they're all just workers and they won't be here when he isn't. And then there's the quaestors who have responsibility for the treasury itself, but-'

'But they're in Dyrrachium?' Galronus hazarded.

'More than likely. Come on.'

Puffing a little with the effort, Fronto climbed the thirty two steps of the grand staircase to the imposing building at the top. Taking the most common Roman form of temple, it consisted of a solid rectangular cella of heavy stone with a pillared portico in front. As they reached the top, Fronto paused, grasping his knees with his hands and bending, finding his breath once more. Galronus, beside him, cleared his throat.

'Who's that?'

Fronto straightened. A shadowy figure in the gloom beneath the portico was almost invisible in front of the great bronze doors.

'Don't know. Come on.'

He strode between the columns and approached the figure. Lucius Caecilius Metellus, tribune of the plebs, stood in his toga in the deep shadow, his face stony and bleak. In his hand was a knife. Not a small eating knife, but perhaps not quite big enough to be classed as a weapon of war and break the sacred laws. He waved the knife at them.

'Caecilius.'

'Go back, Marcus Falerius Fronto. You'll not take the state's money.'

'You're going to be disappointed, Caecilius. Out of the way.'

76

'You are a nobleman of Rome, Fronto. Patrician blood flows in your veins. You can't do this. Rape your own republic to strengthen the army of a would-be despot?'

'Did you not know, Caecilius? He's no enemy of Rome now. The senate confirmed his Proconsular powers until the end of the year. You do have a terrible memory, Caecilius, as I *know* you were there.'

'The man who makes his own senate can grant himself anything, Fronto. It doesn't make him *right*, though.'

'Enough banter, Caecilius. Get out of the way.'

'It'll do you no good anyway, Fronto. There are only two keys to the temple. One belongs to the Rex Sacrorum and is still with him, and the one for the quaestors is in Pompey's hands now. These bronze doors are rightly locked against you.'

''Wooden doors, Caecilius. They might be coated with bronze, but no bugger would be able to pull them open if they were solid metal. I suspect you'll find that half a century of veteran legionaries can make short work of a door, no matter how impressive.'

Caecilius glared at him. 'You would break into Rome's most hallowed temple like some sacrilegious thief?'

'And I will break you in half to get to them if you don't get out of the way, Caecilius. This has been agreed by the senate of Rome. You are in the wrong, no matter what you believe. And don't think for a minute that little toothpick is going to make me shit myself, let alone my friend here or the centurion behind me. We've stood knee deep in blood and bone while German women tried to put barbed spears through us. We're in the right here, Caecilius.'

But somewhere in Fronto's soul, he felt the corrosion taking hold even as he spoke. Just a little sacrilege here, a little trick there. It might not seem much, but he found himself suddenly wondering how his father's descent into drink and misery during the last dictator's rule had begun. He remembered as a boy being forced to study his Polybius and scoffing at the very idea of history coming in cycles. And yet here he was in oddly similar circumstances to his father, wondering whether he had just set off down that self-same path.

'Sir,' called the centurion arriving at the top of the stairs behind him and breaking the rather depressing spell.

'Yes?' he asked, turning.

'The carts are ready and I've brought forty lads up to start work.'

Behind the centurion, legionaries were standing in ranks on the steps, waiting for orders. 'Good,' Fronto said, mentally swatting at the soul-destroying demons gathering at the edge of his consciousness. 'Caecilius Metellus was just getting out of the way, weren't you, Caecilius.'

'Go away Fronto.'

'I'm afraid it appears that the keys have all fled in terror across the sea, Centurion, so we'll have to smash the doors open. Can your men manage that?'

'We've broken open Gallic oppida, sir. I think we can manage a door.'

'Good man. Get to it.'

Caecilius Metellus hurried forward, waving his hands, the knife seemingly forgotten as he sought to dissuade them.

'No, no, no.'

Before he'd really decided what to do about the man, Fronto had grabbed hold of a gesticulating arm and yanked. Caecilius, unbalanced, staggered to Fronto, who nodded at two legionaries as the large cooking knife clattered away across the ground.. 'Be so good as to hold the tribune here still and remove his knife. I don't want him to hurt himself.'

As the two men grasped the tribune by the arms and pinned him in place, Fronto joined the centurion at the door.

'Piece of piss, sir,' the centurion grinned. 'Atticus? Tauro? Get this door open. Stand aside, sir, if you will.'

Fronto moved to one side as two legionaries the size of some kind of ancient mythical monster emerged from the group of soldiers, took a look at one another, nodded and broke into a run. They hit the doors like a runaway wagon, and there was a deep, echoing clong as they ricocheted off the bronze, cursing and rubbing their shoulders. But Fronto had distinctly heard a small cracking noise in the midst of the clong that still reverberated inside the temple.

'Again,' the centurion called. Atticus and Tauro jogged back to the stairs, counted together and ran again. As Caecilius Metellus watched in disbelieving dismay, they hit the doors and with a crunch were through and into the dark interior. The bronze-sheathed wooden leaves crashed back against the inner walls while pieces of the lock clattered across the tiled floor. The centurion bowed and gestured inside.

Fronto and Galronus entered the temple and allowed their eyes to adjust once more. As the two big men who'd affected entry helped one another up and rubbed their shoulders, wincing, other men rushed around lighting oil lamps to illuminate the interior. With the centurion at heel and his men following on, Fronto and Galronus crossed the temple, the Romans lowering their heads and muttering a respectful prayer to the perfect statue of the god at the far end on its plinth, a red cloak over its shoulders, head veiled and feet bound in wool. As the centurion and his men looked over the trapdoor that gave access to the stairs that led down into the podium, Fronto made a quick and very fervent promise to the god to have the doors mended and to raise an altar to Saturn at the first available opportunity.

By the time he reached the trapdoor, the soldiers had it open, and he was the first to descend into the aerarium – the state treasury – that resided within the heavy podium upon which the temple sat. A soldier handed him a glowing oil lamp and he emerged into the vaults carrying it for illumination, Galronus right behind him, then the centurion.

The aerarium, a place few had either cause or right to visit during their time in Rome, consisted of twin vaulted rooms that ran the full length of the temple, openings connecting the two repeatedly along their length.

Fronto could imagine what the place must have looked like in Rome's richest days, before Pompey had ripped out all the gold his pet senate would allow. Still, the number of chests standing in neat, ordered lines down the side of the first room was impressive, enough to buy a thousand country estates with enough left over for a warship or twenty. For these chests were not stacked with bronze or brass or even good sestertii, but packed with bars of silver and even of gold.

A shelf near the stairs held a ledger that contained a neatly written record of deposits and withdrawals. Pausing to examine it, Fronto's eyes widened at the last entry. The figure was large enough to loosen the sphincter of any money lender. It was under the name of the consul Cornelius Lentulus, but then it would be, for Pompey had no authority to remove it himself and would have had to rely upon the consuls to do so. Caesar was bound by no such niceties, of course. One thing Fronto was sure of as he replaced the book and turned, scratching his head: Pompey had taken more money than remained in the vaults.

'Get to work,' he said to the men now joining them in the room. 'Start with this line. Eight men to a chest and make use of the trolleys as much as you can. The legions don't tend to look after soldiers with bad backs that well.'

As the soldiers began to manoeuvre the extremely heavy chests into position, walking them to the purpose-built small trolleys, Fronto strolled into the other parallel room, which was filled with alcoves and niches. Galronus followed him, squinting into the gloom. A light glowed at the far end where what had once been the door now admitted light through a thick and thoroughly burglar-proof iron grille.

'Not just chests of coin, then,' Galronus muttered.

'Eh?'

'Books and metalwork,' the Remi noted, pointing at a stack of bronze plaques carefully stored, with linen to prevent chafing, and the collections of carefully-bound books piled neatly close by.'

'Roman law in all its glory, Galronus. Those are the current official copy of the twelve tables – the root codes of all law. And the proceedings of the senate are all stored in books. If you could be bothered and had the time, you could go back through these books right to the early days of the republic and see what men like Cato or the Gracchi said to one another. Mostly insults if I know the senate.'

'You Romans have a peculiar need to document everything, don't you. I'm surprised you don't have a little book in the latrines to keep track of your movements.'

'Some men do. I know a Greek medic in the city who insists on it.'

'Your people are weird. However did they find time to grow from a small town into this?'

Fronto grinned and walked on down the passage listening to the sounds of soldiers grunting and swearing as they shifted the heavy chests. 'There are things we'll leave, for all Caesar said to empty the place. We'll just take money. That's all. We're not here to pillage the place.'

Galronus nodded. 'Besides, you'd be here for a month filling in your little book with what you've taken. What's that, then?'

At the end of the second room another five large chests stood, their antiquity clear, a thick layer of dust atop them. A single helmet sat atop the nearest chest, and Galronus examined it curiously. It was most definitely the helmet of a Gaulish nobleman, albeit centuries out of fashion.

'The Gallic Defence Fund,' Fronto sighed.

'The what?'

'Rome was sacked by Gauls centuries ago. It's how the animosity all began, really. But there was defiance and indignation in Rome afterwards. They were determined never to let it happen again. A huge fund was gathered and stored here just in case. If the Gauls ever hoved into view again there was enough money here to raise quite an army to stop them.'

Galronus laughed. 'And here we are. A conqueror of Gaul and a Remi prince, close enough to place our hands on it.'

'Better than that,' Fronto snorted and then turned and shouted over his shoulder. 'Centurion? The Gallic Defence Fund is down here. See it gets taken out to the carts, will you?' When he caught the bemused look on Galronus' face, he grinned. 'Well I for one hope we've seen the last threat from Gaul. I figure it's redundant now.'

The pair strolled back, pausing to examine legion eagles from the time of the war against Carthage and other priceless treasures, Galronus quizzing him on various items and then pausing to peer at the books of senate proceedings and the twelve tables of law and pronounce them gibberish even with the good command of Latin he now had.

They waited for the best part of an hour as the men continually removed chest after chest, including the Gallic fund. Only once the aerarium was hollow and echoed to the sound of the legalised robbery did the soldiers leave, clomping up the steps into the temple above and leaving only the centurion with them. As Fronto and Galronus reached the stairs once more, the centurion was busy making careful notes in the ledger.

Fronto peered as the man wrote.

'Fifteen thousand bars of gold, thirty thousand bars of silver, thirty million sestertii...' He grasped the ledger and pen from the surprised centurion's hand, scratched two lines across the new entry and replaced it with the word 'everything'.

'Done. Come on.'

Within the colonnade out front Caecilius Metellus had clearly given up struggling. The soldiers had let him go and he sat with his back to a column, ashen faced and trembling as he watched the value of an empire being loaded on to carts at the bottom of the stairs. Half a dozen soldiers were just shifting the last chest down the steps.'

Shame they couldn't use that doorway downstairs, sir, the centurion mused.

'But if *we* could open it, so could robbers. Better this way, I reckon.'

The officer nodded and followed on.

'So that's it?' Caecilius Metellus said flatly, pushing himself upright. 'You've robbed Rome. Will you and your despot master be going now or do you intend to stay and start stripping the valuables from the other temples?'

Fronto reached out to take the man's arm but he flinched away.

'Don't touch me.'

'It was inevitable, Caecilius. You couldn't stop it, and nor could I. But it's done now. And I don't think the general has any intention of causing any further trouble in Rome. He will not delay. The senate are once more in control of Rome, there are plenty of sources of funds available to rebuild the treasury in the form of absent enemies, this will pay for the forces who defend the peninsula against the forces in the east, and there are matters to be addressed out west.'

Caecilius Metellus ignored him and turned to stomp away. Galronus breathed quietly. 'You think we'll be off straight away?'

'I do. A few days at most and we'll be off to Hispania.'

And the family. Gods, let the family be safe...

Chapter Four

18th of Aprilis - Massilia

18th of Aprilis - Massilia

THE column moved swiftly along the hillside overlooking the great port city. Strangely, the place had come to feel more like home to Fronto than Rome ever had. There were half a dozen new villas on the periphery, outside the heavy, ancient Greek walls, but he could see his and Balbus' ones well enough. Even from here he could tell they had been empty for some time, given the overgrown nature of the grounds. There should still be a few slaves there keeping the place secure, and Catháin and the staff of the business should still be in Massilia. While the family had left, Catháin had remained to keep the trade active. Surely he was using the villa?

He glanced behind him at the men.

Horses. An entirely mounted column. The legions were still following on from Italia, but they would be many days behind, moving through necessity at slow campaign pace, while Caesar had forged on ahead to meet up with his other Gallic veterans who hovered on Pompey's provincial doorstep at Hispania. As well as the officers and scouts, nine hundred cavalry plodded along behind – the horse contingent from one legion and a mixed unit of Gallic and Germanic cavalry they had collected in Cisalpine Gaul on the way.

'Will Massilia be sympathetic?' Fronto asked the general, who turned a frown on him. 'Well, I heard they had spoken openly in support of Pompey and the senate.'

Caesar's eyes hardened. 'I imagine they were testing which way the wind blew. Given my long history with Massilia, the amount of trade I have put through the place and the favoured position I put them in above all other allied independent cities, they will be displaying a dangerous level of ingratitude if they deny me.'

But Fronto harboured his doubts still as they began to descend, making for the red and brown mass of the city that lay between deep blue sky and azure sea. Caesar had visited the place a few times and put a factor in to maintain his supply system, but Fronto had lived there. He had encountered the xenophobic anti-Roman sentiments of some of the traders. He had seen the boule – the town's council – arguing in their chamber and knew them for what they were.

The main roads leading to the gates of Massilia thronged with people, carts and animals going both in and out, but as the long line of armoured riders became obvious, figures stopped emerging from the gates and those seeking entry did so speedily, pushing their way into the city. By the time the newcomers had reached the low grassy slopes outside the walls, where there was a natural dip in the terrain, the last of the travellers and city folk had disappeared through the gates.

Caesar rode at the head of the column in his gleaming cuirass and red cloak astride his white horse, backed by the cream of Roman military command and near a thousand mounted killers.

And the gates were shut.

Caesar's face did not change, but Fronto felt the anger sweep out of the proconsul like a wave.

For his own part, Fronto was less than surprised. Caesar had been generous to Massilia, but so had the senate, and the links between the place and Rome itself were ever tightening. The boule of the city almost certainly still thought of Caesar as an outsider – a rebel. There was even a chance that they had not yet heard that Caesar had re-founded the senate in Rome.

'What do they think they're doing?' Trebonius snarled.

'They think they're supporting Rome against a rebel,' Fronto replied. 'I could almost see this coming.'

'Can they hold out against us if we decide to do something about them?' the officer asked. 'Do they have a strong garrison?'

Fronto shrugged. 'They have *a* garrison. I wouldn't say it's particularly strong, but I *will* say they don't have to do much to hold out against a thousand horse. Had we arrived with the best of the Gallic legions, I imagine those gates would have been open faster than a whore's door on a festival day, but with just this small cavalry column, they have to decide whether to hold to their oath to the senate and consuls or to Caesar.'

'You sound surprisingly sympathetic?' Salvius Cursor grumbled.

'Not especially, but they are rather in the shit. They support Pompey and anger us. They support us, and everything is roses and wine now, but what if Pompey comes west and thrashes us? They would have lined themselves up to be punished by Pompey. If I were them I'm not sure what I would do, that's all.'

Caesar huffed angrily.

'Do you have any connection with the rulers, Fronto? You've spent time here.'

'Not exactly, General. They never really liked me much. I've got people inside, but just traders and workers and scribes. No one important.'

Caesar shuffled in his saddle. 'I cannot afford a delay.'

The other men nodded their agreement. News of events in Rome and of Pompey's withdrawal might not yet have reached Hispania, but if it hadn't, it would do soon. And then it was anyone's guess what Pompey's men would do. Realistically, in order to control the situation in the west, Caesar had to deal with the forces there as soon as possible, while there was uncertainty, confusion and disarray.

'And yet I can hardly ride for Hispania and leave a strong point between me and Italia, that favours the enemy. Massilia must be taken care of. I am in an unenviable position, gentlemen.'

'How far behind us are the legions?' Trebonius asked quietly.

'Two weeks at a rough estimate,' Salvius Cursor spat. 'Too long.'

'Regardless of the urgency of Hispania, we shall need to dally here after all,' Caesar sighed. Across the dip, men were now beginning to line the walls. It was starting to look more and more like defiance rather than uncertainty. 'Let us start to put things in place. If there is any chance of us frightening them into capitulation, then we must try for it. We need to make it clear that defiance in Massilia will not be tolerated and that we are serious about the matter. Fronto, your villa is somewhere around here, if I remember correctly?'

'At the far end of the land walls, Caesar.'

The general nodded. 'Might we prevail upon you?'

'The place has been empty for some time, Caesar, but it should suffice. For the officers, that is. It's a good size, but not big enough to accommodate a thousand.'

Caesar smiled for the first time since their arrival. 'Good. I want to set the cavalry to work on defences, and then the officers can retire to Fronto's villa to plan.'

'The cavalry, sir? They won't have a clue. Not an engineer among them.' Trebonius' brow furrowed.

'It doesn't take years of training to dig a straight ditch and pile up the dirt. And there are officers among us who've watched it done hundreds of times. There's a depot at Aquae Sextiae ten miles from here that's been active since before the Gallic revolt. There will be all the tools and equipment we need there. Have riders go there and retrieve the tools. While they're gone, get some twine and have men start marking out three legion-sized camps.'

'Three, sir?' Trebonius echoed. 'Three legions?'

'Yes, Trebonius. In fact, you're in charge of it all. I want the residents of Massilia to see what we're doing. I want them to realise we're preparing for three legions to arrive and that they mean to stay and deal with Massilia. We'll give them a day or two of watching the preparations to get nervous and realise what it means, then we'll have a little chat with their council and see if we cannot get those gates thrown open.'

* * *

Fronto stood on the veranda of his villa with Galronus, sipping from his wine cup and enjoying the play of sun on his face. Caesar's attendants had done a good job of making the villa habitable, firing up the furnaces and heating the floors and the private bath suite, gathering in foodstuffs and collecting linen and other goods from local sources.

He had been rather surprised when they arrived to find the villa empty. And not just empty of people and valuable possessions, either. Truly empty, as though he had moved out. The bare furnishings were still there, and the drapes too, but no linen, no foodstuff, no supplies, no crockery. What had Catháin done?

Still, it was now liveable, and with the sun still two or three hours from setting, they had been outside Massilia for more than a day. The camps were progressing surprisingly well, considering the lack of experience of both the riders doing the digging and the officers planning the sites. Every few hours the important folk of Massilia would gather on the walls and watch the activity. No one could say what was going through their minds, but Fronto could hazard a guess. Nervousness. Panic, even?

The general emerged, stretching, from the front door.

'Shall we go and rattle someone's confidence?'

Ingenuus and his riders fell in with the officers as they left the villa, a dozen men of Tribunician rank or above, and walked their horses slowly toward the walls of Massilia – slowly enough to allow word to be carried in the city and the councillors to make it back to the walls. Sure enough, as they neared the gate, white-clad figures appeared atop the parapet between the heavy, square towers. Fronto glanced to either side, his gaze taking in the twin bolt throwers of classic Greek design on the towers. Neither had swivelled toward them yet. The moment they even twitched, he wanted to be ready to get out of there.

'Am I speaking to representatives of the city boule?' Caesar called in clear, flat tones as he reined in before the gate.

A voice called out in a thick Massiliot accent in reply. 'I am Pherecydes of the council of Massilia. Say what you have to say, Proconsul, and begone from our walls.'

Caesar leaned back and folded his arms.

'I do not expect your welcome, despite the longstanding alliance we have held throughout my dealings in Gaul. Despite the impressive mercantile growth you have experienced through my patronage. Despite the money I have put into your city. Despite the favoured position I secured it with the republic of Rome. I do not even expect your surrender or capitulation to me. Because despite everything I am one man, and what you should do is welcome *Rome*. Surrender to *Rome*. Just like all of Italia has done before you. Because I am no rebel. I am a servant of Rome, intent on restoring her in the face of the animals that have wrested control from her rightful senate.'

He allowed a pause, half expecting the Massiliots to fill it, but there was only silence.

'If I am required to, I will invest Massilia with siege works and force a settlement, for I cannot suffer such strong opposition sitting directly at the heart of my supply lines. But I would far rather we come to agreed terms now and settle the matter peacefully.'

'Your horses can climb walls now, Caesar?'

Fronto saw the dangerous flash in the general's eyes as he fought to control his temper at that.

'There are a number of veteran legions only a week or so behind me and, once they arrive, Massilia will be looking at hardship, pain and protracted deprivation. Do not toy with me, Pherecydes of Massilia. This is no game.'

'Oh but it *is*, Proconsul of Gaul. It *is* a game, and a race and a wrestling match, and on much closer terms than you realise. And it does sadden us to turn our backs upon a man who has favoured our city. But equally your consuls and Pompey himself have done so in their turn. Pompey granted extra lands to our territory and endowed us with funds for expansion to increase our trade with his provincial ports in Hispania. So you see we are left with a choice of who to disappoint. And while your legions are a week away, we have it on good authority that Domitius Ahenobarbus, carrying the authority of the consuls and senate of Rome, is much closer with a fleet of men to support Massilia. So you see, along with our Albici allies who already drew into the city at news of your approach, we are thoroughly prepared to hold out against you, should you make the unfortunate decision to besiege us.'

Fronto could see the vein throbbing at Caesar's temple, indicating either that a decision was about to be made that everyone would regret or that – more likely – Caesar was about to suffer one of his falls. He turned to Trebonius. 'Get everyone back to the villa.'

'But, Fronto…'

'Now!' As Trebonius turned and gestured for the others to follow on, Fronto yanked on Caesar's reins, turning his horse. Galronus came along the other side of the general and Salvius Cursor and Aulus Ingenuus were suddenly there too.

'Get back to the villa,' Fronto snapped at the tribune, trying to urge Caesar's horse forward as the general rocked gently, held in place by his horned saddle, his eyes half-closed and his body trembling.

'Fronto, what is this?' Salvius asked quietly.

Fronto gave a meaningful look at Ingenuus, who nodded and turned. 'Go, Tribune.'

Salvius gave Fronto a glare as though he'd taken personal offence, and then rode off in the wake of the others. Caesar was starting to shake now.

'Quickly.'

Grabbing the general's reins and hoping the saddle would hold him adequately in place, Fronto, Galronus and Ingenuus escorted Caesar back up the slope of the defile, across the ridge and to a small barn that stood on the edge of some rich man's estate. Ingenuus' riders formed a cordon around the place, and Ingenuus and Fronto pulled Caesar out of his saddle, dragging him into the shed, where they dumped him unceremoniously on a pile of damp, cold straw. The general was starting to shake wildly.

'Hold him down,' Fronto told the other two, then looked around and, unable to find a stick, stupidly on the edge of a farm, he pulled his pugio from his belt, made sure it was the one with the leather binding on the grip, and prised the general's jaws open, placing the knife hilt between them and holding it there.

They held him tight for some time as he bucked and shook, froth and drool flicking from his mouth as he thrashed. After a while, the shaking subsided and the fight went out of the fit. Ingenuus, his expression grave and his face pale, fixed Fronto with a steady look.

'You knew?'

'I've seen it once or twice now,' Fronto nodded. 'And I think it gets brought on when he becomes enraged. I saw it coming this time, in plenty of time.'

'You certainly did. And good job. The Massiliots will be wondering what happened to him, but at least they didn't see this. And neither did the officers.'

Galronus frowned. 'This happens often?'

'Not often,' Ingenuus replied. 'Happened once in front of a Gallic deputation, which was almost a disaster. We managed to convince them he was stung by something and had a bad reaction. The truth of this would make people nervous. They would think him cursed or unlucky, and we cannot afford that.'

A weak voice beneath them said 'I am luckier than most. Thank you.'

A shaky hand proffered Fronto's pugio, hilt first, where the leather was sodden and covered in teeth marks.

'Er… thank you.'

'Next time, Fronto, find a stick. I think I chipped a tooth.'

'Gadfly bite, sir?' Ingenuus murmured. 'It's about the right season now.'

Caesar nodded as he slowly sat up. 'Gadfly. Good. I need to dust myself down and wipe my face and get back to the men.'

'Take a few moments,' Fronto said quietly. 'Make sure you're steady. It's not like anything will change in the next hour.'

'The next *hour*, no,' Caesar replied. 'But the next few days… Damn it, Fronto we're in a race. The legions get here first and we can storm Massilia or threaten them into surrender, then all is good. We leave a garrison and move on. But if gods-damned Ahenobarbus gets here first with his fleet then we have a full-scale siege on our hands, and I can afford neither the men nor the time to deal with that.'

'Ahenobarbus is only days away, and the legions well over a week. Unless there's a freak storm, I think we've already lost the race.'

'And Hispania gains time to prepare,' Caesar sighed. 'Everything is coming unstitched at the last moment, gentlemen. We need to be certain. I need to send riders to find my legions and discover how close they are and whether there is any way to speed up their approach. And I shall have to send a message to Fabius and the legions at Narbo. If we are to be delayed here, then he must move to keep Pompey's legions off-balance. He should move to secure the Pyrenaei and all the border crossings.'

'Maybe you should send Salvius Cursor into Hispania for you, Fronto said. 'The whole place will probably be a charnel house before you can get there.'

'That one I am keeping on a tight leash until he is needed,' Caesar sighed. 'He will have his time and his uses, but it is not yet time.'

* * *

Three days later the riders brought news that Caesar's legions were at Nikaea, a hundred miles to the east and would be three more days even at a forced march before they could hope to join the general. This unhappy news was compounded when that next day, at noon, a fleet of seven warships appeared on the horizon, pulling into the harbour of Massilia by mid-afternoon, their bellied sails bearing the eagle motif of the consular fleet and every foot of space bristling with armed men.

Ahenobarbus had arrived.

Salvius Cursor was unrelenting with his high ground, reminding them all how he had been adamant that Ahenobarbus should not be spared at Corfinium and how now, when they least required intervention, here was the man again with a relief force for the defiant city.

'Well, Caesar,' Trebonius had sighed, 'it looks like a siege after all.'

* * *

Carbo fastened the chinstrap of his ostentatious helmet and glared at Atenos.

'This outfit feels like I'm preparing to play some role in the theatre. Probably a comedic one.'

Atenos laughed. 'Respectfully, Legatus Carbo, you could fall in a pile of horse shit and stand up smelling of roses.'

Carbo gave him the same glare he'd been using all the way from Narbo. The centurion shrugged. 'I've been a warrior, a mercenary and a legionary and now I'm a centurion. I'll never go higher than this, though. You? Centurion, then camp prefect and now legate? What's next? Going for consul after Caesar.'

Carbo grunted as he settled his weighty cloak into place. Caesar's letter assigning him command of the Tenth had come in the winter and he'd been flabbergasted, though on sober reflection – and he hadn't been sober for a few days afterwards – it was a natural choice. He had served with the Tenth for over a decade and had been senior centurion for many of those years. Following his spell in captivity he had come back tentatively to serve as camp prefect, and while he thought he'd been mediocre in the role at best, others said he'd excelled in the position. And Caesar had taken note. So, short of senior officers and with men fleeing his side as he opposed the senate, Carbo was the natural choice.

'I note that the Tenth got the choice assignment again. The Ninth get the tender meat, the Sixth the tasty crackling, and the Tenth the chewy gristle of life.'

'With respect, Legatus…'

'Don't call me that.'

'With respect, I don't envy the Ninth. And the Sixth won't find their task easy either. You can argue assignments when we all meet up and drink wine at Gerunda.'

Carbo grunted again. He wouldn't admit it, but he didn't envy his peers and their legions either. The Ninth had been given the difficult coastal path by Fabius. Their route was coastal and pleasant past Portus Veneris, but by the time they were in sight of Cervaria the terrain would be dreadful. High hills and low mountains reaching down to the coast, then ten miles of horrible travel before they could turn inland on the low pass and make for the flat plains around Emporiae. And in the midst of all that horrible terrain they would find the port of Cervaria, garrisoned with Pompey's men and with fast ships. They would have to take the place fast and preferably without letting ships flee the harbour carrying news. No, he didn't really envy the Ninth.

And the Sixth had boarded every ship that Fabius could impound at Narbo for a landing on the plains beyond the mountains. They would have the critical task of securing the ancient and strong city of Emporiae before the other legions cleared the passes. A siege of Emporiae following a sea journey didn't sound like a lot of fun either. Once they were in position in Gerunda and Emporiae, Hispania would be open before them and Caesar's orders would have been completed.

And yet that did little to diminish the difficulty of their own mission.

Carbo's eyes slid up the pass to the looming monument at the summit. With a sigh, he turned. 'Come on.'

The Tenth stood at attention in the wide, grassy area of what was, otherwise, a narrow and fairly vertiginous valley. He could see the wagons of the artillery and supply train moving slowly up the pass from Narbo in the distance, but the legion was as ready as they'd ever be. The only sounds were the occasional cough, the wind howling and whipping through the mountains and the croak and caw of birds wheeling above. It was almost eerie.

'There's no subtlety to this,' he shouted to the assembled men, each centurion standing at the front of his unit. 'But then we weren't chosen for this because we're subtle, were we?'

A ripple of laughter played across the ranks and Carbo waited for it to die away.

'This is a little piece of Pompey's black heart and it's our job to take it in the name of Caesar, of the senate, and of Rome. Can you see the two peaks?'

He waited as each man's neck craned to look up at the summit.

'On the right hand, slightly lower, peak is a trophy. It was put there by Pompey himself twenty two years ago to commemorate his part in the butchery of thousands of men, both Hispanics and Romans, during the war against Sertorius. It names the eight hundred and seventy six fortresses he claims to have taken. And many of them were held by Romans. Hispania ran with Roman blood for years, much of it spilled by Pompey. Other men spilled plenty of Roman blood in that war, men like Sertorius, Perpenna and Metellus. But only Pompey would think the death of so many Romans glorious enough to raise a trophy on his day of victory.'

There was a collective grumble of malice. Good. He needed them fired up for this.

'So here's what we're going to do, men of the Tenth Legion. We are going to swarm up the other peak to where Pompey has garrisoned a single understrength cohort of men, and we are going to take it and raise the standards of the Tenth over it. There are four hundred men at most there to our four thousand. And they may have fortifications and terrain and rest to their advantage, but we... are... the... TENTH!'

There was a roar, and Carbo grinned. Maybe he could be a good legate after all?

'And then, when that fortress is ours, you know what we're going to do?'

There was a general muttering of uncertainty, and Carbo grinned.

'We are going to piss on Pompey's 'achievement'. Every man in the Tenth is going to drink a hearty wine ration to celebrate our own little victory, and then he's going to go and relieve himself on one of the names of Pompey's victories.'

There was another roar.

'But… and this is important, men of the Tenth. When we take those walls, we will not be killing the defenders any more, and we're not taking slaves.'

There was a moment of confusion.

'Because for all they stand against us, these men are Romans, and we are not Pompey. You hear me? WE. ARE. NOT. POMPEY!'

A roar of approval.

'What are you waiting for, lads? Take the pass!'

At his words, the cornua blew and the standards waved. The cohorts moved off at a steady stomp. Carbo grinned. At such an exhortation to fight and with their blood up, a young legion, or one full of new lads, would even now be running up that slope, bellowing imprecations and waving swords. And when they got to the top, they'd hardly be able to breathe, let alone fight. But the Tenth were an old legion of veterans and they knew what they were doing. Just as eager and just as determined, they were moving at a mile-eating pace yet preserving their breath and strength for when they needed it.

'Well, Atenos, best join your unit.'

The big, blond centurion flashed a knowing grin at the pink-faced legate. 'Be a good officer, Carbo, and go stand with the tribunes looking important. You've done your bit. Now let me do mine.'

As the legate threw him a sour look and wandered off toward the small knot of senior officers, Atenos jogged lightly ahead to the First Cohort's First Century, which was now passing his position on their way up the pass. A moment later he was among them, at the fore of the whole army, looking up at the heights for which they were bound.

The trophy was impressive. Of white stone and the height of twenty men, it towered over the valley and the surrounding peaks. It consisted of a heavy square base with a monumental arch forming a tunnel in the foundations, through which the Via Domitia passed on its way into Hispania. Atop that heavy square base stood a square building like a temple of giants, with false columns built into it and seemingly endless carved plaques bearing the names of Pompey's conquests. The building was surmounted by a pyramidal roof, crowned by a larger-than-life statue of

Pompey himself in a moment of supreme self-aggrandisement. However impressive it might be as a structure, even the sight of it made Atenos feel a little sick.

The fortress stood to one side on a slightly higher peak, guarding the pass. There was no ditch, for this place had been built on the bare rock of the mountains, and the natural slope at each side provided the best defence possible. Stone walls rose to enclose a small fort capable of holding only a few hundred men, with a high watchtower at its heart.

Even as they climbed, a beacon was lit, sending a message to the Pompeian garrisons on the far side of the hills. That mattered little. In fact, the news might just be an advantage. At the last gathering of intelligence, the legions of Hispania Citerior were based around Calagurris to the west, where the ongoing pressure was applied to advance Roman territory to the north coast. Even the concentration of Caesar's legions at Narbo had not drawn them east. Now, they likely *would* come, but by the time they were in a position to endanger the Tenth and their sister legions, Caesar's army would be in Hispania and well-fortified in the eastern strongholds. The enemy would be too late and all that signal would do was tell the garrisons ahead that even the high pass couldn't stop Caesar's men.

Gritting his teeth, Atenos put aside all thoughts now other than their immediate goal.

'Second Cohort,' he bellowed, 'to the left. Third Cohort to the right. First Cohort with me.'

And he began to pick up the pace. They were only two hundred feet or so from the walls, now. Clearly the garrison were legionaries and not some sort of native auxilia, as neither arrows nor sling shots came from the walls, but as they staggered up the increasingly steep slope, Atenos distinctly heard a call for pila within the walls.

'Shields up!' he shouted as they struggled on, and the men of his cohort raised their boards, staggering up the slope with sword in hand and shield high.

The pila came in a single volley and their effect was horrifying. The missiles punched through shields and arms alike and men shrieked and fell, while others cast aside their useless defences and stomped on shieldless. Atenos' worst fear was realised when he heard another call for pila. In battle, each legionary might be expected to have two pila, but in the defence of a fort their only limit was however many were stacked in the storerooms.

'Run!' he bellowed, and the men charged as fast as they could up toward the walls even as the second volley of pila launched out from the parapet and fell among the men, ruining shields and puncturing flesh. The walls were the height of two men. Not high by Roman standards, but enough given the steeply-sloping terrain to all sides.

'Up, lads. Up and over.'

The first men to reach the wall advanced in two different manners. Some grasped the gaps between stones where the mortar had weathered and cracked in the high mountain winds and began to climb, assisted by the very slight slope of the defences. Others leaned against the wall and bent so that men could climb onto their backs and shoulders, the pain of their mates' hobnailed boots dulled by the thick double shoulder layer of their chain shirts.

They hit the walls like a tide of men, wave after wave smashing against the stone, clambering up the façade or climbing onto their mates' shoulders to gain an initial boost. Something smacked into Atenos's shoulder from above and as his head snapped around he was rather surprised to see a bloody gladius bounce off his mail shirt, a severed hand still gripping the hilt. Snarling, he pushed a man upwards where the legionary was struggling to rise from his mate's back. The man managed to get purchase higher up on the walls and pulled, the man on whose back he had been standing heaving in a breath of relief only momentarily before Atenos was suddenly clambering up onto him, blade in hand, silently climbing.

The centurion, veteran of a dozen wars fighting both for and against Romans, waited irritably as the man he'd had to push upwards finally pulled himself further and made room for Atenos. He looked up as the man disappeared over the parapet, yelling and slashing out, only to reappear a moment later, gurgling and clutching at his throat as he fell to the rocky ground, dying.

The face of the man's killer appeared over the parapet, making sure his victim was gone and, his own height added to that of the man on whose shoulders he stood, Atenos stabbed upwards, driving the slender tip of his gladius into the man's eye.

Unspeakable fluids spattered across the centurion's face as the defender shrieked briefly until Atenos pushed extra strength into his arm and shoved upwards, driving the blade into the brain. He had a little difficulty ripping the blade free, and the man's twitching body came with it, falling from the parapet and almost carrying Atenos down to the rocky slope with it.

Allowing himself no time to recover, the veteran centurion clambered up the wall, his fingers gripping the flat stone of the parapet, hurrying to fill the gap made by the fallen defender before it was plugged by one of his mates.

He pulled himself up onto the defences just as another Pompeian legionary hurried forward, brandishing a pilum, ready to jab down into the attackers. The man realised he was in danger of losing his intended place at the defences and stabbed out with the pilum at the figure clambering over the wall, but Atenos was fast and strong. His free hand lashed out and grasped the pilum below the iron head. The man tried for a moment to yank the weapon from the centurion's hand, but as he failed, Atenos pulled in response. The legionary, jerked forward, lost his footing and stumbled. Atenos dropped from the wall into a crouch as the defender hit him and tipped over the top. Even as the man fell forward with panicked momentum, Atenos grabbed the man's flailing leg and lifted, helping him on his way as he fell over the parapet and disappeared with a scream. Two more men were coming for him now, but Atenos took a moment to glance this way and that and take stock.

It seemed he had overestimated the defenders' numbers slightly. He would guess at somewhere between two and three hundred men were rushing to hold the walls. Here and there a legionary from the Tenth was already inside, just like Atenos, fighting to maintain his hold. The centurion marked the one who had pushed furthest by sight. He must have been the first over the wall, and if he lived it would be him who received the decoration from Carbo afterwards. His roving gaze caught sight of Celsus, senior centurion of the Second Cohort, who had just clambered over the parapet on the western side and was busy pulling his blade from a victim. Celsus' own gaze suddenly met Atenos' and the man grinned and started to push forward, bellowing and slashing and stabbing with his gladius.

'Oh no you bloody don't,' Atenos snapped and launched at the two men coming for him even as another legionary from the Tenth climbed over the wall behind. Celsus was making for the headquarters building close to the watchtower, beside which stood a vexillum flag. Atenos was damned if he was going to let Celsus be the man to take the enemy commander.

The veteran centurion hit the two reserve defenders in a shoulder barge, sending one flying from his feet to roll away across the grass. The other staggered and attempted to stick his blade into Atenos, and the centurion parried the blow with an arm-deadening clang.

Pausing only long enough to smash the man in the face with his sword's pommel, Atenos ran on toward that crimson flag with the eagle and lightning motif. Even as he and Celsus raced for the goal, three figures emerged from the doorway of the headquarters. One centurion, accompanied by a legionary, nodded their understanding of something to a man dressed as a tribune and made to move to the defences, then spotted the two centurions closing on them.

Atenos tried not to succumb to irritation as the legionary ran for Celsus, brandishing his blade, while the Pompeian centurion – a man who by very definition would be a tougher customer – came at Atenos.

The centurion leapt at him, slashing out at neck height and, even as Atenos parried, the man was already dropping low to take him in the inner thigh. Atenos stepped back out of reach of the blow and struck down only to have his blade turned by that of his opponent as he rose once more.

'Sorry, brother,' the Pompeian centurion said loudly, and there appeared to be genuine regret in his eyes as his sword slipped from hand to hand and then came in suddenly and unexpectedly from the left. Atenos ducked to the side and almost fell in the desperate need to move out of the way of the blow that missed his armpit by a hair's breadth. It had been an unexpected and very swift killing blow, and Atenos had survived it more by luck than by judgement.

He lashed out with his foot as he struggled to rise to his full height again, the studs of his boot hitting the man on the knee. The metal nails clacked into the man's protective greave but Lady Fortuna clearly favoured Caesar's men that day for, instead of sliding off the metal armour left or right as would most likely happen, instead his boot slid upwards.

The strain his rising leg caused his crotch was eye-watering as the other centurion came on with momentum, the advance forcing Atenos' leg higher and higher into the splits. But for every bit of groin strain the Tenth's chief centurion suffered, Pompey's man had it worse. The sharp nails in the sole of Atenos' boot slipped from the metal greave and slammed into the muscular flesh, drawing blood. And with his forward momentum, Atenos' nailed boot raked upwards, shredding the flesh on its route to the hip.

The centurion cried out in pain and fell, even as Atenos collapsed into a heap. The Pompeian rolled onto his back and Atenos could see the mess his boot had made of the man's thigh, deep furrows gouged in the skin, and blood everywhere. However, he felt a little too preoccupied to feel too sorry for the man, as his own groin was on fire, pulled asunder like never before.

Through a veil of tears, Atenos watched his opponent struggling to rise with the agony in his leg. The man had no helmet and, trying to ignore the pain in his loins, Atenos lunged forward and brought his sword down on the man's head, using the flat of the blade. There was a bony clonk and the centurion collapsed once more, his eyes rolling up into his skull.

'Sorry, brother,' he said quietly, and then spent some of the most painful moments of his life rising to his feet. As he took a tentative step forward and yelped, a legionary from the Tenth, coated with blood, was suddenly next to him.

'You alright, sir?'

'I've been better, soldier, but I'll live.'

He almost argued as the soldier took his shoulder and helped him toward the headquarters, but the pain was so intense he relented and let the man aid him. Looking this way and that he could see it was over. Around the walls the remaining Pompeians – probably still half the garrison – were standing with their arms raised in surrender. Irritation consumed him as Celsus emerged from the headquarters with the tribune at sword point, demanding any remaining defenders lay down their arms. The centurion grinned at Atenos.

'Getting slow in your old age, sir?'

'Piss off, Celsus.' But he winced as he made a rather unkind gesture with his free hand and almost fell again.

'Permission to be the first to piss on Pompey's trophy, sir?' Celsus grinned.

'Granted. I might not be pissing for a few weeks, so you might have to do it for me too.'

* * *

Atenos shuffled in his seat and hissed and winced with the movement. It had been three days since the storming of the pass, and so far the pain in his groin showed no sign of abating. The medicus had snorted at his concern and told him to 'grow a pair', which seemed rather heartless in the circumstances. Apparently the strain would heal in a week or two and he would return to normal in due course.

The legion had spent one night at the fort, burying the dead of both sides with respect, and had allowed the surrendered garrison to leave, heading south and west deeper into Hispania. The men had lived up to their promise, and Pompey's great trophy was no longer pure white when they left, the entire valley tainted with the smell of ammonia whenever the wind dropped.

They had left a hundred men to hold the heights just in case, and had then moved on. Arriving at Gerunda this morning, they had found the Ninth freshly arrived and slightly battered from their own ordeals along the coast, Later in the day as the two legions had exchanged war stories and shared food and drink, the Sixth had finally arrived with the rather haggard-looking Fabius at their head. It seemed that Emporiae had been more strongly contested than either of the other points, and the Sixth had truly struggled to secure their access.

Still, they were here now, and the senior officers and higher centurions rose from their seats in the basilica hall they had commandeered in Gerunda as the senior legate and lieutenant of Caesar entered.

'Sit down gentlemen,' Fabius said wearily, then frowned at Atenos as he grasped the wall and gently lowered himself into the seat. 'Haemorrhoids, Centurion?'

'Pompeians, sir. A proper pain in the goolies.'

The officers around them laughed, and Fabius grinned in response. 'Well, we can all be proud of ourselves, I'd say. Only a week after Caesar's message arrived, and we've managed to secure all the major access points to Hispania.' His face became serious again. 'However, we do not have time to rest on our laurels. Word from the locals is that the legions of Hispania Citerior left Calagurris days ago and turned east. Five whole legions to our three. And if they manage to dig in, they could cause us no end of trouble. And worst of all, if the governor of Hispania Ulterior, who is also Pompey's man, decides to come join them, we will be facing seven. So I intend to march forth and meet the five Citerior legions before they can be bolstered.'

'Sir, is that wise?' Carbo asked quietly. 'Three against five? And these are not green men, but veterans like us. Will Caesar approve of such a forward strategy?'

Fabius flashed an irritated glance at Carbo. 'We have no choice unless we want to see all seven Hispanic legions consolidated against us. I will answer to Caesar when the time comes. But to reassure you that I am not leading some insane push against an army twice our size, couriers bear good tidings. Caesar has sent the Seventh, Eleventh and Fourteenth legions south to join us. They are mere days away, already close to Narbo. We will await their arrival, and then push on to meet the Pompeian forces, which will give us a nominal six legions to their five. The campaign carries a certain level of inherent danger, but I cannot risk Governor Varro marching from Gades with his two legions and joining them. So rest your men for a few days, gather what supplies you need, and heal the wounded. As soon as our sister legions arrive, we march west.'

Atenos and Carbo shared a look.

West. Into Pompey's heartland.

Chapter Five

4th of Maius - Massilia

CAESAR stood on the observation point of the camp and watched the activity around him. Late the previous night, finally, the Seventeenth, Eighteenth and Nineteenth legions had arrived and settled into the camps inexpertly constructed in advance by the cavalry. The senior officers had been ridiculously apologetic, mortified that their tardiness had cost Caesar an easy victory at Massilia, but the general had been magnanimous. No man can move faster than his army's slowest component, he had assured them, and they might have set off even earlier and not bothered stopping to resupply in Latium and so on, but no one could have predicted that Ahenobarbus was going to take a force to hold Massilia against them.

Fronto had caught Salvius Cursor's expression at that and had to admit that the tribune might well have predicted just that had they all listened to him. And yet to his credit, Salvius was not reminding anyone that he had been adamant Ahenobarbus not be freed. Instead, he was already turning his attention to how to root out the man.

Siege was now inevitable. With the bitter and talented Ahenobarbus present to defend the place, the Massiliots were hardly likely to surrender their city to Caesar, and certainly Pompey's attack dog was not going to capitulate.

And so since dawn half the men of all three legions had been at work gathering resources. Already the first few hundred paces of the hillside had been denuded of trees, and stacks of trunks and branches were being created in the huge fortified area facing Massilia across the wide dip. Other men were already at work adzing timber and making planks. Wheels were being created from wood and bound with iron rims. A ram head was being cast by knowledgeable legionary blacksmiths. The land surrounding Massilia was alive with work.

Marcus Vitruvius Mamurra, Caesar's favoured siege génius, who had worked miracles during their time in Gaul, had joined them from Rome and, though his girth seemed to have expanded somewhat, he still wore an officer's uniform, sweating in the morning sun as he pored over charts and plans, lists and notes. He had brought a *capsa* – a leather case – of ideas and theories with him.

'How will you give me Massilia?' Caesar said, his gaze straying across the works.

Mamurra hummed indecisively for a moment.

'It is a difficult proposition at best, Caesar. Given the strength of the walls, the lack of land access and the dip in the terrain between there and here, normally I would advocate the building of huge catapults and the bombarding of the city with great rocks and burning pitch.'

Caesar arched an eyebrow, and Mamurra shrugged. 'But you have made it abundantly clear that the city itself is to suffer as little damage as possible.'

'They may currently oppose me,' Caesar reminded him, 'but they still remain allied to the Roman state in one form or another. They are garrisoned with legionaries, and when this mess is cleared up, Massilia will be required to go forward into the future as a strong, loyal ally, or possibly even part of the province, owing allegiance to the republic. Either way, as ash and corpses all it would represent is good propaganda for Pompey, and I will not have that.'

'Besides,' Fronto added, 'I have a huge warehouse of wine in there.'

He winced at the look Caesar favoured him with.

'Well whatever we decide to do, and I have a number of ideas to ponder,' Mamurra filled the silence, 'we will need level access to Massilia. The dip makes things tremendously difficult. Anything we build on wheels is going to be troublesome descending this side and a sheer nightmare to climb the far side with.'

Fronto nodded. He'd never truly noticed the dip between his villa's position and the city walls before. Probably because even the dip was high above the sea. But now that he contemplated it, it would cause trouble in any siege.

'And we cannot hope to undermine the defences,' the engineer went on, 'for normally we would begin to tunnel far from the walls and out of missile range. But here you would have to be very close to the ramparts to begin the mining, at which point you would lose nine men in every ten just getting the tunnels started. Not a viable option.'

Caesar was beginning to look a little exasperated, but Mamurra was not finished yet. 'Worst of all, it seems to have been a reasonably wet winter for the region, and the dip gathers and retains moisture, so there is a certain marshy quality to the turf. My initial recommendation is aggers.'

'Aggers?' Trebonius mused.

'Yes. Causeways of earth, timber and stone.'

'I know what they *are*,' snapped Trebonius.

'Well, we could build two or more aggers from our side of the depression, crossing the place and meeting the rising ground nearer their walls. That would give us reasonable access to their defences. And a line of investment that follows the near high contour is also required, I would say.'

Caesar nodded. 'See that it's done, Mamurra. The faster we can gain access to the walls, the faster we can finish this.' The general's gaze snapped round to the sound of the tent door opening, and Brutus strode in.

'I realise, General, that this news is unlikely to lift anyone's day, but a small fleet of ships has arrived and is making directly for Massilia's harbour. They are a mix of military and civil shipping, but do not appear to be filled to the brim with men, so we must assume mostly supplies.'

Caesar slapped his hand on the table in anger, causing many of those in the room to jump nervously.

'How can I hope to besiege a city when I dare not harm its populace unduly and they are free to receive supplies by sea?'

'A blockade, Caesar,' Brutus replied simply.

'Indeed, but with what? Every ship in Italia is already serving Pompey, barring the few we seized, which are with Curio and Valerius to secure Sardinia, Sicilia and Africa, the few we have in Narbo I've put under Fabius' command to help secure the route into Hispania, and the fleet we assembled during the war in Gaul is on the damned Gallic coast out beyond the Pillars of Hercules and on the other side of Pompeian Hispania. We have no fleet with which to stop supplies reaching Ahenobarbus.'

'Build more?' Fronto said quietly.

'What?'

'Well, if you have no ships and there are no ships to be had, then there is only one solution: make more ships.'

Mamurra turned on him. 'I cannot claim to know much about matters naval, Fronto, but I do know you would need an experienced admiral to oversee the project, a shipyard of adequate size and a workforce skilled in shipbuilding.'

Other men in the room nodded, but Caesar's eyes were narrowing in thought. 'You may be on to something, though, Fronto.'

'Sir?'

We have neither the facilities nor the skills here to carry out such a task. But fifty miles northwest is the city of Arelate, which is on a wide, navigable river, has an excellent port facility, a sizeable shipyard, and owes me strong allegiance. And Brutus here is a knowledgeable and capable admiral, as he proved against the Veneti some seven years ago.'

'Caesar, the time it would take to manufacture a fleet...' Antonius began.

'Not a full fleet,' Caesar said quickly, cutting him off. 'We do not need a huge fleet. All we need is enough ships to blockade the port under the command of a cunning tactician. I do not like to tarry here too long, but my fate is fixed. I cannot leave Massilia behind me in the hands of my enemy. Fabius will have to keep Hispania under control, and Curio and Valerius will have to do what they must to maintain the frontier and keep Pompey penned in in the east. I will allow one month.'

He straightened.

'One month, gentlemen. One month for Mamurra to build his aggers and invest the city and create whatever technological terrors his febrile mind can conjure. One month for you, Brutus, to travel to Arelate, take command of the shipyard and all its resources and begin constructing ships. Build as many as you can manage in the allotted time, but one month from now, I want you and your new ships out in those waters below Massilia, making Ahenobarbus nervous. Are you the man for the job?'

Brutus nodded. 'I can do that, Caesar. I cannot guarantee how many ships I can produce, since I have no experience in their construction, but whatever the time and facilities allow, I will achieve.'

'Good man,' Caesar announced.

* * *

Atop the walls of Massilia, a figure in drab, nondescript tunic and boots ducked and weaved in and out of the soldiers and nobles. The ramparts and towers seemed to be filled with a mixture of Massiliot nobles and politicians in rich whites and vibrant colours, and Roman legionaries in their madder-dyed reds and rusty russets, chain armour shushing and weapons clanking.

The figure found a relatively clear spot and moved to the battlements, ignoring the glare he received from a legionary nearby. His gaze played across the besieging Romans. A line of the criss-crossed sudis stakes reached from the cliff edge to the north, around the city in a wide arc as far as the uncrossable marshy ground to the south, on the far side of the city's harbour. Behind that arbitrary line that roughly followed the terrain, three camps had been constructed and manned by legionaries, though, since the main force had arrived, a fourth, much larger camp had been constructed further back and higher up; a camp which overlooked the ground in between, and had become the main accommodation for the besieging army, with the three smaller camps filled with workers and forward garrisons.

And every hour he looked out, there were fewer and fewer trees on the hillsides inland, and more and more stacks of logs in the camps.

Neither the forces arrayed outside, nor the prospect of the city's fall bothered the figure on the walls and, though the very idea of the hardships of a long siege were hardly attractive, the figure had endured similar and worse.

But he fumed. Because he was trapped in this stupid and untenable situation. Because he should have got out while the getting was good. Because the idiots running this city might think they were backing the fastest chariot with Pompey, but they would soon enough discover that Pompey's chariot was a two-horse biga to Caesar's four-horse quadriga, and he wasn't half the rider the general appeared to be.

With a sigh, Catháin scanned the tents one last time in the hope of seeing Fronto somewhere out there amid the mess, then gave up. He would go back to the office, settle in and wait out events to see what happened.

And he might get drunk. Whatever deprivations might be experienced in the coming months, one thing was certain: he had a more than adequate store of wine…

* * *

'How many vinea do we have so far?' Trebonius asked from the observation platform at the line of investiture.

Caesar turned an inquisitive look on him. 'Mamurra?' he prompted.

'What?' muttered the engineer as he pored over his drawings. 'Oh. Vinea? Four complete I believe, and four more in production. I've had most of the work directed at the aggers.'

'The aggers will not go much further without the vinea,' noted Trebonius, and pointed.

Fronto and Galronus, standing at the rampart close by, peered into the distance. 'I think he's right,' Galronus said quietly, and Fronto nodded. 'This one doesn't have to get much closer to give us access to the level ground, but the other one will have to get a lot nearer.'

As if their collective anticipation of the moment of conflict had triggered something, there was a dull thud and a dozen pairs of eyes swivelled to one of the heavy, square towers, where a *katapeltikon*, a bolt thrower of Greek design and every bit the match of Roman artillery, had finally loosed its deadly shot. The officers had been nervously eyeing the weapons atop the towers for three days now, waiting for the time they came into play as the Roman ramps crept slowly closer and closer.

The arrow was well-placed, especially for an initial shot. It angled forward and down and obliterated two legionaries busily compacting the rubble at the end of the northern agger. The missile went clean through the torso of the first man and thudded into the shoulder of the second, throwing him from the raised embankment down into the damp, marshy grass below.

Fronto watched in disbelief as half a dozen legionaries formed a shield wall at the unfinished end of the agger while their mates continued to bring up materials for its construction.

'What in the name of sacred Minerva's droopy boobs are they doing?' Fronto breathed.

'I think they believe they can stop the missiles with their shields,' Galronus replied.

'Idiots. If a bolt can go through a man and out the other side, a shield won't do much good.'

Caesar sighed. 'Oh for veteran legions, but all the veterans are committed in Sicilia, Sardinia and Hispania.'

Fronto watched a centurion on the agger trying to get some concept through to one of his men with much waving of hands and finally a clout on the shoulder with his vine staff. These three legions had been formed in small part from the barely trained force who had surrendered at Corfinium, but were largely new recruits from Cisalpine Gaul and northern Italia. They had hardly had time to learn which end of a sword did the damage, let alone how to deal with a siege. They'd looked good cutting logs and digging trenches, but they had never experienced a fight. Fronto wondered how hard the Massiliots would have to push to break a new legion.

'They need proper direction down there,' Fronto noted. He straightened, preparing to go, but Salvius Cursor was there first, drawing his sword and rolling his shoulders. 'Fronto's right. Permission to go put the men in order, General?'

Caesar frowned and pursed his lips. 'Granted, Salvius, but carefully.'

The tribune saluted and jogged away from the platform. Fronto watched him go, then tapped Galronus on the shoulder. 'Come on.'

With the Remi prince in tow, he left the observation point and jogged across to the work camp, which was in a state of semi-organised chaos. Work gangs of burly legionaries unarmoured and in just tunics and belts were engaged in every stage of preparation. Some were ferrying in baskets of rubble on the backs of carts from a temporary quarry on the hillside a quarter of a mile away. They were then offloading them into a large stack, from which men were hauling them, grunting, onto their backs and porting them through the siege lines to the end of the agger to help create the embankment that would grant them access to Massilia. Other men were still working on timbers, creating planks, pegs and straight stakes. Others were mixing up cement, resins and pitch. Others were forging nails. Men were assembling ladders and mobile arrow screens and vineae and even beginning work on a huge, outsized ballista that had drifted into the world from Mamurra's imagination via one of his scrappy pages of designs.

Fronto peered this way and that but couldn't identify an officer. Probably there were several centurions around, but without their armour and weapons only their attitude and a vine stick would identify them, and he had no time to hunt one down.

Since the initial gathering of resources, most of the legionaries had now either been moved into place along the siege works or in the building of the aggers, with half a legion at most working on all this material. Likely the legate of this legion – whoever he was, since Fronto didn't know which legion it was and was unfamiliar with the commanders of them all anyway – had committed his best men to the siege lines and put his newest, rawest men on the work duties. That suggested the latter half of the cohorts.

'Seventh Cohort, form up!' Fronto bellowed, plucking a number from the air. He was rewarded by upturned surprised faces and then a whole swarm of legionaries downing tools and running over to line up.

'Good men,' he shouted. 'Your comrades on the agger are being skewered with Massiliot arrows, and the things they need to protect them are here. Divide into centuries and collect the completed vineae and plutei and move them as fast as you can up to the end of the north agger.'

A centurion appeared from somewhere, his status clear as much from his professional attitude and stance as from his vine stick symbol of office. 'We're with you, Legatus.' He turned to the men. 'First to Fourth centuries, one vinea each and stay inside as you move it else you'll be prey for enemy arrows. Fifth and Sixth centuries, bring the plutei, two contubernia to each. Any men left over are support at the rear to replace the fallen. Now move!'

'They could do with *you* up at the front line,' Fronto said with feeling, and the centurion simply saluted in acknowledgement and began bellowing orders for the men to move their siege equipment.

Fronto nodded at Galronus and the two hurried back toward the siege line. A gate had been constructed in the palisade at the near end of each agger. The south agger had not yet progressed too far, but the north one was closing on Massilia's walls rapidly.

The gate stood open and men were gathered around both inside and outside the siege works, their bodies armoured, but lacking helmets and shields, due to the baskets of rubble and earth they had been carrying, which now sat idly by their feet. The legionaries moved respectfully aside as Fronto and Galronus arrived and strode through the gate onto the agger. It was the first time since the siege had begun that Fronto had been forward of the line of investiture and he had to nod at the quality of the agger. The legions may be too green for real war, but it seemed they had some fine engineers and strong workers among them. The causeway was wide enough for a whole eight man contubernium to travel abreast and had been compacted and levelled so thoroughly that it felt like any major road, rather than a ramp amid a siege.

Over a hundred paces away, toward the walls of Massilia, Fronto could see the red plume of Salvius Cursor's helmet amid a small group of legionaries. Whatever the man was doing, he'd kept a few men with him and sent the rest back to the gate.

'Make way,' Fronto shouted to the gathered legionaries. 'Siege engines are coming through. Make space.' And as the men began to shuffle aside, Fronto beckoned to Galronus and jogged on along the agger.

As they closed on Salvius' position, Fronto realised what the man was doing, though he wasn't sure whether he was impressed or horrified. Even as he watched, the tribune pointed to a spot some fifteen paces from the end of the ramp and a legionary ran across to it and stood there, still as a post. There was a heavy thud from the nearest tower and a secondary, duller thud from the tower to the right. Two huge bolts whispered through the air, the second thudding into the rubble of the causeway about six paces from the legionary, while the first hurtled past him and stuck into the ground behind, passing so close to the legionary that the air current ruffled his tunic. As Fronto closed on them he could see the dark patch of liquid blooming around the soldier's groin. Hardly surprising, being used as target practice by the Massiliot artillery as he was. Salvius Cursor waved the soldier ten paces back and threw a white stone down where he had been standing. There were a number of such stones at the end of the agger in various places and two skewered corpses among them.

'This appears to be their maximum *effective* range,' the tribune shouted, pointing at the stone he'd just cast down.

'Get those men back out of artillery range,' Fronto replied sharply.

Salvius Cursor ignored him. 'I would say that makes their effective range perhaps a hundred paces. And that is with no wind and no adverse weather conditions. With wind to account for, make that perhaps seventy paces, though with a talented artillerist behind it, they might reach up to one hundred and twenty, perhaps even one hundred and thirty paces.'

There was a thud and another bolt thrummed past Salvius and smacked into the compacted earth of the ramp. The tribune didn't even turn, let alone jump, still apparently counting off ranges on his fingers. The legionary who'd leaked a little at the last shot went white.

'And get out of range yourself, you mad bastard,' Fronto shouted.

Salvius Cursor seemed to notice him again now, his lip curling up into the sneer that seemed to arrive automatically in Fronto's presence, and he ambled slowly back away from the walls as another bolt issued and thudded into the ground where his boot had so recently been.

'I believe that with these measurements we can plan the other agger's approach with a little more care.'

Fronto stared at the man, and Salvius shrugged. 'We knew little of the capabilities of their artillery. No Roman has faced a Greek artillerist in living memory.'

Behind them, Fronto could hear the trundle and squeak of wheels and the grunting of men. He turned to see the siege engines approaching along the agger. The smaller plutei came first. Curved shields of timber, one and a half times the height of a man, they rested on two wheels and were manoeuvred by a single steering pole behind. Two came up in quick succession, the men pushing them ducking behind even as they approached, prepared for shots from the walls.

The vineae came along behind, not wheeled this time, but carried by the legionaries. They were covered galleries some twenty feet long, built of a heavy timber frame with a slatted wooden roof and wicker walls to either side, the whole covered with dampened hides to prevent fire damage. Open at both ends, they formed a mobile tunnel, protecting workers from aerial attack. The soldiers lifting the upright posts and carrying the vineae were sweating and grunting with the effort, and Fronto and Galronus stepped aside, almost sliding down the steep side of the bank as the first vinea passed. The men expertly dropped the mobile tunnel at the very end of the agger, the two plutei forming a front for the place. The other men brought further vineae forward and lined them up behind the first, forming an eighty-foot tunnel atop the agger.

'That should have been done when they first approached missile range,' Fronto sighed. 'Oh to have veterans. Still, I suppose everyone starts to learn somewhere.'

Even as he watched, a centurion blew his whistle back at the gate and men began to move once more with their baskets of rocks and earth. The two nearest towers on the walls once more began to release their missiles at the defences. The bolts thudded into timbers and stuck there, shaking the vineae with each strike and knocking the plutei back a foot or so each time. Legionaries moved the plutei back into position. The second tower, off to one side, managed a rather effective shot, its missile striking the side of the vinea, where it simply ripped through the hide and wicker without good solid timber to stop it. Fronto turned and looked back. Half a dozen more plutei were sitting idly on the agger further back.

'Get those inside the vineae, pushed up against the left side as an extra wall.'

The legionaries did as they were bade and wheeled the curved wooden shields into the long tunnel, manoeuvring them into position as an extra layer within. Fronto and Galronus edged their way between two vineae into the tunnel, where Salvius was watching and nodding with satisfaction. The legionaries were hurrying along the defensive tunnel with their baskets and, reaching the end, the men at the plutei would twitch them aside for the count of ten while the assembled legionaries threw their building materials down, beginning to advance the ramp once more, and would then shuffle the shields back into place as missiles thudded down.

Fronto peered through the gap. Only another forty paces or so, and the agger would reach level ground again. Then they would have access to the walls.

Salvius Cursor glanced at them without acknowledging their presence, then turned and strode back along the agger toward the camp. Fronto and Galronus shared a look that suggested they agreed in their opinion of the tribune, then followed on.

* * *

The summer came to Massilia that next week, the chill of the early morning receding and the sun gaining in warmth daily. Scudding clouds became fewer and higher and the sky darkened to a rich blue. Four more days saw the completion of the first agger, and another week witnessed the southern one reaching the high ground beneath the enemy walls.

The various constructions and work gangs were prepared for undermining, scaling and every conceivable method of besieging the place, but all were held back. Fronto and Trebonius took to working with the veteran centurions in setting up a new training regime for the legions so they could prepare themselves for coming battle while maintaining their lines at the same time.

Salvius Cursor daily beseeched Caesar to commit to an assault, yet the general held back. *'Why waste so much time and effort constructing the aggers and building all this equipment if they were not to be used?'* the tribune demanded, but still Caesar refused. The belligerent officer cajoled and demanded, snarling that Ahenobarbus needed to be removed as soon as possible and that any man who stood in the defence of those walls was an enemy by default. By the time another week passed, Salvius Cursor had angered the general with his constant pushing for battle and had been assigned some ancillary duty that kept him busy and away.

For Massilia sat silent and still now that work had stopped. No arrows or bolts flew. And Caesar watched the walls each day, willing the locals to rise up and overthrow their masters, opening wide the gate. He'd not said as much, of course, instead maintaining that he had no wish to throw away lives while there was still the chance that the place could surrender. But Fronto had watched the general throughout their journey through Italia, and he could see how it grieved the man that this city, which had a special connection with him, would not capitulate, while cities in Italia that owed him no allegiance at all had thrown their gates wide, and at Sulmona the Pompeian leaders had even been removed by the populace and the garrison.

The general simply could not countenance that something like that would not happen here if he waited long enough. But at the same time, each day the general looked a little more tense, and he had picked up the habit of waiting at the north-western end of the siege works, gazing out toward Hispania and waiting for news rather than watching the city they had surrounded.

Another week passed, marking the end of the month that Caesar had grudgingly allowed, and finally, on the morning of the fifth of Junius, pickets reported a small fleet of ships coming in from the west. Fronto had joined the other officers in hurrying to the promontory that lay at the edge of Fronto's estate and also at the north-western end of the siege line.

'Twelve. Better than nothing,' Trebonius said appreciatively.

'Can you be sure that's Brutus?' asked Mamurra, struggling to fold an armful of parchments.

'It's Brutus,' Antonius replied. 'He's put Caesar's bull emblem on the sails.'

'Will twelve ships be enough to blockade Massilia? Ahenobarbus has to have more than twelve ships in there.'

Caesar drummed his fingers on his folded arms. 'The city has a narrow enough harbour mouth. So long as Brutus uses his ships well, he can keep Ahenobarbus penned in and prevent anything entering. He will need marines, though. We need to get a couple of cohorts of the best men down to the coast and aboard the ships. And a few heavy weapons if we can get them aboard, too.'

'The month is up, Caesar,' Salvius Cursor said, quietly. 'What are your orders?'

The other officers turned to look at the general, equally pensive, waiting to see what the general planned. Caesar nodded silently, watching Brutus' ships as they made for a small group of islands off the coast, opposite Massilia's harbour.

'The man knows exactly what he is doing. He has chosen his base and will come ashore shortly. Sadly, I will be gone when he arrives. I can tarry no longer. Hispania calls me. I will take most of you and the cavalry and locate Fabius and his six legions. Trebonius?'

The legate, who had acted as Caesar's lieutenant more than once in Gaul, straightened.

'Caesar?'

'Massilia is yours. I am placing you in command of the Seventeenth, Eighteenth and Nineteenth legions. Brutus will work with you as commander of the fleet. Between you I expect you to crack this particular nut by the end of the season. But just like a succulent nut, I expect you to do it without damaging the valuable core inside. Bring me Massilia, but bring me it intact.'

Trebonius saluted. 'Of course, General.'

He was all business, but Fronto could see behind the façade into the officer's eyes, and could see his dismay at being given this troublesome task. Massilia would fall easily enough if he were able to throw everything he had at it with impunity, but being restricted so would make it a much more difficult proposition. Still, he had three legions that were becoming better trained by the week, a fleet with which to blockade the place, and more siege engines than most armies could boast.

Good luck to him.

'We move into Hispania, Caesar, then?' Fronto asked. 'With just the cavalry.'

'There are six legions there awaiting us somewhere between Emporiae and Gerunda under Fabius, and I have already sent scouts out over the past few weeks to our friends in Gaul asking for military support against the legions of Hispania. They will ride south to meet us there.'

Fronto's brow rose. He'd not known of such riders being sent out. Only two years after such a devastating war had ended, could many tribes afford to send warriors to Caesar? Were there any warriors *left*? Still, he had to admit that most of the Gallic tribes now would likely fall over themselves to ingratiate themselves with the general, and being invited by a Roman general to kick other legionaries would be an enticement all its own to the war-hungry Gauls.

Hispania. Tarraco. Family.

* * *

Catháin watched in disbelief.

He'd felt a wave of relief wash over him weeks back when he'd finally seen Fronto. The man had, almost predictably, been out at the very front of the action from the start. As soon as the ramp the besieging army was building came within range of the wall top artillery, the new Roman governor who had taken control of Massilia had given the order to loose their bolts.

There had been some discussion, to put it politely, among those charged with the defence of the city as to whether being the first to draw blood against Caesar's army might close forever a door many would have liked to leave open. In fact, since Caesar's first arrival outside the walls, when the gates had been shut against him, there had been a gradual slide toward the idea of surrender.

The boule of Massilia was split, and though the vote to side with the senate had been won by a small margin, that margin had gradually diminished with the Romans camped outside the walls. In fact, the vocal few who had so loudly denied the proconsul had been outnumbered by those who favoured seeking a peaceful solution, and the city may well have voted to surrender had not this martinet of a mad man, Domitius Ahenobarbus, suddenly turned up with ships full of rabid soldiers and taken charge. Now, the vaunted democracy of Massilia had been stamped down beneath the autocratic boot of a Roman governor ostensibly sent to help them.

The boule had even approached Ahenobarbus with the idea of surrendering the city, but the Roman governor had snarled and snapped like a wounded bear, refusing even to hear of such a thing and issuing an order against the city council meeting unless in his presence. Some believed him to be the sort of Roman, like Pompey or Caesar, who would never back down in the face of the enemy. But there was also a rumour passing around that Ahenobarbus had been forced to surrender a city of his and several legions in Italia because his subordinates had made peace behind his back, and he was not going to let something like that happen again. Having seen and listened to the man, Catháin favoured *that* belief, personally.

But the fact remained that the city was not going to surrender, whatever the cost, at least as long as Domitius Ahenobarbus was in command. And Caesar was not going to leave them to their own devices. So there *would* be a siege. And there would be war. And blood, and fire and death. Catháin had grown up in a native island harbour settlement where death had been dealt out as often as beer, and blood and fire were daily fare, but not on the scale the Roman legions offered it.

So Ahenobarbus had launched his missiles at the Romans building their ramp, and Catháin had stood on the walls and watched. He had been less than surprised when two figures came rushing out to put things right in the midst of a rain of missiles, that those two men were Fronto and Galronus. Well, them and some lunatic Roman officer who seemed to like using his men to test artillery ranges.

And then the missiles had loosed every day from dawn until dusk, and the legions of Caesar had laboured under the deadly hail to build their ramp across the dip until finally, with a surprisingly low casualty rate, they had finished the thing. Then they had built another, southerly, one, off toward the harbour and the marshland beyond. And then, perhaps two weeks ago, they had finished, withdrawn behind their siege lines, and spent time building peculiar wooden contraptions that sat mouldering in a compound.

The artillery had fallen silent and the legions drilled daily and waited. It had been odd, and strangely tense. Ahenobarbus had convened the boule of the city, as though he were some sort of dictator with a council of his own, and had informed them that he believed the time had come to try a sortie against the besieging army. He had been frustrated and angered to the point of red-faced rage when the city's leaders refused to add their soldiers to his Romans for such a move and, moreover, their allies the Albici who had poured into the city to stand firm against Caesar, had no more wish to go out front and knock on the general's tent door than the Massiliots themselves. Lacking the manpower with his Romans alone, the governor's wish for a sortie was crushed, and he returned to glaring at Caesar's men from the towers as though he could peel their flesh with his eyes.

For two weeks now little had happened. Life went on in the city, thanks to a good supply of stores and the freedom for ships to come and go. Knowing what lay at stake on a personal level, Catháin had made enquiries with ship captains at the port about the possibility of leaving the city with his personal effects. After all, he was neither Massiliot nor Roman, so this siege had little or nothing to do with him. But it seemed that Ahenobarbus' eagle-like claws had dug into the port too. Nothing sailed in or out without his approval, and every ship was checked in both directions by his men.

This morning a small Roman fleet had been sighted off to the west on their way to the city and rumour had it that this flotilla was nothing to do with Ahenobarbus, which made them Caesar's by default. Along with half the city, Catháin had scurried up to one of the clearer sections of wall to see. And while he caught an excellent view from this end section of the twelve ships bearing Caesar's sign, he also had a nice position to observe the Roman commanders and officers at their little observation place.

He watched now in dismay. He had been atop the wall for an hour, and had seen it happening, but he could hardly believe his eyes as Fronto and Galronus, along with Caesar himself and most of his officers, mounted up alongside a huge force of Gallic cavalry and rode off into the west, leaving some subordinate to command the legions here.

Once more Catháin cursed himself for not having left earlier. And now it looked extremely unlikely that any Roman officer who made it through the walls of Massilia would be even remotely sympathetic to Catháin and to Fronto's family and business interests.

He was facing the decision he'd been worrying about since arriving in the city.

Clucking irritably, he pushed past the other figures on the wall and descended the long 'stairs of the rocks', hurrying through the area of vegetable gardens and fruit orchards that lay between the walls and the housing. There he began to wend his way down the slope a little until he reached the street he sought, then fumbled momentarily with the key in a lock.

Fronto's warehouse door opened and he slipped inside, locking it again. In the gloom he hurried to light three oil lamps to give him adequate light by which to work, for he had long since taken the precaution of blocking up the high windows. In a time of siege the goods of merchants were often fair game and it would take longer for inquisitive locals to wonder what was inside the warehouse if they had to actually break in to find out. And as soon as they did, months of Fronto's profit would disappear down the hungry gullets of the besieged Massiliots. While Catháin knew that Fronto could afford it these days and that it was small fry in the scale of a besieged city, it offended him to think of the profits he himself had made being ripped away by thieves.

And then there were the *other* contents of the warehouse, as well as Fronto's wine shipments. Stacked neatly and carefully in the alcoves were anything of value from both villas, Fronto's and Balbus'. With both men being Roman nobles, that was worth a pretty sestertius, too.

And the documents. There were Fronto's business records, of course. They would do no harm in the wrong hands, but their destruction or theft would set the business back months in terms of permits, fees and the like.

But the thing that he needed to keep safe, and the thing that was giving him his great dilemma was the leather bag under the desk. And it wasn't even Fronto's. It was the reason he was here, the reason he had come to Massilia even under the threat of war and siege. And he'd retrieved them in good time only to get trapped in the damned place with them. He had been tasked with returning them, but his own sense of security told him that whatever they contained, if they were *that* sensitive, it would be better to burn them than to risk their being discovered.

Not for the first time, he contemplated opening the bag and reading them, but he had too much respect for that. If he couldn't find a way out, and it looked inevitable that Caesar's men would find a way in or even, when the city reached a level of desperation where locals might decide to ravage and loot the warehouse, he might be left with no other choice.

His gaze drifted from the oil lamp with the flickering golden flame to the leather bag full of highly combustible documents.

With a sigh, he slid the leather satchel back under the desk and decided to diminish profits by another five or six cups. In the morning he would see whether the strange stalemate continued and whether there might be someone at the port he could bribe with wine or silver. There *had* to be a way out of Massilia.

Chapter Six

12th of Junius - Gerunda

THE journey from Massilia had been swift, eating away in excess of forty miles each long, difficult day. Fronto's backside had taken every mile of the two hundred and fifty mile journey personally, and he would swear that each mile had implanted a permanent reminder there in the form of sores and callouses. How couriers speed-rode for a living, he would never understand. Most rides of that distance would take twice the time but, resting the horses as much as necessary, they had spent every possible hour in the saddle, pushing hard even over the mountains.

They had passed across the Pyrenaei mountains by the main road and been greeted by the small garrison Fabius had left there, who had little news of the world beyond their tiny domain other than that the Tenth had moved on for Gerunda to meet up with Fabius and the other legions, and that the Seventh, Eleventh and Fourteenth had crossed the mountains soon after, also making for Gerunda. Fronto had taken advantage of their night's stop with the garrison to examine the great trophy Pompey had constructed in the pass, and wished instantly that he hadn't. The place had been used as a latrine for over a month and the flies gathered around it like nothing Fronto had ever seen. He swore the stench of Pompey's glory would remain in his nostrils for the rest of his life.

The next day – the morning of the day before the ides of Junius – they had crossed the green hills of north-eastern Hispania and raced the setting sun to the walls of Gerunda. This fortress town on the main road through the region had once been a settlement of the local tribe until Pompey's year of victory in Hispania, when he settled veterans here and established the Roman town of Gerunda atop the native one, strengthening the existing walls and building the interior anew. That had been almost three decades ago, and already it was largely indistinguishable from many Roman towns.

As the riders, with the large native cavalry contingent following on, passed along the road between the wide, sluggish river and the forested hill toward the heavy city walls ahead, Caesar's mood grew pensive and disquieted. Something was clearly wrong. Even had the three legions sent south from Gaul to join Fabius had not yet arrived, and that would put them weeks overdue lost somewhere this side of the mountains, there should still be a massive encampment of legionaries here, with the three legions from Narbo and their auxiliary support.

No encampment was visible on the plain across the river, the only flat ground large enough to play host to an army that size.

'Perhaps they've camped somewhere nearby?' Salvius Cursor hazarded.

Caesar shook his head. 'Since Pompey first settled this place any force passing through has used the field of Mars across the river to camp and muster. If the legions are not camped there, then they are not at Gerunda at all.'

'Which begs the question: where are they?' added Marcus Antonius.

Directing the cavalry to the far bank to set up camp, Caesar, his cadre of officers and a small guard under Aulus Ingenuus rode on through the gates of Gerunda, where the two evocati veterans who guarded this approach bowed their heads in respect at the party of senior Roman officers. This was not a fortress or camp, with military control. No password or identification were required to enter, and the lack of security strengthened the theory that Fabius and his legions were nowhere in the area.

'Where will I find the most senior councillor of Gerunda?' Caesar asked the two veterans, pausing in the gateway.

'That would be Papirius Cilo, Proconsul. He is the speaker in the ordo and… likes to think he rules the city himself.'

Caesar gave a wolfish smile, and the man went on. 'He will be in the large domus next to the basilica in the forum. There's a wine shop built into the front wall, sir. Can't miss it. Don't buy the wine either. It's over-priced.'

Fronto grinned as they trotted on into the city. With the banks of the Alba river rising into such high hills, sunset came sudden and strong, and Fronto could see the last of the golden light sliding up the higher storeys of the buildings to either side of the street as the shadow enveloped Gerunda.

'Why not just enquire of the veterans, Caesar?' Antonius muttered as they rode.

'*Pompey's* veterans. I am sure they feel themselves beyond such divisions in retirement, but I would find myself beset constantly by niggling doubt if I based my decisions on information drawn from my enemy's veterans. The town's councillors, however, should be much easier to intimidate into clear truths.'

Fronto caught the eye of Salvius, expecting some sour look, given that he himself was a former Pompeian officer, but the man showed no emotion at all.

By the time they reached the forum, the city's workers were out lighting torches in sconces that burned with oily black smoke but relieved the forum of some of its gloom. Taverns and shops and establishments of a more carnal nature displayed open, welcoming doors with lamp-lit golden interiors, but Caesar's eyes were on the columns of the basilica and the wine shop beside it. More specifically on the ostentatious door in the high wall next to the shop. They dismounted as they reached the place and Fronto rolled his eyes at the sight of the expensive cedar-wood doors which had clearly either been imported all the way from the east or purchased at great expense from Numidian merchants across the southern straits. The doors were covered in ornate bronze discs, and the handles were formed of bronze lion heads. Even the bell that hung beside the door was of bronze and embossed with the shapes of exotic animals.

Fronto had never met Papirius Cilo, but already he disliked the man. His hand closed on the pommel of his sword and he realised with chagrin that the sort of mind that commissioned the decorative orichalcum hilt of his own sword was the very same that might desire those doors. His gaze slid to Galronus, who was giving him a knowing grin as though reading his mind.

Ingenuus tugged on the bell and they waited in the warm night air for long moments before the door inched open and a man with an impressive hooked nose that almost overshot his mouth peered out suspiciously.

'Who is it?'

'Gaius Julius Caesar, Proconsul of Cisalpine and Transalpine Gaul,' announced Ingenuus in a clear tone, 'to see master Papirius Cilo.'

The man didn't even blink, apparently unfazed by the impressive title. 'Wait here,' he rumbled, and shut the door again. Caesar and Antonius shared a bemused look. 'Perhaps I should be accompanied with my lictors after all,' the general mused, 'since even doormen seem unimpressed.'

There was a drawn out pause once more, and then the door was flung suddenly open and a man appeared in the opening, bowing obsequiously. His face was flushed and his skin sweaty and over-abundant, covering multiple rolls of fat. His scant black hair seemed to be trying to escape via the rear, leaving much of his head shiny and pink while the back of his skull remained dark and curly, matted hair covering his neck and shoulders without interruption. He wore an expensive toga. Well... *almost* wore. Clearly he had just thrown it on, on his way to the door, and had not had time to let his slaves adjust and settle it. Even as he straightened from his bow, most of his toga tried to escape downwards in sympathy with his hair. Fronto would be able to describe the man only as some kind of shaved ape.

'Proconsul, I am humbled by your presence.'

'Of course you are,' Antonius snorted, earning himself a reproving look from Caesar.

'I do not wish to cause you too much disturbance, councillor Papirius, and I do apologise for having disturbed you from your... ah... labours. I am seeking information as to the whereabouts of my lieutenant – Gaius Fabius Pictor – who was reported to have brought his legions through the mountains and was intending to base himself at Gerunda until my arrival. Might you have further details for me?'

The man's eyes rolled in worry. His toga slid a little more and the sweat literally ran off him.

'General Fabius, Proconsul? He was here some weeks ago. Three legions encamped across the river and he remained with his officers in Gerunda until a further force joined them. Biggest army I've ever witnessed, I have to say. Aggressive, too. We had to put a ban on parties of more than eight men at a time entering the city because of the disgraceful behaviour. I'd hate to be in the Citerior legions with that bunch baying for my blood. Not that I have any love for Pompey,' he added hurriedly, gathering the sliding folds of toga in a growing pool of sweat.

'So Fabius gathered six legions and moved on?' Antonius prompted.

'Why yes. The army left the day after the new legions arrived.'

'Might you have information as to their intended destination?' Caesar said quietly, in a tone that Fronto recognised as the general trying to eke out the last of his patience.

'I am afraid not, Caesar, though rumour says that your lieutenant has moved west with the intent of bringing to battle the legions of Afranius and Petreius, Pompey's *maggot-ridden* men in the province.'

Fronto almost laughed at the stress the men put on the insult, given the extreme likelihood that he had fawned all over both of those men at some point during his tenure at Gerunda. The man was a politician to the core, even when suddenly faced with the most powerful man in the world turning up on his doorstep.

'The last reports I know of,' Fronto piped up, remembering the briefings back in Massilia, 'put the legions of Hispania Citerior somewhere on the other side of Tarraco. Would Pompey's lieutenants not try to hold Tarraco against Fabius, it being the capital of the province?'

Caesar nodded. 'If they are not engaged around Tarraco, they will certainly be in the region, and news of the situation will be clearer in the city. We ride on in the morning, following the coastal route to Tarraco in the hope that Fabius is there.'

He waved to the sweating man in a tangle of toga. 'Thank you for your time, Papirius Cilo. I pray you have a good evening.'

Leaving the trembling councillor on his doorstep, Caesar turned his horse and began to walk it across the forum. Once they were away from the house, finally, Caesar released his temper, thumping the horn of his saddle in anger.

'What in the name of sacred Venus is the man doing? I gave Fabius strict orders to secure the mountain passes and hold the access to Hispania. And we arrive to discover that he appears to have taken it upon himself to launch a war in Hispania. I shall give Fabius a piece of my mind when we track down the man,' he added in a tone that suggested the flaying of a certain officer's skin loomed in the near future.

Fronto shrugged, remembering Fabius Pictor, a serious, intelligent man. 'I don't think he would have exceeded his orders without good reason, Caesar.' He bit down on pointing out the rather glaring parallel between Fabius being sent to secure the passes of the Pyrenaei and launching a war in Hispania beyond, and Caesar a decade ago moving north across the border of his province with the ostensible goal of preventing Helvetii migration and turning that into an eight year campaign of conquest in Gaul. Somehow, he didn't think Caesar would see the funny side of that.

'There is a mansio in Gerunda,' the general said. 'We shall pass the night there and then move on at dawn. Get some sleep. We travel fast again.'

* * *

On the sixteenth of June, Caesar's party arrived at Tarraco to find neither a huge encampment of six legions plus auxiliary support, nor a war in progress. Caesar's knuckles whitened as his grip nearly broke through the leather of his saddle, and Fronto could see the frustration and anger starting to boil over in the general's very demeanour.

As they rode toward the upper city and the governor's palace, Fronto could not help but repeatedly glance over his shoulder, back along the coast, as though he might be able to see the villa he had purchased from the estate of Longinus last year, where his family should at least be safe now, given the fact that the armies of both sides had yet to be located.

He remembered both Afranius and Petreius, the men who would now be arrayed with legions against them – *if* they ever turned up. While Pompey was officially Proconsular governor of both Hispanias, the quiet, inoffensive Varro governed in his stead over Hispania Ulterior in western Gades. And Afranius and Petreius governed in his name in Hispania Citerior, Afranius controlling civil government from the high city of Tarraco, while Petreius controlled the legions in the constant push to add what was left of free Hispania to the Roman provinces. Afranius was an accomplished officer with a string of victories to his name, all in

126

Pompey's service as far back as the Sertorian wars. But for all his military ability, Afranius was careful and pacific by nature. Not so, Petreius, a man given to feats of martial prowess and who hungered for war and victory.

It came as no surprise to any of them to find no real military presence at all in Tarraco, barring once again a few evocati veterans who served as support for the governor's guard. Two of them stood roughly at attention by the main gate to the upper city as Caesar and his officers reined in.

'I am here to see the governor's representative,' Caesar announced loudly.

The two men looked at each other, then one of them cleared his throat.

'I'm afraid, General, that neither the governor, nor his lieutenant, are in residence at this time. The best you'll find in Tarraco is the questor, though he's very busy and might not see you.'

Caesar's eyebrow rose slightly at the faint air of insolence about the men, soldiers who would be Pompeian through and through.

'Might I enquire as to where the governor's man – Afranius, if I am not mistaken – might be?'

Fronto could see the difficulty his commander was having in controlling his temper. He coughed and, as Caesar turned to look at him, gave the general a meaningful look. The last thing he wanted right now was for Caesar to have one of his attacks.

'Governor Lucius Afranius is with General Petreius at Ilerda, kicking seven shades of shit out of your man Fabius,' chuckled the other veteran. Fronto watched, alarmed, as the vein on Caesar's forehead began to visibly throb.

'Even in times of war, there are ways to talk to a Proconsul of Rome,' Antonius snapped, 'and ways that are simply *unacceptable*. For now, be about your business and, when we have put down Pompey's pups in this province and brought their army to heel, I will be back in Tarraco. When I am, I will be looking for your two faces and you have better fucking *pray* I do not find them. Do I make myself clear?'

Something in Antonius' tone or expression seemed to have a profound effect on the two veterans, who straightened and lowered their faces.

'That's more like it. You may serve Pompey, but you're still soldiers of Rome, and *we* are still Roman nobiles and officers. Remember that, you pair of snivelling little scrotums.'

He turned his back on the two chastened men and glanced past Caesar to Fronto. 'You know this city better than any of us Marcus. If we're to ride on to Ilerda and join a war, I personally want a strong drink and a good night's sleep first. Anywhere you recommend?'

Caesar was still seething and the look on his face suggested that his mind was going over everything, processing the information and planning their next move. Fronto grinned at Antonius. 'There are a few good taverns in the city, but if I might suggest, I have a villa a few miles out of town with its own vineyard?'

Antonius clapped his hands together. 'Capital. Now that's the first good news I've heard since we left Rome. Come on, Gaius,' he slapped Caesar on the shoulder. 'If we must stay the night at Tarraco, we might as well drink Fronto out of house and home.'

* * *

Fronto sank back into the couch with the most relief he had felt that entire year.

Every step that had taken him closer to the villa had made him more tense. What if Afranius had learned that one of Caesar's officers had family in the area and had imprisoned them, or worse. What if Afranius and his army had been at work ravaging the area? What if Fabius had ravaged the place in passing, for he would not know of Fronto's property? There were so many ways this could have gone horribly wrong for the family. He could see a similar concern building on Galronus' face as they turned up the drive, too.

In the end, all his fears had been unfounded. Not only had the villa escaped all trouble and even the notice of the anti-Caesarian elements in Hispanic government, the place had actually thrived. Business was good, the crop had been abundant, and peace had reigned. Fronto had almost melted as they arrived, to see Marcus and Lucius, his two boys, running around the villa's lawns with sticks, shouting things about Gauls and barbarians and delivering deadly uppercuts to finely manicured bushes.

It never ceased to amaze him how much the boys had grown every time he saw them. They were marching toward their fourth birthday now, and clearly causing trouble as was the wont of all three year olds.

Lucilia had thrown her arms around Fronto and smothered him in kisses, much to the wry amusement of Caesar and Antonius, who sat astride their horses behind him. Faleria had been considerably more restrained, grasping Galronus' hand as he dismounted and leading him away around a corner, though the end result must have been much the same, judging by Galronus' grinning red face by the time he put in another appearance.

Masgava, Aurelius and Arcadios were looking well, if a little out of shape – the latter two, anyway. Fronto had never yet seen excess fat on Masgava. The man was basically a muscle with limbs.

The only thing that gave Fronto pause was the sight of Balbus as he appeared through the atrium to shake Fronto's hand. The old man had a faintly haunted look, and the sight of Caesar made him pale slightly, though only Fronto seemed to have noticed.

Caesar, Antonius and the other officers were welcomed into the villa as honoured guests, along with the most senior cavalry commanders. As Salvius Cursor cast a disapproving eye over the place, Fronto wondered whether he could legitimately refuse accommodation to the tribune, but decided that the backlash it would create was not worth it. He endured the lunatic's bile day in and day out. What was one more night?

Lucilia and Faleria both bore expressions of frustration as Fronto asked humbly whether they might be able to find somewhere in the villa's grounds for a not-so-small cavalry unit to camp. In the end the auxilia had set up their rows of tents to the east of the villa, on common grazing land at the estate's edge, allowing their horses to be corralled with the estate's animals, a decision made by Fronto's mother who, though appearing to have aged several years since he'd last seen her, was still as much a force of nature as ever.

That afternoon the three ladies of the family set to ordering about the villa's staff while the menfolk made use of the private bath suite in shifts and retired to their rooms, emerging refreshed and in clean, fresh clothes in time for an evening meal that would have put to shame any social engagement held by a senator of Rome. Fronto had eaten until he felt distinctly unwell, and then continued to make himself feel all the more bloated by topping up with several cups of wine.

'This is an excellent vintage,' Antonius complimented him. 'Reminds me more of a wine from the Greek islands than the usual western fare.'

Fronto grinned. 'If you would like to compare, later on this evening, I will take you to the store sheds out back. We have a shipment there of Chian that was bound for Massilia but was rerouted due to the… well, you know.'

'Funny how even a disaster like Massilia can result in the odd unforeseen advantage,' chuckled Antonius. 'Chian is one of my favourites.'

Caesar rolled his eyes. 'If it's red, comes in a jar and dulls the senses, then it's naturally one of your favourites!'

Gentle chuckles filled the room for a moment, then died away. It did not escape Fronto's notice that Salvius Cursor had sat as far away from him as possible, had not smiled once during the evening, and had wrinkled his nose in distaste at the food and drink proffered to him. Indeed, the man had not said a word all night, his eyes peeling layers from everything he looked at… everything, and everyone.

'I must apologise to my gracious hostesses for this,' Caesar said, suddenly, 'but I'm afraid I must ask you a few questions. I came to Hispania expecting to link up with Fabius and the army at Gerunda, receive intelligence there and begin to prosecute a war on my own terms. Instead, I find myself racing around Hispania Citerior in search of a battle that might already be over, and almost every source I can probe for information owes allegiance staunchly to Pompey, so I am somewhat flailing in the dark. Having found such warm and gracious friends here, I wonder if you might be able to clarify a few things for me? Just update me on what you know of the local situation, if you can?'

Aurelius looked at the ladies of the house who gave him an indulgent nod.

'The legions of Citerior were based up near the frontier region during the winter. Once news arrived that Fabius and his legions had taken the passes and moved into Hispania, we heard that Petreius had started marching his legions west. For a while we worried that they meant to consolidate around Tarraco, as it would seem natural.'

Caesar nodded. 'But they did not do so.'

'No, General. Petreius sent messengers to Varro down in Gades, urging him to bring his legions northeast, and then came this way, but before he reached Tarraco, Afranius took all his garrison men, apart from his evocati reserve, and marched off to join his peer. Good job, really, as only a couple of days later, Fabius and his men passed by looking for them. Last we heard, Afranius and Petreius were in joint command, digging in at Ilerda, and Fabius had taken his legions up there to cut them out.'

'I am still vexed that the man moved ahead of schedule,' Caesar grumbled. 'Still, at least we now have at least a vague idea of what is happening. Do you know anything of the makeup of their forces?'

Balbus cut in now. 'Fabius, I presume you know, Caesar, has six legions and perhaps ten thousand auxilia of varying types. From what I know of the Citerior forces, Afranius and Petreius will be fielding only five legions until Varro joins them, but with something in the region of eighty thousand auxiliaries and native levies, they will still outnumber Fabius. And they have the advantage of knowing the territory and its people. Fabius, I would say, is in for a tough fight. And if Varro does come north with his two legions, then that will likely swing the result in Pompey's favour.'

Caesar sighed. 'He moved without waiting for me and my legions. That being said, I have not *brought* the three extra legions I had intended, since I was forced to leave them with Trebonius at Massilia.'

'Fabius has other problems, too, Caesar,' Masgava added. The various officers turned their interested gazes on the big Numidian. 'The lands of Hispania Citerior are almost entirely loyal to Pompey and his lieutenants. There are pockets of resistance, but even the bandits in the hills and mountains seem to have taken sides, focusing their unpleasant attentions on Fabius rather than Afranius and Petreius. Your man set up a very thorough network of supplies from what I hear, but they are not reaching him. There are roving units both regular and irregular, official and unofficial, who are picking off his supply columns. His army will be short of everything already, and their ability to proceed as a military force must be diminishing by the day.'

'What a mess,' Antonius sighed. 'He should have waited. How do you know all of this?' he asked the former gladiator.

Masgava shrugged. 'I spend quite a bit of time in the city for one reason or another. People talk. Besides, most of Fabius' supplies end up in Tarraco, where they're either stockpiled in the governor's storehouses, or sold on to merchants in the port.'

Caesar's eyes narrowed. 'That will have to stop. I think we need to deal with this in the morning before we move off. There are only a few evocati left in the city, and Antonius has already terrified the manure out of two of them, so word will spread quickly. I think we will find surprisingly little resistance from the garrison if we put things right tomorrow.'

The general gestured to the wine with his empty cup and a servant hurried over to fill it.

'Good,' Caesar said. 'At least now I am rather more enlightened as to the situation. Tomorrow we shall resolve the supply problem and put assurances in place to secure the ongoing arrival of food and goods. Then we shall make for Ilerda, which if I remember correctly is two days' hard ride from here. If Fabius has retained an iota of sense, and the gods are with us, we will find the battle as yet unfought and not a field of corpses and crows.'

He turned an apologetic look on the three ladies. 'I must apologise for my turn of phrase. Fruit of time spent among soldiers, I am afraid.'

The ladies brushed the matter off, and the evening returned to the discussion of niceties and meaningless nothings. Less than an hour later, Galronus and Faleria managed to slip out of the room unnoticed by most for some time, and when Fronto finally realised they had gone, he and Antonius shared a sly grin. Salvius Cursor, predictably, wore a look of disgust at the idea of the Gallic noble and a Roman lady together. Fronto had been trying to decide whether a pleasant little time alone with Lucilia might be in order, or perhaps to show the wine sheds to Antonius, when he caught Balbus' eye and the old man nodded slightly at the door.

Fronto rose and slipped from the room, making a comment about relieving the bladder pressure and ignoring Salvius' eyes boring into him as he moved. Outside he strode along the balustrade of the peristyle garden and waited until his father-in-law emerged.

'Not here,' the old man said in oddly tense tones, and led the way through the sultry evening to the steps that led down to the private beach. His sandals flapping on the stones, the old man hurried down halfway to a small terrace that Longina had constructed to sit in seclusion and watch the sea. Slipping onto the cold marble seat, Balbus gestured for Fronto to join him. The younger man stood silent for a moment, looking back up the steps. There was no sign of movement, and he could hear nothing but the whispering of the breeze through the trees and the gentle roll and crash of waves down on the beach.

'Sorry,' he said as he sat. 'I don't trust that tribune – Salvius Cursor – as far as I could spit a piglet. The way he's been watching me all night, I was almost certain he would follow me when I came out.'

'That one? Something unfriendly about him, Marcus. I felt it from the very start. Which is why I waited until Caesar involved him in conversation to slip out, sure that he wouldn't try to fob off the general.'

Fronto chuckled. 'Well played. I should have known you'd have thought of something.' He stretched. 'So why are we out here alone?'

'I may have made an error, Marcus.'

It was an innocuous enough statement, but something about the old man's leaden tone sent a shiver through Fronto. 'Go on.'

'While I was still in Massilia, I was party to the city boule's discussions.'

'So?'

'So I spent some time interfering, in an attempt to quieten the whole issue and defuse the situation. I had hoped to reconcile the sides and keep Massilia neutral in the conflict between Caesar and Pompey'

'That's very laudable,' Fronto said quietly. 'Just what I would expect from you, and nothing for which any man in that villa will condemn you.' He paused. 'Any man except Salvius Cursor, anyway, and I can deal with him.'

'No, Marcus,' Balbus went on, almost in a whisper. 'The problem is that I wrote a number of letters to influential men, both Massiliot and Roman, beseeching their aid in keeping the peace. At the time it seemed so wise. It was only when you rushed us out of Massilia and sent us here, and I was unpacking my personal effects that I realised I did not have my copies of the replies.'

A suspicion began to dawn on Fronto and his brow lowered. 'Who were these letters to?'

'Various people, as I say. Men in the Massiliot boule and in positions of power in the city. And a number of senators back in Rome.'

'Oh, shit, Quintus.'

'And Cicero.'

'Cicero too?'

'And the consuls.'

'Quintus, did you not think what you were doing?'

'They were innocent letters, Marcus. They *truly* were. But with only one side of the conversation, it would be extremely easy to see them in a rather poor light. I am more than a little concerned that I have condemned myself to appear Pompeian at heart if they are found.'

Fronto shook his head. 'I was in the villas a few weeks ago. They were empty. I think you're safe.'

'I hope so, Marcus, but I'm not sure. I sent Catháin back to Massilia with a wine shipment, with instructions to find all correspondence and get it out of the city and back to me. But that was months ago, and there has been no sign of him. I very much fear he has been caught up with the troubles there, and trapped in the city.'

Fronto took a deep breath.

'That, Quintus, is truly shitty. What were you thinking? With luck Catháin will have destroyed the documents by now. But if not.... if he's fallen foul of someone, or been arrested... I don't know. But if Trebonius takes Massilia and those documents are somehow found, Caesar's men will damn well crucify you. He doesn't take kindly to betrayal at close quarters, even if it was done with the best of intentions.'

'I have been considering going to Massilia myself, Marcus. Seeing if I can get in somehow.

'Balbus, you're over seventy summers old. Don't take this the wrong way, since you're fitter than any other grandfather I know, but you're not going to get into Massilia. Believe me. I was there when the siege began.'

He fumed for a moment. 'And I cannot go. I'm committed to Hispania now, with Caesar. Our best hope is to get this fight at Ilerda out of the way as fast as possible, and then get Caesar to somehow post me back to Massilia. If I can get back there before Trebonius, then I can be among the first men into the city and I can find Catháin and get rid of your letters.'

'I'm sorry, Marcus. I only meant to try and make things better.'

'I know you did, Quintus. But the way this has to work now is deniability. We are going back to the villa. *You* are going to carry on here as though nothing was wrong and say nothing to anyone. *I* am going to go with Caesar, beat Pompey's men to a pulp and then get myself assigned back to Massilia, where I shall resolve the problem. Then, with luck, I'll get back here for the winter. Or, if Caesar has other ideas, I'll send word to you.'

Balbus nodded.

'Now get back up those steps with me, drink good wine and try not to look like you've done something monumentally stupid.'

Chapter Seven

16th of Junius - Ilerda

ATENOS and Carbo stood at the edge of the enormous camp, eying the lands around them with no small amount of distaste. Ilerda promised little more than hardship, hunger and privation, and that fact was rapidly settling into the bones of every man in the army.

The six legions and varied auxiliaries of Fabius' army had arrived in high spirits. They had moved through eastern Hispania unopposed, commandeering what they needed from places that had until recently held Pompeian garrisons, and then moving ever on in the direction in which the enemy were said to be gathering. By the time they had passed through Barcino – a port town that reeked of fish and of rotten seafood sauce components – they had learned that Afranius had fled Tarraco and drawn every available garrison to his banner, scurrying northwest to join with Petreius, who had brought his five legions and innumerable native levies west. They had settled at Ilerda and there awaited developments. Fabius had been determined to give them one heck of a development before more legions could come in support from Gades.

They had force marched to Ilerda and there all the enthusiasm had quickly drained from both the army and its commanders.

The city of Ilerda itself – an ancient native site re-fortified by its Roman conquerors decades ago – stood atop a hill with a garrison of legionaries defending it, rumoured to be the site of a massive store of provisions. The main Pompeian army was encamped on another rise perhaps a quarter of a mile from the walls of Ilerda, well-entrenched and twice the size of the city it lay beside. The River Sicoris ran along behind both fortifications, and between the two lay a saddle with a small hill overlooking a solid stone bridge across the torrent. It was a well-protected crossing, overlooked by both Petreius' camp and Ilerda's walls, and approachable only by the saddle between them.

Fabius' army had arrived from the east and, finding the only crossing of the river guarded by Pompey's army, they had moved four miles upstream, constructed two hasty bridges, and then crossed to the same side of the river as the enemy. Scouts had been sent out, but reported only disappointing news. There was no strongpoint for the legions to camp close to the enemy. If they encamped opposite Petreius and Afranius, they would be forced to build on low ground, away from the water and at a disadvantage of terrain. And so they had camped four miles away, close to their new makeshift bridges.

It had turned out to be a wise decision, too. The scouts also reported that this huge triangle of land formed by the River Sicoris, the River Cinga – a downstream tributary, and the mountains to the north, was entirely free of forage. It seemed that the forward thinking Petreius, when he had arrived at Ilerda and settled in, had ravaged the local countryside and taken anything of value, storing it within Ilerda's walls for his own army.

That would not have been such a worry had it not quickly become apparent that the supply chain Fabius had set up was troubled. Only one in four expected caravans of supplies actually arrived, and rumour had it that half of Hispania were rising up with spears, attacking the convoys and stealing the supplies. And so, Fabius' army remained safely by their new bridges where they could cross them and move east to the better forage in that area.

Still, it was not the most favourable situation, and the frustration at their situation grew daily. They could not safely bring any attack against the enemy forces. On this, the western side of the river, they would be fighting from low plains up against a superior force behind strong walls with a good source of food and ready access to more over their bridge. Fabius' army, on the other hand, would be under-supplied and would become more so by the day. Here, four miles away at the new bridges, they could cross to the east and forage enough to keep the army alive, if hungry. But if they moved to Ilerda and besieged it they would be too far from the bridges to safely send out foragers and they would starve.

It was a stalemate, and every day slightly weakened Fabius's army while Petreius and Afranius' forces remained strong and well-supplied. Moreover, since they had moved on without waiting for Caesar and his own supplies, Fabius' financial situation had become troublesome. The men were late being paid, for Fabius' supplies of coin had long since diminished. And while there was nothing here for them to spend wages on, anyway, men waiting for late pay were never in the best of moods.

'Something has to change,' Atenos muttered. 'Half rations make men grumble at the best of times. And when they're unpaid and having to spend every day marching out into fields in unknown territory looking for food, they slide toward discontent every day. You and I know that sedition is only ever one payday and three meals away for any army.'

Carbo sighed. 'But *what* to do is the question. We move to besiege Ilerda, and our ability to scavenge supplies decreases. We leave, and the enemy might receive reinforcements from Varro. So we're stuck here praying for something to happen.'

'I don't *know* what to do,' Atenos agreed irritably. 'Yet *something* has to be done.'

'And something will.'

They turned to see Lucius Munatius Plancus, legate of the Seventh Legion and one of Caesar's longest-serving staff officers, striding up the turf bank toward them. Both men nodded their heads in respect, Atenos also saluting his superior. Plancus had begun his service as an over-eager, green officer, but the years of service seemed to have settled him into a role no one would originally have anticipated. He had become a careful, intuitive legionary legate, earning a great deal of respect from the several legions he had commanded over the years.

'You have news?' Carbo enquired.

'A hasty meeting. Three of us went to see Fabius to urge him into some sort of action. I don't know what the Tenth is like, but if they're anything like the Seventh, then they're about three days from turning on their officers and eating them. Man cannot live on barley gruel alone. We bashed around a few ideas and Fabius has made a decision.'

'Not one you agree with, from the look on your face,' Carbo noted.

'Not particularly. I favoured detaching two legions and stringing them back along the route to Tarraco to secure a supply line from the port. Fabius is not willing to consider such a proposition as it removes a third of his manpower and puts him in greater danger from the enemy. I tried to point out that we were in danger from our own men if we didn't provide supplies, but still...'

'So what *does* he plan?'

'A single, massive forage.'

'What?'

Plancus shrugged. 'It's all well and good sending out half a cohort or a cohort at a time to find untouched grain or the odd pig sty. They're providing enough food to just about keep the legions alive. If we want to face the enemy we need a good solid supply for at least a week at our fingertips.'

'We all know that, Munatius, but how?'

'Instead of committing a cohort to do a swift raid on the far bank, Fabius plans to send a single force out for a day or more across the river, reaping enough supplies to keep the whole army for a week. He plans on sending out two legions with cavalry support. I bet you can guess which legions?'

'The Tenth and the Seventh by any chance?' Atenos grunted.

'Precisely. With horses, oxen, carts and wagons. The whole mess. So that we can gather an army's worth of supplies.'

'That will make us slow-moving and encumbered,' Carbo murmured. 'All it would take was for Afranius to learn of it and have the guts to commit a force and we could find ourselves butchered to a man in some barley field to the east.'

'I know. It's far from perfect. But at least it's movement. At least we'll be doing something other than slowly starving four miles from a content enemy.'

'There is that,' Atenos conceded.

'Well, if that's the plan,' Carbo sighed, 'we'd better start getting ready while it's still early. The longer we wait the less day we'll have to gather supplies once we cross.'

* * *

Carbo approached the bridge with a certain level of trepidation. There was something about pontoon bridges that always set his teeth on edge. A solid bridge, even one formed hastily of new-cut wood, remained still under your feet. A pontoon bridge, no matter how well constructed, always had a certain level of movement, stirred by the current beneath and about each boat. It should not, to

Carbo's mind, be possible to get seasick so many miles from the sea, but a grey face loomed in his future, he was sure.

Ahead, the Seventh Legion was already across, moving out into cohorts and securing a bridgehead just in case, as the scouts spread out over half a mile or more, checking the surrounding countryside. Now, Carbo watched the support train of the Seventh crossing as he prepared to lead across the Tenth.

The bridge was bending and shuddering with each clomp of a horse's hoof and trundle of iron-shod wheel. Carbo shuddered again. It took half an hour just to get the animals and carts across, and Carbo would be willing to swear he was seeing the bridge deteriorate as he watched. Yet, finally, the last of the Seventh's carts reached the east bank and crawled up to join its fellows in the protective arms of the legion.

Carbo sighed. Plancus had tossed a coin to see who crossed the river first, and had won the toss. Or possibly lost. Carbo still wasn't sure which he preferred.

'Ready?' Atenos murmured from nearby, quiet enough not to be heard by the waiting men.

'Not really. I swear I saw a piece of that bridge break off and float away just now. Who built this? It wasn't the Tenth.'

'I've no idea. But it took the weight of the Seventh well enough.'

'Fortunately I'll be accompanying the rear guard, so this joy is yours.'

Atenos chuckled. 'See you across the Styx.'

As he blew his whistle and waved on the First Cohort, Carbo made a warding sign against bad luck, cursing his friend for such a blithe yet dangerous joke. He sat with the tribunes – five young men who couldn't tell a gladius from a bum hole, and one broad stripe who kept looking hungrily at him as though he felt Carbo was just keeping the uniform warm for him. Carbo hated tribunes. Their role in the legion remained largely mysterious to him even now he commanded one. Centurions kept things working from the top to the bottom, in camp, on the march, and in battle. The legate made the grand decisions, along with any imperator in command, and the camp prefect ran the camp. But tribunes? One just waiting for the legate's knotted belt, and five boys who were waiting to get home so they could watch girls swoon over what heroes they were.

Pointless. In months of command all he had ever used the tribunes for was to deliver messages.

He watched the First Cohort cross with the same feeling of nervousness. Every creak of timber or groan of a boat made him shiver. He definitely spotted half a cracked plank float off downstream toward Ilerda as the Second Cohort moved down the bank and tromped onto the timber boards nailed across the boats. Under his breath he uttered a prayer to the deity of these waters, whatever his name might be, that he be kind, and wished that his legionaries were capable of marching gently, without stamping their feet so.

The Second Cohort passed across without incident and the Third followed on. By the time the Third was climbing the far bank and the Fourth already crossing, his fears had faded somewhat. He glanced past the other six cohorts to the wagon and beast train waiting patiently, and the six hundred cavalry who were bringing up the rear. Armies with wagons and oxen moved at a pace that would make a snail cry, and Carbo knew that all too well. Often, during their time in Gaul, Caesar had sacrificed ease of supplies and support for speed, leaving behind wagons and pack and marching just the legionaries at a good pace. Of course, they couldn't do that here when the supply wagons were the whole reason for the crossing in the first place, but that didn't make the coming slow slog through unknown land close to the enemy any more attractive.

The Fifth and Sixth cohorts crossed. Carbo tried not to look too closely, yet still saw two pieces of timber drifting away down the river. He couldn't definitively say they were part of the bridge and *hadn't* been brought this far on the current, but he was willing to bet it.

The Seventh and Eighth crossed, laughing and chattering carelessly, content in the knowledge that nothing nasty awaited them on the far side, with so many fellow legionaries already there and controlling the ground.

Carbo tried to let the tension go out of him, counting up slowly in time with what he wished his pulse to be, and keeping going until his heart fell into step with the rhythm. More relaxed, finally, he opened his eyes.

The Tenth Cohort was now stomping off across the bridge. There was a ligneous cracking noise and a deep groan and suddenly Carbo's pulse was racing again, all his good work undone. He watched, tense, as the men crossed, unheeding, and climbed up the other side. The wagon drivers began to descend one after another and rumbled out onto the boards. Carbo looked back past the now greatly diminished waiting column. He could see Fabius and his legionary commanders standing on the ramparts and watching. His interest was piqued as he noticed the standards of the Ninth and Fourteenth moving out to the north slightly, just at the edge of the camp. What were they preparing for?

The rumble of wheels and snort and stomp of animals drew him back. There was another deeply worrying groan from the crossing.

'Wait here,' he said to the small knot of tribunes, and trotted down toward the bridge. As he reached it, he looked out across it and realised he'd been right. He waved at the next cart. 'Stay there. Don't board the bridge yet.' As the driver saluted and did as ordered, Carbo moved off onto the boards, carefully manoeuvring his horse alongside the slow-moving ox-carts.

'Slow it down and space it out,' Carbo yelled to the drivers. 'You're putting too much stress on the timber at once. You!' he bellowed to the man he'd just passed. 'I know oxen can walk backwards. I've seen it happen. Move back to the bank. Spread out, all of you. Those at the front move up to the bank and thin it all out. I want...'

His voice trailed away as there was a deep groan, as though Gaia herself had failed to digest something. Then, in a heart-stopping moment, there was a splintering noise.

'Get off the bridge,' Carbo yelled. 'Now!'

Even as the drivers went into a most un-military panic, a boat broke away from the pontoon, one side of it ripped out and still attached to the bridge. The boat whirled and bounced along the current a few hundred paces and then disappeared beneath the water. The planks that had been attached to that boat suddenly shot upwards, with no anchor for them, and the wagon on the other end tipped into the interior of the boat below, oxen bellowing and thrashing in blind terror.

Carbo was dismayed to see that many of the teamsters had simply abandoned their vehicles and were running for whichever bank was nearest.

There was another creak and a groan and suddenly Carbo was hurtling through the air. He caught a brief glimpse of his own horse screaming and plunging into the water amid shattered timbers and pieces of boat and then his world went black.

Carbo struggled. The water was cold and dark and pulled at him, dragging him simultaneously down to the riverbed and also south toward Ilerda. Something heavy bounced off his shoulder and sent him cartwheeling through the deep. He managed to unhook his cloak, which was not weighing him down like his armour, but was most definitely trouble, and the crimson wool floated away up to the surface.

He saw dimly in the dark waters a man plunge downwards, touch the bottom and then start launching himself up toward the surface, only to have a mule and half a cart land on him, crushing him back down into the depths.

He struggled with the clasps for his cuirass, even as he realised it was hopeless. He had moments of breath left before his lungs would override his brain and force him to suck inwards, filling them with water that burned despite the cold. He would never remove enough armour and weight to swim upwards and his strength was already starting to flag.

His feet touched the bottom and he bent his knees and launched himself. Not upwards – his armour would never allow that. But toward the bank that he could see only because of a dead horse lying on it, its mane wafting in the current. Three bounding leaps he managed toward the bank, but his limbs were starting to feel like lead and his fingers had gone numb with the cold water as they attempted and failed to work the armour clasps. He had cut his thumb on the metal and the blood bloomed darker in the dark water. One more step.

His lungs tried to pull in air, but he resolutely kept his mouth shut by force of will alone as his body lurched and spasmed with the effort of not breathing.

Suddenly he was zooming through the water.

The dark was replaced with a blinding light and his eyes could not adjust, full of water and dazzled by the glare. Driven by some automatic realisation, his mouth opened and he sucked in air again and again and again, filling his lungs like never before.

A serious face was looking down at him, full of concern. He blinked away the water and his eyesight gradually settled. His broad stripe senior tribune crouched next to him, drenched and with his hair in disarray. The man grinned. 'Good job you let your cloak go, sir, or we'd never have known where you were.'

Carbo coughed and coughed and coughed again and finally, when his body stopped shaking uncontrollably, he grinned.

'So *that's* what tribunes are for.'

* * *

Atenos turned at the sound, and watched in horror as the bridge bucked and tore, folded and collapsed, sending carts and wagons, horses and oxen, men and horses into the river. The Sicoris was no Rhodanus or Tiber, but nor was it some minor stream. Between fifty and a hundred paces across at different places, it was deeper than two men and flowed fast and strong. Any man who went in there in armour was almost certainly a dead man.

He watched as the whole thing disintegrated, broken shards of timber and pieces of board spinning off as debris downstream. His horror abated slightly as he saw the gleaming shape of Carbo hauled from the water on the far bank and nursed back to consciousness, but still the whole thing was an unmitigated disaster. Two legions and the scouts were now on this bank, along with one legion's carts. All the cavalry remained on the far side and the Tenth's vehicles were divided roughly evenly between the grassy slopes opposite and the river bed.

'Shit.'

'Recall the scouts,' bellowed Plancus not far away, his orders relayed by the musicians. The legate hurried over to Atenos. 'Is it worth ploughing on, in your opinion, Centurion? With only half the vehicles and no cavalry support?'

Atenos, effectively commanding the Tenth right now, shook his head. 'We're trapped, sir. The other of our bridges is two miles upstream and the one at Ilerda is four miles downstream. We can't use theirs. I would recommend we move up to our next bridge and send for instructions from Fabius.'

Plancus nodded. 'I... wait. What's going on?'

Atenos turned and peered across the river to where the legate's gaze was locked. Two legions were on the move from their camp: the Ninth and Fourteenth. They had abandoned all kit except their fighting gear, just like the Caesarian legions they were, and were moving at double time north toward the other bridge, the cavalry keeping pace alongside them.

'What are they doing?'

Atenos shook his head. He had no idea. Then his gaze slid slowly toward the knot of officers on the rampart opposite. The commanders there, even Fabius, were gesticulating wildly toward the south, downstream.

Plancus frowned and peered off in that direction. Over the gently rolling landscape he could just see the high bulk of Ilerda rising on the far bank, miles away.

'What have they seen?'

But Atenos was not looking. He was listening.

'The enemy are coming.'

'What?' Plancus turned to him.

'I can hear distant calls – infantry and cavalry. Roman instruments, but not legion calls I know. It has to be theirs. Afranius and Petreius. Somehow they know what's happened and that we're trapped. They're coming for us.'

Plancus slapped his head.

'Debris. It'll take only moments for debris to float miles downstream in this current. They've spotted the debris, I'll bet.'

Atenos huffed. 'They have infantry, which means they can't move any faster than us. If we make for the second bridge, we can be there before them.'

'Not with wagons,' Plancus pointed out.

'Then leave the damned wagons, Legate.'

'Can't do that, Atenos. We've just lost a whole load to the water, and with the supply situation like it is, we need them. We can't let the enemy get the wagons. We have to protect them.'

'Then we're buggered, sir. We'll have to form up and face the enemy.'

Plancus gave him a bleak, humourless grin. 'Well we've been pressing for a fight. Looks like we'll get it. We only have to hold until the Ninth and Fourteenth get here.'

'Only?' repeated Atenos meaningfully.

'I'm not sacrificing the wagons, Atenos.'

The centurion nodded. 'Very well. We'll need favourable ground. And we've got half an hour at the absolute most before they're on us.'

Plancus looked about. 'There's a good sized rise over there.'

Atenos peered at it. Some three hundred paces from the river was a small plateau with a very regular edge. 'Looks like a fort platform to me. Maybe some legion has camped here before?'

'Either way, it's our best chance. We get the vehicles in the middle and defend in orbis form around them. No heroics, no charges, just solid, careful defence with as little waste as possible. We hold them until the other legions get here.'

Turning back to the river, Atenos put his hands around his mouth and bellowed across. 'How many?'

A tribune on the far side did the same. 'Four legions and horse, we think.'

'Shit. That puts us on equal terms even when the others get here. This could go bad for us.'

'Come on, Centurion,' Plancus grinned. 'You're Caesar's glorious fighting Tenth Equestris.'

'Don't feel too glorious right now,' grumbled Atenos. 'Alright. Let's get to work.'

* * *

Atenos gestured to the centurion to his left. 'Spread your men out a little more forward and have the reserve come closer. When the moment comes to rotate ranks I don't want any delay. Quick and efficient, from one line to the next, alright?'

The centurion saluted and began to move his men a little here and there, prodding them as his optio nudged them around with his staff. The wagon drivers and their mates had followed a suggestion of the Seventh's Primus Pilus, and were gathering any rocks they could find from among the dirt and grass and piling them in their wagons.

'Looks like they're here,' Atenos said suddenly, pointing at one of the scouts, who was racing back toward them from the south. Other riders were also appearing at speed, waving and pointing behind them.

'Damn, that was quicker than I expected,' Plancus hissed.

'Indeed,' Atenos replied. 'We'll have at least half an hour to hold until our friends arrive. Hope the men's blood is up.'

Plancus smiled and drew his sword with a rasping hiss.

'Put that bloody thing away.'

'Are we not acknowledging rank these days, Centurion Atenos?' Plancus said meaningfully.

'My apologies. Put that bloody thing away, *sir*.'

'Atenos, we don't have the luxury of sparing me. Every sword counts.'

'And you've probably been practising very hard, sir, but leave it to those of us who've trained all our lives for this. Besides, nothing hits a legion's morale harder than watching their commander take a face full of gladius.'

'Point taken, Centurion. *Blunt* point, but taken nonetheless.'

Atenos waved the legate away and Plancus, distinctly unhappy with the decision, moved through the ranks to the centre of the raised platform where the teamsters had drawn their vehicles into a rough square like a makeshift fort. Clambering unceremoniously onto one, he peered off into the distance in the direction of the enemy.

Atenos flexed his shoulders, arms, fingers, stamped from foot to foot, keeping his leg muscles limber. He turned the sword hilt in his hand, finding the comfortable angle where his fingers had worn the bone of the hilt into shape. The centurions to either side had collected shields – oval ones considerably smaller than the legionaries' great body-shields – from the carts as soon as it had become apparent that there would be fighting. Atenos had not. In his right hand, he held his gladius, and in his left the petrified, knobbly, ligneous vine stick that was his badge of office. Since he had first taken his commission under Caesar, several of his peers had tried to persuade him that the staff was a badge, and not a weapon. A hundred men under Atenos' command would attest differently, having been on the receiving end of it, and *they* were only being clattered for misdemeanours. How might it be used to harm someone who *really* deserved it?

The scouts did not pause, riding past the two legions drawn up on the raised ground and bellowing warnings to the officers. The enemy were right behind them. And then they were gone, north in the direction of the other bridge. Atenos watched them pass. They could do little good other than as light skirmishers anyway, and their job now was to apprise the commanders of the legions hurrying to their aid of the situation, and to exhort them to move with all haste.

Moments later, he caught sight of movement to the south. Shapes were emerging from an olive grove – riders in glinting chain shirts with bright green shields. They swarmed out from between the twisted ancient trees and began to close once more into units.

'Rear ranks be ready to pass your pila forward. We're going to take a pounding from the cavalry first.'

The centurion to his right cleared his throat. 'Can you see how many?'

'You've got eyes,' Atenos replied quietly.

'Yes, but you're about two feet taller than the rest of us. You're almost looking down on them.'

Atenos shrugged. 'Hard to tell. More than a few hundred. Maybe a thousand?'

'Regular or native levy?'

'Both. But it's the natives they'll throw at us. Petreius won't want to push Roman against Roman if he can avoid it. He can't be sure how well his men will react to it. I'd like to say we're better off against the natives, but the Hispanics have been fighting Romans for decades thanks to the *last* civil war, so they know what they're about.'

'So what do we do?'

'They'll try to break us – they *have* to. We launch one volley of pila as soon as they come within range. Then the reserves pass their pila forward and we form the *contra equitas* formation. All of us. The whole square. We deny them the chance to break in, because if they break one side of the square then we'll be in chaos when the infantry get here. Any man who even trembles gets a taste of Antonia here.' He waved his vine stick meaningfully.

The enemy cavalry were coming now. They had formed up this side of the trees and created three units, each several hundred strong. Behind them, the red banners and gleaming chain of Pompey's Hispanic legions were emerging from the greenery in solid, military formation and at a mile-consuming pace. Atenos knew that every man around him was experiencing the same feeling. The Tenth and the Seventh were old legions – Caesar's staunchest and longest-serving veterans. They had fought Belgae and Gauls, Aquitanii and Germans. There was no one of whom they were afraid.

But the men pouring out of the trees across the parched fields of Hispania Citerior were men just like them. Pompey's veterans. As long-serving, as well trained and experienced. As strong and – most importantly – as *Roman*. Civil war.

Of course, Atenos had the benefit of an outsider's view. He may be a Roman citizen, and serving as an officer in the legions, but he was a Gaul by birth, weaned on tribal warfare. In the old days, when he'd been young, civil war was the norm for his people. Tribes fighting tribes was as natural as the morning air. But for the men under his command it would seem unthinkable to plunge their blades into those men beyond the cavalry. Into many of the horsemen too, for that matter.

The three units of riders began to diverge as they approached, the outer units veering off to the sides. The central one was riding straight at Atenos' men.

'A quarter of our lads are going to get an easy ride,' murmured a centurion off to his left.

'There'll be no easy rides to be had today,' corrected Atenos. 'Ready pila.'

The men in the front rank shifted position, bracing their leading leg, their hands changing grip on the wooden shaft as they angled it upwards past their chins, ready to launch. Atenos peered along the line, satisfied that they were in good order.

Every legion had a different way of doing things, and he could just see the men of the Seventh around the corner of the defensive line preparing to follow the same commands. Their pila wavered slightly and were held at much less uniform angles. Many legions preferred to have their heaviest, strongest veterans at the front line, taking the first blows of any combat, and there was a great deal to be said for the advantage that gave a unit. Fronto himself had followed that very system when he'd commanded the Tenth.

Atenos and Carbo had instituted a *different* system. Their first line in battle formation was formed of the legion's best throwers. The *second* line was the heavy veterans. Of course, they'd not had much chance over the past couple of years to test the veracity of this system, though it seemed the time was upon them at last. Now it was about the pila. Then it would be about quick changes in formation and the spacing of the men.

'Wait until they get close. No further than thirty paces.'

His vine stick jabbed out, indicating the line of white stones his optio had placed in front of them, marking the thirty pace mark. Thirty paces was something of a stretch for a pilum thrower to hold any level of accuracy, but his front line were the best he could muster. He'd been careful to have the white stones placed at twenty five paces around the Seventh to allow for their likely lesser effective range.

He could feel the tension building as the cavalry thundered toward them.

The most dangerous moment facing a cavalry charge was now. With that implacable wall of iron and horseflesh pounding toward you at breakneck speed, even the strongest bladder began to leak. Men who thought themselves brave would consider their next few moments carefully and seriously contemplate taking flight. Once battle was joined, things became easier, if more violent. But if the cavalry could somehow rupture the lines, then it would be over in short order. Even Atenos would be unlikely to recover any sense of formation before the infantry hit them and began to butcher. They had to hold.

'Steady, lads. They're only boys on ponies, after all. Not proper soldiers, like you.'

There was a ripple of nervous laughter along the lines. Someone let out a fart that lasted a surprisingly long time and rose in pitch to an impressive squeak. The line roared with laughter and even Atenos smiled as one of his men muttered something about eggs, but he needed them to focus as well as maintain good spirits. 'Calm it down now, lads. Those poor buggers on the horses think you're laughing at them. Ready…'

The enemy were close, their hooves pounding toward that line of white stones. *Please*, Atenos thought, directing his request to whichever gods might be watching the dry fields of Hispania, *please let the lads get this right.*

Closer.

'Tense those muscles. Ready...'

A hoof smashed one of the white stones to pieces as the first horse crossed the line.

'*Iacta!*' bellowed Atenos.

Four hundred pila left his line in near perfect harmony, released at the same time and at almost the same angle. The cavalry were still coming. There was nothing they could hope to do now, at thirty paces, other than attempt to ride down and break the Roman line.

'Contra Equitas!' he bellowed even as the last pilum left loosening fingers. Even as the volley was in flight, every man passed his pilum forward, while the front two lines also slammed their shields into position. The front line dropped to a knee and formed a wall with their shields pushed together into a perfect defensive line. The second lifted their shields and held them at a forty-five degree slope atop the front ones, bending in to brace the line so that the legion produced a wall two shields high and at an angle. Pila were thrust through the gaps between the shields, forming a hedge of perilous spikes along the line.

Atenos heard it all happening, heard the officers telling men to shuffle this way and that. But he wasn't watching. His eyes were on the enemy. The volley of pila had been brutal. The Iberian cavalry were equipped to each individual's capability, which meant that a few wore cuirass with leather shoulder straps, and more wore chain shirts, but the majority wore either a leather shirt over their tunic or no armour at all. Some had helmets, but others had none. Many had shields of one size and shape or another. The only uniform aspect to them were the swords hanging from the saddle horns and the spears in their hands.

There were perhaps four hundred of them at Atenos' estimate, and the initial pila barrage was devastating. Almost every pilum struck a target, between the skill and strength of the soldiers, the distance required and the sheer press of men at the other end. Iron points smashed deep into horses and men, into chests and legs, heads and rumps. Beasts leapt or slumped, crashing to the ground as their riders tumbled from them, equally agonised and transfixed by pila.

A hundred men and their steeds died at that line, and there was a long moment of chaos as the riders behind plunged on through the crowd of fallen and dying creatures, many of them being unseated or felled by the disastrous chaos around them. By the time the riders were past the stones and the huge line of thrashing and shrieking flesh, the legion had assumed their contra equitas formation and were prepared.

From somewhere inside the enclosure of shields there was another drawn out fart and a lot of cursing until a centurion bellowed for silence.

The riders hit the shield wall. They didn't want to, but they had little choice. No horse will willingly charge a hedge of iron, and even the most vicious and brave riders among the Iberians found their horses shying away, rearing or attempting to turn from the deadly wall. But the momentum of the unit was carrying them inexorably forward. Just as they'd been forced on through the crowd of their fallen brothers by the pressure of the mass behind them, so now, even as they reared or turned, they were driven into the Roman formation by their friends behind.

Atenos could see nothing of what happened now. Without a shield or pilum himself, he had ducked down at the last moment within the formation and simply heard the clash from within the enclosed world of the shield-box.

There were screams of men and horses, the sound of pila being snapped, the constant clatter and bang of shields, and the thud of men hitting the ground hard. The centurion felt a man pushed back against him and boot studs painfully grazed his ankle, making him hiss. The formation was being pushed back at his position. Between the men holding the shields he briefly caught sight of bay horsehair and a screaming man. There was a spray of blood that managed to penetrate the shield wall.

'Push back,' Atenos yelled. 'Straighten the line.'

Not an easy thing to do, of course, when a horse has smashed into your shield and fallen dead at your feet. His men lifted their shields and dropped them onto the dead horse, allowing them to move a pace or two forward again, the shield-line now undulating over the fallen beast rather than bowing back behind it.

A centurion nearby beat him to his next command, bellowing out 'Pass your pila forward!'

Those men whose javelins had been snapped as the beasts collided now cast the shattered remains out into the mess and grabbed a new one, passed from behind, jabbing it out through the same gap and thrusting it at any shape that moved in front.

It was over quickly. The remaining native horse had managed to pull back at last and now fled the field in disarray. Light flooded into the formation as a man lifted his shield with a sigh of relief. He cried out in pain as Atenos' vine stick walloped him on the shoulders. 'You break formation when you are *told* to break formation, soldier!'

He waited and, as if to illustrate his point, a last few Iberian cavalrymen threw spears into the mass before racing away. Atenos counted to twenty, slowly, and then gave the order.

'Form into four lines. Front rank cycle to rear.'

As the shields were pulled away and the battlefield became visible once more, the front line, damaged and exhausted, pulled back between their counterparts and formed the reserve, while the second line stepped forward to become the front. *These* were Atenos' strong veterans, like those already fielded among the Seventh. His system had worked. It might not work in straight infantry situations, but now he had his best men out front, fresh and ready for the fight, while the veterans of the Seventh were being rotated to the rear, putting the less experienced men at the fore.

The ground before the legion was littered with the bodies of men and horses. The casualty rate among the cavalry had been extremely high, and no more than a third of their number were now racing for safety. They had held off the first attack. Atenos breathed heavily and turned, surveying his men.

The Tenth had bowed and almost broken thirty paces to his right, a fact clearly stated by the body of a horse and rider within the Roman lines. That had been close, and maybe forty legionaries lay dead in that area. He wondered idly if the man with the horrendous wind had been among them.

Still, the Tenth had lost less than a hundred men and had taken out almost three hundred cavalry in the process. It had been close, but they had to count that a win. Shouts of consternation from the far side of the hill suggested that things had gone worse for the Seventh. He turned and glanced up at Plancus, who stood atop a wagon, engaged in a discussion with a tribune.

'Sir, how's the line?' he shouted, interrupting the conversation. Plancus looked around in irritation and spotting Atenos shouting at him, waved the tribune away. 'Lost quite a few men, but the line held on every side. I don't think we'll see their cavalry again.'

'No, but we've got something else to worry about now.'

He pointed, and Plancus followed his gesture, his face paling and his expression setting hard.

Across the dry brown grass, toward the olive groves, four legions stomped relentlessly toward them in formation. Atenos threw up a prayer to Mars and to his own favoured Teutatus as well, and looked down the line.

'Alright, men. This is going to be nasty. We're not going to try to take them all. We're not here to win. We just stop them getting to the carts and beasts. Hold the line until the relief gets here, and then we'll go home and drink until we can see dancing sprites and big-breasted women.'

There was an oddly subdued cheer, and Atenos watched the enemy approach.

* * *

Atenos felt a fiery line drawn across his flesh as the tip of a gladius dinged off his cheek guard, missed his eye by a finger-width, and carved a furrow in his nose. He caught a brief glimpse of the face of its wielder – a sun-weathered legionary with skin like a saddle bag, before his automatic reaction blow struck, his vine stick swung hard from the left. The heavy, knobbly end, polished on the tunics of a hundred legionaries, clanged into the man's helmet so hard that it sounded like a temple bell. The man fell away, his sword lowered, eyes spinning with the blow. He dropped to his knees and threw up even as he tried to undo the chinstrap on his helmet and free his concussed head. His helmet fell away, and before he could sense relief he was hit in the face with the bronze edge of a shield as a soldier from the Tenth took momentary advantage.

Atenos lashed out with his gladius, slamming it into the armpit of a man who had raised his sword to strike at a Caesarian optio.

It was hell. The unconscionable consequences of civil war had been forgotten from the first moment the Pompeian legion had hit them. Atenos had not been able to escape the irony that it appeared that the unit they were facing also carried a flag labelling them as the Tenth. Only Caesar's bull on their own flag helped delineate who was fighting whom. Worse, Atenos had already twice found men from his own legion fighting one another in the mistaken belief they were deadly enemies. His only consolation was that the same thing seemed to be happening among the enemy. He'd seen two men fighting back to back against a circle of enemies for a dozen heartbeats until they realised they were from different legions, and even then Atenos hadn't been sure who had won that scuffle.

'Reform the line,' he bellowed. 'Tenth Equestris on your banners!'

The lines were holding, but here and there they melted outwards into small melees as men accidentally responded to the whistle calls of centurions from another legion.

A man slashed at Atenos and he knocked the blade aside with his stick, irritated at the dent the blow left, and jabbed his sword into the man's genitals. As the legionary fell, screaming, Atenos stepped back and watched his men pulling away from the enemy and settling into their lines again. The enemy commander seemed to have had the same idea and he could hear calls for the Tenth Virtutis to pull back and form lines.

Virtutis. The brave. There was no denying that, at least.

'Take a look,' Atenos said to his men, 'at the men to each side. Keep them in that position and stick your steel in anyone in front. Don't get drawn out into melees and forget whistles and horns. You all know my voice and that of your own centurion. If the order isn't called in one of our voices, ignore it. Ready, lads?'

There was a roar in response, and swords were clattered against the side of shields.

'For Hispania and for the senate and the people of Rome,' bellowed an officer of their opposing legion. Atenos narrowed his eyes.

'For Caesar, for Rome, and for victory!' he bellowed.

Another roar, and the enemy came again.

Once more Atenos found himself in the thick of it, his vine stick and gladius lashing out together, battering and slashing, parrying and jabbing. His flickering glance suddenly fell upon a man with the pelt of some great beige feline draped across his helmet and his eyes rose to the standard above him. A standard!

Two men beside him were already breaking the line to get to the standard bearer and, despite breaching his orders to maintain the line, he could understand why they would risk it. To take an enemy standard in battle was automatic promotion and free drinks for a year. It was hard to beat as a battle honour unless you could get your hands on their eagle.

The first of the two men fell to the blade of the man on the signifer's left, and the second crumpled as the iron shoe on the bottom of the standard slammed into his helmet. For a moment even Atenos considered putting himself in mortal danger and breaking out of the line to try for the man's heavy burden. Then the reality of what that standard meant sank in. It was a standard from the Third Cohort, but the Third Cohort of the Fourth Legion. That meant that he and his men were no longer facing just one legion, but two. Their odds had just fallen considerably.

'Form up and hold. Just hold. No heroics!'

Again, his world became blood and bone, iron and bronze, as things unmentionable sprayed across him and hit his armour before sliding wetly downwards. His sword sang out again and again with the meaty sound of blows successfully delivered. His vine staff blocked sword after sword, taking notches along its length, and repeatedly dinged people on the helmet, sending them reeling back with their ears ringing.

He felt something cut his thigh but by the time he looked down, whoever was responsible had gone and the only evidence was a red line below his tunic that poured blood down his leg. Something smashed into his left arm and he felt the whole limb go numb. He struggled to keep hold of his vine stick even as he lanced and stabbed, slashed and cut.

And suddenly the enemy were not there anymore. As his sword sliced out, the man he'd been aiming at was yanked away to safety by a friend. He could hear urgent whistle blowing and see standards being waved frantically.

156

A legionary rose from the piles of wounded and dead in front of them, staggering on a damaged leg, and turned a terrified expression on Atenos. The centurion narrowed his eyes. The man was an enemy, but he looked so familiar he could easily have been a man of Caesar's legions.

'Go,' he told the man, pointing toward the retreating enemy with his vine stick. Then, he turned to the rest of his men. 'Let them go.'

He'd had enough of killing Romans for one afternoon, and it was clear that the Tenth Virtutis and the Fourth were pulling back and running for Ilerda. The other two enemy legions were falling back too, reforming out of pilum reach and preparing to retreat in good order.

Atenos didn't have to wait long to hear the sound he'd been expecting from the moment the legionaries had started pulling back: the calls of the Ninth and Fourteenth legions, coming up from behind. Petreius had been willing to commit when he had hope of an easy victory, but once the numbers were more even there would be an indecisive bloodbath, and nobody wanted that.

Atenos heaved in deep breaths and dropped his vine stick and sword, rubbing his numb arm and trying to massage some life back into it as the enemy fled. They would be back in Ilerda shortly and the legions of Caesar would return to their own camp. It felt like a victory to have held them off, but in truth all they had done was avert disaster and return to the hopeless stalemate they'd endured for days already.

Something had to change soon.

Chapter Eight

22nd of Junius - Ilerda

FRONTO reined in alongside Caesar, Antonius and Galronus, peering across the gently undulating open ground toward the river as the other officers rode forward to join them.

'A bridge,' Salvius Cursor noted, a hint of disbelief and exasperation in his tone. 'They've been here for weeks in the heartland of the enemy and they're camped in the middle of nowhere building a bridge.'

'There might be more to it than that,' Fronto countered, watching the men of his own former legion, the Tenth, busily constructing a heavy timber crossing.

'There was a disaster here,' Galronus said in an odd, quiet voice, drawing frowns from the others. He shrugged and pointed at the river. 'Half a boat. A few broken timbers. And over on the grass beyond the camp there is a new burial mound. Either a fight happened here, or a disaster.'

Caesar nodded, turning back to the bridge. A small party of officers had emerged from the camp beyond the river and was riding toward them. The riders reached the river and there was a short discussion between them and the engineers before they rode gingerly out onto the not-quite-complete structure. As the last of them crossed, wide eyes on the timbers beneath them, they walked their horses toward the new arrivals.

Fronto was relieved to see not only Fabius, but also Plancus and a few other legates, including Carbo. Fabius reined in opposite Caesar with the other officers behind him, and bowed in the saddle.

'You seem to have had a problem?' prompted Caesar with one dangerously raised eyebrow.

'Greetings, General. We are constructing a new crossing. The pontoon bridge that had been here previously collapsed under the weight of carts and animals and was swept away. The bridge is required to secure forage, you see. Our men were caught, trapped on this side and the enemy came. It was hard fought, but we drove the enemy off and managed to secure our position once more.'

Caesar's face had been growing slightly more disapproving with every word.

'The next time I distribute orders to my lieutenants, will it be necessary for me to have them illustrated with maps and clear images, Fabius?'

'Sir?'

'I gave you instructions to secure the crossings from Narbo into Hispania. I gave you six legions to hold those crossings for our approach. Instead, I discover that you have taken it upon yourself to launch a campaign, forging one hundred and fifty miles southwest into the province in search of an army that might well be strong enough to flense you and send you running back east once more. Might I enquire as to what prompted you to disobey your orders to such a grand extent?'

Fabius was slightly taken aback, partially at the edge to the general's words and partially at being upbraided so publically, with the common soldiery of the Tenth within earshot at the near side of the bridge. To his credit, he rallied well. Straightening in the saddle, he replied in a clear, commanding tone.

'Our intelligence – while unconfirmed – was important enough to warrant a change in the plan in my *professional* opinion, Caesar.'

Caesar's raised eyebrow notched up a little higher, but he remained silent.

'We know that Varro has two legions,' Fabius went on, 'in Hispania Ulterior, who remain staunchly Pompeian but have not yet been committed to this region. Our reports suggest four things. That the local commanders have petitioned Varro to send his forces to join them and oppose us, and if we allow him the time and opportunity to do so, then every day our opposition becomes stronger. Also that Varro has been raising local levies since the day we crossed the Rubicon, so we would not be facing a further ten thousand legionaries, but more likely an additional thirty thousand men, including slingers, spearmen and cavalry drawn from the Iberian tribes.'

He paused for breath.

'Thirdly, that Varro has already sent men to take control of the Gallic fleet that has wintered off the west coast of Gaul. If that fleet is brought south and through the Pillars of Hercules, then Varro and the local commanders have the freedom to rove across the Mare Nostrum, giving them access to Italia, Sicilia and perhaps even to Pompey's army in the east, which I felt would solidly undermine our position. And finally that the local commanders are at loggerheads. Petreius is a forthright military man who favours outright war and field campaigns and seeks to bring us to battle. Afranius is countermanding half Petreius' decisions, as he is more concerned with the stability of their provincial control. And, I believe, he is afraid of the consequences of civil strife. So I felt it important to press these two arguing commanders and keep them busy before they reach a solution and become a decisive and singular command. If I have misread the situation or offended, Caesar, then I will unknot my general's ribbon and hand it to you alongside command of your legions.'

There was a long, tense, silence. The general's accusatory eyebrow had lowered once more and he wore a thoughtful look. He looked around the assembled officers. Most remained carefully expressionless. Fronto cleared his throat.

'It was a judgement call, Caesar. We've all done it, yourself included. And I can't say he was wrong, just as I can't say he was right. Only time will tell.'

The general nodded, turning to Salvius Cursor who was breathing heavily as though preparing to charge. 'Given the circumstances, I laud Fabius for his forethought,' the tribune muttered. 'Too many officers would sit back, relying on the knowledge that they were safely obeying given orders, while the enemy strengthened their hold. It takes a good man to bite the bit and move on the enemy regardless.'

Caesar sighed. 'Very well. I accept your assessment and judgement call, Fabius. Next time I would take it as a professional courtesy if you would do everything in your power to keep us informed of your movements before you commit. We were somewhat in the dark, bumbling around Hispania looking for you.'

Fabius threw a sour look at the new arrivals. 'In truth, Caesar, I have sent couriers to you five times since we left the mountains and Gerunda. You should have been well aware of each move we

160

have made. However, we are finding a great deal of resistance from the populace of this region. The decades seem to have robbed them of the memory of the violence Pompey inflicted upon them. They appear to have an unshakable loyalty, and Afranius is surprisingly popular as a governor. Couriers and supplies keep disappearing, as well as those units we send out to locate them. I am not at all surprised that no word has reached you. Similarly, precious few supplies have reached us and we have been forced to rely largely on forage.'

'You moved too fast without securing your support lines adequately,' Caesar admonished quietly.

'The issue, Caesar, is one of supply and logistics. On the west side of the river where the legions are encamped, Petreius and Afranius very much raped every last resource before we arrived, so we have been forced to forage on the other bank – this one – hence the bridge. Petreius commands the real stone bridge at Ilerda.'

Caesar nodded and Salvius Cursor's eyes narrowed. 'So where *is* this Ilerda and the enemy?' the younger man asked.

Carbo pointed off to the southwest 'Ilerda is around four miles that way, on a ridge to the west of the river. Most of the enemy's supplies are held by a loyal garrison within its walls. The main enemy force is encamped a few hundred paces southwest of that on a similar ridge. Between is a small hill they use as an observation post, which overlooks the bridge.'

'And might I ask why you are camped four miles away in the countryside rather than treading on the enemy's toes?' Salvius grunted, earning a warning glance from Caesar. The tribune, Fronto noted, was only happy when overstepping his bounds and promoting violence.

Fabius cast a withering look at Salvius. 'The situation there is untenable. They have the strong heights and control of the bridge. If we camp there we are too far from a viable crossing and the forage and supply issue will become a critical concern. And,' he turned back to Caesar, 'there is the issue of pay. Our funds are exhausted and the men are beginning to become... concerned. Throwing them against a strong enemy while they are already disgruntled could be an unwise move.'

Caesar nodded. 'Fortunately, the money I had put aside for the legions remains at Narbo. I had intended to bring it with me to the crossings and distribute appropriately, but you moved too far inland and I have only cavalry with me, so I brought it no further than Emporiae. Now we shall have it brought up and made available. But in the meantime, we must keep the men happy. The centurionate owe their commissions to us and their support to their legionaries, and it is uncommon to find a centurion who has not put aside a sizeable sum of their own. Have the centurions stump up any coinage they can and divide it among the men. Note down each grant and give each centurion a chit promising a return of their money on the arrival of the chests, with an extra ten percent interest.'

Fronto frowned. Would they go for that? Of course they would. They needed the men's loyalty and they were themselves loyal to their general.

'Very good, Caesar,' Fabius replied.

'I believe I have the supply situation dealt with also, which will free us to press this campaign, but first I need to familiarise myself with the field of battle.'

'Caesar?' Plancus stepped his horse a few paces into the fore. 'You said you brought only the cavalry? We were anticipating the arrival of further legions?'

The general took a deep breath, rising in his saddle. 'Unfortunately, Massilia has been claimed by the hand of Pompey and holds against us, so I have been forced to leave three legions there under Trebonius to bring the siege to a satisfactory conclusion. Still, with six legions, my additional cavalry, and various auxiliary units we should have adequate numbers to bring down Petreius if we use them wisely. I still hold out hope of a solution that will not rely on committing steel to flesh, regardless. And I have sent word to our allies in Gaul, so I hope to see tribal units coming to join us any day. Now let us put an end to this troubled meeting and instead ride out across the terrain and see what we face.'

* * *

The small group of officers, accompanied by Ingenuus' Praetorian guards and a few scouts, stood atop a dusty, brown-green hummock scattered with stones and parched, sharp plants.

Before them stood a green plain all the way to the river two miles away. And across that river rose the twin ridges that marked the strongholds of Petreius and Afranius, with the small mound between giving the location of the solid stone bridge.

'Clearly there is no value to assault from this angle,' Caesar mused, earning a knowing nod from Fabius. Camping west of the river would give them ample access to the forage that covered the lands in this area, but the presence of the sizeable torrent would make any real assault against the enemy extremely difficult and costly, if it were possible at all. Funnelling men over that bridge into battle was the only feasible option from this direction, and that would just be throwing men away on a grand scale. Fabius had been right to encamp east of the river. And with their visit around that side of Ilerda in the early afternoon, it had been clear that Fabius had also been correct in his assessment that it would have put possible forage at risk. Of course, now that Caesar had secured the supplies and supply lines, that should no longer be an issue, but the value of good forage could not be ignored even then.

The officers turned en masse to look the other way. Beyond this small hillock, the verdant fields and orchards stretched out toward the great Iberus river.

'It is a shame we cannot cut them off from this source of forage,' Antonius mused. 'Maybe if we destroyed the bridge we could seal them in?'

Fabius and Caesar shook their heads in unison.

'It would cost far too many men to attempt to destroy that bridge right under the enemy's walls,' the general countered.

'And from what I understand,' Fabius added, 'the stores in Ilerda could keep Petreius and Afranius and their men comfortably for many months. If the campaign lasts that long then Varro will be here, will have the fleet in southern waters and we will have lost.'

'Denial of resources,' Salvius Cursor murmured.

'What?'

'Deny the enemy their supplies. We cannot break the bridge for fear of losing troops, the general says.' Was that a hint of a sneer Fronto saw on his face there? 'But we can equally deny them forage very easily by taking all that we can and burning and razing the rest.'

The officers turned to him with a disbelieving look, and Salvius shrugged nonchalantly. 'Fill our wagons and take them to the camp and then burn all the crops for twenty miles or more. Right the way to the Iberus if we have to. Butcher the livestock, fell the trees. Lay waste to the land and make it unyielding.'

'I think you missed my point,' Fabius spat. 'They have good supplies in Ilerda.'

'I missed nothing,' Salvius snapped in reply. 'But we could then concentrate on Ilerda. From what I've both heard and seen, the massive bulk of the enemy are encamped on the other hill. The walls of Ilerda are held by a lesser garrison. We do not immediately need to engage the enemy legions. If we breach Ilerda, take the supplies and burn the town we deny the enemy all possibility of supplies. They will starve their way into surrender.'

'What is it with you and burning?' Fronto grunted angrily.

'You have a problem with the prosecution of a war by the most expedient means, Fronto?'

'If those means include razing the land and salting the earth, then yes. Salvius, these are Romans. Well, provincials, but they pay their taxes, honour the gods and speak our tongue. They are as Roman as you or I. And they are innocent. No matter our quarrel with Pompey or his legions, that does not give us the right to destroy and loot farms and townsfolk.'

'War is like the fires of Tartarus, Fronto, fiery and destructive. You're soft. We can't all afford to be as soft as you or the war is already lost.'

'Children,' shouted Antonius, glaring at the two arguing officers, 'pipe down. Cultivate a stoic calmness and listen to your father.' With a fierce smile, he gestured to Caesar, who was looking at both Salvius and Fronto disapprovingly.

'This will not be resolved through supplies and starvation,' the general said, finally. 'We must find another way. There will be an option that lies somewhere between slowly starving them out and a costly and uncertain main attack. An assault across the river is not feasible, so Fabius was correct in his positioning. However, since our supplies are now on the way, guarded by Gauls and a few regular cavalry, including a good supply of wine donated by Fronto here, and with the pay issue temporarily resolved too, there is nothing holding us back from moving against the enemy at

Ilerda. Be reminded, all of you, that this is a state of civil war, and that everyone we face is Roman. To that end, full-scale warfare is the very last option I will take. I do not believe we can negotiate with the enemy, and we do not have the luxury of time to force them to capitulate. But we may yet bring forth in them such fear of facing us that they surrender and back down. If this can be done, it is what I seek. I would rather see the officers hand me their swords and the men go free than a field of thousands of dead Romans. Are we all clear?'

There was an affirmative chorus that left only Fronto and Salvius glaring at one another. Without taking their eyes from each other, they both agreed.

'Wonderful,' Antonius said with only a touch of sarcasm. 'Then perhaps it's time we got back to camp and started making arrangements. With luck, Fronto's wine will have arrived.'

* * *

Fronto shifted his backside in the saddle, trying to massage some life back into it. War, he reflected – for an officer, at least – consisted largely of sitting on a variety of different hills and waiting for things to happen. This particular hill didn't really deserve the appellation. It was more of a crease in the otherwise relative flat. But it was the best observation point as the legions assembled. Caesar was back with his other officers organising their legions, but Galronus, Antonius and Fronto, having no direct commands, were sitting ahorse on the rise and observing the opening stage of what would likely be a brutal battle.

Off to the left he could see Ilerda on its rise, strong walls recently reinforced, with the gleaming figures of men atop them. The defences followed the high contours closely and made Ilerda as much a fortress as a city. A saddle separated Ilerda from the main camp, though a small hill rose like a pimple at its centre, upon which a small unit of Pompeian soldiers were dug in, overlooking the bridge.

Petreius and Afranius' camp, a huge affair housing vast numbers of men, filled a second hill only slightly lower than the one upon which Ilerda sat. Its earth and timber defences were good and positioned well at the top of a deadly slope. Fronto was starting to doubt the wisdom of facing the enemy here. These were no tribal force who were incautious and direct. There was no chance they would trip themselves up by failing to consider the enemy. These were Roman veterans, as experienced and as skilled at war as Caesar's army. There would be no easy victory to be had in this war.

Behind the three of them, six legions and various auxiliaries fell in, forming up as though offering battle. Which, of course, was precisely what they were doing. Almost all Caesar's manpower was here, with one cohort from each legion left behind at the camp to secure the bridges and the supply route that was already bringing in food, drink and equipment.

'Will they attack?' Galronus asked.

Antonius and Fronto glanced across him at one another.

'Perhaps,' Fronto mused. 'Perhaps not. They have the advantage of terrain and probably of numbers. But they know we are veterans and determined, and they know we're fresh from the Gallic campaigns. They have to be suffering some small amount of uncertainty. And if what we hear is correct and Afranius is reluctant to commit, then Petreius might not be able to launch an attack. They share a joint command, and to commit the full Pompeian force would require the assent of both. Dual commands rarely work out well.'

'I'm not sure whether I want them to or not anyway,' added Antonius. 'Just as they're likely worried about what we can bring to a fight, neither can we underestimate them. These legions have been fighting to push the edge of Roman-controlled territory back into the northern Hispanic tribes for years, and before that they were involved in the previous civil war out here. Caesar's legions have an impressive reputation, and rightfully so, but these legions we face might well be a match for them.'

'Caesar will have a plan,' Galronus said quietly.

The other two turned to him. 'What?'

'Caesar always has a plan.'

Antonius nodded. 'When he is the one setting out the board he always thinks several moves ahead and can work out a winning position. But since the days of Alesia and Uxellodunum, things have been changing. Despite being the ones to cross the unthinkable river and start it all, we are now playing games on boards set by Pompey and the consuls and their lackeys, so Caesar's planning is limited. Brundisium took us by surprise. Massilia took us by surprise. Fabius' campaign took us by surprise. He cannot plan for surprises. This now, though, is the pivotal point. We must take control here and win. We must secure Hispania and then turn back east before everything goes wrong and we find the whole world arrayed against us. Caesar knows this and he will do whatever he can to finish this soon, but we also cannot afford to utterly waste our men, so we are rather hampered in our options.'

'Caesar will have a plan,' Galronus repeated, with a tone of assurance.

Fronto hoped so. He really did.

A moment later they were startled by the sounds of horns and whistles from the hillside above. The three men watched, tense, as the gate of Petreius' camp opened. Caesar and his officers cantered over to the rise and joined them as the first legionaries spewed from the gate in good order. More were issuing from the exits at either end of the camp and filtering round to the hillside facing Caesar's army.

'I half expected them to stay behind their walls,' Plancus said, joining them. Antonius nodded his agreement.

The tension built as the moments passed, Caesar's legions settling into their formations and awaiting the enemy's advance, the officers now gathered together watching Pompey's army forming up. The legions of Hispania were shifting into good formation on the hillside before their ramparts, no more than a quarter or a third of the way down the slope. Finally, the last of the legions moved into position, and then the auxiliaries began to emerge, equipped with horses and spears, or with swords or slings, forming up at the flanks of the heavy infantry in an age-old strategy. It took perhaps half an hour for the last man to leave camp, and the only people still visible on the rampart were officers, observing the slope just as Caesar and his men did below.

Fronto swallowed his nerves, trying to look professional and unconcerned, though he could see the fractures of doubt cracking the many serene, commanding faces around him. There were so *many* of the enemy. They really did outnumber Caesar's army, and that was without the men in Ilerda itself or on the little hill in between.

Only Galronus felt the freedom to whistle through his teeth.

Silence fell. The world waited.

On the hill above and on the gentle rise behind Fronto and his fellow officers, they could hear the billow and snap of flags in the breeze. A faint succession of jingles here and there announced men shifting position slightly in one army or the other. The sound of patient horses snorting and stamping echoed out across the land and, oddly, the noise Fronto could hear loudest, atop all the sounds of men prepared to kill and to die, was that of the endless cicadas in the long dry grass.

The two armies sat watching each other warily for some time and eventually Antonius clucked his tongue irritably and reached up, removing his scarf and scratching his hot, sweaty neck.

'This is ridiculous. If nobody moves soon we're going to start taking root. Somebody is bound to have some wine. Send it my way.'

Fronto, his cheeks reddening only slightly, unhooked a flask from his saddle and passed it to his fellow officer.

'They're not coming,' Caesar sighed.

'We could go to them?' Plancus said quietly. Salvius Cursor nodded. 'Not the best option, but the surprise we instil in them might just balance out the terrain problem.'

Caesar shook his head. 'No. Assaulting up that hill against a superior force would result in just the sort of bloodbath I'm trying to avoid. They are not coming, and we shall not assault them.'

'If they have no intent to attack, why come out at all?' Fabius murmured. 'Tactically, it makes little sense to me.'

'It's about confidence,' Fronto replied, accepting his wine flask back from Antonius considerably lighter. 'They wanted us to see how strong and numerous they are. And they wanted us – our legionaries in particular – to see that they are not afraid.' He turned to Caesar. 'I will tell you one thing, General. This is not going to resolve the way you hope. You're going to be faced with a choice here. Either you accept what you're trying to avoid and we initiate that bloodbath, which will be quick and likely decisive, but extremely costly, or you continue to avoid pressing battle, but that will drag out more and more and it may be months before you can tie up anything here. Petreius and Afranius are not going to hand victory to you. You will either have to tear it from them or wear them down. One way is short but very costly, the other: uncertain, but even if you win, it will take a long time.'

He caught Salvius looking at him and couldn't quite make out what the man was thinking from his expression.

'I shall not push up the hill,' Caesar reiterated. 'This place has all the characteristics of a small Gergovia and the gods love to toy with patterns. I will not tempt them to repeat upon me that disaster. Something will occur. The information drawn from a few scouts we've captured lurking around by the bridges suggests that Afranius and Petreius argue with one another constantly. Sooner or later one of them will make a mistake and we must be ready. In the meantime, let us prepare our forces. The afternoon wears on and there will be no fighting today. We shall fortify our position on the low rise facing them. Have the orders disseminated among the officers.'

Antonius nodded and gestured to several of the men on the hill, beckoning for them to follow him back to the legions.

Caesar turned to look at Fronto. 'That was a succinct appraisal. The answer as to which choice I would select, though, is a given. While I would like nothing more than to secure Hispania in a single week and then march back to find Massilia taken and content and Italia settled, I will not waste lives whether they be those of my men or those of our opposition. They are, after all, still loyal Roman soldiers, even if Pompey is their commander. If the need is there, I will proceed slowly and carefully and gradually bring them down. Trebonius will just have to deal with Massilia and we will have to hope that Varro does not feel safe moving beyond his borders in Hispania Ulterior.'

Fronto nodded. While it was far from ideal he could hardly do anything but approve of the general's decision.

'It is time, I think, to assign you a command. The Eleventh is currently under the control of Quintus Fufius Calenus, but the man is a much better logistical officer than he is a legate. I fear his talents are underused and I could very much use his advice in other areas. Fronto, I'm giving you the Eleventh for this campaign and removing Fufius to my staff.' He turned to Galronus. 'And you? Well you are now one of the equites and a senator to boot. As such we can't have you all trousered and whooping and the like with the auxilia. Antonius is my overall cavalry commander, but I have need of him for now, so you shall take the rank of *Praefectus equitus,* my Remi friend, and command the army's cavalry for me.'

Galronus blinked in surprise.

'Don't look too grateful,' Fronto grinned. 'That might yet prove to be something of a barbed honour!'

* * *

The officers' briefing that evening was an uncomfortable affair. They were not residing in a fortified camp and, though the enemy had returned to their own fortress at sunset, the knowledge that a larger force who felt no fear of them hovered at the top of the hill opposite, and could sweep down with little notice, set every man's teeth on edge.

The soldiers of the six legions had been set to work digging in, but the sun sank earlier here at the edge of the Pyrenaei foothills, and the ground was extremely hard and rocky, so even with a strong compliment of men they had managed only a single deep and wide ditch by dusk, cutting across the land before Ilerda, separating Caesar's army from that of Pompey's dogs. The knowledge that only one side of the camp site was adequately secured made sleep and rest nervous, and the number of pickets and watchmen had been tripled for this night.

And while the soldiers lay twitching in their drab tents in ordered lines all across the low rise, the officers had gathered in the rather hollow empty command tent, which as yet lacked anything in the way of décor and even much in the way of furniture.

The officers were slowly polarising. Fronto had seen it before when two paths lay open before an army. Two groups of opinion would begin to form and their possessors would tend to cluster together with the few undecided sometimes standing with one and sometimes the other. The group that generally advocated a quick and violent solution outnumbered the patient crowd by roughly two to one in Fronto's estimation. At the fore of their opinionated group stood a surprising trio Fronto could not have seen working well together at any other time. Salvius Cursor was no surprise, of course. That man could be relied upon to select the bloodiest route through any problem. Marcus Antonius was more of a surprise. Usually the man to stand at Caesar's right hand and argue in favour of any choice the man made, Antonius had apparently now begun to favour action. And Fabius, who had been so cautious prior to their arrival, had moved to a position of decisive action too. Of course, Antonius was known to be headstrong, and might just be following the pulsing of his blood, and Fabius had explained that though he had been reluctant to offer battle previously that had been due purely to the supply situation, and that now Caesar had solved that issue, Fabius would like to tan some Pompeian hide.

At the other side of the room stood the advocates of slow erosion, including Plancus and Fronto, Galronus and Varus, who had arrived in camp at sunset, having overseen the escorts for the supply train put in place, and who now found himself commanding the regular horse under Galronus. To his credit, given that Varus had been a senior commander since the first year of the war, the man greeted Galronus warmly and seemed to have accepted the situation without question. Fronto wondered how balanced these two groups would have been had Trebonius and Brutus been here. Or even Labienus.

Salvius Cursor was glaring in their direction once more and Fronto, with a devilish glint in his eye, winked at the man and raised his cup in salute. No words had passed between Salvius and them, but none had been needed to make clear how the man felt. Galronus, who Salvius did not trust and thought to be little more than a well-shaved barbarian in Roman costume, had been granted one of the most senior and crucial roles in the army. And Fronto, who he so clearly hated utterly, had been made legate of one of the six legions once more.

Fronto had been torn, upon hearing the details of his assignment, between laughing to the very verge of insanity or weeping at what the gods – and more specifically Caesar – had dropped in his lap. With the Thirteenth Legion now resident in Italy watching for Pompey's first move, a certain tribune had been left without a unit. Having reached the end of his patience with Salvius Cursor's repeated opinions in staff meetings, the general had assigned him as the senior tribune of the Eleventh. Fronto's deputy. Such an appointment could only have been the general's deliberate choice, and Fronto couldn't decide whether it was done to punish him or Salvius. Either way, it would result in both.

The other five tribunes of the Eleventh were the usual lot of noble children from Rome who would likely cut themselves to pieces if they ever had cause to draw their swords and who kept having to ask who people were. At least he could rely upon the centurionate. The primus pilus, Titus Mettius, who people called *Felix* due to his repeated bouts of bad luck, had been in charge of the Eleventh throughout their time, and Fronto had seen the man fight through most of the great battles in Gaul. Pullo and Vorenus, also, he had seen in the Gallic campaign, and both had reputations as solid centurions.

But Salvius Cursor, of all people...

The tribune was even now throwing a look at Fronto that could have melted through an officer's cuirass – wholly inappropriate for a Roman officer looking at his commander. Still, Fronto would let him have his attitude. It was easier to let him seethe than to fight it. As long as the man did what he was told, Fronto would manage.

'So that, in a nutshell, is our situation, gentlemen,' Caesar concluded. 'Thoughts?'

'Do we put in siege works?' Plancus asked. 'This area is sparsely forested. If we are thinking of building rams and vinea and the like we should start gathering and construction pretty much immediately, as it might be a long job.'

Caesar shook his head. 'There is little opportunity to use such equipment against such a lofty target. To make them viable we would have to build a long ramp, and that just creates numerous other problems. Our greatest hope for a clean victory here is to drive the enemy to panic. We must never appear to be struggling – always controlled and confident. We must gradually move to reduce their supremacy in any area. To that end I want each of you to think of ways to gradually tip the balance toward us so that we can undermine the enemy's confidence and perhaps, with luck and the favour of the gods, turn the soldiery against their commanders. We have seen it happen already in Italia more than once. Yes these are more experienced veteran legions, but every man has his breaking point.'

'One short assault would break them, General.'

Fronto turned a disbelieving look on Salvius. The man was still pushing the agenda despite Caesar having refused such a plan. Caesar opened his mouth to reply, but Antonius interrupted. 'Hear his idea, General.'

Caesar's face darkened and his expression remained stony, but he nodded in the face of such a request from his old friend.

'We know they are divided in command,' Salvius said, spreading his arms and appealing to all in the room. 'We know that they are not happy committing to an act of civil war, the same as all sane men.'

That rules you out, Fronto thought nastily.

'The simple truth,' the tribune went on, 'is that no one here wants to be the man to draw first blood against other Romans and that reluctance puts an army on the back foot. We can capitalise on both the division in command and the reluctance of the soldiers if we launch one full-scale, sudden, unexpected attack. And to make it the most brutal possible, we could send a legion or two around over our new crossings to advance across the enemy's stone bridge. I know you denied an attack from those quarters, but that was given the theory that the enemy would be able to concentrate on defending that quarter,. If they are suffering attack from all sides at once, they will not be able to protect the bridge as vehemently. I do believe, and so do a number of my peers...'

Peers? You arrogant little prick!

'... that such a sudden action from several sides would break the morale of the defenders and force a surrender.'

'And if it doesn't,' Fronto said suddenly, turning on him, 'then you have divided our forces and committed a smaller army against a larger up a steep slope and against solid ramparts. I'm a betting man myself, Salvius, but I wouldn't be willing to risk a whole army on it.'

Caesar was nodding. Salvius and Antonius shared a look, aware that their argument was losing momentum, and that Fronto's comment had stolen it all.

'Then emulate the Macedonian King Philip,' Salvius said hurriedly, jabbing a finger at Caesar. 'Divide and conquer. Take Ilerda and remove the army's supplies and control of the bridge.'

Fronto saw Antonius' face and almost smiled as he caught the reason. Salvius Cursor had been so urgent in pushing his argument that he'd overstepped his mark and forgotten to even grant the general any kind of title or honorific, instead wagging a finger at him. Antonius or Brutus, or even Fronto, might be able to get away with such unseemly familiarity because they had all known the general since before his rise to power. Salvius had no such advantage, and Caesar looked faintly peeved. The tribune's desperation had led him to trip himself up and even Antonius knew they'd lost the argument now.

'General?' prompted Salvius, frowning at Antonius.

'Quiet,' Marcus Antonius told him in a subdued tone.

'But…'

'Quiet.'

'We shall consolidate our camp and settle in for the duration,' Caesar said finally. 'I shall ponder further moves, but that is all for now.'

The meeting was over, and the officers immediately began to disperse, heading back to their own units. Galronus nodded to Fronto and the pair left the tent, heading toward the Tenth's lines. Though Fronto would have to return to his new command shortly, Carbo had invited him for a drink to catch up with old friends, and Fronto had readily accepted. He's not seen the hulking Gallic primus pilus Atenos for far too long.

'That was low,' snapped a voice behind him and Fronto stopped, turning on his heel with Galronus beside him, the balmy evening air loaded with passion flower and hibiscus doing nothing to mask Salvius stepping closer like the bad smell he so clearly was.

'Forms of address for a superior officer aren't your strong point tonight, are they, Tribune Salvius?'

The man's nose wrinkled in distaste. 'That was low, *sir.*'

'That was a frank and free exchange of opinions. I tore down your argument with such ease because it was constructed of straw and nothing more. The general does not favour your bloodthirsty approach and, if you persuade him toward your way of thinking, he will lose that edge of respect and favour he has received in so many quarters since we crossed the Rubicon. His magnanimity has won him several extra legions, the love of towns that had been arrayed against him and has avoided the spilling of a sea of Roman blood thus far. I am no idiot, and I can see that this war will yet witness violence and bloodshed – it can only be resolved that way – but let's try and save that until we're facing Pompey, and not carve a bloody trench through people who need not necessarily be our enemies.'

He stopped, breathing heavily, realising he'd gradually raised his voice as his anger at the man built. He looked around. Soldiers and officers alike were watching them. Angrily, Fronto turned to the nearest tent, which belonged to a unit of Ingenuus' guardsmen. He strode over and threw open the flap.

'This tent is being commandeered for a few moments. Step outside, gentlemen, and make yourselves scarce.'

Three horsemen emerged swiftly, bowing to Fronto and hurrying away. 'Get inside,' he snapped at Salvius Cursor, who did so, bristling with indignation.

'Permission to speak freely?' Salvius said darkly once they were inside and the tent flap back in place. Galronus stood outside the door to ward off those who might eavesdrop.

'I've not noticed you having a problem doing so thus far,' Fronto replied acidly.

'I am aware that you are my commander and I could be disciplined for insubordination, and I wouldn't put it past you, either, sir,' the tribune hissed.

'Very well, Salvius. Speak freely.'

'I do not trust you, Fronto. I think you are weak. You're clearly too old for command…'

'I'd be careful not to say that around the general,' Fronto interrupted.

'…and you've gone soft. They say you don't even like to keep slaves and that you have mostly paid servants. I've seen you whisper honeyed words into the general's ear ever since Ravenna. And I have yet to see you do a single thing of value or note. You are a has-been riding on the reputation you made long ago when you were still vital. You have no strength left and no value in this army. At best you are weak and cowardly. At worst you are a traitor, either imposing yourself on Caesar's staff in order to ruin this campaign, or possibly even placed here by your good friends like Labienus or Galba. That's right. I know how many of your friends are now siding against Caesar. You will prove the downfall of this army, Marcus Falerius Fronto, and I believe in Caesar and his success to my core. I will not let you destroy everything the general has built.'

Fronto stood, narrow-eyed, waiting for another outburst, but there was just a tense, seething silence as Salvius glared at him.

'Now listen to me, you insolent, arrogant little turd,' Fronto growled like Cerberus emerging from the gates of Hades.

'Now…' began Salvius.

'No. You've had your say. And not as officer to officer. As man to man. Now it's my turn.'

He stepped forward so that his face was remarkably close to Salvius', Fronto's stale-wine breath clouding the tribune's features as he spoke.

'I *am* old. Yes. Nearly as old as Caesar. But if you think for one minute I'm past command or fighting, you are in for something of a shock, and any time you want to take up a wooden training sword and test my mettle I will happily break a limb or two and put you on your soft downy arse to prove the point. You want to fight, then you just ask any time. As for my beliefs, friendships and motivations, I will tell you this. We are in a state of civil war. Yes, I have friends who now serve Pompey. And yes I once even considered it myself. But in our army are men who once served Pompey, yourself included. In a civil war there will always be friends facing friends across the field of battle, and brothers facing brothers. And, yes, it may be necessary, but whether necessary or not, such a thing is not to be relished and certainly never sought if there is any alternative. Outside our borders are a plethora of enemies waiting to pick over Roman bones. The Gauls of Britannia. The Germans. The Iazyges and the Parthians. The African tribes. Every Roman who kills another Roman is doing the work of the republic's enemies. Weakening Rome. So yes, I want to avoid as much killing as possible. But the time is coming. Until then you can hate me all you like, and you can even question me in the privacy of your own head, but if you once speak out of turn in front of other people, I will smash that glib tongue of yours through the back of your skull. Now, I am your legate and you are my senior tribune. We have to work together. The Eleventh are as committed to this fight as any other legion, and we *will* do what is required with efficiency and spirit, and any time you stand before that eagle I want a smile of pride and an expression of deference on that smarmy face of yours. Am I clear?'

'As spring water,' snarled Salvius Cursor, '*sir!*'

'Good. Now get out of my sight before I decide that being one tribune down could actually be a benefit to this army.'

Salvius Cursor gave a stiff salute, unable to prevent his lip curling, and turned, leaving sharply. Fronto waited a while, getting his breathing under control, and then followed him out to find Galronus grinning.

'I don't know what you said to him, but I would avoid getting caught in the latrines alone with him for a while. That was a face of murder he wore.'

'I'm not frightened of him,' Fronto said quietly.

'You should be. Lunatics harbour dangerous strengths. Take it from part of a family of them.'

Laughing, Galronus clapped an arm around Fronto's shoulders and steered him toward wine.

Chapter Nine

23rd of Junius - Ilerda

THE legions worked hard, toiling in the already hot sun, steam rising from the ground where the minimal dew had almost evaporated. Birds cawed and bees hummed as a thread of sound woven through the tapestry of soldiers fortifying a camp. The hack of a dolabra – the soldier's standard-issue mattock – striking dry earth and rocks and pebbles, the slicing sound of shovels cutting into turf and dusty mud. The grunt and panting of men labouring, along with a few quietly-sung songs traditionally accompanying such work.

Over the top of it all, the calls and complaints of centurions and engineers as they adjusted the work and corrected minor faults that no one but an engineer would ever know had been perpetrated.

There was no wind. The banners hung limp as men paused in their work to mop their faces with scarves that now hung from their armour rather than sitting tight around their neck as padding for the metal. Common practice when forming camp defences was for the men labouring to remove their armour, helmet and weapons and work in just tunic with perhaps a straw hat to ward off the sun. Not so here and now. Orders had been clear: the men would work in their armour, albeit unarmed, and their helmet, shield and sword would be within fingertip reach at all times.

Because the danger remained.

At the top of the hill the army of Petreius and Afranius remained contained within the walls of their fort, but they were strong and unafraid. They were an ever-present threat.

The defensive ditch was now crawling slowly across the landscape back away from the enemy at both sides of the camp, while a lesser party had already begun on the rear defences some distance back. Other men were forming a low rampart with the dirt removed from the ditches, while a third group formed a sharp fence from the sudis stakes carried in the wagons and set them atop the rampart as a wall of sharpened timber.

Fronto stood with Felix, watching as the men of the Eleventh raised the rampart at the front, facing the enemy camp across the ditch dug the previous day. The centurion had made one concession to the heat of the day. He had swa

pped his wool helmet liner for the felt and linen one he carried as a spare. His armour gleamed and his helmet, topped with a transverse crest of red-dyed feathers, glowed in the morning light. He wore greaves embossed with some unidentifiable god's image and a cuirass of the traditional sort bearing a medusa head for luck. The pteruges that hung from shoulders and waist beneath the armour were of long-hardened leather and his vine stick looked as old as time. Fronto approved. Felix was the quintessential centurion.

In fact, Fronto had emerged from his tent that morning in light kit with just a linen tunic and leather subarmalis, fringed with decorative pteruges. One look at Felix stomping around the camp and smacking slovenly legionaries with his stick while his armour shone like a jewel had sent Fronto scurrying back into his tent to re-emerge quickly, this time in full armour. Once more a legate, he had been assigned a body slave and two tent slaves, as well as two clerks, a barber/bath attendant, a musician, a courier and six bodyguards. He had spent an hour finding things for most of them to do to keep them out of the way, had instructed the six guards to keep watch on his tent and not himself, and had, by the morning, trimmed his active and attentive staff down to one tent slave and a clerk. He had nothing against a bodyguard, of course, and even missed Masgava and the others, who had remained in Tarraco to watch over the family, but as often as not bodyguards got in the way rather than providing protection.

And so, dressed in the armour polished by his tent slave, Fronto had come down with Felix to encourage the men. Legionaries may respect their most senior commander, but they didn't always like them, and Fronto knew that to have the heart of his men, he had to be among them, one of the legion. It was something Caesar had taught him, and something that both Pompey and Crassus had overlooked in their commands.

Felix barked out a series of expletives at a soldier who accidentally threw a shovel full of dry dirt across the centurion's foot and Fronto couldn't help but smile, his gaze turning away and sliding along the defences until it fell upon something that killed his humorous mood instantly.

Salvius Cursor stood on the raised mound at the corner of the camp, his face sour as he stared up at the enemy fortifications. The tribune had busied himself early in the morning flitting around the staff officers until he managed to see Caesar and Marcus Antonius, whom he attempted once more to persuade into precipitate violence. Antonius had shooed the man away before Caesar had too much opportunity to lose his temper, and Salvius had returned to the Eleventh in a foul mood where he had proceeded to avoid Fronto and any level of communication. It suited Fronto down to the ground, and he wondered idly what the enemy's range was with a catapult from up on their ramparts and whether if Fronto painted the tribune purple they might helpfully put a steel-tipped bolt through him.

Behind him, he heard the rising cascade of honks that announced the first morning break. Toil would continue across the camp, of course, but all around the works small groups of men would move with amphorae of cold water and wooden cups, and baskets of bread with pots of butter that would already fast be becoming oil. As they moved around the camp in ripples, men would pause and down their tools to chew on something hearty and sluice it down with a cup of chilled water. Otherwise, throughout the day they would be able to rely for refreshment only on the tepid water in their flasks and the hard, dry *bucellatum* biscuits from their packs.

Fronto didn't hear the first call. The musicians of the six legions were honking all over the hillside, warning the workers that water and bread was coming round, and it was only when the enemy gates opened that Fronto realised the enemy calls had been timed to meet their own, masking their intentions.

Fronto shouted the alarm, but his voice was drowned out by their own musicians. He saw Salvius Cursor waving frantically at a centurion, and next to him, Felix was gesturing to his standard bearer and cornicen who were standing nearby waiting for orders.

The signal having finally been given, Fronto's attention rose once more to the hillside.

It was not a full-scale assault. That much was instantly clear. The men who had emerged were native levies – the auxilia serving with Petreius. Hispanics and Iberians with a variety of weapons and armour, they had to belong to a number of different units. They poured down the hill from the camp at a pace the legionaries would not be able to manage due to their equipment and formation. These men were equipped as light skirmishers and could travel at an impressive speed. Here and there one would tumble, but they were agile enough that it would not cause a mass slip, and they were closing on the Caesarians fast.

The men of the Eleventh and Seventh – the bulk of the men working on this rampart had been drawn from those legions – were in levels of disarray as they scrambled to prepare themselves and follow the calls of their units. Some had been in the ditch affixing sharpened points, while others were sat with their bread and water. Men were now hurrying across to their shields and trying to tie on their helmets with numb fingers while every man looked this way and that to locate their standards ready to fall into line. There would not be enough time to form on standards before the swift natives hit them, and both Fronto and Felix had seen as much.

'To the rampart,' Fronto shouted. 'Forget your standards and form on Felix.'

Other officers took up the shout, bellowing to the men as they armed and ran to 'form on Felix'.

Fronto returned his attention to the approaching enemy. They were coming in a mass rush without formation, but he could identify three distinct lines to their approach. At the front were men with javelins and small, round shields, much like the *velites* of the ancient days. Behind them were men with larger shields and the native Hispanic swords from which Rome had borrowed the gladius design. Finally, at the back were men in white tunics and belts with no visible weapon, but a pouch at their side. Fronto knew damn well what they would be.

'They have no intention of engaging. They're coming to shower you,' Fronto shouted.

'Shields ready,' Felix urged. 'Prepare to receive a volley.'

Across the rampart, Fronto heard a bellowed oath to Minerva and could see Salvius gathering men to him. What was the lunatic doing? Still, Fronto didn't have time to consider it. He allowed the shield wall to close in front of him since he was carrying no shield, though he drew his sword ready, as did Felix beside him.

A discordant din of honks and toots blared out from the camp atop the hill and Fronto frowned at the mess. He was familiar with every legion's calls in the rule book. He had served with more than one unit in his time, and while each legion individualised their calls, there were common themes among them so that an experienced officer would likely be able to ascertain what the calls of another unit meant. The noise blarting out from the hill above was like nothing he had ever heard. What in the name of Apollo were they trying to do?

'Do you hear that?' Felix asked him as he watched the enemy close on them.

'Yes. What the shit does it mean?'

'It's two calls at once. Half the musicians up there are calling a cohort forward and the other half are sounding the retreat for the auxilia. Talk about confusion!'

Fronto dropped his gaze once more to the approaching enemies who were clearly either ignoring that call from above or unaware that it had been given. He smiled. It seemed that the division in command between Petreius and Afranius was more troublesome than they had dreamed. If this was the level of disagreement and chaos they could expect from the enemy, then perhaps there was a chance to end things quickly after all.

'Incoming,' bellowed Felix, and shields rose slightly along the rampart. Behind Fronto, who stood in the second line, a legionary lifted his shield to cover his commander.

The javelins had been loosed not in a cloud as would have happened with better organisation, but rather in sporadic fits as each man reached a certain distance. Fronto could see it happening between the shields. The javelin throwers were running to a position perhaps ten feet back from the ditch and hurling their weapons. The javelins were light and sleek, unlike the heavier legionary pila, and they arced up easily and fell among the shield wall. It was not as effective as a steady assault would have been, but still there were cries of agony here and there as a man was transfixed through with four feet of wood. Men were pierced in the thigh or the midriff, the chain shirts inadequate protection against those sharp points at such force. In places along the line the shields had not yet formed, men still running into position. There the javelins had a more brutal impact, the speed and unexpectedness of the enemy assault having caught them off guard.

Fronto could see through the spaces between shields that the javelin throwers were a one shot attack. As soon as they cast their missile, they turned and raced back up the hill. As they did, the second group of auxilia stopped at the bottom of the slope opposite the Caesarian lines and formed a rough shield wall of their own. Behind this meagre defence, the slingers skidded to a stop, fishing stones and bullets from their pouches and fitting them into the leather straps.

There was a series of offensive calls from the far left and Fronto braved the storm as he rose above the level of the shields to look along the line. Salvius Cursor had formed a century of legionaries at the far end into a testudo and was even now moving out across the ditch toward the enemy. *No, you lunatic…*

'Pila forward,' Felix bellowed. 'Send for the archers!'

Fronto watched the heavier missiles being passed through the crowd from those who had access at the rear, and the second and third lines took a step back, allowing the second rank room to angle the weapons and prepare. The first sling shots began to ring out, thudding against the wooden shields and occasionally dinging off helmets and clonking into leather greaves. There were cries of sharp pain from a few men who had caught well-aimed bullets. These slingers would be from the *Baleares*, whose people were renowned across the republic with the weapon. Sure enough they were finding their targets despite the legionaries' armour and large shields.

'Iacta!' bellowed Felix, and several hundred pila arced up over the shield wall. Many of the heavy missiles fell short due to the distance, but perhaps one in eight struck the line of men protecting the slingers. Up the slope the cacophony of mixed signals continued as the commanders argued about what to do, and to the left, Salvius' small armoured tortoise was already rising from the far side of the ditch and approaching the enemy. They had left four men in the ditch, two dead and two screaming from the wounds the slingers had inflicted, but more than seventy men continued to approach the auxilia.

The chaos caused by the enemy officers began to manifest in the forces arrayed at the bottom of the slope as several of the slingers and some of the swordsmen turned and began to climb the slope once more in answer to the retreat call, while others stayed put and continued to loose bullets and stones into the Caesarian line.

'They're ready to break,' Fronto noted.

'The archers are coming,' Felix replied, hooking a thumb over his shoulder.

'Then it becomes a war of attrition. I want to save men. Damn it, but Salvius might just have stumbled onto the right approach.'

His gaze slid left and he could see the fight breaking out. Salvius' testudo had reached the lines of Hispanic auxiliaries and carved their way through with little resistance. Even as he watched, the tribune ordered melee and the testudo broke open amid the slingers and swordsmen, exploding outwards like a drop of blood hitting a marble surface. The damage they were causing was devastating.

'Screw the archers. Sound the advance.'

Felix looked for the briefest of moments uncertain, then nodded and relayed the order to his signallers. The new call rang out and, accompanied by centurions' whistles, the lines advanced down into the ditch and crossed it, rising into a sporadic hail of stones. Here and there men fell, but the enemy were taken aback by this advance and several groups broke and began to race back up the hill. Others prepared to receive Caesar's force.

Fronto stomped along in the second line, keeping pace, wondering what his new bodyguards would say if they could see him advancing in a shield wall while they guarded an empty tent. A stone clanged off the raised point of Fronto's gladius and he felt the reverberation all the way through his hand and up his arm into his shoulder. Despite the slight numbness it caused, he bared his teeth and marched on, allowing a slight space to open in the lines so he could shake out his arm and sword and bring feeling back to the limb.

He should be back with the officers. He knew it. No other legate would be taking the field like this. Lucilia would be horrified if she could see him. Masgava would slap him. Caesar would roll his eyes. And it was entirely unnecessary. He told himself as he stomped that it was important for a new commander to be seen to be one of his unit and to boost the morale of his men. But somewhere deep inside he had the nagging feeling that he should have let Felix rely on the archers and that the reason for his committing to battle was a selfish need to prove something.

He hadn't realised that Salvius' little jibes about his age and ineffectiveness had got to him until now. Had he committed unnecessarily purely to prove something to the arrogant tribune?

The time to ponder such things passed in a moment as the legionary in front of him cursed loudly and braced, jabbing out. There was a scream as an Iberian swordsman met the soldier's blade. Then more. The man to the fore-left suddenly shouted in pain and fell back clutching his sword arm, which displayed a long deep cut from wrist to elbow, his own blade lost in the press. The man in the second line moved to fill the gap, but Fronto was there first. He almost submitted to panic as, before he could even swing a blade, a sling bullet clanged into his cuirass, leaving a noticeable dent and sending a numbing vibration across his whole torso.

A swordsman came at him and he dodged slightly to the side, jabbing out with his gladius into the armpit of the man even as he lunged. The blade sank in deep – one of the killing blows taught to every soldier. The Iberian shrieked and fell, though Fronto had little time to celebrate as a well-placed blow from another native came close enough to severing his hand that it took the flesh off the top of three knuckles. Hissing in pain, Fronto lashed out. His sword met that of the enemy repeatedly as they parried and struck. A sling stone whizzed past at a bladder-loosening closeness, drawing blood on his upper left arm with a hot point of pain. Finally an opening showed, and he stabbed the Iberian in the shoulder. The man would live, but he fell back with a cry, clutching at his wound and retreating from the fight. Suddenly, in response to a whistle, the line surged forward two paces and Fronto found himself among the slingers. His sword lanced out again and again into unprotected flesh and then he was stabbing empty air as the enemy fell back, shouting, running up the slope to their camp. The auxiliaries were in a rout.

He let them go.

Felix called out the order to halt and then pulled the line back to the ditch and rampart. Fronto delayed, his gaze wandering along to the far end of the defences, where the men led forward by Salvius Cursor were throwing rocks at the retreating auxilia and jeering. He couldn't see the tribune and wondered whether the officer had fallen in the fight. For just a moment he almost prayed it had happened, but stopped himself in time. A man shouldn't toy with the gods like that. His hand went up to the twin figures of Nemesis and Fortuna at his neck, but they hung beneath his cuirass and he couldn't touch them.

A few moments later, he was inside the camp, watching the last enemy soldiers disappearing into their gate and the great timber leaves closing with a thud. The cacophony of mismatched calls had ended. A capsarius hurried over and yanked the sword from his unresisting fingers before applying some sort of salve to the bloodied burning knuckles and binding the hand with linen wrap. The soldier looked at the wound on his arm and shrugged, moving on to find someone with a more pressing wound.

Fronto staggered wearily through the crowd, leaning slightly as the wound Verginius had given him last summer pulled and ached. He was as healed as a man could be from the carefully-placed injury, but still extreme exertion brought a tight reminder that it was there. He'd had rather a lot of wine last night with Atenos and Carbo, and he hadn't felt hung over until now, but the sudden burst of violent activity so early in the day and brought on a thumping head that almost drowned out the aches and stinging knuckles. He rubbed his hair vigorously and stopped suddenly, almost walking into the figure before him.

It was a figure straight from nightmares. The tribune was coated head to toe in blood, and other fluids. Flesh hung in ragged strips from the brow of his helmet where he had driven it into a number of faces. His sword hand was a sort of purple-red colour and slick and gleaming and unspeakable things had caught on the various raised portions of his armour. The last time Fronto had seen such a gruesome figure was in the arena.

Or at Alesia, of course…

'I see you had cause to draw steel, sir,' Salvius said, and Fronto was too tired and pained to even try and work out whether there was sarcasm in the tone.

'I did my part.' Fronto regarded the man with distaste. He had seen common soldiers and centurions on occasion with such an uncontrollable love of combat and lust for blood that they'd come back from a fight looking like that. But this had been a quick and light skirmish. Salvius looked like he'd bathed in a pool of gore. And he was a tribune. A senior officer.

'That was good work,' he said. It irked him to send any praise in the direction of the man, but Fronto had the suspicion that if he properly investigated what had happened out there it would turn out that Salvius' push against the enemy had been the thing that turned the auxilia and sent them running, rather than the calls from above.

'Thank you, sir.' The tribune's expression was entirely neutral as he saluted and walked off, hopefully to bathe.

That was it. First blood with the army of Pompey's Hispanic generals. Oh, not the true first blood, of course. Fabius had had that honour before they had even arrived. But this was the first blow struck for Ilerda. It would not be the last.

* * *

Fronto stood with the men of the Eleventh, flags wilting in the hot sun. The calls went out and they moved across the ditch.

It had all come as rather a surprise to Fronto. Somehow, word of Salvius' actions had filtered through to the commanders and despite days of being reined in by Caesar, the tribune was once more in the general's council. Three days has passed since the first skirmish, and the camp had been rapidly completed, with two more brief testing forays by the enemy that had come to naught. The cost of that first clash had been acceptable to Caesar. Ninety four dead or disabled legionaries and seventy one walking wounded. The count of dead native auxilia in front of the ditch had passed five hundred, and Salvius, Fronto and Felix had received the congratulations of the other officers.

But somehow Salvius' newfound celebrity had made people pay attention to him again. With Fabius and Antonius alongside, he had pressed for a retaliation and, despite three plans being swept aside by the general they had persisted until a compromise had been reached.

Fronto was unsure, but he could at least see the strategic sense behind it.

Three legions would move to take the small hill between Ilerda and the camp of Petreius and Afranius. If the Caesarian army could manage to get a garrison in command of that hill, they would cut off the army in the camp from both the bridge and from the supplies in Ilerda. An assault on the camp would be horrific, and simply waiting until their supplies ran out would take months. But if they could seize that single position, they could cut the enemy army off from their supplies and forage routes in one go. That would make a siege to starvation a much quicker proposition.

There had been some discussion as to the size of the force to commit. Clearly, the more men they put into the fight, the more chance there was of success, but with the saddle between the two stronghold being only three hundred paces across, there was a limit to the space into which men could be poured. The figure of three legions had been settled upon by the more strategically minded officers, and now the Seventh, Tenth and Eleventh legions were arrayed in full battle order, ready to march. The enemy couldn't yet know what they intended, and the most likely target would be the camp, but whatever the case, the Pompeians would work out what was happening before the legions reached their objective, and would be able to field men quickly in response. It would be a hard fight, whatever happened.

The horns blew with centurions' whistles for counterpoint. Standards dipped, and the legions marched forth. Salvius Cursor had been ordered not to throw himself into the front lines, but he was close enough that there was little chance of him ending this day not coated in gore again. Similarly, despite convention, Fronto had placed himself only one century back from the front line at the legion's centre.

Fronto fell into step, his gaze occasionally straying to the red plume of Salvius' helmet among the press of men. He could see Carbo and Volcatius, the legates of the other two legions, on their horses at the rear. Fronto had opted to move on foot despite the urging of his bodyguards and centurions. Partially there was the worry that Bucephalus might be injured or killed in the action, but in truth he had always felt more comfortable marching than riding. It was one thing that he apparently had in common with Salvius who had also opted for boot leather, unlike his peers in the other legions. What that said about the pair of them, Fronto refused to consider. He would put it down to common sense given the gradual steepening of the terrain.

Amid the clank and rattle of armour and weapons, the clonk of wooden shields, the grunting and muttering of men and the occasional shouts of the centurions, they moved at an oblique angle to the enemy fort, making for the gap between there and Ilerda. A small enemy garrison of perhaps two centuries had been in place on the small hill for some time, but as Caesar's legions moved on up the gentle incline toward the saddle that dominated the bridge, the gates of the main camp opened, accompanied by the blare of horns, and the legions of Afranius and Petreius emerged, hurrying toward that low hill to intercept the attack. This time there was no conflict in calls. Both the Pompeian commanders had clearly seen the danger and agreed upon the response.

The army marched on and Fronto could hear Felix at the front shouting at his men to hold their line and ready themselves. Upward they went, though the slope was as nothing compared to the incline that rose to the fort. Fronto caught glances here and there of the enemy legions rushing to stop them, but not enough to estimate numbers.

Fronto felt the incline change slightly as they rose toward that knob of a hill where the two sides would meet in their first full engagement. His calves began to feel the pull, the tendons at his ankles stretching with the effort. Thousands of nailed boots dug into scrubby brown-green grass punctuated with crumbling rock and dry, sharp shrubs. Men grunted in irritation as the undergrowth scratched their legs while they climbed, leaving narrow red lines and occasionally drawing blood. Fronto smiled to hear it. It was in the nature of soldiers to concentrate on the immediate – the small things. Atop the hill sharp steep blades awaited their flesh, but they took such a threat stoically while vocalising their displeasure at the irritating lacerations of thorns and sharp leaves.

Over to the left, the Seventh began to clatter their swords on the rims of their shields as they climbed, forming a rhythmic thumping that challenged the nerve of the enemy every bit as much as the Germanic *barritus* roar or the Gallic *carnyx*. To the right, the

Tenth joined the rhythm. A few soldiers at the front of the Eleventh joined in, but Felix quickly put a stop to it.

'Save your energy for the fight,' he shouted. Fronto nodded his agreement and gradually, as they ascended, the other legions fell silent once more. A more muted thumping continued, and Fronto realised that the Pompeian legions atop the hill were clattering swords on shields in exactly the same manner. This truly was a war of brothers. Felix dropped back for a moment, allowing his men to sweep around him, and Fronto soon caught up with the senior centurion.

'Are you in this fight, sir? I can't persuade you to move out to the rear?'

Fronto nodded, his breath coming in heaves as his body dealt with the effort of the climb.

'For the record, I don't approve, Legate Fronto. But if you're going to be involved, I need you to work with us just as any centurion would. I will be guiding the overall fight, so you have control of my century.'

Fronto blinked.

'Don't screw it up and get them killed, sir,' Felix added.

Fronto grinned, but the smile quickly faded as he realised that the centurion was quite serious and not simply ribbing him.

'I'm throwing forward three centuries at a time in six rows, with the front twenty as the heavy shield wall, the second twenty in similar formation to provide push, and then four rows of ten in looser formation to plug gaps as they appear. At each burst of three and then three whistles, the front two ranks will swap, and at two and then four whistles, the entire century will drop back, forming gaps for the next century to move up. That way we keep a fresh line against the enemy and everyone gets a rest. Alright?'

Fronto nodded. How was the man able to keep such a constant flow of chatter up as he climbed. The man was almost Fronto's age, and the legate could hardly manage a yes without an explosion of breath.

'Good.' A spare whistle was thrust into Fronto's free hand.

Felix moved off to the side, between his century and the next, identifying a capsarius in the ranks by his leather satchel, sending him to the rear and taking his place in the ordered lines.

Across the hillside, the whistled orders came. Fronto was not yet quite used to the calls of his new legion, but they were familiar enough for him to anticipate the commands. Felix followed suit and the front lines slowed slightly, their concentration now on holding tight formation rather than climbing safely. Another call and the front centuries began to fall into formation. The call was repeated throughout and Fronto lifted the whistle and echoed the command for Felix's century. The front ranks formed two rows of twenty men in shield-to-shield spacing, while the next four spaced out ready to move as required. Now it would be down to Fronto.

He frowned. Centurion level combat was a different matter to both high command and to individual fighting. The fluid strategy of the battlefield became his task and the lives of eighty men his responsibility. He was relatively inexperienced at such things, but his martial abilities and knowledge of the legions and their capabilities made him the equal of most recently appointed centurions at least.

He shuffled forward through the ranks, finding the place in the second row that had been left for him when Felix had vacated. Of course the centurion had been at the front, but either he or his legionaries had decided that the legate should be in the second line at best, preferably further back.

Battle was joined unexpectedly for Fronto, and he realised in a heartbeat why his men had relegated him to the second rank and what a mistake he had made.

While Petreius and Afranius' legions had been lined up and presumably given strict orders to hold formation and wait, given the advantage of terrain, some centurion had clearly broken those commands. A small bulge of enemy legionaries broke out of their line and crashed down the hill into the centre of the Caesarian line, straight at Fronto's century, and he cursed himself for his lack of foresight.

It was natural for any enemy of the legion to make serious attempts to cut down any man carrying a standard or wearing a centurion's crest. The death of either crippled morale, of the former hampered their ability to effectively relay orders, and of the latter removed that level of command altogether. Every warrior facing a legion went for the standards or the centurions. But Fronto had changed the dynamic. He was still wearing his officer's helmet in the old Attic style with a straggly plume of red and black horsehair. He was a senior officer, marked as such by his attire, and in the second line of the attack. He was just too tempting a target for the enemy, and they had broken ranks in an attempt to kill him.

And so, while across the hillside the Caesarian legions stomped upwards and the Pompeians awaited them with braced legs and gritted teeth, the centre of the enemy force poured down and crashed into the Eleventh in an unanticipated move.

Felix's century took the force of the attack and proved their worth as the First Century of the legion, the strongest veterans to be found in the Eleventh. Despite the terrain disadvantage and the relative speeds, as the Pompeians hit the line, only three men had fallen back with the push, and they were quickly replaced by the men in the second tight line, the lightly spaced rear ranks shuffling to fill in and help the fallen men up. Fronto saw brief snatches of battle-hardened Hispanic legionaries between the two men in front of him, desperately stabbing and chopping, trying to get at the officer with the conspicuous crest. Men were already falling and dying.

The world became a commotion of ringing metal, screams, bellowed rage, oaths to a hundred gods, the chopping of shield boards, the sounds of carved meat and the crunch of chain shirts taking the blows of iron and bronze weapons. It took a count of ten for the stench to begin, rising like a miasma from the fray. The sharp, metallic tang of blood with the acrid stinging scent of fresh raw meat mixed with the odour of opened bowels and urine. The great writers of the world never mentioned such aspects to battle in their heroic sagas.

Fronto felt himself being pulled and pushed in the press, unable to do little more than hope, then suddenly a gap opened as the man in front of him disappeared to the side with a cry of agony, three swords sheathed in his torso as desperate Pompeians fought to get at the crested officer.

Fronto felt the shield of the man next to him move slightly, protecting him from several blows even as the legate struck, his sword clanging off that of the maddened enemy and tearing a few links from his chain shirt. He drew back the blade and struck again. The enemy legionary fell away, his face oddly more disappointed than agonised, and suddenly Fronto felt a man pushing past him trying to fill the gap. With a snarl, Fronto took a step forward and began to stab and slash and hack. There were flurries of blows, several coming close to ending him, but none quite striking home, and he realised only at that moment, as another man leapt to his death attempting to deflect a blade meant for the legate, that his men were seriously endangering themselves in an attempt to save their commander. He was being selfish in taking such a part as he was, and Felix had been right to disapprove. His very presence here was costing the legion.

Perhaps he had given them one advantage, though? After all, the enemy *had* broken ranks to push at him…

His gaze rose for a moment over the battle and he was disappointed to see that the gap formed by the disobedient Pompeian century had quickly sealed up as more and more of the enemy poured from their camp to defend the hill.

Fronto thrust twice more, catching a man in the upper arm, and ducked to avoid a dangerous blow, then allowed the man who had been trying to push past to fall into position in front. He staggered slowly back a pace, the legion flowing round him to push onwards The legate's gaze met that of Felix, who nodded and blew new commands on his whistle. Fronto dropped back into the ranks, safely away from the front lines, the men opening up a gap for him as he went.

Wiping blood from his brow – his or someone else's? – Fronto heaved in ragged breaths as he emerged from the rear of the advancing legion and took stock of what was happening. Any advantage they might have gained from the impulsive attack of their enemy had quickly disappeared as the gap they left had been plugged with ease. Although that century of Pompeians had been almost obliterated now, many more waited atop the hill. The rest of the fight was becoming rather mechanical as the two lines met at the crest, like a formal dance.

Both sides knew the capabilities, strengths and tactics of their enemy and now that the initial bloodthirsty charge had ended things had settled, the legionaries on both sides far more concerned with staying alive and keeping formation than killing men who wore the same uniform. There were deaths and there were screams still, but it was oddly muted and sporadic as both sides did what they had to with a distinct lack of enthusiasm. Shuffling to the side, Fronto found a large grey rock and sank down gratefully onto it. His side ached where the wound had so recently healed, and his knuckles burned from the skinning they had taken the other day. The bandage wrapped around his hand was deep pink, but there was enough blood splashed and spattered across him that he couldn't tell whether his hand had bled freshly into the wrappings or whether the stains were from someone else.

He closed his eyes. Oddly he could still hear the hum of bees over the din of the fight up the slope, and wondered at the resilience of nature even through man's destruction. How long he sat there with eyes shut listening to the drone of war and the hum of nature he couldn't say, but it was almost like being awakened from a dream when a familiar voice nearby addressed him. His eyes shot open and he straightened.

'We almost had them,' Salvius Cursor said again.

'There's a long day ahead yet,' Fronto reminded him, noting once more with distaste the gore coating much of the tribune, whose sword was still raised as though expecting the fight to go on even here.

'But now it is becoming a war of attrition,' Salvius spat. 'I was surprised to see you so visible and so far forward, sir. It was a good ploy,' he added with a clearly grudging admission. 'To draw them out like that. It almost worked, but their reserves plugged the gap too quickly for true advantage.'

Fronto toyed with the truth. Telling Salvius that it had been unintentional and that he had made a mistake and endangered his men would hardly help, but lying always rankled, almost as much as agreeing with the tribune. Whatever he said, the fact remained that his presence in the front lines had almost won them an advantage, but the Hispanic legions of Pompey were every bit as experienced and strong as Caesar's and even the failures of one century would not compromise the whole. They had quickly reformed. Now the fight was very much a stalemate, the two lines cutting and shoving at the crest of the hill, but there was no likelihood of advantage, and the numbers seemed to be more or less even. Three legions or thereabouts had been committed from the Pompeian camp.

Salvius Cursor was correct: it was now simply a war of attrition. He remained silent, contemplating the mess they were in.

'This is what happens when the high command are too skittish to commit to a fight,' Salvius grunted.

Fronto turned disbelieving eyes on the tribune. 'What? This was *your* idea. *You* pushed for an attack. Those of us who knew what it would cost fought against the decision, but you won. You got your attack, and it's turned into a systematic thinning of Roman ranks on both sides.'

Salvius looked around, perhaps checking they were alone as the legions fought on up the slope.

'Respectfully, Legate,' he said in a tone almost entirely devoid of respect, 'this is *not* what I advocated. I spoke up for a full push against the Pompeian camp. A single decisive strike. With the division in their command we stood a chance of taking their ramparts before they could adequately respond. This was a smaller scale push to take a secondary target with the given likelihood that they would field adequate defence. It was doomed to turn into this mess.'

Fronto felt the ire rising once more and forced it down. Getting angry with Salvius would do little good now.

'Our only hope is that someone makes a mistake,' the tribune said.

Fronto nodded. 'But we both know that's not going to happen. The centurions on that hill are as good as our own. The meat grinder will go on.'

Salvius leaned against the other side of the rock and the two men fell silent, watching the fight on the hill as Romans fell to Roman blades in wave after wave of butchery. After a time, a small group of support personnel appeared, three slaves with them carrying buckets and jugs and trays. Fronto and Salvius washed off the worst of the blood from their arms and faces, tipping jugs of water over their heads. A capsarius looked at Fronto's knuckles, applied fresh salve and rebound them, treated a small cut on the tribune's forearm, and someone supplied a platter of bread and butter and a cup of water each.

The two men watched on as the sun rose to its zenith and then began to descend, the legions at the crest never moving, just reforming here and there so that the freshest men moved to the front, a steady stream of casualties carried or limping back from the fight, the ranks becoming noticeably thinner as time went on.

'I need to stop this,' Fronto said finally and was surprised when the tribune nodded and made to follow.

The two men moved swiftly back down the hill and made for the small knot of senior officers on the rise watching the fight. Caesar and his staff were arrayed around a small table that held fruit and meat and bread and jugs of wine and water as though they were watching a day's games in the arena. Fronto coughed loudly as they approached. The general turned and nodded at him.

'It would seem we are evenly matched,' the general mused.

'And gradually becoming less numerous,' Fronto added. 'Time to call off the attack. We're gaining nothing here other than bodies on both sides. We'll never take the hill, and they don't quite have the strength to drive us back.'

'We cannot withdraw now,' Antonius said. 'All it will take is one small advantage and the whole fight will change. One centurion makes one mistake, and we will control the hill.'

'Not if that centurion is ours,' countered Fronto. 'Their men are every bit as good as ours.'

'There is still time,' Antonius persisted.

Fronto glanced at Caesar, who seemed undecided, and opened his mouth, but Salvius Cursor cut through from behind him.

'The prize there is not worth the loss, General. Had we committed to a full attack on…'

'Enough,' Caesar said quietly, silencing them all. 'This entire strategy needs to be rethought. There is no simple decisive victory to be had, whatever you advocate, Tribune, neither at their camp nor at this hill or the town. And I cannot watch the systematic attrition of legions for no appreciable gain.' He turned to Fufius Calenus. 'Order the Ninth to the hill in a support capacity and have the three assaulting legions withdraw using the Ninth as cover to prevent a rout. Get the men back safely to camp while we still have an army to field.'

Fronto sighed with relief and cast a quick glance at Salvius, nodding his appreciation for the unexpected support. Their motivations may be different in almost all matters, but their agreement had seemingly swung Caesar to ending the costly struggle.

* * *

'So you're not going to lead from the front again, then?' Galronus mused.

'I should have anticipated what would happen. I'd looked across the lines and spotted Salvius by his red plume. If I could find him that way, any man could find me the same. But as for taking part? I'm not sure. I have absolutely no desire to kill Romans, no matter who they call imperator, but how can I expect my legionaries to fight Romans if I'm not willing to do it myself? It's different when you're facing barbarians – pardon the term – because a legionary feels that what he is doing is for the good of Rome. But when the men in front of you are also Romans? Well, half the motivation melts away.'

'But they fight for love of Caesar and the desire for the loot he promises,' noted Galronus.

'You'd be surprised how brief the love of Caesar flares when facing fellow Romans, and financial incentives have to be freshly remembered to carry much weight. This war is anathema to most Romans, and so they need every motivation we can give. Oddly, while I still think Salvius Cursor is a continual danger to his own army, sometimes that headstrong berserk nature of his actually works in our favour.'

'What will Caesar do now?'

Fronto shrugged and poured himself another wine before proffering the jugs to his friend.

'We're at an impasse once more. He needs decisive action, but any decisive action is horribly dangerous and could easily result in defeat. Unless the gods drop a solution in his lap I just cannot see how things will change.'

Both men fell silent.

'Did you hear that?' Galronus said after a while.

'What?'

Then he heard it too. A sporadic drumming on the roof of the tent. Rain.

'Well that settles it,' Fronto sighed. 'Nothing will happen while it rains anyway. Time to lick our wounds and wait.'

197

Chapter Ten

26th of Junius - Massilia

CATHÁIN stood on the top of the port tower, the salty sea breeze whipping him repeatedly in the face. This tower was one of the widest and stoutest along the entire length of the city's fortifications, yet was rarely occupied by the military. The entrance to Massilia's great port, which occupied a natural cove or inlet, was protected by twin towers a little further along from here, the far one a singular turret disconnected from the system across the water. A chain was habitually slung between the two at water height to bar access to shipping at dangerous times, though the legions Caesar had left to besiege the city had partially demolished that far tower and therefore disabled the chain during the early days of the conflict.

The walls of the city proper, though, continued in along the cove a little way, and the last two towers overlooked only the water within the cove, and so were in no direct danger from the Caesarian legions. Consequently they were rarely occupied except by port officials. Of course they were still kept from public access, for they held artillery designed to protect the city from seaborne attackers, but with the distinct unlikelihood of sea attack, they were unmanned and stood silent and still. Catháin had managed to obtain a permit for access to the walls through his more dubious connections, though if the authorities scrutinised it too hard they might decide he had no real reason to be on the walls.

The permit had been hard to acquire, but had been important to him. If he was ever going to find a way out of Massilia, he needed to be constantly aware of the external situation, and he could only truly understand that with his own eyes and ears. He had fretted over many days, peering out and down from one tower or another in an effort to spot a way out that would not see him either pinned by the arrows of the besieging army before he could explain or thrown forward into a ditch, skewered by a huge bolt shot from a tower top.

Finally, he had decided that his best chance would be by water. There were a few small rowing boats still in the city, privately owned, but all had been documented and impounded by Ahenobarbus in his defensive system. All but one, at least. It had been overlooked as a wreck by the authorities, and there was little doubt that it would leak the moment it dipped into the waves, but Catháin had been in boats all his life, and he knew a vessel that would float and a vessel that would not. The small rowing boat standing in a yard three streets back from the port would eventually fill and sink, but it would take at least half an hour, which should be ample time to make it across the cove or out past the walls, and bailing out water as he went would extend that lifespan.

The only issue he had was that the waters of the inlet were observed by both Massiliots and besieging Romans. He was as likely to be killed by either side while rowing as he would sneaking across the grass. But the water had the advantage of not having to cross the walls first. It was the answer, but he had to figure a way to make it across unobserved.

Hence his concentration on this tower.

Here, beside the port, he had an excellent view of the entire inlet from the towered entrance out to open sea right to the dangerous marshes that lay inland, adding an impressive level of defensive capability to the walls at the other end. There had to be a solution, and if it was to be found it would be found here.

The morning was chilly, though that would soon change as the sun rose higher, and soon even the sea breeze would be little more than refreshing relief from the heat. Gulls wheeled and shrieked, and some minor port official with his scribe chattered away on the other side of the tower, looking down at the dock.

Perhaps if there was enough of a distraction, he could slip across unseen?

A racket suddenly drew his attention and his gaze tore from the gently lapping waters below to the tower behind him as voices gradually increased in volume, figures climbing the steps from inside onto the tower top. He felt the tiniest flush of worry as a man in Roman officer's uniform emerged onto the parapet, but quickly it settled. Nerves only ever caused trouble. You had to control them or they'd undo you for sure.

The officer was not alone. Two other Romans emerged, and Catháin's eyebrow rose a little at the sight. He'd spent long enough around them by now to recognise their uniforms. The first man was a tribune of broad stripe status, probably a legionary man. The second wore a blue tunic beneath his cuirass and was bearded, which seemed to be almost unheard of among Romans. He was an officer of a Roman ship or some other naval rank. The third man was the bastard himself: Lucius Domitius Ahenobarbus.

For just a moment – the blink of an eye – Catháin wondered whether he might be able to end this entire thing if he simply ran around the rampart a little and pushed the gangling, long-limbed lunatic over the edge to plummet to his death on the quayside below. In fact, despite the presence of the other two officers, he was fairly sure he could do it. But Romans were resilient and nothing if not bloody minded. Ahenobarbus would die, but almost certainly one of those others would take his place, and there was always a possibility they would be worse. Besides, Catháin would die for his efforts, and he hadn't come all this way and lived such a successful and profitable life to throw it all away now on some heroic attack. Oh, and Fronto and Balbus' paperwork would fall into enemy hands then too.

The three officers were followed by half a dozen local nobs in their expensive himations and fine sandals, and then by another half dozen soldiers along with an optio. These latter immediately went to the artillery piece and began to check it over.

His eyes narrowing at the sight, Catháin turned and looked along the wall. Sure enough more soldiers had emerged at the other two waterfront towers and were testing the efficacy of the weapons atop them. *Something was afoot...*

With a sharp bark of command, Ahenobarbus sent the port official and his clerk scurrying out of the way and took their place, looking down at the port, his companions close by. As he found the place he desired, the Roman commander's gaze played around the tower and settled on Catháin.

'Who is that?' he snapped.

'Some local engineer,' the tribune by his side replied dismissively. 'You see him all over the walls. I gather he's something to do with the crew that patch up the cracks and replace the masonry.'

Catháin sent a small silent thank you floating into the abyss for the cleverness of his contact who had acquired his permit. Good man. The Roman glared at him for a moment with a furrowed brow.

'He looks untrustworthy to me.'

'We've no engineers or masons with us, General,' the tribune replied. 'We have to rely on local talent.'

Ahenobarbus harrumphed and, apparently dismissing Catháin from his mind, turned back to his work. The northerner paid attention to his role, producing a wax tablet and checking the mortar and any cracks in the parapet to allay suspicion. As he did so, he moved to the tower's corner. Closer to the Roman officer and his party, but not so close as to seem suspicious.

'How many in total?' Ahenobarbus asked.

'Seventeen warships, sir,' the naval officer replied. 'All the ones you can see at the jetties plus two in the sheds at the end. Eleven of them have fighting decks. Then there's a total of twenty two sizeable civilian ships we can take, all smaller than the warships, but adequate. Thirty nine vessels in all. Quite a fleet, given our circumstances.'

'Good. A good distribution.'

Catháin felt a chill running through him. Something big was most definitely afoot. The danger he was currently in began to insist itself upon him, and he started to edge quietly and unobtrusively back along the wall away from the small Roman group and their local nobles. As he did so, he could not help but notice figures moving through the port below. He paused. Sailors, both Roman military and local civilians, were carrying goods aboard every ship on the quayside now, and small groups had formed in front of the warehouses. He recognised the figures of the Albici, the local Gallic tribe who had thrown in their lot with Massilia. They were archers, those men. Checking out the ships. There was no good reason for Albici archers to be examining the ships unless they expected to be on them at any moment.

His heart began to thump.

Trouble was most definitely afoot!

As unobtrusively as possible, he paced back around the tower, skirting the crew now tilting and turning the great bolt thrower, and reaching the stairs. As he took the first ten steps into the gloom, he paused, his ears twitching.

'Where did that engineer go?' Ahenobarbus murmured.

'No idea. Must have moved on.'

'Good,' the general grumbled. 'Will all be ready at first light?'

'Ready and waiting,' came the reply.

Catháin shivered and began to pad silently down the steps away from danger. His thoughts turned to Caesar's blockade. The redoubtable Brutus had brought twelve ships to seal in Massilia. The city's defenders had watched as the young Roman admiral had taken his small fleet to the island that sat outside the harbour mouth and there formed a small naval base. Twelve ships. And no matter how many men the admiral had for each ship, twelve vessels against almost forty was a foregone conclusion, especially when they would be taken entirely by surprise.

Shit. Things never stayed simple, did they?

* * *

The darkness was almost total in the cold room. Catháin had found his way in with relative ease. His weeks of exploring the walls and defences had given him an almost unparalleled knowledge of the system, and he had climbed one of the lesser bastions far from danger, slipping along the wall-walk and nodding at the odd bored and tired guard, displaying his permit. The chances of his movements reaching the general from the mouth of these bored watchmen were minimal. They had not been told to keep out those with official permission and would not think to mention it to their superiors.

After almost half an hour, he had reached the great chain tower at the port's entrance. This was one of the most important and most occupied towers in the whole system, and he had been very careful as he reached the entrance from the wall top. He had slipped through the first room, rather blasé, and nipped into the corner stairwell, where he had climbed past a room of chattering and laughing soldiers. Crossing the stairwell without drawing their attention had been a nerve-wracking gamble, but he had reached the small room he sought unobserved and had removed the key, opened the door, entered, and locked it behind him.

He was alone in a room just five feet across. It was claustrophobic to say the least. And dangerous. More dangerous than walking into a drinking pit back in Īweriū and telling the denizens that you'd never been beaten in a fight. And his chances of success were small, reliant upon whether anyone was paying attention and whether they would know what they were seeing even if they were.

It was a longshot. More than that: it was a sequence of longshots with only one chance of success. But the poor bastards on the island with their twelve ship fleet had to be warned. He had to try.

He approached the window. The room was unused now, due to its current empty purpose, for it had been the sighting window for the chain. Here one could look along the line of the long gone chain and into a matching window at the far, now ruined, tower. But if you looked at an oblique angle to the right, you could also see the island outside the harbour mouth. And due to pure chance of design, from nowhere else on the city walls could an observer quite see this window.

Working quickly and with his breath controlled and slower by far than his heartbeat, Catháin produced from his belt pouch a small oil lamp and flask, filling it. He placed a little dried grass and a few twigs on the window sill, the night breeze ruffling them but not strong enough to blow them away. Striking iron to flint, he worked until a spark caught, then carefully lifted the lamp and lit the wick, then quickly tipped a small phial of water onto the smouldering grass. With just the glow of the lamp, he lifted it and placed it on the stone of the window, then fished in his pouch again. The convex mirror was his pride and joy, formed of perfect orichalcum and smooth as a baby's behind. He placed it behind the lamp and gave a few test movements facing into the room, watching the light flash around in the darkness, illuminating the wall. It took a moment for him to remember that he needed to invert his signals, else they were displayed upside down. But still they were strong and bright. He hadn't done this for a while. Not since he'd worked with a Roman smuggler from Narbo.

Returning to the window, he tried to run through the signals in his head. It had been a few years, but they had been so critical in that illicit trade that he had burned them into his memory for all time. So far so good, but now he was reliant upon the island noticing and being able to read the signals.

He held up the lamp and mirror facing the island and flashed the light up, up, down.

Nothing. He waited for a count of thirty, and then repeated the signal.

His heart thumping, he continued to wait in his gloomy cell. This small oil lamp burned for just less than a quarter of an hour. He might – *might* – be able to replenish the oil reservoir once from his flask without it going out, but it was a tricky process. And he had no spare tinder.

Again and no response.

He waited, attuned to every slight sound from the tower around him.

Again. No response.

Pause and try, pause and try, pause and try.

He almost missed the reply when it came.

To be sure, he tried again. Up, up, down.

Down, down, up.

He grinned like an idiot. The Roman navy might think themselves all noble and mighty, but some devious bastard out there under admiral Brutus knew the smugglers' codes.

Down, down, down. *You are in danger.*

Up, up, right. *Pirates?*

Left. *No.*

Up, up, left. *Warships?*

Right. *Yes.*

Left, left, down. *How many?*

Right, down… right, down… right, down… left, down… down… down… down… down. *Thirty nine.*

Why did it have to be such a long damn number?

Up, right, up. *Armaments?*

Left, right, left. *Arrows.*

Left, left, up. *When?*

Right, Right, Right. *Dawn.*

Down. *Understood.*

There was no signal for 'good luck', so Catháin simply wished it silently and waited. No new signal came. Finally, his lamp guttered and began to fade. Hopefully he had done enough. At least Brutus had been warned and the fleet could flee before Ahenobarbus' force emerged. Roman lives could be saved.

* * *

The northerner was up before dawn again, but this time he was not alone in that. Massilia had woken early and burst into life, a hive of activity. The city garrison had taken their place around the walls as usual, but now the defences at the port end were seeing unusual levels of occupation too. As Catháin hurried through the streets, even an hour before dawn the people of the city were up and about, stirred from their slumber by the activity of Ahenobarbus' men.

A few streets back from the port, he dropped by the alleyway where the dilapidated rowing boat rested. He had already identified, a street away, a small wheeled trolley used by some trader to transport goods through the narrow alleys, and had reasoned that he could take it to the boat and manage to tip the vessel onto the trolley. He had even worked out a route through the less visited backstreets that would bring him to the waterside far away from the dock, near the potters' district, where he could slip it into the water with the minimum of fuss. It was heart-stoppingly dangerous, but whenever the nerves pinched at him, he remembered how perilous it would be to simply be in the city when the walls fell to enemy legions. Rome had something of a reputation for the way defiant cities were treated when captured.

He would check the port and make sure all eyes were on the fleet first. Then, if there was even a chance of slipping across the inlet further down the waterside, he would go back and fetch the boat. Accompanied by the rising odour of brine and the increasing concentration of gulls, he emerged nonchalantly at the port, sauntering from a roadway as though on everyday business.

The huge fleet had moved out from the jetties and now sat in the harbour, riding at anchor, already loaded and crewed, awaiting a signal. Archers from the Albici filled the decks, testing the efficacy of their bows in the salty damp air of the port, making sure the strings had not stretched, and securing their positions on the decks or among the rowing benches on ships with no deck.

The quayside was alive with humanity, though the activity that had seen the fleet's preparation had long since ended. Now those soldiers and civilians who had loaded ships, untied and coiled ropes, cleared jetties and the like, simply stood on the dock and watched the fruits of their labour bobbing and floating, waiting for the order to move. Catháin's heart sank. Half a thousand eyes played across the water, and while they were largely centred on the fleet, they had a clear view inward right past the potters' district and to the marshes at the far end. There was no unobserved stretch of water after all.

Inwardly, he cursed. It seemed that the concentration of attention on the fleet would make any attempt impossible. His plans scuppered, he fumed impotently for a moment, finally deciding that, given the lack of opportunity for escape, he would instead pay attention to what was happening with Ahenobarbus' fleet. With luck, Brutus' ships had taken the opportunity to slip away from the island under cover of darkness. And then there would be another chance for the leaky little boat, for when the Roman officer had regained control of the sea approaches there would be less focus on the water.

Catháin turned from the port and made for the walls, noting the Roman vexillum of Ahenobarbus on the chain tower. Carefully, he selected the turret two along from that, well out of sight of the Roman commander, just in case, and climbed to the top, showing his permit to the various legionaries or Massiliot guards who stood in the way.

The bolt thrower atop the tower was manned and ready. A few men lined the parapet, but not enough to fill it. The city's garrison was not that large, and most of them were still concentrated in the areas facing the legions outside. Locating a suitable spot, Catháin rested his elbows on the stone. He took out his wax tablet and stilus but did nothing else, assuming that there would be enough interest in the proceedings that no soldier would expect a civilian to work without watching. If the men in the port were allowed to stand and watch, why not the wall maintenance engineer the soldiers were so used to seeing around the defences?

The sun was not yet up, but dawn had more or less broken anyway. The presence of the high hills behind Massilia meant that the sky became light some time before the golden disc made its first proper appearance. First the low peaks along the coast began to glow, and then the wine dark sea far out took on an indigo hue, lightening as the sun climbed as yet unseen. There was a subdued blast of a horn somewhere in the city and the entire fleet raised their anchors and began to move with expert coordination. Their trierarchs were good. In just moments they were moving through the port entrance and heading toward the island that was still as yet in shadow, little more than a mound of black against the purple waters.

Catháin held his breath.

The sky lightened further as the ships emerged, and the island began to become more visible, the observers able to pick out details in the glow as the first arc of yellow finally appeared above the peaks. The northerner blinked, certain his eyes deceived him. No, he had not been mistaken. The sunlight was now picking out white sails before the dark mound of the island. Twelve ships. The fleet of Decimus Brutus had not fled after all. In fact they had, during the hours of darkness, put to sea and come around the island, arrayed in a spaced out line before the shore and facing the city.

What was Caesar's man doing? Was he mad?

The lighter it got, the worse things looked. Catháin shook his head even as the soldiers across the tower top laughed in relief. Not only were the Caesarians outnumbered three to one, they were also clearly outclassed. From what Catháin understood, the blockading ships had been newly built at Arelate, and crewed only by what sailors could be found among merchant vessels there at short notice, unlike the naval professionals working for Ahenobarbus. Catháin knew his ships. The hastily recruited sailors would likely be inferior and slow, but so would Brutus' vessels. They were heavy, of newly hewn and unseasoned timber and would be slow to manoeuvre. This fight looked over before it had even begun. Ahenobarbus' ships were faster, stronger, better crewed and piloted and far more numerous. Unless *Manannán mac Lir* – or perhaps Poseidon, given where they were – popped out of the water and plucked a few Massiliot galleys from the fight, Brutus stood no chance.

The city's fleet would be able to outrun and surround the blockade vessels, peppering them with arrows. They might even be able to take out banks of oars if the Roman crews were slow or unprepared enough.

For just a moment, Catháin wondered whether the wily young Roman had set these twelve as fire ships in an attempt to destroy the Massiliot fleet. But, no. He could see them moving now, heading to intercept the city's ships, taking the massive force head-on. What was he doing? He had to have some sort of mad, reckless plan. While Catháin had only personally met the young Roman a couple of times, Fronto had often talked about Brutus – about his impressive defeat of the Veneti sailors in Gaul half a decade ago. Could that same genius be displayed here, against his own people.

Bellows of triumph were echoing along the walls at the sight of the two fleets converging, and Ahenobarbus had calls blared out from the chain tower. They were picked up by musicians aboard the ships and the various trierarchs began to manoeuver in response. The ships of the Massiliot fleet separated. The smaller ones with fewer archers drifted out to the periphery, leaving just twenty four ships – the strongest and best crewed – making for Brutus' fleet. It was a sensible tactic, and Catháin had seen the results at times, when pirates had taken some unsuspecting merchant in this fashion. Two ships to each enemy, gliding in alongside, trapping them between twin groups of archers. The arrow storm would come from both sides and the death toll would be appalling without too much damage to the vessel itself. Why was Brutus letting it all happen? It was as though he had *planned* this, given the wide spacing of his ships. Was he mad, or was he incredibly clever and had seen something Catháin had not?

The northerner watched, his heart in his throat.

Sure enough, as the moments wore on, the two fleets converged. As each pair of Massiliot ships neared one of Brutus', they shipped their oars, their momentum carrying them into position, the vessels slowing, through natural water resistance and the skill of their crew, to come alongside. Brutus' ships did the same, the fleets drifting toward one another and slowing, oars raised and then pulled inside. No ship who intended to live through an engagement left their oars protruding when another vessel came alongside. If there was even a chance the enemy hull might touch the oar blades it would mean the end. The oars would be smashed, and the portion of the long timber beams that remained inside the ship would be pushed back, crushing and smashing the rowers between them into agonising deaths. No. Any sailor worth his salt shipped his oars as another vessel came close to move alongside.

And so, as though they were docking at a jetty, the Massiliot ships ran alongside the Caesarian ones, drifting expertly to a halt. The Albici archers began their barrage as soon as they judged they were in good range. In Catháin's opinion, the trierarchs of their ships could have kept them outside oar distance if they'd desired, but in order to give the archers their best effective range, they had closed on Brutus' vessels.

Catháin squinted. At this distance, it was not quite so easy to make out the finer details. Was that some kind of construction on board each of Brutus' decks? Some siege work of some sort? It looked like a great crate or even a low vinea.

He realised what they were with surprise. They were overlapping shields, the familiar red designs hidden beneath their leather travel covers, perhaps to preserve them from the salty air, or perhaps to keep the nature of the formation hidden from the enemy as long as possible. A testudo, like the ones the army made, keeping the bulk of the men within safe from the arrow storm. Equally, as the enemy ships had pulled alongside, the oarsmen had hunched down and pulled spare covered shields over themselves. A few men would have fallen to the arrows anyway, but not half as many as the Massiliots had been expecting. Every man had adequate cover, even the rowers. And as the archers finished their first barrage, a few letting off sporadic loose shots as the majority nocked a new arrow, the Caesarian fleet responded.

On each of the twelve outclassed ships, the testudo unfolded like a flower opening to the sun. Strong sailors hidden within hurled grapples and lines. In the blink of an eye, the whole battle changed. Where a moment ago, the Caesarian ships had been pinned beneath twin sources of arrows and had seemingly stood no chance, suddenly they were on the offensive and the attackers knew that something was going horribly wrong.

The heavy iron grapples flew out, four from each side of each ship, and more than half of them struck home on target. Before the Massiliot crew realised what was happening and rushed to free the pointed menaces, massively-muscled men on Brutus' ships were hauling on the lines. Those cables that had missed were hauled back and thrown again.

Panicky archers had dropped their bows now and were trying to dislodge the grapples, nervous fingers scrabbling at the pitted iron hooks as their owners' eyes remained fixed warily on the soldiers aboard the Caesarian vessels. There was no hope with the grapples so well pinned. A few of the more forward thinking among the archers began to draw swords and daggers and hack and saw at the ropes, trying to free their ships, but Catháin knew how much effort that would take. A sailor knows better than any land ape that a salt and brine-strengthened rope is as hard as steel and a man can cut easier through a hull than through a proper rope.

Catháin watched in wonder the arrow clouds thin and then fade to virtually nothing as the rest of the archers began to join the desperate attempts to free their ships. Relatively safe from arrows now, the Caesarian sailors rose, adding their own muscles to the ropes as the marines who had formed the testudo split into two groups, one facing each ship attacking them. Forty men facing a ship of roughly as many archers. But the men Brutus had fielded were not unarmoured archers, nor even the lightly armoured marines of the Roman fleets. They were true heavy legionaries, geared for war. Catháin almost laughed, but then remembered upon whose walls he stood and contained his glee behind sullen brows.

As he watched in growing disbelief, the sheer muscle exerted on the ropes dragged the Massiliot vessels sideways through the water, a feat that would take Herculean strength. A few of the ships finally managed to get themselves free before they were inexorably dragged into Brutus' trap. Often the only way was brutal, the sailors hacking at the strakes of their own ships, braking away the rails and timbers so that the grapples attached to them fell harmlessly into the sea even as other men used oars to push themselves away from the horrible, terrible Caesarian vessels and their cargo of armoured killers.

Catháin made a count. Nine vessels remained trapped by Brutus' ships a few moments later, even as the attack foundered and failed. He could hear Ahenobarbus raging and bellowing even two towers away. Arguments broke out there and a musician was summoned. A call to retreat went up, summoning the entire fleet back to the city.

Those ships that had moved to the periphery turned swiftly, unhampered by grapples, and raced back to the safe harbour of Massilia at a surf-cutting pace. Those who had managed to free themselves from Brutus' ships struggled back, trying to turn and get away. They had time, Catháin noted, for Brutus ignored them, concentrating on the nine ships he had pinned.

The true brutality of Brutus' plan then unfolded.

Unable to break enough ropes or remove enough grapples, the Massiliot ships were drawn in with a series of deep, wooden crashes against the Caesarian vessels' hulls, and even before they had finished jostling back and forth in the water, the boarding ramps had been run across and forty bloodthirsty, bellowing veteran legionaries crossed the boards and threw themselves into each group of archers like a hot coal into a slab of butter. Optios and Centurions moved among them as they mercilessly butchered their prey. Here and there a Caesarian or a Massiliot would tumble, screaming into the gap between hulls, where they would be mercilessly crushed as the hulls bounced, jostled and ground against one another like the *Symplegades* – the 'clashing rocks' of Argonaut legend. Catháin had watched that happen before in sea combat. It was one of the worst ways to die he could imagine.

The entire compliment of soldiers now on board the enemy vessels, the archers fell like wheat. It was appalling to watch even at this distance. Catháin had seen fights up close, and death too. He knew what it would be like on those ships – like a hot night in Tartarus – and was immensely grateful he was on this airy tower top watching the grisly display from a distance.

Those Caesarian ships who were not part of the fight, whose opponents had managed to cut loose and flee, made valiant attempts to chase them down, but while their sailors might be inferior, the trierarchs were clearly good men, following a plan. They chased the fleeing Massiliots only as far as the edge of the fight, then let the enemy run rather than follow them into danger.

It was over in a hundred further heartbeats. Catháin watched, stunned, the legionaries returning from three now dead hulks even as the ruined hulls began to fill with water, dipping down into the waves, sinking with their crews of the unburied damned on board. Those lines were released, and the three vessels slowly disappeared from view, swallowed up by the briny deep.

The other six remained afloat, though their crews fared no better. Whether it had been part of Brutus' plan or just a side effect of angry, beleaguered soldiers, the legionaries on board had given no quarter. Not a Massiliot sailor nor archer from those nine ships lived out the morning. Catháin watched in cold understanding as the bodies were tipped into the sea and the crews of the fleet reorganised so that the captured vessels could be sailed away.

The northerner shook his head and cast silent 'thank you's to half a dozen gods – some of them even Roman ones – as he watched Brutus, victorious. Thirty vessels were even now racing back in through the welcoming harbour mouth of Massilia – the smaller and less occupied ships. The biggest and the best of the Massiliot fleet had been committed and had been lost.

And Brutus, who had sallied forth against insane odds with twelve ships, was now turning his fleet and sailing back to his besieging harbour on the island with eighteen, including six of the best, most manoeuvrable vessels the city had boasted.

Ahenobarbus was beside himself. His shouting was, to Catháin's mind, most ignoble and un-Roman. Some poor bastard tried to calm the raging general down and the northerner watched the unfortunate tribune tipped over the parapet, where he plummeted to the water below. It was a death sentence. A fall, even into water, from that height would have broken every bone in his body. The tribune sank beneath the surface and disappeared.

As the wall top and the towers became hives of activity, Catháin moved to an opening and disappeared down a stairwell, finding his way out through the defences and into the city. He kept his composure through the forum, where horrified Massiliots were wailing over their loss, and all the way to Fronto's warehouse, where he unlocked the door and disappeared inside.

He found one of the best vintages in a huge amphora, pulled up a chair beside it and poured himself a large unwatered wine. He drank it, then another, and then another. And only when the pleasant fug of Bacchus was beginning to drift into the periphery of his vision did he allow himself a burst sigh of relief and then a peal of slightly deranged laughter.

Gods love that young man. He was everything Fronto had said and more.

Brutus was a lunatic. But he was a genius with it.

Catháin fell asleep some time later, comforted with wine and dreaming of his soggy, northern homeland.

Chapter Eleven

6th of Quintilis - Ilerda

IF he hadn't lived through it, Fronto would never have believed it. Had he been back in Rome and someone had told him it had rained in Hispania in high summer for ten straight days, he'd have called them a liar. Junius and Quintilis in the region were the hottest, driest months and even a day of showers was a rare treat to savour. Ten days of almost torrential downpour was unimaginable.

Fronto rolled over irritably in his bed and wrenched the blankets up higher, as though the problem was a chill. It wasn't. It was the incessant drumming of rain on the tent roof, which had kept him awake for hours each night, or would have done had he not somewhat slid into his old ways. The enforced stationary situation, as both armies huddled in their camps battered by the rain, had left little to do, and Fronto's wine consumption had reach an all-time high, or perhaps the equal of those days in Gaul before Lucilia and the strictures of age had toned it down somewhat. At least going to bed in a nice mental blanket of Chian red helped him sleep through the downpours.

Most of the time.

And then on some occasions, the insistence of the weather drummed through even the thickest of heads and left him tossing and turning in his bed, working through problems and failing to find solutions even as he kept trying to clear his mind and fall asleep again.

He'd tried to solve the rain-noise issue by having spare blankets stretched above the tent to deaden the rain before it hit the leather roof. The relief lasted around a count of fifty and then the weight of the water brought the blanket slapping down onto the tent roof and the problem began again. He'd consulted the engineers and they had told him that there was nothing to do about it and perhaps he needed to pray to Jupiter Pluvius for the rain to stop as many were now doing. He'd told Galronus too, and his

Remi friend had come up with the helpful suggestion 'go and campaign somewhere else?'

With a sigh, he kicked the blankets aside and curled into a ball, where he lay for a while, worrying about Balbus and his brilliant incriminating documents back in Massilia. He straightened and an insistent itch began just below his shoulder blade. Try as he might, he couldn't quite reach it and the more he attempted the worse it got. With a snarl of irritation he rose from the bed and crossed to one of the tent struts, put his back against it and began to rub this way and that like a bear on a tree.

His sigh of satisfaction turned into a howl of incandescent rage as the pole shifted slightly with the pressure and a small torrent of icy cold water tipped down the inside of the tent, soaking his hair and back.

He leapt into the centre of the tent, dancing this way and that, trying to peel off the clingy sodden tunic and stopped in shock as he saw a figure standing in the tent door. On the cusp of an indignant demand to know what in Hades the visitor was doing, he recognised the shape as Galronus and sagged.

'Our druid used to do a ritual dance a bit like that on the solstice,' the Remi prince snorted. 'And my cousin once did it when a wasp got trapped in his trousers. Is this something you do often when you're alone, and does Lucilia know?'

Fronto wound himself up to a blistering retort, but something about his friend stopped him. The ribbing was Galronus as usual, but the Remi's expression was dour and concerned.

'What is it?'

'Broken timbers in the river. One of the guards alerted a centurion and it got back to Carbo, who sent runners to warn the officers.'

'The bridge again?'

His friend nodded. 'We presume so. Hardly surprising given the state of the river now.'

Fronto nodded. The river had been worrying the engineers for days and had been one of the prime reasons for so many offerings to Jupiter Pluvius recently. The first two days had seen little change, but then each successive day of continual downpour had strengthened the flow of water in the Sicoris such that now it was even beginning to threaten the camp. Surges had led water to slop over the banks and brought the dry dusty soil down so that the verges were wearing back and becoming dangerous. More than one legionary had fallen foul of the treacherous riverbank while going for a surreptitious piss and struggled to drag himself clear of the torrent. One man had gone missing two days ago and it was assumed that the river had claimed him for good on such an occasion. Even the ditch around the camp was fast becoming a moat, the water in it almost hip deep.

But while the engineers had been very vocally worried about the river, no one had specifically mentioned the bridges until now. Fronto hadn't given them a moment's thought. They were not temporary pontoon bridges now, but good solid timber constructions.

Or at least, they had been.

He didn't like to contemplate what the possible consequences of this might be.

'Get dressed. Caesar is gathering the officers at the equisio's enclosure.'

Fronto nodded and hurriedly found a dry tunic, started to slip into it, paused and used it as a towel on his back and drenched head, then found another and pulled it on. He belted it and slipped on his boots, then found his most waterproof cloak and flung it about him, fastening the brooch and pulling the hood forward.

'Come on, then.'

Dressed in light kit, for this was not combat and the weather was playing havoc with the army's iron equipment, he hurried out with his friend, airing yet more irritated language as his feet sank into the boggy mud that more or less formed the ground of the whole camp now. Squelching and slipping, accompanied by horrible sucking sounds, he staggered through the rain, which came down like solid rods, toward the horse enclosure where the chief equisio, Flavius Pinca, kept the officers' horses separate and better cared for than the bulk of the mounts. As he found the first slight incline, Fronto felt his foot slip and caromed down the slippery slope, landing flat on his back and continuing to slide to a halt. He rose to find Galronus grinning like an idiot, and sent a couple of choice curses into the air, drawing shocked looks from the few nearby troops who had call to be out in the rain in the middle of the night.

Caesar and Antonius were already present and mounted when they arrived, and two of the other legates were busy waiting for their horses. Fronto found cruel glee in the fact that Salvius Cursor had been omitted from the gathered personnel, which called only for staff officers and legionary and cavalry commanders.

'You look like an upright turd,' Antonius snorted. 'Did you bathe in mud on the way?'

'Thank you. And piss off.'

The angry retort just made Antonius laugh out loud and turn to Caesar. 'See what I mean, Gaius? No matter how bleak things look, Fronto can always find something to amuse.'

'I'll amuse that smirk right off your face in a minute,' grunted Fronto as he pulled the cloak tight and watched Bucephalus being led out. The magnificent black beast looked depressed and damp already. Fronto knew how he felt.

Caesar seemed anything but amused. He turned his piercing aquiline features on Antonius.

'You would laugh at a Plautus comedy, Marcus.'

Antonius shrugged, but Fronto simply frowned. He would laugh at a Plautus comedy too. Farces, pratfalls, fart gags... what was not to like? Better than the stuffy high-brow playwrights that the nobility seemed to prefer, anyway.

'I myself fail to find much to laugh about,' Caesar added, 'over a legate covered in mud. Our issues are serious business, Marcus. This could spell the end of our campaign in Hispania if we cannot recover the situation somehow.'

Fronto nodded his understanding as Bucephalus was led toward him. The legions had recovered from their near starvation through Caesar's timely rescue, his recovery of the supply routes and the steady stream of goods they brought. But that relied on the two bridges upstream.

'If we're lucky,' Fronto muttered, feeling about as lucky as a drowning man being handed a bucket of water, 'only one bridge will have gone, and the other will be stable.'

'Not likely,' put in Mamurra, Caesar's chief siege engineer, sloshing through the ankle deep murk and wrapped in a cloak on his way to join them.

'You have further information?' Caesar pressed, leaning forward.

'I've been observing the wreckage in the water. There are two very distinct varieties of timber floating down. One is older, of dark oak, and the other of beech, light and already showing signs of rot. Since the two types of wood are drawn from different sources almost a mile apart in the area of the bridges, the chances of both timbers being used in one bridge are minimal. I am certain we are seeing the wreckage of two separate bridges at the same time.'

'Damn it. That leaves us deep in the mire,' Caesar murmured. 'If the only crossing is once again the stone one under Petreius' nose, then our supply line is effectively cut until we can construct a new bridge. And we are expecting a particularly large delivery that has been held up by the weather. The longer the train of supplies languishes out there across the river, the more chance there is of the food rotting or the local bandits finding some way to gain control of it. Plus there should be a unit or more of support coming from Gaul, who might well be floundering around out there unable to cross.'

'We'd best go and look at it, then,' Fronto suggested. 'Survey the damage.'

The small party waited for the last of the legates to join them, and then rode out through the east gate of the camp, between the water-filled ditches and then, some distance out, past a pair of Roman pickets sitting under a tree, bedraggled and rubbing their hands together for warmth.

Once they passed outside the protective cordon of the camp's outriders and pickets, Ingenuus and his cavalry escort moved out into a ring, protecting the general and his officers. The land here, once the mounds of Ilerda had been left behind, was resoundingly flat and open, studded with small copses of trees, traditionally the perfect land for riding, but more than a week of rain had left the whole place very boggy and spotted with mires and small impromptu lakes that made navigation for the riders problematic. Though they tried to follow the usual route from the camp up to the former position of Fabius' legions and the bridge there, they repeatedly had to backtrack and work around a small swamp, unwilling to test how treacherous it might be in the circumstances.

Going was slow and it took half an hour to reach the first bridge, two miles upstream. The sight was enough to destroy any good humour remaining among them. The bridge had gone in its entirety. All that remained to be seen were two pieces of smashed timber jutting from the earth on the far bank and three piles driven into the river, one of which was leaning at a forty-five degree angle.

'That, I presume,' Fronto grunted, 'is not a repairable bridge.'

Mamurra rolled his eyes. 'Three days to put it back. Three days under good, dry, helpful conditions, that is. Any less than that and it would be even flimsier than this one. If we have to do it in this weather, more like a week.'

Caesar exhaled loudly. 'The gods send us what they will, and on this occasion they send me disaster. Let us move on to the upper bridge and see if it can be salvaged.'

Once more, the small party, now even more sullen and travelling in unhappy silence, rode the two miles to the upper bridge in a further half hour, backtracking here and there en route. Finally, they moved toward the river once more, and the site of the second bridge. The mood deteriorated even further as the officers' eyes fell upon the half dozen torn timbers jutting from dirt and water. The only surviving section was a short platform perhaps six feet long that protruded from the near bank at a slight angle.

Harrumphing his displeasure, Caesar dropped from his horse and crossed to the timbers. Gingerly, he pressed the toe of his boot on the timber. It did not move. Mamurra, also dismounting, scratched his chin. 'Some of the piles are still in place and if this end is still well anchored, we might be able to build on existing structures.'

Caesar nodded and made to step forward but a hoarse, crackly voice with a thick Hispanic accent said 'I wouldn't do that, Chief.'

Caesar and the other officers turned in surprise, and Ingenuus and his cavalry, discomfited at having missed a potential danger even in the troublesome night of rain, hurried over, drawing their swords. Fronto peered at the slope near the river.

A leathery-looking native was sitting next to three goats, two of which looked bedraggled and miserable, the third still and seemingly lifeless, its appearance suggesting the man had dragged it from the waters. The cavalrymen relaxed a little, their swords still in hand, but less prepared for a quick kill.

'Dangerous?' Caesar asked the farmer.

'Orrible, Chief. Sima here fell off it into the water. It rocks when you gets out a few feet.'

'You have my thanks,' Caesar replied, gesturing to the man. 'You have likely saved me an impromptu bath.'

'Saved your arse more like,' grinned the man. Ingenuus made to step forward and curb the man's insolence, but Caesar simply chuckled and waved the bodyguards back. 'Indeed, my friend. Did you see the bridge go, perchance?'

'Like a spider being hit with a hammer, it were,' the farmer said. 'Messy. Bits everywhere.'

'You are just the most charming conversationalist, aren't you,' laughed Antonius.

'Says it as I sees it, Chief,' the man shrugged. 'Seen a few crossings go in my time. Specially in the arse end of winter when the snows melt and the rivers run high. This was one of the best though. You Romans like to build things big. Just means they're more impressive when they come down.'

Again, Caesar smiled. Fronto did too. It was hard not to be oddly charmed by this man.

'Your goat has died?'

'Aye. Poor girl.'

'You will miss her?'

'Only 'til tomorrow. Then she goes in the pot. Three days good eatin' for the whole family. Not enough for a legion, mind,' he added, meaningfully, looking around at the assembled horsemen.

Again, Caesar laughed. 'Be at ease. We will not impose upon your meal. Aulus, give this man something for his troubles.'

Ingenuus reached into the bag that hung from the saddle and produced a small purse of coins, which he threw down to the man. The farmer caught it and looked inside. His eyes rose again, suspiciously. 'I ain't for sale in that kind of way, if that's what you're thinkin'?'

Another chuckle. The purse was probably more coins than the man had ever held. 'Call it a gift for your aid, and compensation for the goat. It was, after all, our bridge from which she fell.'

'Aye, well, you're right there, Chief,' the man replied, tucking away the purse before anyone might think to take it back.

'How long to replace this one, then?' Fronto asked Mamurra.

'Same, I reckon. Three days in the dry. A week in this nightmare.'

'Things are looking less than bright, aren't they?' Fronto murmured.

'Another day,' the farmer said in a firm tone.

'What?'

'One more day o' rain. That's all. By sundown tomorrow the ground'll start to dry. Two more days even the pools'll have gone.'

'You're sure?' Caesar probed.

'Sure as shit, Chief. I seen many a flood. All the signs are there. One more day.'

'You have truly earned your money,' Caesar smiled, then turned to the other officers. 'Alright. The legions sit tight for one more day. As soon as the rain clears and the river starts to drop again, two legions are to replace the lower, closer bridge. That means four days and we should have working supply lines again. But I am still concerned about the supply wagons that are overdue, and our Gallic allies. Galronus? I want you to take a small cavalry force and look for them. It would take the infantry or wagons forever to move far enough upstream to find another crossing, but you can take spare mounts for each man and move swiftly. Head up to the first ford or bridge you find and cross the river. Locate my supplies and direct them to the lower bridge.'

Galronus bowed his head.

'Anyone want to buy a goat?' asked the farmer hopefully.

* * *

Galronus and his men reined in their mounts in the shade at the edge of a copse of birch and elm. It had been a gruelling two days for the cavalry. Dispatched by Caesar as soon as the bridges had been surveyed, Galronus had ridden back to the camp and gathered a full ala of horsemen, mostly Gallic or Belgic auxiliaries, but with a few small units of regulars among them – each type of horseman had their own unique methods, after all. They had set off to the northeast in the driving rain, leading a spare horse each – most of the cavalry's excess mounts, in fact. The drenched men and horses had ridden at a good, mile-eating pace for the rest of that day and the morning of the next before finding the first crossing of the Sicoris, a ford constructed by the local tribes in ages past.

They had then turned back south and raced on, changing horses periodically to give them adequate rest and pausing for breaks as often as Galronus felt safe. Fortunately, that afternoon, just as the goat-herder had predicted, the rain cleared and the sun returned to Hispania, burning the moisture from the land in thick banks of mist. The riders had spent the night under makeshift shelters, gradually drying out, and this morning they were comfortable for the first time in days, though many had caught chills and coughs from the conditions of their journey. A constant chorus of snorts and choking noises accompanied the cluster of three hundred riders.

Finally, here amid the steaming land and the verdant trees, Galronus rested. He had called a two hour break for a mid-day meal, the longest rest they'd had during the day since they'd set out from the camp. The horses were tethered with long leads amid some of the richest grass they had seen, green turf given strong life by the combination of gleaming Hispanic sun and days of heavy rain. The men collapsed onto logs, rocks and turf and unwrapped their bucellatum hardtack biscuits and the meagre remains of bread and cured meat they had brought with them. There would be enough left in the packs for two more days. What would happen then no one could predict. Galronus grumbled to himself that he'd not halved the rations yesterday, but he'd believed there would be enough to see them back across the river if they stretched it. And there would. If they turned back soon. But it all depended upon how long they needed to be out here. He didn't like to think of the consequences of failure and returning to Caesar empty handed.

He chewed the pork, wincing at the saltiness, and washed it down with a flask of extremely watered wine, barely registering a taste it was so weak. Some preternatural sense made him look up just as one of the *exploratores* scouts emerged over the crest of the hill a quarter of a mile away, moving at a fast pace. The hairs prickled on the back of his neck, and without needing to hear whatever the man had to say, he rose and swallowed his mouthful.

'Arm up. To horse.'

Around him there was a moment of blinking surprise, and then every man discarded his bread and biscuit carelessly, grabbing swords and helmets and running to their horses.

'Leave the spare mounts tethered. Looks like trouble.'

Men were hauling themselves into their saddles and unslinging shields from where they had been tied for travel. Galronus pulled himself up onto Eonna and settled himself between the horns of the saddle. Everywhere was the grunting and coughing of men, the shush of chain shirts, the snorting and whickering of horses and the clonk of spear shafts and shields. The rider was getting closer now and if Galronus had needed any confirmation that he had been correct in his anticipation it was the speed and desperation of the man's ride.

'Form turmae!'

As the riders moved into their units ready for action, rather than staying as a loose travelling formation, Galronus trotted his mount out a few dozen paces toward the approaching rider. Two more of the exploratores were closing, too.

As the man reached the cavalry, he reined in urgently and gestured over his shoulder.

'What is it?' Galronus demanded in the native Gallic tongue, his accent these days an odd combination of Belgic and Latin.

The man heaved in a deep breath.

'Supply convoy. Aedui and Ruteni, I think. Under attack.'

'How many?'

The man's face hardened and Galronus felt a twinge of worry at the expression. 'Maybe two and a half thousand warriors – archers and horse. As many civilians again as that. Half a hundred wagons, too. They've pulled back to a hill.'

'But how many attackers?'

'Many. A flood of cavalry, mostly Hispanic. And legionaries too. I saw the standards of two different legions, but there were so many men it must be at least three.'

Galronus whistled through his teeth. Possibly twenty thousand Pompeians, and only three thousand warriors to fight them off even if Galronus joined in. A horrible moment of decision fell upon him. He had served both the Remi and Rome as a leader of men over the past decade, but never had he experienced a level of command with such momentous choices weighing upon him.

To rush and help the beleaguered convoy would be to court disaster and might mean the end of them all. Certainly the odds were horrifying. But to leave and return with news for Caesar would be to condemn those Gauls to death and to deny any hope of supplies to the legions. His eyes rose to the featureless blue sky.

'Great Cicolluis, Mars of Rome, father of war, place your hands around us today.'

He nodded and gestured for the scout to move out of the way.

'Officers to me. Ride on.'

As the three hundred strong cavalry unit pounded off at a trot in the direction whence the scout had come, the various commanders left their men and converged on Galronus out to the side, keeping pace.

'The odds are heavily against us,' he shouted to his men over the pounding of hooves. 'They have retreated to a hill. From what the scout says they are half civilian and half warriors, those warriors being Ruteni and Aedui. Many of you have fought against or alongside those tribes, and we know how they prosecute war. On the defensive they will have drawn up the wagons and tribesfolk at the high point and surrounded them with Ruteni archers. What foot they have will be defending the archers. The cavalry should be harrying the enemy, but in the circumstances they will either be dismounted and holding the hill or lined up on horseback fighting the enemy off.'

They had to be brave and strong to have made it this long against such a force, but they would not last much longer.

'I can only presume that the Romans are paying a heavy toll in souls to the Ruteni archers and are keeping their distance. As soon as the archers run out of arrows, it will be over in heartbeats. If the Roman commander is wily he will be delaying, letting the Ruteni expend their arrows on the Hispanic horse and waiting until they are helpless to send in his legions. We have one advantage and one chance.'

It was a small chance. But if it worked, it would be the stuff of legend. The sort of thing Fronto would do...

'We do not know the enemy commanders, but they will be Pompeians and probably aristocrats. They will not be with their legions, but standing at a highpoint to direct the battle with just their Praetorian units to guard them. Most Roman officers fight thus. One well-placed sword blow to the neck of the army's senior commander could break the attack.'

A regular Roman cavalryman shook his head. 'That won't work, sir. The whole system of tribunes and centurions is designed to keep the army fighting even when their senior men fall.'

Galronus nodded. 'During ordinary circumstances, yes. But this is civil war. This is a war of commanders. The troops seem to have little heart for fighting their own people. The directions of the generals are critical here. With their seniors dead and the new attack flying Roman banners, we will see just how tied to Pompey's skirts these men are.'

The decurion looked less than convinced, but nodded anyway and fell silent.

The officers dismissed back to their units, the ala rode on, after a short while cresting the hill whence the scout had come, and Galronus' breath caught in his throat. The land perhaps a mile ahead was awash with men. A sea of figures. As the scout had said, perhaps five or six thousand were gathered on a hill with their wagon train, but three times as many were lined up on the flat land before them. The legions stood in neat squares, three of them, if a little understrength in Galronus' estimation. They must have slipped from Ilerda during the storm, unnoticed by the Caesarians. The native cavalry they had brought were riding in three wide, loose circles, continually moving, coming close to the defenders and throwing the occasional javelin, then riding back out of danger. Their tactics might be troublesome to infantry, but they were taking far more numerous casualties than they were causing, their javelins killing a few, but the Ruteni arrow storm plucking rider after rider from his saddle.

Sure enough, at the rear, some distance from the reserve lines, a small knot of men on a low rise were surrounded by horsemen. The commander and his staff and bodyguard.

Some quarter mile behind them, back toward the river, there was a long, low ridge. Galronus grinned.

'I think we can find other ways to break their morale,' he shouted to his men. 'Direct your men without loud signals. We head west and into the defile. That ridge will keep us out of sight until we are almost on them.'

Unnoticed as yet by either side in the battle, Galronus' cavalry ala veered sharply away from the crest of the hill and back out of sight, making first for a scattering of trees and then for the low valley that ran toward the rear of the enemy. Some time in the days following the birth of the world, the gods had moulded the land here into a series of parallel ridges, like spines bulging from the ground. This was one such fold, and would hide them from the action until they were upon it.

'Send me the regular cavalry musicians,' he shouted to the nearest Roman officer.

* * *

Publius Cassius Bucco was not happy. A year ago he had secured his tribunate in the military with the patronage of his father's friends and had looked forward to his term of service, a first step on a road which could even lead to consulship in the future. He'd had dreams of gleaming armour and red plumes, of sipping good Falernian while his legion romped through the ranks of some barbarian horde and earned him a reputation.

His dreams had been shattered repeatedly since then. Assigned to a legion who supported Pompey, he had been hopeful. The fat old oligarch was supposed to be the saviour of Rome, so the opportunity for glory had seemed likely. Then he had been sent to Hispania to serve under an angry man, while Pompey had hoisted up his toga and run like a chastised child to Greece, leaving Rome in the lurch.

Since arriving with the Second Vernacular as one of the five junior tribunes he had suffered constant disappointments. The legion were not gleaming Romans. Half of them spoke Latin with a notably Hispanic accent, having been locally recruited. Petreius, their overall commander was a man with a tongue like a scourge and a temper fit to burst through walls. And then they had joined with Afranius and the legions had gathered. The two commanders seemed to hate each other and disagreed on everything, the only thing holding them together being their allegiance to Pompey

Then they had moved to this gods-forsaken dung hole and shut themselves up in a camp next to Ilerda, where they had waited until first General Fabius arrived with his legions, then Caesar himself. And while they had managed to stay in command of Ilerda, the two generals had constantly promised their men that the siege would flounder and fail and that Caesar would run out of food and have to leave. Yet the cursed proconsul clung to Ilerda like a bad smell, and his legions were going nowhere.

In the privacy of his room, Cassius had pondered more than once whether perhaps his father had hitched his family's cart to the wrong horse with Pompey.

Then, in the midst of that horrible twelve day storm, scouts had brought word that Caesar's supply column was approaching, and three legions had been dispatched secretly in the mire and the downpour to capture or destroy them.

And now here they were.

Cassius' legate, the ex-consul Gnaeus Cornelius Lentulus Clodianus, was the senior man in the field, a close friend of Pompey's and at sixty five years one of the most experienced and longest-serving commanders in the army, and as such had been given command of the entire force. And while Cassius had to admit to being no great tactician, he felt certain Lentulus Clodianus had got it wrong. Privately he grumbled the old stories that Lentulus had been resoundingly beaten by Spartacus during the servile wars. He seemed to be displaying similarly poor military qualities here.

The native horsemen were dying in droves with little noticeable effect on the Gauls on the hill. And while they were all barbarians up there, some of them were flying *vexillum* flags bearing Caesar's infamous bull emblem, so there was no doubting these were fighting for Rome's populist hero. They did not look like a force that were worried or about to be broken.

And now, steaming under the hot sun, Cassius was learning what the main duties of a junior tribune were – apparently mostly holding the legate's cloak or his helmet, fetching things for him, running errands or playing messenger. It was demeaning work for a man supposedly in high office.

And he should be on a horse. A tribune was a senior officer. It looked bad for a senior officer to be on foot. Yet here he was struggling up the slope toward the legate and his staff, carrying a dispatch from the primus pilus who seemed to treat him like a clerk.

The Praetorian guards stepped to the side to allow him through, and Cassius approached Legate Lentulus, who was sipping wine and engaged in light hearted banter with the commander of one of the other legions. Damn him.

'Legatus, a dispatch from the primus pilus.'

He handed over the wax tablet and the legate opened it, ran his gaze down the scratched marks, nodded, scribbled a quick response and then slapped it back into Cassius' hands. That was it! Dismissed without a word. Assuming the fresh scratching was a reply, Cassius turned and pushed his way down the hill between the guards once more until he had his back to everyone and could glower the way he felt he needed to.

Grumbling things about clerks and slaves and messengers and doddering consular revenants who had no manners, he began to make his way across the open ground toward the legions, who still waited in their ordered ranks.

He had covered a third of the distance, not hurrying lest he be given an even more onerous task, when the gods unleashed the river of death upon the plains of Ilerda.

A scream announced the attack. Cassius turned in shock and his eyes bulged. The Praetorians guarding the officers were being cut down mercilessly by a large force of cavalry bearing more of Caesar's bull banners. Even as he watched in horror, Cassius saw the legate of the Eighth Cantabrian disappear in a welter of blood, some Caesarian horseman whooping a victory call.

In moments the hilltop was no longer the Pompeian command tribunal, but a charnel house commanded by howling horsemen.

Cassius blinked in shock. What should he do?

His eyes slipped back to the three legions and their native horse besieging the hill. They had not even noticed yet. The noise of their own fight had effectively drowned out what was happening behind. Even as he panicked, the legions finally realised what was going on, and desperate calls began to blare out.

A centurion emerged from the rear of the Second, running toward him and waving at the hill.

'What's happening, Tribune?'

Someone was asking him? Deferring to him?'

'Errr....'

'Tribune, who are they?'

'Caesar's men. Cavalry. Lots of them.'

'Not just cavalry,' the centurion replied bluntly, without using rank, title or honorific.

'What?'

'Listen,' the centurion said. 'Can you hear those calls? They're legion calls. This is just the vanguard. Caesar's legions are coming.'

Cassius' blood ran cold. Really? Here? It seemed impossible, but then the sounds he could hear did sound a lot like the calls he'd heard from the legions at Ilerda.

'Errr…'

'What do we do, Tribune?'

Cassius blinked. Why was the man asking him? Legates made the decisions. Or in their absence the senior tribune. Or, he supposed, when they were both gone…'

He realised with another chill that there was every likelihood that three legates, seventeen tribunes and a number of prefects had been cut to pieces on that hill by Caesar's men. Was it possible that he was now the most senior man of Pompey's on the battlefield.

'Sir?' insisted the centurion.

He felt sure that he could turn the situation to his advantage and wipe out the men on the hill if he could just think, but there was no time. And if Caesar's legions were closing, ready to trap them…'

'Sound the recall,' he told the centurion. 'Pass it to all three legions and the cavalry. We move at a double march. We break directly south and move until we know we are clear and then turn and retreat to Ilerda.'

The centurion saluted and ran off to his musician. Cassius swallowed nervously, looking at his army, then at the Gauls on the hill and the cavalry flooding the rise where the officers had been. It could very well mean the end of his military career. A still-born career, in fact. But at least this way the legions would survive and the two squabbling commanders could use them again. He *could* attempt to lead some heroic action here, but what would happen then if his three legions were crushed and butchered by Caesar's men? No. Better that they live.

The Pompeian calls went up and the army broke off its attack in moments, turning in order but at speed and leaving the field.

* * *

Galronus grinned as he watched the legions depart.

'That might be the most chancy, audacious move I have ever seen, sir,' the regular cavalry decurion laughed.

'I've certainly never seen infantry outpace cavalry before,' Galronus grinned. 'Magnificent attempt at saving their own skin, I'd say.'

The decurion chuckled and saluted, then returned to his unit. Galronus heaved a sigh of relief. The calls the cavalry musicians had made, hidden behind the ridges, had sounded a lot like legionary commands. Of course, none of them knew the true melodies for such, but they'd heard them often enough to be able to roughly mimic them, and it seemed the Pompeians had bought the ruse and fled, fearing they were facing Caesar's legions, and not just an ala of three hundred horsemen.

The force on the hill was beginning to descend and sheathe weapons, setting their carts moving, and a small group of noblemen were ahead, riding to meet their saviours.

'Greetings,' said one of the horseman in thickly-accented Latin. 'I am Cisiambo, Prince among the Aedui and ally of the Roman war leader Caesar. We bear the same standards. I believe you are his men?'

Galronus smiled at the arm-ringed, braided Gaul regarding him with an odd expression. Something that was a mix of Celtic distain and allied camaraderie. It was a weird combination.

'Greetings,' Galronus replied in turn. 'I am Galronus, prince and war leader of the Remi, staff officer of Caesar and senator of Rome.'

An odd thrill ran through him. It was the first time he'd ever said those words. It had always felt to him as though it would be an empty honour to be a senator. A title without strength. But being able to say it to someone felt oddly impressive. And when he combined it with his exalted rank, Caesar's name and his own lineage…

The Aedui was wrong-footed, unsure whether to be impressed or not.

'We have supplies and reinforcements for Caesar. We reached the river, but the bridges were gone. We turned and found ourselves pursued.'

'Pompey's dogs,' Galronus snorted. 'They run when true warriors face them. You did well, my friend, prince among the Aedui. We have had bad rains, and the floods have taken the bridges, but the matter is already being attended to. Follow me and I will lead you to Caesar.'

As the newly-arriving troops moved the supplies off the hill and the two forces joined, Galronus watched, implacably, from the hill. It was odd. The Remi were a tribe of the Belgae, almost as Germanic as they were Gallic. These were Aedui, southern Gauls who had been influenced for ten generations by Rome. And yet while they should feel a certain blood tie, all Galronus felt was natural superiority. He was Remi, but he was Roman. He had ridden with his tribe to join Caesar's army in their early days in Gaul. They had been honoured for it. The Remi had emerged from a decade of war stronger than ever, with ten times their original influence, cities where their villages had been, and Roman citizenship for their nobles. He had lost something of what he had been, but what he had gained had more than filled the gap. He was part Belgae, part Roman, and in many respects better than either. Certainly, he knew he was better than Cisiambo, which was a thought that would never have occurred to him a decade ago. Was this part of what it was to be Roman? Was this what powered their self-possession and strength? It was an impressive feeling, deep into the bones.

In an odd moment, as he welcomed the Ruteni and the Aedui to Caesar's army in the name of the Senate and people of Rome, Galronus had an epiphany. He was Roman now. No matter what he might call himself, he was now as Roman as Fronto. Probably more so, he snorted.

It would take too long to bring the supplies via the upstream crossing they had found, and the wagons might not make it, but with luck Caesar would already be working on a new bridge. Galronus would lead the supplies to the lower bridge site and hope that things were underway.

* * *

Fronto stood behind the sudis stake defences and watched the enemy come. Behind him, Felix and the Eleventh Legion braced themselves.

Already, even early enough in the morning that the sun was still just a ribbon of gold above the peaks, work on the new bridge proceeded apace. Mamurra had set three entire legions to work on it, one procuring the necessary materials, one turning those materials into usable components and the third assembling them into a good, strong bridge, as strong as a timber crossing could be and far better than the ones the storm had demolished. Work had begun yesterday at dawn, and had proceeded slowly and with great difficulty, for Petreius and Afranius had sent auxiliary troops to the far bank, where they had lurked behind wicker screens and launched arrows, spears and sling bullets at the working legions.

Caesar's irritation at the slow pace, which Mamurra had admitted would stretch out the production time to more than a week, had driven him to finding a new solution. The legions had been turned to a new project for two hours, manufacturing light wattle-and-hide-sided boats of the sort they had seen in Britannia a few years earlier. Then, during the night, the Eleventh had been ferried across the Sicoris in those boats a few miles upstream and out of sight while the enemy retreated to the safety of Ilerda for the hours of darkness.

Fronto could imagine the surprise among those Pompeian troops this morning, as they laughed and joked and sauntered off to the river to cause trouble for the working legionaries again, only to find a full legion encamped on this side of the flow waiting for them.

The Pompeians were not legionaries. Mainly they were Balearics, Carpetani and Oretani – slingers, archers and sword-bearing infantry in tribal groups.

'Shields up,' bellowed Felix beside him, watching the approaching auxiliaries. 'Ready those pila.'

He cast a meaningful look at Fronto, who nodded and stepped back. He was not wearing a red plume now, but he would still easily be identifiable as a senior officer by the rest of his attire, and he had learned a harsh lesson about that now. He stepped back and watched as the Eleventh confidently lined the makeshift fence of pointed timber and pulled their right arms back, the points of the pila lined up with their ear along their arm, ready to throw. Some men had the shaft gripped less than half way along. Others favoured a heavier variant and clutched it closer to the head for balance. Still others used the old Greek method, a throwing cord wrapped around both weapon and fingers to give extra lift during the throw. Each to their own in Felix's legion. Whatever worked best for the man.

The Hispanics approached the defences, their confidence melting away as they realised what they were up against. Some native leader shouted a command and the front lines of spear men stopped and threw their javelins. It was a shambles. They had stopped far too early, worried about the coming barrage of pila, and so their missiles almost entirely clattered and slammed into the ground many paces short of the Roman line.

There was no homogeneity of command among these auxilia, led by their own tribal nobles and not by a Roman prefect, and each unit fought independently as though the others were not there. The swordsmen pushed between the spears and, spotting the pila ready to throw, ground to a halt, their rather inadequate small shields coming up defensively. Fronto could see the men of the Eleventh straining, desperate to throw.

'Hold them steady,' ordered Felix. They would not waste the missiles on these infantry.

Sure enough, the slingers and archers were now approaching, some filtering out to the right to make for the river bank nearby where they could take opportunistic shots, others heading for the makeshift fortification and Fronto's men. The legate found himself muttering under his breath, urging the primus pilus to give the order, but Felix knew his business. Finally, as the sling stones began to whip out and thud into shields and greaves and ding off helmets, he cleared his throat.

'Iacta!'

Four hundred pila arced up and over the intervening ground, past the enemy javelins lying harmless in the dust. Felix had been precise with his timing. The archers were drawing back the strings of their bows and raising them, sighting ready to release, as the pila struck home. Archers and slingers fell all across the enemy force, pinned to the ground or to each other, shafts through torsos, limbs and heads. Mis-shot arrows launched up into the air at odd angles, or down, or even into their friends nearby. All was chaos. The attack floundered instantly.

'Pila to the front,' Felix shouted. Fronto nodded his approval as across the line another four hundred of the deadly missiles were fed forward to the men at the defences. Even now he could see out of the corner of his eye another batch being moved up ready, and more were being transported across the river for their use.

The enemy saw the pila being handed to the men and readied, and Fronto could sense their tension, their readiness to break. A single shout of alarm started it. Somewhere among the archers, someone cried out and in moments the Hispanic auxiliaries exploded outwards like a drop of rain on a marble slab. Many fled back toward Ilerda, mostly archers and slingers, unwilling to face a second such barrage. They had no heavy infantry support, no legionaries, and were largely defenceless. It was one thing to stand beside a river and play huntsman, picking off Roman engineers. It was another to face a legion able to fight back.

One of the enemy leaders had different ideas. While the missile troops scattered, the swordsmen of Carpetani origin rushed forward, seemingly intent on removing the threat at the sudis barriers rather than evading it.

The men of the Eleventh faced this meagre threat with confidence as they steadied their missiles.

'Now,' Felix shouted, and another four hundred pila arced up, the angle considerably lower this time, aimed at the advancing swordsmen. They were brave, Fronto had to give them that. Despite the slew of deaths they came on, launching themselves at the defenders who, at Felix's next command, had drawn their swords and were ready.

Fronto watched, never even for a moment considering the possibility that his men might lose. The Eleventh held their makeshift barrier with ease as the Carpetani swordsmen pushed and hacked, trying to negotiate the dreadful points of the sharpened stakes, only to find themselves prey to the Roman blades. They fell like wheat to the sickle, and by the time a dozen heartbeats had passed, the attack broke and the infantry were rushing back along the river bank toward Ilerda. As the legionaries relaxed and watched their enemy run, Felix gave the orders to sound off. It transpired, as Fronto listened, that they had lost twenty-some men in the press, while the ground beyond the defences was littered with Pompeian dead and their thrown or discarded weapons.

Fronto stepped regretfully past a young legionary lying lifeless near the stake fence, his helmet dented so deeply inwards from a sling bullet that it had smashed the skull and driven into the brain, and strolled back toward the river and watched the work.

Three days at most now, as long as the Eleventh could continue to hold the bank and protect the workmen. He felt confident in that. With three legions at work here and one protecting them, there were still two legions in the main camp facing Ilerda. Fronto could not imagine a general worth his salt committing a sizeable force to stop the bridge and thereby endangering his stronghold. No, the bridge was not worth that risk. The Pompeians were willing to commit a small auxiliary force to irritate and slow Caesar, but they would not send their legions here.

With a sense of satisfaction, he toured his makeshift camp, Felix falling in alongside him. His mood soured a little at the sight of Salvius Cursor standing at the camp's southeast corner with two more centurions. Bracing himself, prepared to grit his teeth and not argue in front of the men, he approached Salvius.

'How are things going, Tribune?'

Salvius Cursor saluted. 'Well, Legate. Permission to begin work on a more permanent defence?'

Fronto mused for a moment. With only half rations, and short on sleep after their night time crossing, the legion could do with rest. But it *would* be helpful to have better defences here. He was sure Petreius and his men would not come at the moment, but circumstances might change, and having a fortification at this end of the bridge could certainly be useful.

'Agreed, but only in small shifts. Take a cohort at a time for the work and do it in two hour shifts so the rest of the men can rest.'

Salvius Cursor saluted again, his face registering his disapproval and disagreement, but his mouth remaining mercifully shut tight.

'Hello, what's this?' Felix murmured, gesturing out from the fence of stakes. Fronto followed his gaze and spotted the dust cloud. The three men stood silent for a long moment, watching.

Fronto could feel the primus pilus tensing, ready to give the order for his men to fall in at the defences again.

'Are those Caesar's flags?' Fronto muttered.

There was another long pause, and then Salvius Cursor nodded. 'It is the cavalry returning. And it looks like they found the supplies.'

The men watched with a wave of relief breaking over them. Three hundred cavalry had left the camp four days ago, but the approaching column, moving confidently and swiftly below the red and gold bull flags of Caesar, numbered more than a thousand horsemen, with thousands more on foot, a line of wagons stirring up immense clouds of dust. Moreover, there seemed to be a huge number of cattle being driven alongside, adding to the grime.

Even as they watched, a small group of horsemen broke away from the front of the column and rode off toward them. Half a dozen legionaries scurried across at Felix's barked command and dismantled part of the sudis fence, leaving a gap for a gate. Fronto, Felix and Salvius stepped out through the open section and into the wide ground before the camp. They were on foot, for horses had not been ferried across, given the small size and light construction of the boats they had used.

It became clear as they approached that the majority of the horsemen were decurions of Gallic nobles, but the two riders at the fore were the leaders. As they approached and reined in, Fronto nodded a greeting, grinning at Galronus.

'Caesar will be pleased to see you, my friend. You found the supplies, then?'

'That and more,' laughed the Remi noble. We've a few thousand reinforcements under Prince Cisiambo of the Aedui here,' he indicated the other rider, who bowed his head. 'We routed a sizeable force of Petreius' men, and on the way back we stumbled across a party of Pompeian foragers. They ran like the wind when they saw us, so we gathered up their cattle and grain and added it to the supplies. I reckon the legions will eat like kings for a while.'

Fronto sighed with relief. 'Good, 'cause my lads are getting a mite hungry now.'

'How's the bridge?'

'Getting there, but it'll be a couple of days yet. We've been having trouble with enemy archers, but I think we have it under control now. You'd best get the caravan into the camp and rest everyone.'

He turned to Salvius Cursor. 'You'd best get to work on your defences, but string it out and double the camp size. We have to make room for our guests, now.'

Things were finally looking up. Now all they had to do was find a way to break Ilerda.

Chapter Twelve

16th of Quintilis - Ilerda

FRONTO leaned back in the tent and sighed with relief, wiggling his toes as he poured another cup of wine and water. Galronus and Felix both followed suit, though Antonius remained sitting upright in the campaign chair, his cup barely registering emptiness before it was full once more. His consumption was the subject of amazement among the others, given that at the end of the night, having drunk enough wine to float a liburnian, he would stand, stretch, and then go about his duties as though naught but water had passed his lips. In fact, water most certainly hadn't passed his lips, the wine he drank entirely uncut. Knowing that Antonius had intended to join them, Fronto had requisitioned two extra jars of wine. But he could hardly blame the man. Everyone was in a celebratory mood.

The last five days had seen fortunes begin to change. Following a period of dangerously low supplies, hunger and increasing discontent, the new sturdy bridge had been completed, the supply chain reactivated and reinforcements and a wealth of food and goods arrived. Then, in an unexpected turn, a number of ambassadors had arrived from various local towns and tribal centres, renouncing their allegiance to Pompey and his officers and taking their oath to Caesar. Two units of native warriors had come over to join them, one of whom had been serving as roving foragers for Petreius, even, working out of Ilerda across the river.

It seemed that the ongoing conditions of siege and the resilience of the Caesarian force were beginning at last to have an effect on the defenders and their subjects. While it had not brought Caesar's army any closer to taking Ilerda itself, it had strengthened their position and weakened that of Pompey's men. As long as the two Pompeian commanders maintained their huge supply base in Ilerda town and access over that bridge to the rich forage lands beyond, though, the siege would go on interminably.

'I'm surprised you're not with Caesar, though,' Fronto said, gesturing to Antonius. 'He likes to keep you close when he's planning things, and I saw his expression earlier. He's planning furiously now, because he can feel victory almost at his fingertips.'

Antonius rolled his eyes.

'Not always. You know the old man. Sometimes he plays things so close that no one but him knows what's going on. After the briefing I hung around to see if he needed me and I was all-but dismissed. He had that glint in his eye, though.'

Fronto nodded and the four men gradually wound down the night until finally Felix yawned, stretched and rose, bidding farewell to all and heading back to his own quarters. Galronus followed shortly after, and some time after midnight, Fronto finally managed to turf out Antonius, who, he noted, took that remaining jar of wine and a cup with him.

Alone at last and with a comfortably fuzzy head, Fronto shuffled down onto his bed and lay flat. He dozed off quickly and spent a strange time lost in a dream where he was chasing the boys through the streets of Massilia, waving papers at them and having to leap hurdles that all bore Caesar's bull emblem.

How long he'd been asleep he couldn't say, but when he woke it was in utter confusion. The interior of the tent resolved in the gloom and he couldn't reconcile it with what was happening in his head, which was still in Massilia trying to catch the boys. A figure blurred into vague shape and it took a long moment for him to realise it was a full-grown adult figure and not little Marcus.

'Wha…'

'Get up, Marcus.'

Fronto blinked a few times. Galronus. It was Galronus.

'What?'

'Get up.'

Accepting the offered hand and using it to pull himself up from the cot, Fronto rose unsteadily to his feet. 'What's going on?'

'Just come on.'

'I need my boots. My cloak…'

'It's warm and the turf is dry. Come on.'

Still utterly confused, Fronto followed his friend from the bed and out through the tent. As they stopped, the Remi noble pointed off toward the left hill – the walled town. Fronto squinted into the night. His eyes shot open as he realised what he was looking at.

'Fire?'

Galronus nodded. 'It's been going for a quarter of an hour at least. One of the decurions woke me. Caesar's down by the camp gate. The men who came over from Petreius' army say it's the granaries.'

Fronto peered at the orange glow from behind the walls of Ilerda town and the roiling black smoke pouring into the purple sky, golden sparks rising on the plume of heat. It was a conflagration of impressive proportions, and the thickness of the smoke suggested that the inhabitants were trying desperately to extinguish it with bucket after bucket of water. They were clearly failing. That was the problem with wooden structures filled with grain. They burned hot and powerful.

A suspicion washed through him.

'Only the granaries?'

'Apparently.'

'That's a very selective conflagration, isn't it?'

Galronus shrugged and Fronto folded his arms. 'Stay here. I'm going to belt my tunic and put on my cloak and boots.'

A few moments later he was out once more and attired respectably. 'Come on.'

With Galronus at his heel, he made his way through the camp toward the gate where Caesar would be standing and observing this lucky turn of events. All across the camp, men had emerged from their tents and were gazing up at the burning of Ilerda. Many were smiling with relief, for it meant another change in their fortunes, though no one would cheer, for the burning of a Roman town was not in truth a subject for joy.

A small knot of officers stood atop the gate, watching what was happening at Ilerda, and Fronto had to nudge his way between other staff officers.

'They're containing it well,' Antonius noted, gesturing with his wine cup, the dark contents sloshing about but not quite slopping over the rim.

'Not well enough,' Fabius replied. 'That's the bulk of their supplies. Now they'll be at least as reliant on forage as us. More so, with civilians to keep fed as well.'

Fronto narrowed his eyes. 'I would hate to think we had stooped to starving civilians just to gain the edge militarily.'

Caesar turned an unreadable expression upon him. 'I can assure you, Fronto, that I gave no such order.'

I'll bet, thought Fronto in the privacy of his head. No such order. A few well-placed hints or suggestions to those former Pompeians who had come over to their side would have done the trick without the need for an order.

'This changes the whole siege,' Antonius smiled.

'How so?' Caesar frowned.

'They don't have a huge supply of grain to fall back on.'

'While that is certainly true, they have good forage and excellent access to it over their stone bridge. They can still hold us off for many weeks.'

'Then we need to cut off their access to forage,' Fronto murmured. 'Or make foraging difficult and dangerous for them. They don't have much in the way of cavalry, while we have plenty. We could harry them and stop their forage parties. Galronus proved that when he brought in the cattle from that little raid of his.'

The Remi, next to him, shook his head. 'With just the bridge a few miles away it takes hours at best to get a sizeable cavalry force across, and if we run into trouble we might get trapped, unable to cross back at speed. I have no desire to waste the entire cavalry force trapped on the far bank as we try to feed two men abreast across the bridge while four legions butcher us. Remember what happened to the foragers before we arrived?'

'Then if the bridge is inadequate, we need a better crossing. Mamurra?'

The siege engineer turned, his brow creased in thought. 'Building endless bridges is an inelegant solution.'

'Then find me an elegant one,' Caesar said, that glint back in his eye once more.

* * *

In fact, It had taken Mamurra but the blink of an eye to decide upon his elegant solution. Within the hour he had set upon an idea. Three further hours of riding with a Praetorian escort had provided him with the location for his plan, and a further three hours had ensued persuading Caesar and the staff that it would work. The famous siege engineer had a reputation unsurpassed and few men – even veteran engineers – would argue with him, but this latest idea had seemed ridiculous.

Two days now the work had been going on, but this morning Mamurra had summoned them to his work site three miles upstream. It was, he said, almost time.

Fronto stood with Galronus on the podium, formed by the spoil heap from the works, Caesar, Antonius, Fabius and the other officers all present. Mamurra looked confident. The morning already sizzled in the searing sunlight and the sounds of nature – bees, cicadas and birds were audible as part of the tapestry, woven through the gurgling flow of the Sicoris and the tense sound of cohorts of men waiting.

Fronto cleared his throat. 'Look, I know you know your engineering, and I can hardly claim to be grounded in any kind of science, but it seems to me that water always stays at the same level. You just can't make it lower in one place. It doesn't work like that.'

Mamurra turned with that long-suffering expression borne by all engineers when they had to explain their works to the uninitiated. 'That is most certainly true, Fronto. But the fact is that the same quantity of water pours along the Sicoris no matter how wide or narrow, deep or shallow it is. Floods, meltwater and drought can change that, of course, but no matter, it will still throw the same volume of water along its course. And what happens if you empty a small, deep bath and use the water to fill a wider bath, Fronto?'

With a sour face, aware that he was being treated like an idiot student, Fronto sighed. 'The bath will be wide but shallower.'

Precisely. The Sicoris here is too deep for the cavalry to cross safely, as could be said for its course all the way from the confluence many miles up into the hills. But here, the surrounding ground is low, almost at river level, the ground is soft, made even softer by the many days of rain, as you can see from the number of landslides along the banks. Easy digging. And here there are rocks in the river bed, which my scouts have seen from the trees. Those rocks have, over the years, gathered sediment and raised the river bed a little. If there is to be a crossing, this is the place. All we had to do was take this narrow bath and make it a wide one, if you understand my thinking.'

Fronto grunted an answer that could have been anything and went back to watching.

'Are we ready, then?' Antonius asked.

'All is in place. Watch carefully, gentlemen.'

At a single blast from a horn, the work parties bent to their final task.

Two days of labour had seriously scarred the landscape. A single channel some thirty feet wide and almost a thousand paces long, at a depth of just five feet, now ran parallel to the river, separated by just ten feet of untouched ground. Two more channels had been constructed parallel with it, narrower and slightly shallower. A single cohort had moved across the bridge and created a similar channel on the far side. All these four new channels were currently dry and empty, but at each end, where they met the river bank, the water had been kept out with a single wall of tightly bound timber.

As the officers watched with a mix of scepticism and wonder, the soldiers hauled on ropes and tugged those wooden obstructions from the large channel with some difficulty. River water surged into the thirty foot channel the instant the timbers moved, almost carrying the temporary wall and the soldiers holding it away, though by some miracle they managed to hold position and lift the wood from the water. Other men waited only until that channel was full, then tugged away the board walls to the next, smaller, narrower channel, allowing the event to repeat on a slightly smaller scale. Then the third channel was opened, and across the river: the same.

Fronto watched, impressed. The ten foot earth banks that had separated the channels were almost swept away immediately, eroded and turned to sediment before his very eyes. In half a hundred heartbeats, he watched the Sicoris widen from eighty paces to around one hundred and twenty. And as the waters spread out, the river bed became visible, particularly since it was rising slightly with the muck washed into it in the process.

'The God of the Sicoris favours Caesar, I believe,' Mamurra said grandly, flinging out his arms to the river theatrically.

The general, his eyes narrowed, turned to Galronus. 'What say you?'

The Remi noble peered at the river. 'Unless anything changes, that presents no problem as far as I can see. I'd say at the deepest it would reach the shoulder of most cavalry horses. And wide enough for the best part of a turma to cross at a time. Should be a swift route to the far bank.'

'Good. Are your riders rested?'

Galronus shrugged. 'As rested as they can be. They are ready for action, certainly.'

'Very well,' the general smiled. 'Take as many of the cavalry as you feel can reasonably be controlled in a single column, equip yourselves for several days, and cross that river. I want you to range far and wide, find any of Petreius and Afranius' foragers and deal with them. I want their food supply to grind to a halt. Can you do that for me?'

'We can, Caesar.'

'Good. See to it.'

* * *

21st of Quintilis

21st of Quintilis

Galronus waved his men forward with just a touch of nervousness. Caesar had, after all, told him to 'range far and wide', but Galronus felt he was very much at the limit of what the general had intended. By his estimate he was now between twenty five and thirty miles south-west of Ilerda, into the hills and away from the good grain lands.

He had split his force once they had begun to harry the Pompeian foragers, two alae in each group. One had ranged the lands north of Ilerda, toward the Caesarian supply lines. Another had the remit to continually circuit and patrol the fields south of Ilerda, making grain harvesting impossible for Petreius and Afranius' men. Galronus, with the third, had followed a lead that was intriguing, if dangerous.

At the southern edge of the grain lands, they had found a small supply depot of Pompeian soldiers. The infantry had swiftly surrendered at the sight of six hundred veteran cavalry bearing down on their tiny compound, and had offered the information that they were part of a chain of such posts between Ilerda and some town by the name of Octogesa. They had refused to reveal anything further and Galronus had accepted that, certain that Caesar would disapprove of torturing legionaries for information every bit as much as he himself did.

But the knowledge that there was some sort of supply line leading off to another town was too interesting to pass up the chance of inspection. Leaving the other two forces to ravage the Pompeian foragers, Galronus had taken his men and forged on in the direction of this other town.

It had taken a few attempts, by trial and error, to trace the route of these outposts. Once at the edge of the flat lands, the hills rose like a series of upturned bowls creating wide flat valleys with seasonal streams. It was something of a natural labyrinth, with identical looking hamlets of weathered natives in many, none of whom spoke much in the way of Latin and most of whom had never been further afield than the next valley. Still, with some searching they had managed to pin down the trail of the Pompeian supplies and had located another small depot who had fled into woodlands at the sight of the approaching cavalry, melting into the landscape in places the cavalry could not go – groves of crabby olive trees and copses of tight-knit vegetation.

Galronus and his men had moved on, and the lower, bowl-like hills had gradually given way to larger slopes that rose like backbones, creating deep, green valleys. They had tried two such dales before they had found signs of Roman life. A Roman trader with a cart. His wheel had broken and he was far from reticent when faced with Caesar's cavalry. The rest of his caravan – four carts – had gone on with an escort to a village he knew four miles further on where a wheelwright lived. They would be returning with him soon. In the meantime, the trader waited. His vehicle was empty, but he knew from bitter experience that even a broken cart or a lame horse was a valuable commodity among the locals, and if he left the cart and walked on, it would be in some farmer's shed within the hour.

When his role in this Pompeian system was queried, he'd had little to tell. He was a wine merchant from Octogesa and had been delivering his wares to the garrison at Ilerda. Now he was taking his empty carts back. Where was Octogesa? Perhaps another eight or nine miles through the hills. It was a thriving little port town where the Sicoris met the Iberus. Had he any useful information? Well, when he'd left there were more ships in Octogesa than usual, but not *military* ships. Other than that, he told them the location of the next depot and then went back to waiting placidly for his wheelwright.

Galronus had ridden on with his men into the higher hills, following what appeared to be the route for Octogesa. Finally, they had come to a small village with a strangely ill-fitting Roman mansio built at the foot of a high spur. The road they had been following split here, and with the afternoon already greatly advanced, the Remi officer had encamped his men for the night and had taken a small unit to the mansio.

A little conversation, some exchange of silver, and further information had been forthcoming. The route to Octogesa was one easy day's travel to the north side of the spur. The other route led down to the Iberus via another valley with a narrow, swift river. Why was the road so well used? Because it led to a tiny settlement on the Iberus with a dock. Logging was a source of income for the hill folk there and the timber was taken down the valley to that dock and shipped downriver to Dertosa for sale up and down the coastal region. Galronus had almost consigned the logging valley to the heading 'unimportant', but had caught sight of something in the innkeeper's expression. A small fortune in silver changed hands once more, and it was revealed that a large number of soldiers had passed through only a few days ago and had taken that smaller, lesser valley.

Thanking the man, Galronus had returned to his camp and had conferred with his officers. The decision was simple. The northern path was a simple trade route from Octogesa to Ilerda and, from the geography he had gleaned thus far, small ferries or boats would transfer traders from one bank to the other, though that was across the Sicoris to the town itself. There was nothing surprising in that. But soldiers taking a logging trail toward a small hamlet with a dock on the great Iberus – Hispania's biggest river? Well, *that* was worth investigating.

And so, as the sun climbed clear of the Earth's ribs, the cavalry had ridden on into the narrower valley. And as they had ridden, several things had become apparent to Galronus. Firstly, he could see the small logging communities up on the slopes, as well as the bare patches that stood testament to their work. For ease of transport, the loggers had set up mileposts along the road. The first Galronus saw labelled the destination rather grandly Portus Iberus and suggested it was five miles distant. The valley, of course, wound back and forth, so likely it was less than three miles as birds flew. And the sense of tense expectation built with every hoof beat along that valley. The loggers were watching them from the slopes in taut silence. Galronus felt certain they were riding toward something important or dangerous, or both. He began to slow the pace of his men and to keep to the blind side of the valley as they approached each bend. Then, at the three mile marker, he called a halt.

Another conference. Whatever this was, it had not been advertised. The chances were they had stumbled across some Pompeian secret and if they wanted to maintain the advantage, they would have to keep themselves unnoticed until they knew what they were dealing with.

That was why, just now, when the alae had rounded the bend in the valley and spotted the enemy, he had made the snap decision to ride them down. None could escape.

They were legionaries and auxiliaries, though he couldn't see their flags to try and identify a unit. There were less than a hundred of them – Galronus suspected half a century of each, which meant the other half century of each were likely stationed somewhere else nearby. They had built a small stockade by one of the river's tributary streams, but with no officer present and no anticipated danger, they were generally sprawled about on the grass in just tunics and boots, some with swords close to hand but very few armoured and prepared. They were gathered around two men who were clearly engaged in a boxing competition – one Hispanic auxiliary and one legionary, likely for the honour of their units. Everyone was drinking and laughing.

It was appalling, and Galronus felt slightly nauseated at the attack. Rome might often take the most pragmatic path in any war, but the Remi were a tribe of noble warriors, who traditionally challenged their enemy to single, fair combat. To ride down such a crowd was far from heroic, but it did seem prudent.

Six hundred horsemen pounded toward the gathering, swords and spears ready, mouths closed, silent barring the jingle and shush of weapons and armour and the thunder of hooves. The small Roman garrison panicked and exploded into activity. Some ran for the stockade, probably not for its defensive capability as much as because it was where their weapons would be. Others charged for the narrow river or the slopes, where the treeline was perhaps two hundred paces from the valley bottom. Very few ran toward the horses.

Galronus, at the fore of his men as always, rode down the first man, bones smashing and shattering beneath the heavy beast, and thrust out his spear, taking another legionary in the throat. The sudden jerk of the blow forced him to let go of the spear, still jammed in the dying Roman, and draw his sword. He chose a man even as his riders flowed across the valley like a tide of gleaming, thundering death.

Ahead, a soldier had managed to find a shield and spear. He was one of the auxiliaries – a Hispanic with swarthy skin and dark hair and beard, his mail shirt studded with decorative bronze whorls and his shield bearing some design of a stylised horse. The man gritted his teeth and braced behind his shield, holding out his spear.

No horse will willingly charge a formation of such men. A hedge of points and steel. One man on his own? He could still do plenty of damage with that point, so at the last moment, as the man inevitably closed his eyes, braced for the collision, Galronus veered off to his left. The collision never happened, as the Remi officer thundered past the brave auxiliary's shoulder. Galronus' sword, however, was sweeping out. At the last moment, somehow unwilling to dispatch this brave soldier, he twisted his blade. The flat of the sword clanged into the soldier's forehead, throwing him backwards. He would be out for hours and awake with a stunning headache and possibly other side-effects, but there was every chance he would live, at least. These men were only the enemy through a name on a pay chit, after all. In any other circumstance, they might be fighting side by side.

Another poor bastard in a Roman russet tunic fell flailing beneath Galronus' hooves as he struggled to draw a sword. Then there were no more. The Remi noble had ridden down one man, speared another, and brained a third, and in that short space of time, his six hundred brutal cavalrymen had mown through the other soldiers like a scythe through long grass. By the time he had called the men back, there were just three enemy survivors, huddled within the illusory protection of the stockade. Half a dozen riders dismounted, swords held ready and expressions grim as they closed on the small defence. Galronus halted them in their tracks.

Dismounting and stepping with distaste across the battlefield, trying not to tread in any of the filth, the gore or the opened bowels, he approached the men.

'Bind them tight and gag them, as well as any other survivors you can find. There will be others who will come across them in due course so they won't starve. Wolves or bears might find them first, of course, but that would just be nature at work.'

The three terrified soldiers didn't know whether to look panicked or relieved at this reprieve from certain death by the sword to take their chances with the local wildlife instead. Still, a chance was a chance, so they did not struggle as the horsemen bound and gagged them.

'We should just get rid of them, sir,' said one of the decurions.

'We're not in the business of killing men unless we have to. Bear in mind that these are your countrymen.'

'Not mine, sir. I'm from Narbo, of Volcae blood, way back.'

Galronus laughed. 'I knew there was a reason I liked you. Who'd credit it, eh? A Remi telling a Volcae to be kind to his Roman brothers. Strange world we live in, Decurion. But the fact remains that this little war of Caesar's will be over within the year, as soon as he stamps on Pompey, and then these men will be our brothers again. Let's avoid unnecessary bloodshed as often as possible.'

The man nodded and saluted. 'What now, sir?'

Galronus pondered for a moment. 'To move on down the valley seems foolhardy. If they have pickets and outposts about then there will be more like this and I don't want to have to reap our way down the valley just to see what all this is about. Clean up here as best you can, and then pull most of the cavalry back to the fourth mile marker. If you see a roving patrol you'll have to take care of them, and if you come across anything that might cause trouble, you'll have to pull all the way back to that mansio. Wait for us there if necessary. I'm taking a turma up into the hills to see if we can get a good view of what lies ahead.'

The decurion clearly disapproved, but saluted anyway and began to call the men back to himself. Galronus gathered his personal bodyguard turma. 'We're going to find a way up into the hills. Two scouts will lead the way. This is not a fight. We are going to climb high enough to see what is going on without having to slaughter our way down the valley to do it.'

Half an hour later, the scene of the horrible massacre was almost lost to sight for Galronus and his small unit of thirty three men. They had climbed one of the clearer logging trails, the two scouts ranging ahead to find the best tracks. Continually they had climbed, past a small logging hut where the native woodsman pulled his family away from the approaching horsemen and hid in the building, watching suspiciously as the men passed. Here and there, as the trail bent and curved back on itself in its ascent, they could see down into the valley.

The decurion had done a good job of clearing up, given the time and resources. From this high point, they could see that the bodies had been gathered and thrown into a natural depression in the ground. They would be covered with turf deep enough to stop scavengers getting wind of them. The bodies couldn't be properly burned for fear of attracting further attention, but at least burial would afford them some dignity. Little could be done about the mess on the turf, but that would clear eventually. Idly, Galronus wondered whether his men had reverently placed a coin in the mouth of each of the dead. Some of his men – particularly the regular cavalry – clung tightly to the belief that the ferryman would turn aside those who couldn't pay and they would wander forever as unsettled spirits. Most of his Gallic and Belgic cavalry were content to sing a prayer-song to Dis on behalf of the dead and then drink themselves insensible.

Whatever the case, Galronus forced himself to ponder no further on the Roman cost.

The trails were not wide, but finally, after another hour of riding, they emerged from the edge of the trees, and Galronus was halted in his tracks by the sight of one of the scouts. The man had dismounted and was standing behind a thicket of gorse and juniper. He had his hand up to stop them and was gesturing down the slope. Galronus murmured the order for the entire turma to halt in the trees, uncomfortable though it was, and slid from the saddle, dashing across the open ground to the scout.

He came to a halt behind a sprawling juniper and his gaze slid down the hill. His heart thumped loud and fast and his skin prickled at the sight.

From this impressive vantage point, he could see the small river they'd been following open out into the great Iberus river below. And he could see the small village with its logging dock. He could also see a small fortlet that the Pompeians had built on the shore. But more impressive was the work under construction. The Iberus here was a quarter of a mile across and yet, looking up and down the flow, it was still clearly the narrowest part within sight. The legionaries were at work moving ships into position and lashing them together to form a great pontoon bridge across the massive river. Galronus could just see what must be Octogesa upstream, on the 'V' shape where the Sicoris joined this impressive torrent. Ships were still being guided down from the place, toward the growing bridge.

Galronus understood in an instant.

Petreius and Afranius meant to run. The burning of their supplies and Caesar's sudden control of the best foraging lands had made their position under siege suddenly truly untenable. And the fact that local tribes, towns and units were starting to come over to Caesar was making it ever worse. But the further south and west they went, the more staunchly pro-Pompey the populace would become, and eventually they might meet up with the governor of Hispania Ulterior and his legions. If the two Pompeian generals managed to get their army across that pontoon bridge and then cast it adrift, it would take Caesar weeks to come anywhere near them again. At best it would be like starting Ilerda from scratch. At worst they would find themselves in thoroughly unfriendly territory and against growing odds. They had to stop the garrison of Ilerda from crossing the Iberus, or this fight alone would go on all year.

Breathing deeply, Galronus gestured at the scout and then trotted across to his horse. Mounting, he motioned to the decurions.

'We ride back at speed. Gather all the cavalry and return to Caesar. Petreius and Afranius intend to leave Ilerda and take their army across the great river. We have to warn Caesar. They need to be stopped immediately.'

* * *

The cavalry closed on Ilerda at speed, but even as the twin mounds of Pompeian resistance came into clear perspective, Galronus could see how things had changed in his week long absence.

The last time he had seen the stone bridge across the Sicoris from this side had been early in the siege. The terrain kept this area out of sight from the main Caesarian camp on the far side of the enemy forces. As such, unless the general's scouts were coming dangerously close to the enemy position, it was very possible that Caesar was as unaware of this new development as he was of the pontoon bridge being strung across the Iberus.

Two Pompeian legions, he would estimate, were on the south bank now, constructing a whole new smaller fort beside the other end of the bridge. Having seen the pontoon, this made perfect sense to Galronus. It might not have done to a less informed observer.

If Petreius and Afranius meant to abandon Ilerda, they would have to do it across the stone bridge. Defending the far end and already moving out two legions ready was eminently sensible, especially now that Caesar's cavalry were at large on the far side. But it also meant that the time for their moving was nigh. The Pompeians were preparing to leave.

In his head, from his now vast experience of the Roman army on the move, he calculated the size of Caesar's army and the speed it would travel. It was not a happy result. Galronus could see no way that Caesar could move his legions across the Sicoris in time to stop the enemy leaving. He would have to use the bridges, which were further away and narrower, restricting the flow of men and slowing crossing immeasurably. It was troubling.

'What now sir?' asked a decurion, pointing at the distant works. Almost simultaneously a call went up among the Pompeian legions, warning of the cavalry's approach.

'Nothing we can do about them here and now. They form contra equitas and we're pretty much powerless. Legions know how to face cavalry, and there are ten thousand of them against eighteen hundred of us. Let's hope the ford's still crossable. We need to get back to Caesar as soon as we can.'

Eighteen hundred horse was a fearsome fighting force, now that he had recombined the three roving units, but Galronus was under no illusion as to what their chances would be when facing two full legions of veterans.

'Ride for the ford and cross. Skirt the enemy widely.'

They did so, and Galronus kept his gaze on the enemy even as they raced out of Pompey's reach. He had to respect them. There was no fear or panic about the legionaries building this new fort. They may be deserting Ilerda, but none of them saw it as a defeat. It was a tactical change of position to achieve a new strength. The enemy were resolute.

So was Galronus.

The ford was a hive of activity. Far from leaving it as the rough crossing Mamurra had manufactured for the cavalry, the engineers had been hard at work in their absence. The cavalry reached the near bank and plunged down into the water, despite the lack of obvious pursuit, fearing the possibility that two legions of Pompeian veterans would catch them on the bank.

The near half of the ford was just the same as it had been when they crossed a week ago. If anything, it was worse. The flow of water had begun to wash away and spread the excess sediment, so it was deeper now, and the river bed less stable. The other side, though, was already a vast improvement. Mamurra and his engineers had been working on the crossing, implanting huge boles of trees in the river bed to give it a solid, slightly raised surface. They had also widened the crossing even further with a new trench to lower the flow. The Caesarian bank of the river was now carefully built up and secure.

The cavalry flooded across the ford and made for the camp, and Galronus pushed his mount out to the front once more, arriving at the gate where Caesar and the staff had gathered, and slipping from his exhausted horse, wobbling only a moment as he found the strength in his legs and feet.

'General,' he saluted.

'Galronus. You arrive at speed?'

'I have much to tell, General.'

Caesar beckoned, and the group hurried up the slope to the command tent at the camp's centre. Once safely inside, where they could talk and with Ingenuus and his men standing guard outside, Caesar gestured for the Remi senator to go on.

'The enemy are leaving, Caesar. Their location is no longer strong, and they are making for more forgiving lands with better positioning.'

'How do you know this?' Antonius queried.

'Two legions have already crossed the Sicoris, presumably at night and unseen by your men. They are building a bridgehead fort at the far side of the bridge. There is a series of depots in a line from that side of the bridge all the way to the town of Octogesa, but a couple of miles downstream from that place, a cohort or two of Pompeians are constructing a pontoon bridge of impounded vessels across the Iberus. There can be no doubt that they mean to run, and soon.'

Caesar took a deep breath and turned to examine the map of Hispania on the wall. His finger ran down the vellum from Ilerda, found Octogesa and then continued on across the lands to the south.

'That will take him deep into the Celtiberian heartland. There the staunchest supporters of Pompey remain, as well as a number of fortresses that have remained unbroken since the time of Scipio. If Petreius makes it there we will be fighting over the winter, and even then success is far from certain.'

Galronus nodded. 'Respectfully, General, if they cross the Iberus, then this campaign is likely lost.'

Again, Caesar nodded. 'And if they are prepared to defend the bridge, with two legions across, they are ready to go.'

'Quite so.'

'Hades take the man, but Petreius is clever. He knows when to run and won't let some sense of nobility stop him. I suspect Afranius is less sure, but clearly they have settled on this course together somehow. To move all our legions and support across the bridges will take the better part of a week. We could move on without the support, but we press ever deeper into Pompeian territory and we've all seen, with the arrival at Ilerda, how lacking support affects an army.'

'Send the cavalry,' Salvius Cursor put in. 'They can move fast, can cross the new ford and we have thousands of them.'

Galronus glared at the tribune. 'But there is simply no chance of the cavalry, even if I take every last horse, stopping them. It has to be a full force, including legionaries.'

Caesar met Galronus' gaze. 'But you *could* slow them down and irritate them. Buy time for men to cross. I know you have just returned from a very hard, yet fruitful, expedition, my Remi friend, but I must prevail upon you once more. Take every rider we have across the river. Harry them and badger them. Do not allow them time to think or prepare. Do *not* put yourselves at risk, though,' he added pointedly. 'I do not intend to sacrifice my cavalry. But slow them where you can. In the meantime, we move carefully. Petreius likely does not know that we are aware of his plans and will be working to his own schedule. If we make it clear we intend to stop him, he might simply run ahead of schedule. We need time.'

The general turned to Antonius. 'Have the legions fall in one cohort at a time. Tell their officers to leave quietly, without fuss or musicians, through the far gate travelling quickly and at distance. Get them up to the bridge one at a time and start them crossing. The more men we can get across before Petreius leaves, the better our chances of facing him.'

Fronto, who had been silent and still throughout, straightened.

'Why not take the infantry across the ford?'

Mamurra shook his head. 'The depth and current are too dangerous. Even if the men crossed successfully the death toll would probably be appalling. No, the ford was carefully planned to lower the water enough for cavalry.'

'Too deep,' the legate mused. Fronto's eyes narrowed, and Galronus almost laughed out loud. Whatever his friend might say, the Remi knew that Fronto was already seeing himself slogging across the torrent with a shield above his head.

'Very well,' Caesar said. 'Legions slowly moving out and to the bridge, cavalry over the ford to keep the enemy busy. That is, I believe, the best we can do at this particular moment.'

But Fronto's eyes were still narrowed as he calculated.

Chapter Thirteen

25th of Quintilis - Ilerda

FRONTO was starting to think about sleeping in his full kit, since it seemed that every time he bedded down for the night, someone woke him and made him leave his tent. Now, as the legionary Felix had sent hovered outside, Fronto hurriedly fastened his belt, threw his cloak about his shoulders and pinned it, and slipped into his boots, giving them a quick tie and then emerging into the sultry Hispanic night beneath a blanket of black, studded with glittering silver stars.

'Come on, then.'

With the legionary escort, he hurried across to the command tent, which was already rumbling with the conversation of officers, a gold glow peeking out around the door. Rubbing his eyes and stretching, the legate of the Eleventh nodded to the Praetorian guards to either side and then entered. Many of the officers were already gathered, and a weary looking cavalryman stood by the general's table. Caesar looked untouched by sleep, which was nothing new.

Over only a short wait, others arrived and took their position. Once everyone was present, and Antonius ran a quick head count and nodded to Caesar, the general stepped forward to the table and leaned on it with balled fists.

'Before we proceed further, gentlemen, I am going to let Figulus here repeat the account he delivered to me a little over half an hour ago. Figulus?'

The cavalry soldier stepped forward and rolled his shoulders.

'The enemy are all-but gone.'

There was a general murmur of disbelief and derision among the officers, but a single glare from Caesar, and Antonius' clearing of throat, soon put a stop to it and Figulus continued.

'From the camp's vantage point, very little has changed, I can see. The cook fires still burn and the men are still on the walls. But

I can assure you, sirs, that the bulk of the army of Petreius and Afranius have quit Ilerda. The cavalry have been keeping the two legions across the river penned in their new fort since we crossed, though there was little we could do to actually harm them. They have solid defences and a good working Roman knowledge of contra equitas tactics. But we harry them and keep them hungry, preventing forage, and we've watched them.'

He sighed and stretched. The man was paying little of the due deference one would expect in the presence of senior officers, but then Fronto had seldom seen a man look so weary and dishevelled. The rider had been in the saddle for days with precious little rest.

'Our scouts caught sight of the sneaky bastards a couple of hours ago. They had opened up a small postern facing the river, unobserved by the various pickets and outriders. The legionaries were leaving in a small but steady trickle, crossing the bridge quietly and joining their mates in the new fort. In fairness, Prefect Galronus had questioned why the camp had needed to be so big if it was just a bridgehead. We managed to catch one of their scouts and a bit of judicious slapping revealed that they've been doing that for three nights. Only a small rear guard remains in the camp to grant you the illusion of full defence. Even before I was sent back here with the warning, the enemy legions in the bridge camp were preparing to leave. Almost certainly they're on the move by now.'

Caesar nodded to him, and he stepped back.

'So there you have it, gentlemen. Petreius and Afranius are cleverer than we thought. Faced with growing odds against them and a lack of supplies, they decided to quit and move west to more friendly territory. They have set up a pontoon crossing of the Iberus which they can destroy afterwards and effectively cut off any pursuit. They have a system of depots in place from Ilerda to the crossing, which means they likely have sufficient supplies to see themselves to safety no matter what we've done to them. They have made a solid defence of the far side of their stone bridge and moved the bulk of their men out to it under our very noses. Now they are leaving that fort, with only a minimal rear guard left to slow us. If they reach that pontoon bridge, then this campaign has failed. And if this campaign fails, then the knock on effect will be disastrous. If we are bogged down here in an endless fight with

Pompey's men, then Pompey himself is at leisure to return to Italia and regain control, at which point we will be in a worse position than we were in Ravenna at the start of all this.'

'No pressure, then,' said Fabius, earning himself a glare from the general.

'We are left in somewhat dire straits, gentlemen. We need to stop them, but we simply do not have the time.'

'Can the cavalry not stop them once they leave the fort and are on the move?' Plancus mused.

'They will certainly slow them a little,' put in Varus, a man more than familiar with the capabilities of the cavalry. 'But no, they number perhaps a third as many bodies as the army they face, and the enemy know how to deal with cavalry. At best they will be able to harry them and irritate, pick off scouts and wagons, create trouble for them. They will cause casualties, but to actually fully commit against them would be more or less suicide.'

Plancus nodded his understanding.

'What about the legions who've been crossing the bridge to the north, General?' Fabius said. 'There must be two legions assembled there by now.'

'There are,' the general answered with a nod. 'But they're a few miles further away. They can catch up and commit, but even in conjunction with the cavalry they would be facing insurmountable odds. The only way we can hope to stop them reaching that bridge is by fielding a force against them strong enough to make them turn and face us. We need to get most, if not all, of our men against them and before they can reach the Iberus.'

'Can you not now take the stone bridge?' Mamurra mused. 'If only a small rear guard remains in the camp, they must be inadequate to protect the bridge. And if the enemy have used it, then why not us?'

'A good thought,' Caesar conceded, 'which had occurred to me, but there are three problems with it. Firstly, although it is a wider and stronger bridge than our ones upstream, it still acts as a funnel and it will take our men quite some time to cross it. Also, though we know they have left a rear guard, we cannot be certain what it entails. I doubt Petreius has entrusted his back to a force inadequate to protect it. If our men move across the saddle toward that bridge, I suspect we will find burning tree trunks rolled down on us and the like. Walking into the unknown could be carnage. And there is every chance that the enemy have slighted the bridge as they left, anyway. While we've had no intelligence to that effect, it is what *I* would do, so I have to assume the same of them. A few well-placed blows to weaken the bridge and then the first attempt to cross sends half a cohort of men to their death. No, the bridge is too risky a proposition.'

The room fell quiet again.

Fronto had been listening to the debate with growing irritation, and almost jumped when he realised Salvius Cursor had moved around the room and was now standing at his side. The tribune leaned close, his voice a sibilant whisper.

'I know what you're thinking, Fronto.'

'You do?'

'And you're right. For once, I damn well agree with you. Make them see it. The general listens to you.'

Fronto turned, half expecting to see some sly expression on the tribune's face, this being a move in one of his games, though there was nothing but earnestness in his expression. That worried Fronto more than any opposition from the man. If Salvius agreed with him, then there was a good chance that what he was thinking was criminally insane. But it had the single advantage of being the only option.

'Come with me,' Fronto said, loudly, and turned and walked from the tent.

There was a series of surprised murmurs in the room, and Fronto was already striding down the Via Principalis of the camp with Salvius Cursor at his heel before the first of the officers emerged from the tent.

'Fronto, stop being so theatrical,' shouted Antonius, though there was humour in his voice as he and Caesar hurried down the road after the legate. By the time they reached the equisio, Fronto had grabbed a horse from the corral and mounted, not bothering with a saddle. Salvius joined him and they rode out through the camp gate.

By the time they reached the site of the ford, three miles upstream, the rest of the officers were on horseback and catching up. Fronto approached the ford quickly, the water glittering in the moonlight, silver sparkles on a bed of black. He swallowed. It looked a lot deeper and faster now than it had in his head.

Four cohorts of men were encamped next to the ford, with pickets out, but no proper defences – the workforce who were strengthening the ford. As the bemused staff officers reined in behind them, Fronto slid from his horse, Salvius right behind him, and stomped down to the eight man tent party who stood watch over the ford.

'You,' he shouted to one of them.' Strip to your tunic and belt.'

The man, shocked, stood unmoving for a moment, then realised who it was who had given him an order and, with the help of his mate, unfastened his helmet and sword, dropped his shield and then peeled off the mail shirt. At Fronto's gesture, he stood back. To the general amusement of the gathered officers, Fronto crouched, tipped the shield face down and piled the rest of the soldier's gear onto it. Bracing himself – it took little these days to remind Fronto that he was no longer a young man – he lifted the shield, the burden dreadful, the large curved board supporting a weight in iron and steel and bronze and leather. Grunting, and wondering whether he was being brave and foolhardy or just plain old and foolish, he hefted the shield and slowly, trying not to look too much as though he was struggling, lifted it above his head. Parts of his body issued alarming creaks.

Finally, he settled it in place and, though his arm muscles screamed at the weight, it was better with them raised and locked than it had been actually lifting the thing. He could remember less than a decade ago in Cremona, just before Caesar had taken them north into Gaul, lifting this weight and more and barely breaking a sweat. Gods, but he'd become old in Gaul.

'Fronto, don't be an arse,' Antonius grinned from the turf above the ford.

'Fronto, the water is too deep,' Fabius added, echoing Mamurra's words as the old engineer nodded his agreement.

'If it's too deep, then it just means you're too short,' Fronto snapped, and turned, walking into the river.

It was all he could do not to shout out in shock as the freezing cold water closed on his ankles. It was like sloshing into ice. He shivered and stepped forward again. To his dismay his leg sank in almost to the knee at the second step, and he almost lost his balance, teetering on the submerged log surface. Slowly righting himself, he moved on. Fortunately that was the steepest drop for a while, and he slogged through the numbing cold of the Sicoris until he was twenty paces out from the bank. There, he stopped and turned, intending to grin to the watchers and confirm how easy it was.

His face remained immobile. The officers on the bank were watching, full of concern. Three soldiers had stripped down to their underwear, preparing to dive in and swim to his rescue. The only one who seem to have any kind of confidence was Salvius, who, fully clothed, had followed him into the water and was four paces behind.

'Bear in mind,' Fronto shouted, 'that after this cold bath, I shall want a warm one!'

There was no laughter at his comment. Just more concern.

Turning once more, Fronto moved on. Another five paces and the river bed dropped away again, the water sliding up his tunic and touching his nethers, making him wince and wonder if it was possible to pee through a frozen prick.

On he moved. He could no longer feel his feet. It was like lifting appendages encased in lead blocks. The water was providing more and more resistance the further out he moved, and he could feel the current trying to pull him down toward Ilerda and beyond, to the great River Iberus.

Again, somewhere around a third of the way across, the water rose once more and he found himself submerged to the waist. The going was becoming incredibly slow now and required every ounce of effort he could muster to heave his way through the constant, battering torrent. Still he slogged on, aware of Salvius Cursor just a heartbeat or two behind him. If there was one thing he was not prepared to do, it was fail in front of the tribune.

He found the end of the new work rather suddenly as his foot left the heavy timber boles and sank into sludge. For just a moment, he was almost gone downstream. He tipped to the side, his other leg flailing in the water and then slapping down into the soft river bed. Even as he swayed and the weight on the shield above his head threatened to send him under, the soft bed gave a little under his feet and his head vanished beneath the surface.

He panicked, then fought the panic, then panicked some more, but a moment later managed to free a leg and took a step forward, his other foot coming up. One found a rock and managed to steady him as his face emerged from the water and he coughed wildly. The water tasted of silt. And worse. He heaved in several deep cleansing breaths and took another pace forward, the water lapping at his chin, the shield still miraculously dry and held over his head. It was odd how you could trick your body into forgetting its woes by introducing it to new ones. The pain in his arms holding up the shield had been forgotten with the cold of the water, and now that had been consigned to history with the terror of the depth and sinking beneath the surface. Sadly, he couldn't imagine what new horror waited to make him forget *that* problem. Perhaps there was a pike in the water the size of a horse? That would do it...

Though it was febrile imagining, the sudden thought of what living terrors a river could hold made him push on with fresh force. He glanced over his shoulder. Salvius was still there, and he could see the other officers at the riverbank beyond. He was over half way across the Sicoris.

Determination flooded through him at the realisation and he ploughed on through the pulling torrent, struggling, finding the few hard footings he could and fighting every foot of the way. He fervently wished he could touch and kiss the small figure of Fortuna that hung on the thong around his neck, but both hands were occupied with the heavy load on the shield.

When his foot suddenly found higher ground and he stepped forward, feeling his chest emerge from the water, he almost cried with relief. Then, another five paces and he was up to his waist. Now, the going was easier and, combined with his triumphant relief at being across, he slogged quickly through the remaining shallows, first his groin, then knees emerging from the water. Finally, he was out and stomping up the bank, where he gratefully lowered the shield to the ground and rubbed his aching arms.

Salvius Cursor sloshed out of the water and stood beside him.

'Thought you were screwed for a moment.'

'So did I.'

'I nearly had my legateship, I reckon.'

Fronto almost laughed, presuming it to be a joke, albeit a poor one, but as he looked at Salvius the man was not smiling, and he suddenly wondered if the tribune had been serious. Trying not to think on it further, Fronto, shivering like a leaf in a breeze, waved at the distant figures on the far bank.

'I'm not tall and I'm not young. If I can make it, so can the legions.'

There was a distant burst of cheering from the cohorts on the far bank.

'You're insane,' bellowed Antonius.

'And cold,' replied Fronto. 'Can you send someone over with a hot towel and a jug of wine?'

* * *

Dawn greeted struggling men and barked commands as the legions slogged across the ford. Though Fronto had been joking and had intended to find an easier way back across, Antonius had taken him at his word and over the next half hour had sent big, burly legionaries across the ford with towels, dry clothes and cloaks, food and wine, and finally two tents. Fronto had passed out to catch a last couple of hours of sleep before the day broke in a tiny encampment of twelve men, with two tents and a cook fire.

Up once more at dawn, and yawning with every other breath, Fronto had been impressed with how quickly Caesar had moved during the night. Clearly the general had not rested. He had brought the legions to the crossing, while Mamurra and Antonius had kept the cohorts here at work through the hours of darkness, hurriedly dropping what timbers they could into the deeper stretch in an attempt to help.

By the time the first man crossed – in no danger, since it was Fabius on horseback – Fronto had eaten a dry, small breakfast and was standing barefoot in fresh tunic and cloak on the turf, his boots still hanging on the tent post, drying.

As the men struggled into the water behind Fabius and began the mammoth task of crossing the Sicoris, the biggest and most stable men first, marking out the best route and any dangerous sections, Fabius reined in.

'We're leaving one legion behind to secure Ilerda and the enemy camp and bridge. The two legions up at the north crossing are already coming down to join us here.' He grinned. 'It was one of the strangest sights I've ever seen. Four legions lined up on the flat ground, while the centurions went down the lines and tapped anyone who was too small. All the short, stocky men were separated out and formed a temporary legion. They're staying here with the weak and the infirm to secure the place. Any man crossing the Sicoris is the best part of six feet tall now.'

Fronto rolled his eyes. 'Wonderful. That makes me officially the shortest person in Caesar's army now.'

Fabius dismounted and opened his mouth to say something pithy, but Fronto shook his head. 'I've got to go for a piss. Too much water and wine for me overnight.'

'Go downstream, or you won't be popular.'

Fronto snorted and sauntered off to a more secluded spot a hundred paces downstream toward Ilerda, where a scrubby thicket of bushes masked a dip down to the water with a small gravel beach. His heart sank as he rounded the bush and spotted Salvius Cursor busy fastening his subligaculum and straightening his tunic. He then dipped his hands in the river, upstream from his current position and, causing Fronto to frown, reached down into his belt pouch and pulled out a small unguent jar which he opened and began to apply to his hands.

It seemed odd to see a man who seemed utterly at home covered in blood and shit and filth pampering himself with balms and oils after washing in a river. Stepping back behind the bush, Fronto cleared his throat and then emerged again down to the beach. He nodded at Salvius, who continued to apply his ointment, nodding back casually.

Wondering at the strange variation in the world of men, Fronto stepped past him, pulled up his tunic and tucked it into the belt, yanked aside his subligaculum and let out an arc of steaming yellow with a sigh of blissful relief.

He almost covered himself in his own urine as a commotion broke out upstream at the ford and, quickly pinching off the flow and dropping his tunic, Fronto stepped out into the water, his bare feet baulking once more at the chill. A man had fallen while crossing the river. Two other men had obviously dropped their own burdens and leapt to help. One of his would-be saviours was struggling to stay upright. The other had similarly slipped and followed his friend into the water. Neither of the men wore their mail shirts – that would have been stupid – but their shields and all their gear had gone, tipped into the deep or floating off downstream, and the two men were in serious danger.

It sounded like a simple thing, crossing a river without armour on. But having done it during the night, Fronto knew different. The chill of the water and the constant batter and pull of the current stole the strength and sapped the will, and the longer one fought the water, the worse it got. The first man was already barrelling downstream at pace, probably unconscious, maybe even dead. The second was half-carried, half-swimming, after him, screaming and cursing, the sound intermittently dampened as his face dipped below the surface.

Before he knew what he was doing, Fronto had run out five paces into the river and then thrown himself into the deeper torrent. Ignoring Salvius' bellowing voice behind him, he swam hard, angling upstream to fight the current, making to intercept the two unfortunate legionaries.

It seemed to take forever, but finally he was close. He could see the man bobbing left and right as he was carried fast toward him. His heart sank as he registered the fact that the man was already dead. Regretfully, he changed his focus to the second man, who was still screaming and still dipping under the water.

Something tugged at him and Fronto turned his head in surprise to see Salvius Cursor, pounding the water and yanking at him.

'What are you doing?'

'Don't be a fool, Fronto. The man's gone.'

'If he's shouting, he's alive.'

'He's dead. He just doesn't know it yet. And if you try and get him to the bank, you'll go with him.'

'Piss off.'

Salvius let go of him and began to swim back to the bank. 'Leave him, Fronto. Don't be an idiot.'

Fronto watched as the panicked, shrieking man was carried past him, and then, finally robbed of the last of his strength and unable to fight it any more, disappeared beneath the water. The last Fronto saw of him was a couple of limbs flung up out of the torrent by the flow. Feeling the cold numbness now beginning to settle into his own limbs, Fronto turned and swam back to the shore.

For some horrible reason, watching the poor bastard drown had brought back a welter of unwelcome emotions and the dreadful memory of Florus, the young medic who had been swept overboard, crossing the channel on that stupid foray to Britannia six years ago. The lad had become something of a pet project of Fronto's following their first battle against the Helvetii, and still, on the anniversary of his passing, Fronto would find time, whatever he was doing, to pour a wine libation into a spring or stream somewhere, along with a prayer that Neptune be kind to him.

Now, he was blisteringly angry. At the soldiers for dying. At Petreius and Afranius, and Pompey, for starting all of this, at himself for failing, but most of all at Salvius for distracting him and losing him a slim chance of saving the man. Oh, when he looked deep into his own heart, he couldn't help but admit that the fallen soldier was almost certainly a goner anyway. There was only the faintest chance that Fronto could have caught him and stopped him flowing away. And as he staggered onto the gravel, he knew he had barely made it back himself, and that if he'd had to help a man on the way they'd almost certainly have both drowned. But just because Salvius was actually right didn't take away the anger.

Salvius Cursor returned his angry glare but neither man spoke as Fronto stomped past him and back up toward his small camp where he hoped there was still a towel and some spare dry clothing.

* * *

They caught up with the enemy late the next day.

It seemed that, despite their limitations, Galronus had been thoroughly effective at slowing the enemy column as it left Ilerda. The baggage train of Petreius and Afranius' army was relatively speedy, put together for pace and not content, relying mostly upon the depots they would pass, but the massive force had been picked at by the Caesarean cavalry throughout and had found downed trees or fallen rocks in the way – obstacles that had clearly been the work of Galronus' outriders. They had moved slower than they had hoped.

And the combination of moving without the support of wagons and artillery, and having crossed the river en masse earlier than expected had brought Caesar up behind them much faster than they had expected. They were only a few short miles southwest of Ilerda when the two armies came into sight almost a mile apart now.

Fronto had half expected Petreius to drop his supplies and run for the bridge. Given the stakes they were all playing for now, the Pompeian commander had to realise that this was his last chance to get away without conflict at Ilerda. And being caught on the run played havoc with trying to mount an effective defence. Realistically the man had to either cut and run and hope to cross the bridge, or gird his loins and turn to face Caesar in the field.

The fact that, upon sight of Caesar's army catching them up, conflicting calls went up among the enemy suggested that they were once more prey to disagreements between their two commanders. Likely the ones sending their men *ad signum* – to the standards – were Petreius preparing to take the Caesarian bull by the horns and poll it. And the calls to double time would be Afranius, ever wishing to avoid this conflict and making for the bridge at speed. The result was that the lead elements moved off at a hurry for the pontoon bridge on the Iberus, while the baggage train and the rear elements came to a halt.

Caesar, eager to take advantage of the confusion, pressed his men onward and the legions marched at speed, but before battle could be joined the latest argument between the enemy leaders apparently resolved itself and the entire army came to a halt at a low hill half a mile from Fronto and his men. As they stomped and hoofed forward, they watched the enemy forming. Someone among them – probably not the two generals, given their unwillingness to cooperate – knew what they were doing. Even as the Caesarian force bore down on them, the carts and wagons were drawn up onto the rise, the auxilia and support with them, and the heavy legionaries were shuffled forward to take their place defending the slope.

In the time it had taken Caesar's army to force march a quarter of a mile, the enemy had turned flight and confusion into a solid line of defence with missile support. Fronto watched Caesar, sitting astride his white mare at the fore of the army, and knew immediately what was coming. A moment later the general's arm rose and the call went out from the First Cohort's musicians. The army came to an abrupt halt, the only noise across the plain the jingle and clatter of weapons and armour and the huffing and stretching of men and beasts. At the call for *consilium*, the senior officers gathered on Caesar's position.

Antonius huffed irritably. 'We almost had an easy victory there.'

The general shook his head. 'There will be no easy victory against these men. Even when the generals argue, the legions are veterans and know what to do. We are left with a decision.'

'Not a tough one, Caesar,' Salvius Cursor scoffed. 'We have them pinned on a hill.'

Fronto frowned. He hadn't invited Salvius to the officer's meeting, and tribunes were not expected to attend. Caesar seemed not to notice, or perhaps not to care. 'True, but the outcome of any push here is truly in the hands of the gods.'

'They are on the defensive, General,' Salvius pushed, 'and they ran by night. They will be tired and in poor morale. After all, they have run away once.'

Antonius gestured to the hill. 'They did not run away. They are seeking a more favourable location to defy us. It matters not how you see it, or even how Caesar or I see it, but that is how every man on that hill sees it. They know they've done the sensible thing, and there is no cowardice among them, and I daresay very little fear either.'

'But they *are* tired,' persisted the tribune. Fronto could see the flash of anger cross Caesar's eyes and, to head off a coming tirade, he turned to Salvius. 'So are our men. They were also up during the night. They have slogged across the dangerous ford and lost friends to the waters. They have force marched to catch up with the enemy. Their spirits might be high, but their strength is not. They need to rest, else we chance everything by throwing tired men against tired men.'

'But...'

'Go back to the Eleventh, Tribune, and have a rider sent to find the cavalry. Bring Galronus and his men back in.'

Salvius glared daggers at Fronto, but saluted and stomped off back toward the legion.

'What *do* we do, General,' he asked, when the tribune was gone.

Caesar sighed and stretched.

'We do the unexpected. For now we rest the men. Let them have the afternoon and the evening.'

'And the night,' added Antonius.

'Ah, no. For the night, I have plans,' smiled the general.

Chapter Fourteen

27th of Quintilis – south-west of Ilerda

PUBLIUS Cassius Bucco, now senior tribune of the Second Vernacular Legion, had reached the limits of his patience. He was, by nature, a peaceful and fairly lazy individual, and he was a young man – almost certainly the most junior in the generals' consilium that night. As the son of a well-to-do family of ancient blood and property wealth he had never had to suffer a task more onerous than playing *nomenclator* for his father, or learning his Herodotus. And he was no violent soldier. He was a serving Pompeian officer, but not because he hated Caesar. He had met Caesar precisely as often as he had met Pompey – to whit: never. He was simply playing the role the Fates had laid out for him.

But his path had recently taken weird turns. He had suddenly found himself the senior officer in the field at that hill where the staff officers had been butchered by cavalry and the Caesarian legions had come to put an end to them. He had run away and taken the legions with him. He had brought the troops back to Ilerda to acclaim by the commanders. He'd half expected to be lynched for cowardice. But it seemed to be the considered opinion of everyone of import that he'd saved three legions. He'd been given some sort of crown that was itchy and heavy and he didn't know what to do with.

It had been said in the end that the whole thing was a ruse and that Caesar's legions were not there. But somehow that didn't seem to matter. He had done the right thing based on the information he had. He had been promoted to senior tribune. That was something that didn't happen. Junior tribunes were assigned by the senate for a short stint. Senior tribunes were career officers with a history who were ready to step into high command. You didn't move from the one to the other. But then, the situation here was hardly normal.

He couldn't be made a legate, of course. That would be *too* much of a step. But until a man of appropriate breeding and history could be found, Bucco was the de facto leader of the legion anyway. As such, he had entered the whole new world of the senior officer, and he was already so sick of it, he was beginning to wish he'd been born an insignificant pleb.

Afranius and Petreius could not even agree on the colour of a summer sky. The army was lucky to have lasted as long as it had. It would not last much longer. Half the officers didn't hate Caesar, and many of those men had oddly fond memories of when he had served as questor or governor in Hispania. Their dubious loyalties did nothing to close the divide between the two commanders.

Then they had left Ilerda. Seemed like a sensible choice to Bucco. And they'd done it with cleverness and subtlety despite everything. All was prepared, and yet suddenly Caesar's cavalry were everywhere, causing disasters and slowing them, and Caesar's infantry, who should have been bogged down on the other side of the river, were instead chasing them across the plains south-west of Ilerda, heading for the mountains.

Then they had finally stopped on the hill. At the moment of crisis, Petreius had almost struck Afranius. One had been all for marching on through the night and crossing the pontoon. The other had, almost certainly correctly, advocated turning to face the enemy since Caesar would clearly do anything in his power to stop them. No one had seemed to know what to do. Oddly, it had been Bucco's comment that had saved the day, yet again. He had railed in relative privacy about his seniors' failure to keep the army together, and his own camp prefect had told him 'quite right' and had given the orders for the signals for every legion. The Second had been responsible for pulling it all together, and while Bucco had not given the order himself, he knew he was the reason it had been given.

Now here they were, sitting on a low hill, not far from the valleys that would spell relative safety from the cavalry, while Caesar's army sat on another low rise opposite, the two like alley cats on fences each waiting for the other to howl first.

Yet despite the proximity of danger, the officers of the Pompeian force had called for consilium and, instead of planning what to do next, had used the past half hour to sling insults at one another. There was no homogeneity of command. No solidarity. Just the sort of chaos that even Bucco, whose military experience had all been born from being thrown into the shit this past month, knew would only end in defeat. He listened to one of Petreius' men – a career soldier with a leather face and a caustic voice – heap insults on Afranius' heritage. He listened to Afranius' senior legate tell Petreius that he was 'just a soldier' and should have stayed in Lusitania where the strongest enemy were the whores waiting to lighten his purse. They almost came to blows again and Bucco found himself stepping angrily out of the tent and away from the mess caused by his commanders.

No one seemed to notice him go. Half the men were busy weighing in with their spite and bile on behalf of one general or the other, and the rest were trying not to become involved, considering the future of their career instead.

Breathing deeply of the warm night air, he stepped away from the command tent and walked until he could no longer hear the raised voices. What kind of way was that to run an army? When even the auxiliaries in the latrines could hear the generals calling each other names. Trying not to be dismayed by the situation, he continued to the standards of the Second Vernacular, which stood proud at the high point of the hill. With a wedge-like shape, the lower end of the mound was commanded by the cavalry with a legion in support, for the horse could operate best there if the enemy suddenly decided to come. The high end, where the Second were encamped, was of such a height that he imagined he might still see Ilerda during good daylight.

Right now what he could see were the glowing camp fires of Caesar's army. They were not in a besieging position. They were camped on another rise close by. Perhaps they would have been wiser to try and besiege the Pompeians. Here, the legions had no access to water, while an unnamed stream ran right past Caesar's army. But even Bucco, with his very limited military knowledge, knew why Caesar was not attacking. His men would be as tired as the Pompeians, if not more so. They needed a night to recover.

And no matter how much Afranius and Petreius might argue, they would naturally settle on the decision to move in the morning. After all, they had been planning this departure for so long, everything was in place. The legions would leave and would move to the bridge, with Caesar nipping at their heels, and would cross. There was a good chance their rear guard would end up in a fight with Caesar's vanguard while the pontoon bridge was destroyed and cast adrift, but that could not be helped. The man was fast and tenacious. But the bulk of the army would escape, and then the Ulterior legions would join them and the various native levy units of central Hispania would ally, and suddenly Caesar would be vastly outnumbered and would have to either run or face defeat.

The young tribune nodded to the signifer who stood on guard at the standards, which rested in bases specially constructed for such times, each pole with its own socket. A small honour guard of legionaries formed a protective ring around the sacred symbols, and Bucco smiled to see the respect and sense among his men. The senior officers might be like a bunch of ferrets slung together in a sack, but the legions were still the pride of the republic.

He came to rest at a frame where earlier cooking pots had hung, and leaned on the sturdy timber, looking out into the purple world. It was not a bright night. Despite the warmth and heat, high, scudding clouds obscured half the sky, blanking out the twinkling stars and hiding the waning gibbous moon. He had stood here earlier, before the officers had been called to the meeting, and peered out at the enemy camp. It had made his breath catch in his throat. Caesar's wolves were organised and impressive, and the man had brought his army at incredible speed with virtually no supplies. At the time, the moon had been out and the enemy camp had been abundantly clear. Now, Bucco could see little but the many glowing fires across the hill.

He found himself questioning his earlier certainty. *Would* they get to the bridge? Would they manage to cross? They *should* do. They had every advantage. But Caesar had proved himself to be more than just a thorn in their side at every step so far, and it would be complacent of them to assume safety now. Of course they were moving into the hills, and within an hour's march they would be in valleys between high peaks where the threat of the proconsul's ever-present cavalry would be largely nullified. Horse could not operate effectively in such terrain.

Bucco's gaze strayed across the enemy camp once more, picking out the large darker areas where there were no fires, where the cavalry had their horses corralled. Something odd struck him as he did so, but it was one of those thoughts like the touch of a butterfly, which dusted the edge of his mind and was gone in an instant. He frowned.

He repeated his scan, his eyes playing across the enemy force from left to right, from the northern edge, where he knew from earlier observations the latrines to be concentrated, across the camp, toward the southern end, where the general had placed his most impressive veteran troops.

No, he still couldn't quite catch it. What had he noticed?

No fires? No, that wasn't it. The areas without fires were corrals, as he had noted. So what was it? The fires were blazing, which was reasonable, despite the heat of the Hispanic night. There would be men drying clothes, cooking late evening food, sitting round them and laughing, with no fear of needing to keep their fires hidden. Both armies knew the other was there, so there was no need to go short on anything.

Both armies knew the other was there.

Blazing fires.

He was hurrying back past the standards a moment later, finding a different vantage point. He had to be sure. He couldn't interrupt his seniors mid-childish argument without being certain. Pausing at another position, where two crates rested atop one another, he peered off into the gloom with hungry, narrowed eyes. Too dark. Just too dark.

The moon broke through the cloud for the briefest of moments, a shining blast of silvery light that played along the landscape and was gone in a trice. It had been enough. The enemy ranks were thin, and the tightly-ordered area of veteran legions at the southern end was now occupied by the ranks of the cavalry.

It had all been seen in the blink of an eye, but he knew he'd been right, now. What he'd noticed was that he could see the fires *too* clearly. They were not obscured by crowds of men, as they should have been. The soldiers were not at the fires and it was not yet late enough for them all to be abed. So where had they gone?

The slopes opposite seemed to be covered in camp fires and spread out groups of cavalry. The infantry had gone.

'When did they go?' he said, grabbing a startled legionary guarding the supplies. The man blinked in incomprehension.

'Caesar's legions. They've gone. They're not in the camp. That's just the cavalry. They cannot have moved out without being seen. You *have* to have seen them leave. When did they go?'

The legionary shrugged in perplexity. 'I… no idea, sir.'

Bucco released the man and turned, running back across the slope toward the command tent. He couldn't hear the arguing now, but that might be because of the blood thundering in his ears as he pounded across the grass. Two guards made to stop him as he approached the tent, but recognised him as the young tribune who'd recently ducked out, and they stepped back, saluting.

Bucco burst into the tent to see the two generals at a table, arguing over a map of the area, various officers clustered around them, but the conversation stopped and every face looked up, turning to this intrusion.

'Caesar's on the move,' he said in a burst of words between heaving breaths. His seniors' faces creased into frowns. Swallowing and taking one deep, preparatory breath, he tried to slow his pulse. 'The camp opposite is almost entirely cavalry. The legions have gone.'

'Gone?' replied Afranius, his face pasted with disbelief.

'They were there two hours ago, sir,' Bucco replied. 'I saw them with my own eyes. But since then it's clouded over. I think Caesar has used the cover of darkness to slip out of the camp. His infantry are gone. He's left just the cavalry there.'

'You're sure of this?' Petreius said in a quiet voice.

'Yes, sir. I've just seen it for myself.'

He stepped forward into the gap that had opened up among the officers. Petreius and Afranius looked at one another, their previous disagreement now forgotten, then peered down at the map.

'Why would they go?' Afranius muttered.

'*Where* would they go?' replied Petreius.

There was an uncomfortable silence. 'They must know about Octogesa. The bridge.'

Petreius' frown deepened. 'They can't. Their cavalry have been concentrated near us, harrying our foragers. Caesar's been behind us all the way.'

A man in a prefect's uniform on the far side of the table cleared his throat nervously. 'That might not be true, sir.'

'Go on?'

'Well, sir, one of the units that had been on patrol in the valley above Portus Iberus was fallen upon and slaughtered a few days ago. Seventy men or so, both legionaries and auxilia.'

'And why am I hearing about this now?' Petreius said, a dangerous edge to his tone.

'The hills hereabouts are always dangerous, sir. Bandits and tribes who still resent Roman peace being settled upon them. There are such men all around, and it's not unheard of for small units to be killed by such men. That's why we rarely keep such minimal numbers out in patrols. We naturally assumed they had pissed off the logging communities or disturbed a bandit camp or some such.'

'But it is possible,' Afranius put in, 'indeed, highly likely given this turn of events, that it was Caesar's men who killed them and that he knows about the route of our travel and that the pontoon bridge is there?'

'I suppose so, sir.'

Petreius nodded to Afranius and the two men looked down at the map again.

'If Caesar knows about the bridge and his men have been in the valley, then they probably know that's the only viable approach. He would have to take his men on a wide circuit to get round us safely and unnoticed, and the terrain he'd have to cross is not good, and gets worse as they move south. He cannot hope to beat us there in a race.'

Petreius shook his head. 'I disagree. His legions are unencumbered. They did not bring supply wagons and the like. They travel like Marius' Mules, with everything they need on their back. They're hardened veterans, and we know how damn fast they can move. They should still be on the other side of the Sicoris panicking about catching us up. Instead they caught up with us in less than a day. Caesar knows where he's going, and he's no fool. If he's making for the valley and the bridge with his legions, then it's no desperate attempt. He believes he can do it. And if he believes he can do it, then he probably can. We need to drop our supplies and move fast. He has anything up to two hours' head start, and might have been slipping men away earlier than that, like we did at Ilerda. Damn the man, but he's used our own strategy against us.'

Afranius turned to the camp prefect. 'How long will it take to get the army moving?'

'Properly, sir? Two hours.'

'And if we leave the tents and everything we don't need?'

'An hour, sir.'

Petreius shook his head. 'Another hour for Caesar to move. And he's left his cavalry for a reason other than just the look of things. The moment we move, they'll be on us like a cloud of hornets, irritating and troubling us, slowing us down. We have to move now and we have to leave the wagons.'

Afranius straightened. 'Don't be ridiculous. Quite apart from the food, they contain all the weapons, spare armour, the pay for the men, the artillery and all the miscellaneous equipment. We can't afford to just throw it away. Caesar will certainly make use of it.'

'How much damned use will it be if Caesar's men seal off our route and we're trapped on this side of the Iberus? Every day in Ilerda another unit went over to the man. Soon our own legions will start to desert to the enemy.'

'And if you starve them and lose their pay it'll happen all the sooner. We need those wagons.'

Petreius rounded on his fellow general. 'Then your legions can guard them. Mine are making for the Iberus at full speed.'

Bucco sagged. Even now his commanders could not decide on a course of action. What it must be like to be an officer in *Caesar's* army...

* * *

Caesar stood on the slope of the valley with a satisfied smile. Four legions were arrayed across the mouth of the vale that led down to the enemy's pontoon bridge. They were tired. There was no denying that. But they were also resolute and knew that they had turned the tide, and spirit can, for a time, replace rest.

They had slipped away in the darkest hours of the night and moved through valleys parallel to the one in which the two armies had camped. The going had been dreadful. Even with Galronus' advice and the scouts ranging ahead, they had been forced to cross awful terrain. Down steep valley sides, skidding and losing their footing, up steep valley sides, staggering, and hauling on undergrowth to aid the climb. On one notable occasion, they'd even had to descend a jagged rocky slope, which had cost the lives of a number of men. Yet Caesar and his officers had borne the worst of it along with their soldiers, and the enthusiasm of the army flagged only rarely.

Arriving finally in the valley just as the sun neared its zenith, the officers had been concerned that the enemy might have beaten them. If they had learned of the deception quickly enough and had discarded the slowest and most cumbersome elements of their column, they might even now be on the bridge. Upon their arrival, Caesar had sent a fast unit of riders down to the Iberus, and they had come back with confirmation that the enemy had not managed to get ahead of them. As they returned from the river, they were chased by small units that had been set to guard the valley, but once they caught sight of the four legions, they broke off pursuit and melted away into the trees.

In a small attempt to rest his exhausted men, Caesar had sent scouts out to keep an eye on the approaches and give them adequate warning of the enemy's approach, and had then let all four legions fall out and rest, if in position and with weapons and armour to hand.

They had managed almost an hour before the scouts came back, bellowing their warnings.

Afranius and Petreius' army put in an appearance a quarter of an hour later. Their vanguard, formed of Hispanic cavalry units with a few regular turma among them, emerged from another shallow valley and onto the wide 'Y' shaped plain where the road forked. The small village that rested at the foot of the hill had evacuated at the sight of Caesar's army, the population now somewhere safe, probably observing proceedings with bated breath. Whether they favoured Caesar or Pompey, or neither, the fact remained that any battle fought here might destroy their homes and livelihood.

Fronto, standing not far from Caesar, with his Eleventh Legion arrayed before him, watched the enemy carefully. The vanguard flooded out onto the plain but drew up in groups far from contact with the waiting legions. There appeared to be some sort of confab occurring, and the Caesarian officers watched with interest as the rest of the Pompeian army began to arrive, the officers near the front. More consultation, more delays, and a decision made. Turning aside from their original path, the bulk of the enemy veered off to their right, making for the slopes of a hill on the far side of the low depression.

'Are they turning back?' Plancus murmured? 'Returning to Ilerda?'

Caesar shook his head. 'By now the small force they left there will have fallen and our men will control Ilerda's heights. They must know that. They are uncertain as to their next step. They cannot have anticipated us reaching this place ahead of them, though they have moved remarkably slowly. Galronus and his cavalry must have been excelling in their work during the night and the morning, slowing the enemy. They seek another defensive position like their last while they decide how to deal with us. But like their previous position, they select a hill in desperation and will find shortly that they, once again, have no access to water, while we have the stream that feeds the village here.'

'They will move quickly,' Fronto said.

'Sorry?'

The officers had turned to look at him, and Fronto folded his arms. 'Despite setbacks and troubles, and with leaders who can agree on nothing, someone at least in that army can pull their arse back out of the flames. We nearly had them at the hill yesterday, but someone managed to pull them together. It's happening again. Look.'

The other officers followed his gaze. A unit of auxilia several hundred strong from Petreius' army had suddenly burst into motion, breaking away from the main force and racing to the northwest. They were Hispanic auxiliaries from the look, lightly armed and armoured, but swift because of it.

'Where are they going?' Antonius mused.

'From what Galronus said, that would be the road to Octogesa.'

'They'll find no help there.'

'No,' Fronto agreed, 'but if they can secure the route, they can take the army that way. It doesn't help them head into the territory they desired, as they'll still be on this side of the Iberus, but if they can hold us in that valley long enough to ferry much of their army across to the town, that puts the Sicoris between us and them again.

And you remember how much trouble that river's already caused us.'

Caesar nodded with a serious expression. 'Can we stop those auxilia?'

Fronto shook his head. 'We're all heavy infantry, and exhausted ones at that. We'll never catch them in time, and our horse are just a few light scouts.'

'Then we must stop them consolidating. If the rest of their infantry move off that hill, I want two legions to deploy across the gap covering the road to Octogesa.'

'General,' Fabius said quietly, 'if you do that then neither route is safely held. They have five legions. We have four, though numerically we're about matched. But then whichever route they choose to make for, there will only be two legions to stop them.'

'Fabius, think in broader terms,' the general said quietly. 'Two legions will lie between them and freedom, but whichever route they commit to, the other two legions can close upon them like a gate and they will be trapped between both forces. With luck that will not happen anyway. We must make their options *too* unpalatable.'

'Why?' demanded Antonius.

'Because I would still far rather we accept their surrender, save lives on both sides, and end this with negotiation than with bloodshed. We are all Romans.'

There was a silent moment of uncomfortable acceptance of that fact.

'But if they manage to secure that route first, it matters not what we plan,' Fronto murmured.

Now, the main enemy force was beginning to move up the slopes of their chosen hill across the flat ground, once more attempting to command heights against them. Again settling for land with no water. Fronto let out a sharp breath.

'The cavalry.'

Indeed, as the Pompeian force cleared the valley ahead, its rear guard were fighting a desperate running battle, protecting wagons as they came. Galronus' horse were on them constantly, cutting at them, swiping at the army again and again. Fronto remembered seeing their wagon train as it was pulled up onto that hill the previous day, and by his estimate at best half of it remained. The rest had either been abandoned for speed issues or had been captured by Galronus and his men as they advanced. Either way it meant more hardship for the Pompeians.

And as that moving battle closed on the hill and Petreius' legions came out to help defend their supplies and pull them into place, so part of the Caesarian cavalry force broke off the attack and rode out at a tangent.

Fronto smiled, looking forward to seeing Galronus once more, but it did not appear that the officers were the Remi's goal. A single ala of cavalry, mixed Roman, German and Gallic, raced off around the flat ground, skirting the enemy force and following the Pompeian horse as they rode off toward Octogesa.

Fronto shifted position and peered around the hill, trying to watch what was happening. It was then he realised that the auxilia were not running for the Octogesa pass, but had made instead for a small, high peak that dominated that other valley.

'They're trying to secure that mountain. If they can, nothing will shift them and they'll be able to pour down arrows, bullets and rocks at will. Petreius and Afranius will be able to use their positioning to move the rest of his force that way.'

'Then should we not deploy the legions there now?' Fabius urged.

Caesar shook his head. 'That weakens our guard here and opens the route to the Iberus for them.'

'Don't panic,' Fronto grinned. 'I think Galronus has this one.'

* * *

Galronus urged his men on. They were tired, and the horses more so, but he needed a little more from them all yet. They had spent night and morning harrying the rear of the Pompeian column as they fled to the south-west, but Galronus had been sensible and spared the horses as much as possible. Each time he ordered two alae in to attack the rear guard and the wagons, he sent the rest ahead with a wide berth, so they could spend half an hour resting before they were required. Then, as they caught up with the rested men, two more alae would be chosen and begin the attack, while the tired warriors joined those moving ahead to rest. It had allowed them to maintain a constant attack on the column, yet still with relatively fresh horses.

For the last mile or so, though, things had been different. The enemy, sensing they were near the valley and safety, had sped up, and Galronus' men had had no time for rest.

The Remi didn't have a god of luck. The gods controlled things in their own sphere of influence, of course, but no one could claim to control luck. That was in the very nature of it. Men made their own chance. But since meeting Fronto, Galronus had been steadily coming round to the idea of his friend's favourite deity. And if anything yet had given him cause to believe in Fortuna, it had been the last few moments.

As the enemy force had changed course and made for their rise to defend once again, Galronus had taken a single ala and ridden out around the edge of the Pompeians, making for Caesar and his officers to discuss their next move. But as soon as they had cleared the valley and the manoeuvring army, he had spotted the cohort or so of native light infantry making for the Octogesa pass. Though he'd no confirmation of what they planned, there could be little doubt that they were meaning to secure it and head for Octogesa, with the Iberus path closed by four legions. Caesar's force couldn't stop them in time, for sure. Thanking Fronto's beloved goddess for this turn of events, Galronus had redirected his riders and raced after the infantry.

The enemy were on foot, but swift, and were already climbing the slope toward the high peak that dominated the pass, and indeed the entire area.

'Fast as you can. Take them.'

He urged his own horse on, pushing her relentlessly. Caesar's army couldn't stop those men, and once they commanded the heights it would take the god Taranis and all his thunderbolts to shift the bastards. And once they hit the *real* heights, the cavalry would be useless, for their horses couldn't manage the slope. He had one chance.

They were close. He could see the enemy as individuals, now. They were a mixed group – spearmen, swordsmen, slingers, archers. All native auxiliaries, but all from different units or tribes. And they had been sent with no warning and little organisation, for they were not moving as units but all in one mass, each man trying individually to reach the safety of the heights. That would be the start of their undoing. Men running and fighting as individuals were never truly effective in the field.

The first of the auxilia fell. He was a slinger, armed only with the leather missile weapon and a pouch of stones, armoured only with a white tunic and light calf-skin boots. A rider's spear plunged into his back, and the momentum as the man fell and the horse ran on snapped the shaft at the entry point. The dying, shrieking man fell away with the head of the lance still buried inside him, falling silent only as he was smashed and crushed under the hooves of several horses. The victorious cavalryman simply discarded the broken shaft and drew his sword.

Another man went down to a sword blow, then another to a spear. A Hispanic head rolled free, a native disappeared beneath hooves, bellowing curses and pleas. More enemies died, and then a horseman joined them, transfixed where he sat with a native spear that passed through him, from the hip beneath his chain shirt up through the torso, emerging near the liver and punching through the iron rings from the inside.

A man bellowed something in their rough language and the enemy stopped running, some quicker than others, and turned to face their attackers, brandishing their weapons.

'Wrong choice,' shouted Galronus as he swept down his blade and took off an arm just above the wrist, the sword falling away still tightly clutched in the fingers of the severed hand.

And it *was*. While they were running they were dying, but some might have reached the higher slopes where the horses couldn't go and would have been safe. Now that someone had called for them to stand against the enemy, none would survive. Perhaps they felt secure in that they outnumbered Galronus and his men by almost two to one. If so, they were due a rude awakening. Precious few of them were armoured, and few even carried shields, whose who did sporting just a small, round affair like the ones Galronus had seen gladiators using.

The Remi noble put out a call to his men to surround the enemy, but it was entirely unnecessary. They were already doing so, riders plunging on ahead, then turning to take the lead-most natives. Galronus felt the satisfaction of an assured victory flooding him as his sword rose and fell, biting into leather, or wood, or bronze, but mostly into flesh. He cut and swiped, thrust and chopped, and men fell like chaff before a strong breeze.

It was over in a matter of heartbeats. Hundreds of lightly-equipped Hispanic auxilia lying in heaps, dead or dying, weeping and whimpering the most insistent noise, the metallic tang of blood and the pungent stink of ruptured bowel an overriding cloying stench. Galronus looked around. He could see few riderless horses and there were a few beasts lying among the dead, but those who had gone to the underworld in overwhelming numbers mostly belonged to the enemy.

Despite the noises here, slowly the Remi became aware of another sound, and he turned, wondering at the strange, discordant harmony that warbled along in the background. It was *two* noises, in fact, from *two* sources, which was what caused such discordance.

One was the cheering of the Caesarian legionaries blocking the valley to Portus Iberus. They were in loud voice, showing their support and appreciation of the cavalry and their swift and brutal success. But at the same time, a low moan of despair flowed across the valleys from the hill where the Pompeian army now sat, pulling up their wagons into safety and forming a defensive line just as they had on a similar hill some miles away the previous day. The rest of Galronus' cavalry had now broken off their attacks and come forward to rejoin Caesar's army.

That was it. The enemy had lost the race to the pontoon bridge and, despite some clever devil's last minute decision to change course and run for Octogesa, Galronus had destroyed their hope of securing the pass. Even as he watched, the Remi noble could see a large unit of men departing Caesar's lines and making for his own location. Several centuries of heavy legionaries and a few units of archers and slingers. Not only had Petreius and Afranius lost the chance to control that peak and secure the route for their army, now Caesar was garrisoning it against them, sealing them off from Octogesa as surely as he had done from the bridge.

They had lost the race and were trapped on this side of both rivers. Their best hope now would be to return to Ilerda, but they must be aware they would have to fight Caesar's rear guard legion there to retake control. They were damned no matter what route they took now.

With luck the commanders would see that and discuss terms.

* * *

'No,' Caesar replied, his eyes flashing angrily.

'General, we are on the cusp of victory. We have them trapped, demoralised, low on supplies, cut off from water. Their men must be all-but ready to put an end to their own officers by now. I know the men are tired, but they will have one night of rest and that will be enough. In the morning, they can storm those slopes and finish the Ilerda legions for good.'

Caesar was trembling slightly as he regarded the defiant figure of Salvius Cursor.

'For the last time, no! Tribune, you have been advocating blood and fire since the day we crossed the Rubicon. I know you to bear only loathing for Pompey and I appreciate having your vehement support among my officers, but I maintain the position I have held throughout. If Roman lives can be spared, then they must. The time will come for blood and iron, for Pompey will face me and do so with an army at his back, but out in these provinces the legions serve the name of Pompey, not the man himself. They can be turned and saved, and by all the gods, I will do that before I draw one unnecessary drop of Roman blood.'

'General, don't dismiss him so readily,' muttered Antonius, stepping closer.

'I thought *you* had unhitched your cart from Salvius' horse, Marcus?'

'Prudence calls for action, Gaius,' Antonius breathed quietly. 'Salvius Cursor is far from the only man seeking an end to it all. This has gone on for months, and we have seen setback after setback. This is the closest we have been to victory, and is likely the closest we will *ever* be. Even if Afranius is prepared to make a deal, we both know Petreius will not. Many of the officers silently share Salvius' opinion, though they do not possess his somewhat forthright attitude, so they will not push for it. And take it from me that even much of the centurionate among the legions is ready now and waiting for the order to unleash Tartarus upon the enemy. You risk alienating your own legions if you will not give them the chance to finish this. They did not train to run around harvesting grain and scratching their arses. They trained to kill the enemy, and they are right now awaiting your command to do just that.'

Caesar's angry glance tore from Salvius, lit briefly upon Antonius, and then slid to Fronto. With a startled frisson, Fronto realised that the general was running low on support among his officers, and he had turned now to Fronto as the one man in the tent he felt sure would support his pacific, conciliatory stance. Fronto, he knew, would agree with avoiding Roman bloodshed if possible. And he also knew, clever old bastard that he was, that Fronto had pretty much put all his eggs in the general's basket and could hardly afford to turn on him.

Yet even now, at this dreadful moment of decision, Fronto was struggling. Perhaps it *was* time to end the ongoing fight for Ilerda. If they let this chance go, would they have another? Might a careful strike now save many lives in the long run? It made him feel sick to even think of agreeing with the warmonger Salvius, but the fact that Antonius and the other officers were coming around to the same idea did not escape him. And Antonius was right. The centurionate *were* ready for the fight and *did* want Caesar to unleash them. Felix himself had told Fronto as much. Shit, Felix was *one of them* who was ready to take that hill. And there was more. Every night, when Fronto laid down on his cot, he drifted away from this nightmare campaign and saw Lucilia and the boys, Balbus and his friends. They should be safe, but he had not heard from them in weeks, and they *were* in Hispania, after all. And then there was the issue with Catháin and Balbus' incriminating letters. Things required Fronto's urgent attention elsewhere and he could not protect his family or help Catháin while he was still following Petreius and Afranius around Hispania, failing to stop them.

The temptation to argue for a fight was almost overwhelming.

Which is why his next words came through gritted teeth.

'*We* are good men. *We* are the wronged who are putting Rome right. *Pompey* is the sort of man who would climb that hill right now with a knife in his teeth ready to slit Roman throats. Caesar is not, and for that we should all be proud of our service. Any man can kill. Brigands and thieves and beggars. But it takes a great man to be merciful. Any fight we start here kills only Romans. Remember that, when you bow before your altars in your tents. Senatus Populusque Romanus. For the senate and the people of

Rome. What value do we place on that vow if we espouse it as we kill those same people. I say no. I say Caesar is right. They are close to breaking. What we need to do is not kill them but push them over the edge into surrender.'

'Caesar,' Antonius said, glaring at Fronto, 'the men will not take well to another protracted siege.'

'The men will do what they are paid to do,' Caesar replied coldly. 'And if they mutter dissent, their officers can remind them that they are well paid and well fed, and have plenty of water. Point to the force on that hill and explain how Petreius and Afranius have no access to water. No stores of food barring a few wagons they escorted hither. And with us now in control of Tarraco, what chance do they have of pay?'

Mamurra cleared his throat. 'All good points, Caesar, but only if they can be truly starved. We could not besiege them properly at Ilerda for they had control of the bridge and the river. Here, they are on a single hill. From there they will be able to range across the nearby slopes and find water. If we hope to end them here, then we must prevent that.'

Caesar nodded. 'We have four legions in place. Two will remain in position blocking the passes. The Seventh and Ninth, however, will split up and search around the enemy's position. Find any source of sustenance and secure it. I want fortifications here that make Alesia look like a child's sand fort. Both routes to the Iberus and Octogesa fully fortified, and no water or food within reach.'

Fronto saluted, trying not to feel irritated at the withering, bile-filled looks he was receiving from Salvius and Antonius, as well as the clear disapproval emanating from other officers in the tent.

He tried not to be irritated with himself too. His sentiments had been noble, but he'd almost choked on them. He'd had the chance to end it here and within a few days he might have been back with his wife, planning how to solve Balbus' problem. Instead, he had drawn out the campaign once more and prevented anyone from going home.

He was going to drink a lot of wine tonight.

Chapter Fifteen

28th of Quintilis – south-west of Ilerda

FRONTO closed the tent flaps and stepped away, Antonius at his side.

'He will be well. He's been this bad before.'

Fronto nodded, though in truth he was considerably less convinced. Four times now over the years he had seen Caesar fall to his recurring illness, but this was by far the worst. His personal medicus was watching over him now – the knowledge of his condition was still a tightly guarded secret and even the medical sections of the various legions knew nothing of it. The fit had ended, and Caesar was resting, but it had lasted so long and been so violent, Fronto had wondered if it would be the end this time. The fit had finally subsided, much to the relief of he and Antonius who had been with the general when it struck, but it had left Caesar weak and exhausted and he could do little more than lie in his cot and rest as the medicus checked him over and applied pointless poultices.

'I still say it is because he shuns sleep so much,' Antonius grumbled. 'No man can exist on the paltry hours Gaius keeps.'

'I think it goes deeper than that,' Fronto replied. 'I wonder if his father suffered the same?'

'Anyway, other matters demand our attention,' the staff officer noted, pointing across the camp at a small group of men approaching with a legionary guard. They were wearing the uniforms of officers, but the vexillum behind them was not one of Caesar's. It bore a 'II' and a horse in gold.

'Deputation from the enemy. Well timed, with the general down.'

'Let's see what they have to say,' Antonius replied.

'But somewhere private.'

The legionaries escorted the small party forward. The enemy deputation had been allowed to keep their weapons and standards.

The lead man was a tribune and, Fronto was surprised to note, a rather young one – far too young really to be wearing the broad stripe. With him were a narrow-stripe tribune, four centurions and a prefect, as well as an honour guard, though they had been kept at a small distance, just in case.

The deputation stopped in front of them and the officers inclined their heads respectfully. The senior tribune cleared his throat. He sounded nervous to Fronto, and clasped his hands tightly, probably to control trembling by the looks of it.

'Proconsul?' the man enquired, looking at Antonius. The curly haired officer chuckled.

'I wish. No. I have the honour to be Caesar's lieutenant and confidante, Marcus Antonius, and this is the esteemed legate and hero of the Gallic Wars, Marcus Falerius Fronto. Might I enquire of your name?'

The young man coughed nervously again. His eyes darted this way and that. 'I am Publius Cassius Bucco, senior tribune and interim commander of the Second Vernacular Legion. This is my colleague Gaius Afranius, son of the general. I trust the traditional rules of war apply and we are in no danger?'

Fronto frowned. No danger from *him*, certainly, or from Antonius. In fact, in no danger from anywhere in this camp, but two junior officers coming to Caesar rather than the senior generals was interesting, and Fronto would bet any danger to them would be posed by the junior tribune's own father when he found out about this.

'Of course,' Antonius replied smoothly and reassuringly.

'I would rather speak to the proconsul. It is he we came to visit.'

'The proconsul is indisposed at this moment,' Fronto replied, but be assured that we have the authority to speak for him in all matters. Come.'

He gestured to the headquarters tent and the party followed. At the door, Antonius waved at the centurions and Ingenuus' dismounted cavalrymen who formed the core of the escort. 'The guards can stay out here, along with most of the officers. If the two tribunes will join us for a cup of wine?'

Bucco and Afranius nodded their assent and the four men entered the tent.

'I bring you greetings from the camp of the Ilerda legions,' Bucco said as he took the indicated seat. Antonius collected a jug of wine and four cups from the cupboard. Fronto glared pointedly at him as he put them on the table and, with a grin, Antonius returned and collected the water too. Pouring four cups, he sank into his seat.

'You have a proposal for us?' he said.

Fronto, still with narrowed, suspicious eyes, held up a hand. 'Your camp numbers at least four legates, numerous senior prefects, several ex consuls and two generals. I don't intend any insult here, but might you explain why we are speaking to two tribunes?'

Bucco and Afranius shared what appeared to be an extraordinarily guilty look. Fronto's suspicions seemed well founded.

'There is,' the senior tribune said, skirting a reply by some margin, 'a strong sense in our camp that we are setting lines to go to war with our friends. Many of the officers and men of the Ilerda legions, regardless of this current nightmare and our allegiances to the governor, can claim at least distant blood ties to the men of your own legions. Some are closer than that. My own camp prefect has received a missive from his father warning him that his cousin serves as a senior centurion in your Eleventh Legion. And this is not an isolated case. We have fought three or four skirmishes now, but as yet the blades of the legions have not been too sullied with Roman blood. There is a feeling that this whole situation could be resolved before that happens.'

A nice speech, Fronto smiled. The delivery suggested that the lad had been rehearsing it word for word all morning. Educated and clever, then, but still unsure and lacking that strength of a veteran commander.

'This is ever the case in a civil war, Tribune,' Fronto replied, 'and it is highly regrettable. Unfortunately no matter how much all concerned might wish for peace, in order to achieve it one side must capitulate. And you have to be aware that we are in a vastly superior position. Your army is starving and going thirsty. You have minimal supplies and nowhere to run. We, on the other hand, now control Ilerda, Tarraco, and the routes to Octogesa and the river. Caesar has no reason to capitulate. I ask you again, why two tribunes, and not a senior ambassador?'

Again, the two men looked at one another, and this time it was the junior tribune who spoke.

'My father might consider terms.' He sighed. 'He is certainly in favour of avoiding unnecessary bloodshed among Romans. But Petreius is like a savage dog. He sees only enemies, not brothers. Petreius is the one who needs persuasion. But many of the centurions and officers in our camp would seek terms, given the chance.'

'So your father sent you out without informing his fellow general?'

'Not quite,' Bucco croaked. 'The two generals took a force to try and secure water where your Ninth Legion are preventing them. In their absence, there has been a debate among other senior officers. We were sent as a deputation, for my father is a friend of Cicero's and was present at his meeting with the general earlier this year, and Afranius can speak for his own sire. The question that I fear plays highest in the minds of our men and officers is: can your general be trusted.'

Antonius' face took on a slightly offended look. 'Did you come here to insult us?'

'Nononono. The fact is that Caesar's name has something of a mixed reputation here in Hispania. Some see him as one of their own, from his time in the south, and others see him as a man who came here only to rape the land for his own gain.'

Fair comment, thought Fronto, rather privately.

'And that reputation, which is embedded in the Hispanic legions, is somewhat increased by the general belief among the supporters of Pompey that Caesar is a war criminal, a would-be-king and a despot.'

He saw the ire building in Antonius' eyes, and made mollifying motions with his hands. 'I am forced to tell the truth as it is seen. But the fact remains that over the weeks in Ilerda, we have seen your army repeatedly pass up chances for slaughter. Caesar might have the reputation of a bloodthirsty conqueror, but what we have seen speaks more of a man seeking a measured and peaceful conclusion. Am I off the mark?'

Fronto shook his head. 'Very much on the mark, in fact.'

'Would Caesar agree terms that are beneficial to both sides?' Bucco asked. 'Other than a blanket surrender, I mean.'

'He would need the terms to secure Hispania and remove the danger of a Pompeian surge against him.'

'I believe such a thing is possible,' Bucco mused. 'We cannot speak for the governor of Hispania Ulterior, of course. Hispania Inferior could come to terms.'

'But those terms would involve the generals going free,' young Afranius blurted, earning him a despairing look from his companions.

Antonius was shaking his head, though Fronto was already thinking it through. To let Petreius go was to invite future troubles, but the same had been said about Ahenobarbus, and Caesar had still freed him. But then, perhaps the general had learned from that mistake. After all, Ahenobarbus had gone on to fortify Massilia against him. Yet if Petreius and Afranius going free was the price of peace, it was worth considering, certainly.

'You understand what we wish?' Bucco prodded.

'We do,' Antonius replied in flat tones. 'I cannot promise anything at this moment, but I will take your proposal to the general and see what he says. Return to your camp and speak to your people. We will send a deputation within the hour.'

Bucco and Afranius nodded and, taking a token swig from their untouched cups, rose from their seats and departed the tent. Antonius looked at Fronto.

'Afranius we can deal with. I don't think even Caesar will let Petreius go, and if he considers it, I'll counsel him against it.'

Fronto winced. 'Let's not be precipitous. Peace is worth a high price. It needs considering.'

Antonius threw him a sour look and moved around the table, downing the two largely-untouched cups of wine and straightening.

'Let's go talk to the old man, then.'

Emerging from the tent, they could see the Pompeian deputation making their way back to the gate to return to their own forces. Fronto gazed after them, and then followed Antonius across to the general's private quarters. A quick rap on the woodwork and the staff officer entered, Fronto at his heel. Caesar was partially upright now, seated on the edge of his cot. He held a plain earthenware cup and was looking into it with a foul expression.

'How do you feel?' Antonius asked.

'Much improved, thank you,' the general replied. 'Though on this occasion, the cure may just be worse than the illness. I saw him crack a large, spotted egg into the cup, and whatever else he's added still had bits of fur attached. In order to cure my head, dear old Atticus seems determined to empty my stomach.'

Fronto snorted. 'Medics. They're brilliant with wounds - I've been stitched back together more or less from head to foot – but anything they give you in a cup I've learned to avoid like the plague.'

Antonius nodded his agreement. 'Three glasses of unwatered Rhaetic, and you'll be right as rain.'

Caesar took the tiniest sip from the cup, pulled a face and placed the vessel on the table nearby. 'I think I prefer the thunder in my head. What brings you two back so quickly? The medicus says I need several hours' rest yet.'

'It seems the divisions in the enemy camp run deeper than we even suspected,' Antonius replied. 'Apparently Afranius is all-but ready to come to terms, though Petreius wishes to fight on. But regardless, while both are out of the camp trying to cause trouble for the Ninth, their officers sent us ambassadors. They are willing to discuss terms on certain conditions.'

'Conditions?'

'That the terms are favourable to them, and not total submission,' Fronto replied. 'I believe the subtext to be that the legions wish to retain their standards and honour and to remain stationed in Hispania.'

'Their officers would have to change,' Caesar noted.

'Agreed. And they want the two generals to go free.'

'Which is unacceptable,' Antonius pointed out. 'Afranius, if he is the one seeking peace, we can deal with, but Petreius must be handed over.'

Caesar's left brow rose.

'You know I'm right,' Antonius grunted. 'That bastard needs to be chained or he'll be another Ahenobarbus. He'll turn up somewhere in the future, standing on strong walls and calling you a cock.'

Caesar rolled his eyes and pinched the bridge of his nose. 'It is worth considering all terms at this point.'

'Afranius' son was one of those who came to us,' Fronto noted. 'So he should know his father's mind.'

Again, Caesar nodded. 'I cannot go to them. Quite apart from the fact that I am weak as a kitten and need considerable rest before I move out of my tent, I would no more walk into their camp than Petreius would walk into mine. But we do need to agree terms. If this can be ended well, then it is our duty to Rome to do so. The question is, I believe, whether the generals can be persuaded to this. You say their officers are in favour of terms?'

'That was what our young visitors said,' Antonius replied.

'I need to be sure of the will of their officers and the chances that their commanders will agree. Fronto, take a deputation in reply. Tell them I am willing to consider terms that favour the legions remaining in control of Hispania, on the condition that they renounce all ties to Pompey and their senior officers, tribunes, prefects and legates, all step down from their commands to be replaced by neutrally-aligned personnel. If they are willing to do that, then I will guarantee the freedom of all officers to head back to Rome or to their homes and the legions may return to garrison. The stumbling block might be the two generals, but see if you can gauge their likelihood of surrender and whether they would be willing to do so without a guarantee of total freedom.'

Antonius smiled. 'We'll get them to agree.'

'Not you,' Caesar said. 'There are times you can be a little direct and impolitic. Fronto is calmer. He can do it. You need to be visible in the camp in my absence. I will be out to address the soldiers at the evening watch, but I must rest 'til then.'

Antonius, disapproval on his face, nodded. As he and Fronto emerged once more, he turned to the legate of the Eleventh. 'You will take an honour guard from your legion, Fronto.'

'Of course.'

'Including your senior tribune.'

Fronto sighed.

* * *

The approach was tense, to say the least. Fronto and his guard, along with Salvius Cursor and Felix, rode purposely through the gates of the Pompeian camp. They dismounted inside the ramparts – hastily thrown up mounds of earth little more than a couple of feet in height, surmounted by a fence of sudis stakes drawn from one of the surviving carts, augmented by whatever obstacles could be procured. It would not hold off an attack for long, Fronto was sure.

Their horses were taken by men of some unknown legion and tied to a hitching post near the gate before being given feed bags to keep them busy. Fronto and his men strode on up the sloping path toward the centre of the camp, between ordered rows of tents. It was ridiculous, really. He could as easily have been in their own camp, but for the nervous, suspicious looks of the legionaries around them.

One notable thing, though, was the lack of barrels and cauldrons. In his own camp, every few tents there was a cook fire with a cauldron of water for boiling foodstuffs. Here, water was rare in the extreme, and no such pots were in evidence, nor the troughs and barrels the men used for washing and cleaning up. A consequence of that was the unshaven, dirty appearance of the men and the odour of sweat that clung to the hillside. A further consequence of water deprivation was detectable as an undercurrent to the sweat that only increased as they moved through the camp. With no water, there could be no cleaning of latrines, no flushing away of urine. The stench of the stale latrines was beginning to permeate the camp after only half a day. What it would be like in a few days' time was the stuff of nightmares.

Never before had Fronto been so acutely aware of the depravities that a siege placed upon a camp, and in particular the absence of water. Certainly if this was *his* army, he'd be considering terms by now.

A consilium of officers awaited them in the command tent on the hill. Two were legates, as well as three prefects and various tribunes, including both Bucco and Afranius. As they entered, Fronto inclined his head and his men saluted. There were, he noted, no seats set out for them here. Fronto folded his arms.

'Be aware,' he said, quietly and with a dark undertone, 'that without the presence of your commanders, discussing terms with the enemy is seditio. I'm sure I don't need to remind you all of what that means. Before I speak further I need to know you are serious.'

There was a long pause. Legions rarely revolted against their generals but it had been known, and almost always resulted in harsh repercussions for those responsible. Fronto had to gauge how committed they all were to the idea.

'It has been discussed,' one of the legates said. 'But there are mitigating factors. If we make terms with the proconsul, we break only our oaths to Pompey. Our vows to Rome and the senate remain intact, for the senate is now in support of Caesar, being almost entirely populated with his men.'

There was a touch of bitterness in the man's words, and Fronto realised that the legates had probably been senators, or were expecting to be so when they laid down their commands.

'Lucius Afranius is loyal to Pompey, but he is also a true Roman and has intimated to his fellow officers a number of times that war against other Romans does not sit comfortably in his heart. If you can offer us reasonable terms on behalf of the proconsul, we will see that the general accepts them. Then there will be no seditio. Marcus Petreius is more determined to prevent Caesar gaining a foothold in Hispania, though I believe him to be deluded, for the proconsul clearly already has that. Petreius will deny it to the end, but he will have no choice but to capitulate when his fellow general and his officers all favour terms.'

Fronto nodded. 'The general's terms are these: Each legion is to renounce their oath to Pompey and take a new one to Caesar. Their tribunes, prefects and legates are to step down from command and return to Rome or to their homes and be replaced by new officers, though they will go with honour for their years of service and take their servants, slaves and all goods with them. The legions will return to their garrisons with their standards intact and no further action will be taken. A new governor will be installed in Tarraco by the decree of the senate. Both your generals will be faced with a choice. If they willingly lay down their arms and surrender, they will be permitted to leave Hispania with their personal retinues, but without any military force at their command. They may return to Rome or their estates if they are willing to submit to the senate's rule and to renounce their allegiance to

Pompey. If they are unwilling to do so, they may flee to Pompey's side, but Italia and the west will be closed to them and their estates will be impounded by the senate as enemies of Rome.'

There was silence as he finished, while the assembled officers took all this in. The terms were generally very favourable, if not for the senior commanders.

'And what offer will Caesar make to those who are willing to swear a new oath to him?'

Fronto frowned. The general had not covered such an eventuality. His thoughts drifted back to the various commanders across Italy he had seen granted clemency by the general. Almost certainly, Caesar would be willing to extend the same offers here. Before he could open his mouth, a voice piped up beside him.

'You have heard the general's terms,' Salvius Cursor snapped. 'You will step down and retire to your homes, or no terms will be granted, and the legions of the proconsul will irrigate this hill with the lifeblood of Pompeians.'

Fronto turned and tried not to stare in disbelief at his tribune. The moron!

Closing his eyes, he turned back to the assembled officers and opened them again. Their expressions had all hardened. *Oh well done, arsehole.*

'Your terms are understood, the legate said bitterly.'

Fronto took a breath. He could override his tribune and suggest that Caesar might be open to negotiation, but the damage had already been done. If he about-turned now, he would look weak and indecisive, and the officers here would not trust him anyway because of Salvius' words.

'Consider the options and speak to your generals,' Fronto said loudly. 'When you are ready to talk, send ambassadors.'

He turned his back on the men. With Salvius' ultimatum, the atmosphere had changed entirely, and he no longer felt like an embassy to an ally, but more of a lone wolf in the den of another pack. Taking a deep breath, he walked out, with the others at his heel. As they emerged into the sunlight, Fronto checked they were out of earshot of enemy officers and leaned close to Salvius.

'If you ever get the urge to set your own terms in the middle of my negotiations again, bite your tongue very, *very* hard, or I will have it torn from your head and nailed to the standard of the Eleventh.'

Salvius Cursor simply sneered, and Fronto fought his temper as they began the descent toward the gate. Trying not to pay too much attention to the all-pervading odour of sweat and latrines, Fronto found himself listening to the sounds of life in the camp as they walked, and it was because of that he picked up some sort of commotion in the distance. Shouts of alarm. What was it? Surely Caesar's men couldn't be attacking? The general knew they were here and even on his worst day Antonius wouldn't launch an assault while their own men were inside.

Pounding feet.

Fronto turned to see a familiar figure running down the slope behind them – the broad stripe tribune Bucco. The man was waving at him.

'Run,' the tribune shouted between heavy breaths.

Fronto frowned, his eyes widening as he realised the cause of the man's urgent cry. At the crest of the hill, a man in a senior officer's uniform, armoured to the teeth and with sword in hand, had reined in to look around, a group of heavily armoured horsemen cresting the hill at his back.

The man wore a general's ribbon, and while it could as easily be Afranius as Petreius, somehow Fronto knew that it wasn't.

Petreius spotted the Caesarian ambassadors on the grassy slope and with a shout to his horsemen, kicked his steed into a dangerous pace, charging down the hill toward them.

'Go, sir,' Felix shouted, waving toward the gate. Fronto turned. It was touch and go whether they would reach their horses in time as it was. 'Don't be so bloody noble.'

He tugged at the centurion's chain shirt as Felix was busy calling his men to stop. A bodyguard of eight men and a centurion. Not the standard bearer, of course. He was already running for the horses. No soldier willingly let his standard fall into enemy hands, and any man who held this position was a dead man. Petreius rode with a score of men, all ready for war. Felix had eight.

'Contra equitas!' he bellowed.

The eight men formed into two rows of four in good order. The front men knelt and braced behind a shield wall, their pila held out forward between the cracks. The second stood behind them, resting a slanting line of shields atop the lower wall and angling forth their own pila. It was a gamble. Horses did not willingly charge a hedge of spears, but a row of four men was not quite the same level of defence.

'Felix!' shouted Fronto urgently, but the centurion was paying him no heed, pressed into the rear of the formation, adding the weight of his own shoulder to the brace. Fronto glanced around. Salvius Cursor was making for the horses, the standard bearer close behind. The tribune had drawn his sword and wrapped his cloak around his left hand as a makeshift shield.

Fronto was torn. The very idea of leaving Felix was appalling, but the notion of being ridden down beneath the hooves of Petreius' horse was no more appealing. With a last regretful glance at the centurion, he turned and ran, ripping his own sword from his scabbard and following Salvius' lead with his cloak.

Petreius was not the first to reach the hasty formation of legionaries. One of his men rode straight at them, but his horse had other ideas. As he closed, the beast veered to the side and reared, throwing him from the horned saddle. The man was good, one of the general's bodyguard, and he hit the ground well, rolling and holding his sword out of the way to prevent injury. He came to the end of his roll and rose to his feet already moving with the momentum. Fronto caught the incident out of the corner of his eye as they ran.

Another man came rolling past the formation, his horse having done exactly the same. This guard was less agile in his fall, but with shouts of agony and shaking out a pained arm, he rose and staggered on. Fronto glanced ahead again. They were closing on the gateway. The soldiers there were dithering, apparently unsure whether they were supposed to be helping their general or letting the ambassadors leave. Salvius was already nearly at the gate.

Something made Fronto turn before it happened.

One of the riders' horses was made of bolder stuff. The beast hit the nine-man defensive formation like a boulder striking a stick sculpture. Men were thrown in every direction, exploding outwards. Three unfortunates were simply crushed beneath the horse, but the others were not faring much better. He saw one dispatched with a sword slash to the back, broken chain links and blood flying through the air.

Felix was down on one knee at the side, in front of a legionary tent, struggling to hold off a rider who was chopping repeatedly at him.

Fronto, his heart in his throat, turned and ran on. Salvius and the standard bearer were making for the centre of the gate.

'The horses!' Fronto shouted.

'Fuck the horses,' the tribune yelled back as his feet pounded into the gateway. Three men seemed to have decided that their senior commander was the one to support and were drawing swords and running for Salvius as others carried stakes ready to seal off the gateway.

Fronto's gaze tore away from them and to the twelve horses tied to the post near the gate. Third from the end was Bucephalus, the magnificent black beast he had inherited eight years ago from Longinus. Not even for a moment did he consider the possibility of leaving the animal.

Behind, the enemy were busy. Petreius was yelling something at his men about getting the standard, and pointing at the gate, but his riders were being slowed by the need to fight their way through the wounded and dying legionaries. Even nursing shattered arms, limping and unable to raise a shield, the men of the Eleventh were fighting on, buying precious time for their legate and their standard.

Hardening his heart, Fronto ran for the horses.

The equisio reached up to untie the beasts, but a legionary appeared from somewhere yelling something about stopping Caesar's men. The groom dithered, uncertain what to do, and the legionary turned on the approaching legate. Perhaps he thought a man in senior uniform and with more than a touch of grey in his hair would be no trouble, but he launched an almost negligible attack on Fronto, the sword lancing out in a simple move, clearly expecting his opponent not to be competent with his own weapon.

The legate flung his left arm out, catching the sword on the wrapped cloak and pushing it aside. His own sword swung out at head height, blade flat on. The soldier had hurried from whatever he was doing to join the fray and had not found time to locate his helmet. The sword caught him on the temple with a dull clonk and sent him spinning away to the floor. It was not that Fronto felt any urgent need to preserve enemy lives at that particular juncture, but more of a combination of a head blow being the quickest way to put the man out of the fight, and the chance that the equisio might look upon him favourably for his mercy.

As the man thudded to the ground unconscious, Fronto reached out and unhitched Bucephalus.

His eyes rolling, face twitching nervously, the equisio untied two more horses and proffered Fronto the reins. The legate paused for just a moment. The temptation to leave Salvius fighting for his life was almost overwhelming. Certainly life would be considerably easier without the insane tribune around. With a sigh, Fronto grasped the reins and turned Bucephalus.

He moved with slightly greater urgency as he caught sight of the scuffle back up the hill. The legionaries were all on the floor now, Felix included, and only one was still fighting back. Even as Fronto turned, Petreius' blade arced down and smashed into the legionary's head, all-but splitting it in two. The horsemen were veering round him and coming on, racing for Fronto and the two other fleeing Caesarians in the gateway.

Concentrating on his course, Fronto turned and raced for the exit. Men had put stakes in the way to close much of the gate, but they could not seal the centre, for Salvius Cursor was fighting like an enraged bear there. Of the three men who had run to stop him, one was already on the floor, moaning and clutching at a huge gash in his side that had been so powerful it had even carved through the leather subarmalis he wore. Another was fighting, but staggering, one of his legs already useless and sheeted with blood. The third man was being cagey and had yet to be wounded, but Salvius was clearly ascendant. Fronto's gaze slid past him. The standard bearer was out of the camp and running down the hill toward freedom. A native Hispanic auxiliary at the side of the gate was busy nocking an arrow to his bow.

'Salvius! Horses!' he bellowed, and released the reins of the other two, guiding them in the direction of the tribune even as he let go. Bucephalus, he angled slightly left.

Fronto knew how to ride a horse. On the whole he still felt more comfortable walking, but a boy did not grow up in a patrician house without learning to ride. He'd never been good with jumps, though. It was something about his timing. He was never quite right.

He couldn't afford to get this one wrong.

Even as Salvius Cursor put his blade through the neck of an opponent in the gateway and turned with a roar on the cagey one, the remaining legionary broke and fled back to the side. Salvius grabbed the reins of the horse running at him and twisted, pulling himself up with the dexterity of an athlete. He couldn't settle properly between the four horns of the saddle with the desperate move, and found himself in front of the saddle, sat forward on the shoulders of the beast, almost on its neck. To compensate for his position and the slope, he leaned back and slapped the animal on the rump with the flat of his gleaming, sticky sword. The horse raced away out of the camp, down the slope, with the tribune balanced precariously on its back.

Fronto caught all of it only out of the corner of his eye. He prayed as he judged as best he could his position. Bucephalus had managed only five strides to build up speed, but there was no choice. He leapt. The archer raised his bow, sighting and pulling back.

Fronto had had grand ideas of his jump being perfect and both front hooves smashing the brains out of the archer before he released. In fact, his jump had been, as always, slightly mistimed, and only the will of the goddess who clung to his neck on a thong saved the standard bearer. The very tip of one hoof clipped the extreme top end of the bow at the instant of release.

For a horrible moment, the arrow was in flight directly underneath Bucephalus' chest, then its speed made the difference. The missile arced out ahead, and Bucephalus landed with only slight awkwardness, and ran on, picking up speed as he fled the hill. The arrow arced high, almost on target, but fell to earth with a thud some eight feet from the running standard bearer.

He rode on, in the wake of the standard bearer and the tribune.

'For the love of Minerva, weave as you ride,' bellowed Salvius back at him, and Fronto realised in a moment of blind panic that he was riding in a straight line, while the tribune was moving back and forth all over the place. Realising why, Fronto veered wildly to the right and almost weed as an arrow whirred past him, right where he'd been, and thudded into the turf.

Ten heartbeats later, Salvius slowed, let go of the reins of the second horse he had somehow picked up in their mad flight, launched it in the direction of the standard bearer and with more dexterity than any man had a right to, manoeuvred himself back and plopped down between the saddle horns.

Out of range now of chance archers, the three men paused and looked back up at the hill. Petreius and his horsemen were at the gate, raging and pointing. The chances of the general accepting Caesar's terms had never seemed further away.

* * *

29th of Quintilis

The army of Petreius and Afranius set out the next morning. In yet another unexpected move, they had apparently prepared everything in the night and left even as the first lavender strains of the coming morning began to infect the deep, dark sky.

They moved in an unanticipated direction, too, along a narrow valley almost directly opposite Caesar's camp. By the time the various pickets to the north-east of the enemy's hill had become aware in the predawn that the Pompeians were leaving, there was little that could be done to stop them. The couriers carried the message around to the camp and Caesar and Fronto and the other officers were warned of their departure, but even by then most of the enemy legions had already descended the hill and were forging northwest. By the time Caesar's forces could get round to that valley they would already be gone.

They had left their sudis stake defences. They had left their tents and cook fires and wagons. They had left everything but men and horses and the weapons and armour they wore, and had run.

'What are they hoping to do?' Fabius snapped irritably, still wiping the sleep from his eye.

'Given the direction,' Fronto noted, 'they are either bound for Ilerda or Tarraco. They could, in theory, reach either, so long as they moved fast and were willing to suffer hardship.'

He tried to speak over the lump in his throat as he sent up a silent prayer to Fortuna that they never reach Tarraco. Lucilia and the others were but miles from that city.

'Tarraco will not be their destination,' Caesar said, as though reading his mind. 'They cannot know how strongly defended it is against them now that it is ours. And it is more than twice as far to Tarraco as to Ilerda. They have no supplies and are moving at speed. They know we will be nipping at their heels within the day. They are making for Ilerda. Though we now hold the place with one legion's worth of men, with another legion close by at the bridges, our men will have gathered all our supplies together there. I would be willing to wager my arm on the fact that Petreius intends to return to Ilerda, defeat our garrison there and take control once more, impounding our supplies and making them his own.'

'Sneaky fart bag,' Antonius snapped.

'Do not underestimate our enemy,' Caesar reminded them. 'We are not fighting maddened German kings now, but Roman generals with a history of military success. Petreius is only in his position because of years of intuitive command.'

'So what do we do?' Plancus asked quietly.

'We do what we have been doing thus far: we pursue him, bring him to a halt and prevent him from returning to Ilerda. You saw yesterday how close they are to breaking. A little more pressure and even Petreius will not be able to prevent his army cracking like an egg. We dispatch one cohort to Octogesa to take control of the ferries there, and one to Portus Iberus to dismantle the pontoon bridge and send the ships away. That way we cut them off from here for good and prevent a repeat of this escape attempt. And now that we know the terrain and what we're up against, we send out Galronus again to slow them and harry them, while the legions move to catch up.'

'We should have taken them while we could, Gaius.'

All eyes turned to Antonius, whose expression was uncharacteristically severe.

'And by now the landscape would have acquired two more hills, beneath which lay the honoured dead of two armies, both of whom are Roman. No. Yesterday proved that Petreius is harsh, defiant and resourceful. But it also proved how close we are to resolving this without a sea of blood. We go on. A few more days, gentlemen. A few more days and we will have them on their knees, begging for terms.'

* * *

Fronto passed through the gateway with his spirits deep in his boots, catching sight of the mass of Galronus' cavalry racing around the outer slope, making for the rear of Petreius' army. Everything was still in place, where the enemy had left it, from tents to cook pots to the carcasses of animals. There was the post to which Bucephalus had been tied.

The sky was still only beginning to lighten, faint traces of gold threaded through the pale mauve. The ground was gloomy and Fronto had to check each step carefully for what might lie underfoot. The bodies of the nine men from the Eleventh were not there. He'd half expected them to be left where they lay like the rest of the camp, but they had gone.

The men of his chosen cohort moved into the camp behind him, spreading out by tent party, looking for anything of use or import. The army would be on the move within the hour, following Petreius back toward Ilerda, but while the rest of the men made ready to leave, Fronto had given one cohort the task of searching the hill. No one had argued with the right of the Eleventh to do so, though every man in the camp would be twitching at the thought of potential booty to be had. Their primus pilus had fallen in this place, and everyone knew what that meant to a legion.

For a further half hour, the men scoured the hill, secreting away anything of value they found, gathering any supplies or weapons left behind, searching lockers and chests for anything important. Fronto made his way to the crest of the hill, leaving them to it. There he found something for which he'd not been prepared. Fourteen funerary urns sitting in a row, each with a neatly inscribed label. Behind them was a large area of ash, where the pyre had been lit. The Caesarian troops had not paid it any attention during the night. The enemy had their own dead to burn, of course. But the fact was that they had paid deference to the dead of the Caesarian army, too.

Fourteen meant other men had died as well as his own nine. Were they Petreius' cavalry or some others? He found Felix's urn easily enough and sighed as he lifted the heavy jar. "Lucky". He'd been named that for years. Given how the republic was going, maybe it was ironic and he had been *lucky* to be out of it so soon.

'There were others,' said a voice. 'Too many to burn and honour properly. These were your men and a few scouts and pickets the general had taken. He had them executed in front of the headquarters, before the whole army.'

The voice belonged to a man in a centurion's uniform who stood in the doorway to the command tent.

'You did them honour.'

'They were Romans,' the man replied. 'We put a coin in every mouth to pay the boatman. They deserved no less.'

'And you alone remained?'

'Hardly,' the centurion said, and stepped out to one side. A steady stream of men emerged from the tent, mostly centurions, with occasional optios, three tribunes and a prefect. Fronto noted Bucco as one of the men.

'We almost had peace,' he said, nodding to the tribune.

'We did,' Bucco replied. 'And we still will. Afranius fought our corner well. He is ready, though he went with Petreius anyway. He is not willing to leave his legions to his fellow general.'

'Good man.'

'And because he went, so did his son.'

Fronto sighed. 'But because they went, there is still a chance for terms.'

'This war needs to be over,' Bucco said sourly. 'I am new to the legions, and already I tire of the killing.'

Fronto gave the man an odd smile. 'That might just make you a good officer.'

Chapter Sixteen

1st of Sextilis – near Ilerda

'WHY don't we just use the scouts, find a quicker path and get ahead of them?' Plancus muttered as he watched the latest dead being ferried back on stretchers. Fronto, sitting astride Bucephalus next to his fellow legate, sighed.

'A whole number of reasons. Firstly, what happens if we get ahead and block their path, but they change direction and decide to press for Tarraco? Our army sits in the hills all day and waits for an opposition that isn't coming while they get a good head start. Then there's the trouble in doing so. These hills aren't that high, but they're spotted with protruding rock ridges and covered with olive groves. Cavalry would be in trouble crossing them, and we learned how troublesome the terrain can be when we went ahead near Octogesa. No one wants to repeat that journey across the rocks.'

'But if we can't get ahead of them, they might make Ilerda and wipe out the garrison there.'

Fronto shook his head. 'Once we get out of the hills and into the open we can manoeuvre properly and stop them. Caesar's confident in that, and *I'm* content we can contain them then. Besides, the general is happy to move slowly for now. Our scouts have located the only few sources of water in these hills and none of them are in Petreius' path. Every hour his troops spend moving back toward Ilerda, they get more and more thirsty and parched. And I can guarantee you that every hour more and more men and officers in that army are thinking of turning on their commanders. An army can go without pay for some time, and on tight rations for a stint, but no army can survive more than a few days without water. They've not had access to fresh supplies now in more than three days and, without their wagons, they must have used up what water they were carrying.'

Certainly there were signs to that effect.

Every hour of the journey small knots of Pompeian soldiers fled their own lines and ran toward the Caesarian ones, waving their arms in supplication, seeking asylum within Caesar's ranks in the hope of slaking their desperate thirst. Their companions who remained in the enemy lines did nothing to stop their friends' defection, which said a great deal of the current atmosphere in Petreius' army. And every few hundred paces they moved at this interminable slow speed, men simply dropped to the ground, their weapons and shields discarded, too weak to continue.

Those men close to dying of thirst found succour among the enemy. Where a Pompeian legionary lay parched and choking in the wake of his army, Caesar's men would pause in their pursuit to give the man a small flask of water and make sure he could swallow. This was truly a war of brothers.

But the pursuit was costing Caesar's army, too. They had moved just seven miles the first day, leaving the passes of Octogesa and moving through the hills. And though Caesar's legions had swiftly caught up with the Pompeians, every pace of that journey had been a fight.

The enemy kept light and swift auxilia to the rear, and their native cavalry and archers next, with the legions to the fore. Every time they reached an incline, they would slow and, as soon as the Caesarians got too close, the archers would loose arrow clouds above the rear guard. Every time they reached a downwards slope, the auxilia would swiftly move aside and the enemy cavalry would make a charge, slowing the pursuit as they dealt with the threat so that Petreius' men could move on.

Seven miles of repeated arrow storms or cavalry charges, interspersed with pushes against the auxiliary rear guard that were half-hearted at best. Men were dying on both sides and no one had the leisure to collect and dispose of the dead. The bodies had been, through necessity, left where they fell. That first night, when the two armies made camp facing one another, Petreius yet again on a parched dry hill, search parties had taken the precious few horses and wagons they could muster – many taken from the deserted Pompeian camp – and gathered up the dead along the seven mile route, shooing off scavenging beasts and the birds of twilight pecking out eyes and other soft, juicy meat. They had loaded up with the dead of both sides to bring back to the camp for cremation.

That night had almost been a disaster. Before dawn the next morning, the bodies were prepared for the rites, and cohorts were sent hither and thither, some hunting water for the army, others foraging where they could, and more collecting wood for the numerous pyres.

The enemy had once again made a surprise break for it, while Caesar's army was still widely dispersed. The general, irritated at being so duped, had ordered the army into immediate pursuit. Tents were left where they were, along with most of the supplies and the soldiers' effects. Scouts were sent out after the forage and water parties with orders that they follow on with all alacrity, and the legions moved off swiftly, once more on the heels of Petreius and Afranius.

Now, another seven miles into the second day of pursuit, things were coming to a head. With an estimated six miles left between the Pompeians and the bridge to Ilerda, the pursuit was about to change. Just ahead, the hills ended and the land dropped to those rich, fertile plains of grain. There, Caesar's army would no longer be constricted by terrain, and Galronus' cavalry would once more come into their own, able to rove wide and harass the enemy. And even if, by some miracle, the army of Petreius reached the Sicoris at Ilerda, there would not be enough time to feed their army back across the bridge and retake their camp. Caesar's forces would be upon them, trapping them against the river.

Here, in the last few valleys, Petreius had his men fighting back hard. Despite the desertions and the men dropping of thirst, the enemy were numerous and strong, and their general had them defiant still. Whether through loyalty or fear, the results were the same.

Fronto watched as a cohort of the Ninth and another of his own Eleventh broke into a run, charging the rear guard of the enemy. The Pompeian auxiliaries once more formed a dense shield wall, their spears projecting as archers behind them loosed arrows at will and a few cavalrymen joined in, casting their light javelins over their compatriots and into the pursuing force.

Once more, the two cohorts took a few casualties, caused a few, and pulled back into position. It was all very half-hearted on both sides. The Caesarians pushed for a fight constantly in an attempt to shatter the failing spirits of the enemy and force them to terms. The Pompeians fought back only as much as they needed to in order to protect themselves, for they had neither the inclination nor the energy to kill other Romans.

Yet the fighting went on, through stubbornness and necessity.

Horn blasts rang out suddenly from the enemy force ahead and Fronto rose in his saddle, peering into the late afternoon sun, trying to identify the cause of the call.

'They're stopping again. It's late afternoon. They must be securing themselves for the night.'

Hoof beats announced the approach of several horses and Fronto turned to see Caesar, Antonius, Mamurra and Fabius riding forward to join them.

'They're going to make camp on another hill,' Plancus announced, pointing ahead at the enemy.

'Not *much* of a hill, is it?' Antonius noted, eyeing the low, figure eight-shaped mound. 'Not exactly the most formidable defensive position.'

'It's a matter of necessity I think,' replied Fronto. 'We can't be more than half an hour's march away from the flat lands now. This is their last opportunity to camp in the hills with relative safety. After that they're in the wide open.'

'More than that,' Mamurra added. 'I've been looking at the maps, and by my estimation we're little more than a mile from the Sicoris now. We've been gradually closing on the river. You know what that means.'

'Petreius is within reach of water.'

'No,' Caesar said in a dark voice. 'They are so close to breaking now. We have them over the fulcrum and we just need to apply a little more pressure. They are starving and parched dry. They are trapped on this side of the Iberus, too far from Tarraco to be of any help, and now they realise they cannot make Ilerda without us trapping them at the bridge. Tonight there will be a council of officers in that camp, and Petreius will find it almost impossible to keep his men under control. They are ready to break, but we must – *must* – continue to apply that pressure.'

He turned to Mamurra. 'How quickly can you put fortifications in place?'

The engineer shrugged. 'Enough to stop a tired and thirsty legion? A few hours.'

'Good. Take the Ninth and Eleventh and seal off the northern side of that hill. Any approach from there toward the Sicoris is to be shut. Use the legions to guard the passes and to build your rampart, but I don't want a single man from that hill to reach water. This is it, gentlemen. We are on the cusp, at last.'

Fronto nodded. In truth, he'd felt they were on the cusp more than once already during this never-ending slog around the Ilerdan hills, and as yet to no avail. Until this week he'd never considered the possibility that there could be more than one cusp.

'This now comes down to their commanders,' he said, thoughtfully.

'Fronto?'

'Hmm? Oh, thinking out loud. What happens next is down to Afranius and Petreius. The last two days have taught us that no matter how desperate they are, their generals still have control. Afranius might just be ready to deal, but what I've seen of Petreius first-hand suggests he would skin himself and go swimming in a salt bath before surrendering. But the army is commanded by them both, and they no longer have anywhere to run. In the morning, they have a simple choice. Capitulate and seek terms, or lock shields and try to destroy us.'

'Let us pray, then, that desperation and Romanitas win out in their debates,' Caesar said quietly. 'Now take your legions around the north of that hill and seal off the approach to water.'

Fronto and Plancus accompanied Mamurra as the legions deployed. The remaining forces began to encamp opposite the hill and fortify their position, while the Ninth and Eleventh set off, skirting enemy missile range, and moved toward their temporary position covering the northern valleys. The three officers, with a cavalry escort, moved a little closer to the enemy position, risking potential arrows in an attempt to get a better picture of the opposition.

'They look dreadful,' Plancus said with a touch of revulsion.

They did. The enemy were uniformly dirty and unkempt, miserable and exhausted. Fronto watched with distaste as a horse was dragged forward just behind the enemy lines, his cavalry rider protesting and struggling as half a dozen legionaries cut the beast's throat and drained the blood. Even as some began to butcher the animal for meat and more soldiers went to drag another cavalryman's horse into the open killing zone, Fronto averted his disgusted gaze while legionaries drank the thick warm blood in a desperate attempt to maintain the strength to walk and fight.

'This cannot be over soon enough,' he said, his gorge rising as they turned away and made for the saddle between two hills. Scouts awaited them as they moved into position, the legions following on close behind.

'The enemy have already been through here, seeking water,' one of the riders told him.

'That was quick,' Fronto muttered. 'When and how many?'

'They were probably moving ahead of the enemy force. They will have been out of sight, making for the Sicoris even before the enemy positioned themselves on the hill. I would say, from the tracks, maybe two turmae of cavalry.'

Fronto nodded. It made sense. Send out the men to gather the water before you arrive. And cavalry could bring more back with them, and faster, than infantry.

'Then they'll be coming back any time.' He waved at the approaching column and gritted his teeth as Salvius Cursor came riding out ahead in response.

'Get the men moving at speed. Space them out right around the hill and down to the Ilerda direction. Enemy riders will be coming back from the river at any time and trying to break back into their camp. We have to stop them.'

Salvius saluted and, without a word, rode back to join the First Cohort of the Eleventh. Moments later the front cohorts of the legion broke into double speed, jogging and jingling as they moved to half-encircle the enemy position. Fronto turned to Plancus and Mamurra.

'Get the Ninth covering this end and beginning work on your fortifications. I'm going to take the rest of the Eleventh around the hill and make sure the enemy don't get that water.'

Plancus nodded and he and Mamurra began to point at features in the terrain and discuss matters as the legion closed on them, while Fronto rode back toward the rest of the Eleventh, five more cohorts of men moving into position. A junior tribune sat almost regal and aloof on his horse, though he had the grace to look a little less pompous as he saw Fronto bearing down on him.

'Legatus?'

'Take three cohorts and spread them out to reinforce the rest of the men. Watch for any movement from the enemy camp and repulse it, but keep an eye out behind you, too, for enemy riders carrying water.'

Without waiting for acknowledgement, Fronto gestured to the lead century's officer. 'Have your cornicen give the signals. I want the Seventh and Eighth cohorts to follow me at triple time. We have the hill half-surrounded, but the enemy will make use of any access they can get, and I have an idea.'

* * *

Half an hour later, Fronto stood on a small hillock, squinting into the glow of the setting sun. Lines of men led off from here in a wide arc around the enemy hill, all the way to Caesar's position, though he couldn't see the main army from here. He turned about-face and peered into the distance. There were still a mile or so of gradually diminishing hills and, though he couldn't spot the plains, the river or Ilerda, he fancied he could just see the faint golden glow of the town's lights and fires over the hill tops. They were that close.

And they were close to the end.

The sounds of construction reached him across the landscape. Even as night fell, the men of the Ninth, and the furthest groups of the Eleventh, were busily digging and hammering, adzing and heaving, putting up a rampart and a low fence to seal off access to water.

His gaze dropped to his own men. Two cohorts of the Eleventh. The arc of defence formed by the legions under Plancus and Salvius ended several hundred paces west of here. He could see the termination of the line. His own cohorts – understrength, but still numbering over six hundred men, waited quietly, seated in the lee of the low rise.

The enemy came so suddenly Fronto almost missed them. Sixty or so horses thundering out of the darkness to the north, racing back from the river with paniers of life-giving water. They had clearly scouted out the Caesarian lines, for they had come out of the north, angled just right to clear the end of the Roman line. There they would have to ride like mad to make it to the Pompeian camp, for the Eleventh and Ninth would have their scorpions ready, but they could do it.

Or so they thought.

As soon as he spotted them, Fronto dropped to the ground and waved frantically at Albinus, the senior centurion of the two cohorts. Albinus waved back and began to give silent and whispered signals to his men where they sat in the shade of the hill.

Fronto turned his gaze back north. Sure enough, the horsemen were making almost straight for him, angling slightly so that they would round the far side of this small hillock, putting the rise between themselves and the Caesarian lines. Another quick gesture to Albinus to indicate where they would come, and Fronto threw a last look out across the grass to the approaching riders before dropping back down the slope and re-joining his men.

Dangerous work, but the riders had to be stopped.

The distant drumming of hooves on turf became slowly louder and louder as the horsemen approached. Gestures from the various centurions. The forces lay ready.

Albinus judged the time right and gave a single blast on his whistle.

The men of the Eleventh emerged from the lee of the hill at a run.

The Pompeian horsemen, taken aback by this sudden impediment, faced a choice. They could either attempt to ride over or through the Caesarian troops who had appeared from nowhere, or they could swing suddenly wide at the last moment and attempt to ride round them. In the darkness and the confusion, their plans changing even as they rode, chaos broke out among the horsemen. Some jerked on their reins and broke right, heading for the gap between Fronto's men and the main arc of the Caesarian lines. Others instead hauled left, planning to wheel around the new arrivals and seek open ground to get to their camp. Yet more simply hunched down onto their horses and rode directly at the hastily assembling legionaries.

Fronto's men were ready. Five centuries fell into the contra equitas formation, a two-tier shield wall, with the second level angled back, pila extended through the gaps like an iron hedge. Each century formed a single line eighty men long, with the third rank joining in the hedge of pila and the fourth and fifth ready with only swords, adding their shoulders to the bracing of the formation.

Twenty two cavalrymen charged the unit, though many of those desperately reined in or swerved when they realised what formation was assembling. Those who didn't have time were largely thrown from desperately refusing horses or plunged into the shields, men and horses on both sides dying dreadfully.

Those riders who had broken left and right to skirt around the sudden appearance of legionaries fared no better. From the lee of the hill and the shelter several paces behind the shield wall, the remaining seven centuries pulled back their arms and marked their targets. Riders and horses alike were suddenly pinned and impaled with several hundred pila.

Fronto looked this way and that, saw a straggler from the enemy cresting the hill, and ran for him. The rider had spotted an opening, where Fronto's men had all committed one way or another, and was racing desperately for the gap. Fronto knew there was little he could do to stop the man. A decade ago he might have attempted to jump up and haul the rider out of the saddle, or stick him with a sword. He was not fast or agile enough for that now. And with only his gladius and no shield, the only way to adequately wound the beast to stop it was to get underneath and likely be trampled in the process.

A thought occurred to him as the rider bore down, ignoring the paltry danger one poorly-armed officer posed, and he glanced across at the nearest fallen horse.

With a grin, he set his legs wide, braced, ready to move. The rider saw his position and brought his shield down to cover his side and his leg as he rode directly past Fronto. But the shield was in the wrong place. Fronto's sword lashed out just once, at neither rider nor horse. He might not be as agile or strong as he once had been, but he *was* clever, and he damn well knew how to use a sword.

The rider pelted on, whooping triumphantly, making for the Pompeian camp on the hill. He managed almost a hundred paces beyond the insane Roman defences when the strap holding the paniers full of water to the saddle snapped, having been almost entirely severed by Fronto's sword thrust. The critical, life-giving containers slid from the back of the horse and thudded to the grass in the beast's wake. The rider rode on, whooping, for several moments before he realised what had happened. He slowed his horse, turning, ashen faced, to look at the fallen water containers. Just for a moment, he started to trot back toward it, but three pila fell in his path, one punching straight through the leather panier and bursting its contents, water splashing out in every direction. His face registering his dismay, the lone rider turned and made for his camp, the only survivor of the water carrying expedition, and his bags empty.

Fronto turned and examined the results. A number of his men had died in the shield formation, but most had survived, and barring that one man, no rider had made it past. Several horses, wounded and unwounded, were wandering aimlessly around the grass and a number of fallen cavalrymen were rising, groaning and limping, holding wounded limbs. The legionaries were rounding them up at sword and pilum point, and Fronto cleared his voice wearily.

'Let them go. Any man who wants to can return to his camp. Any who don't, escort them around to our main force and deliver them to Marcus Antonius to deal with.'

The man nodded and moved to carry out his orders. Fronto let them get on with it and turned to look at the camp. It would all be over in the morning, one way or another. The enemy had failed in their last attempt to acquire water. Now all they could hope to do was surrender or fight.'

* * *

The second day of Sextilis dawned bright and clear, the hum of bees and chirrup of birds rising early. Fronto, once more back at the main camp ready for the morning briefing, stood with a cup of chilled water, leaning on a stack of shields and watching the camp on the hill. The place was a hive of activity.

'What are they doing?' Galronus murmured, tearing a grape from the bunch in his hand and popping it between his teeth where he crushed it and savoured the juice.

317

'Who knows. Running. Fighting. Surrendering. Three unsavoury choices.'

Both armies had slept under the stars, each having departed a camp without taking the time to pack their tents. Both had eaten what little supplies they had, though Caesar's army had been supplemented by carts emptying the various Pompeian depots they had found, while Petreius and Afranius' men bit miserably into the *bucellatum* hardtack biscuits, their parched throats raked by the dry crumbs as they dreamed hungrily of cold water such as that in Fronto's hand.

Musicians on the hill opposite began a cadence and the army of Pompey in Hispania moved to obey the call. Fronto straightened, ready to move. The swarm of men on the hill were falling into formation in their various units, standards to the fore. As the men turned *ad signum*, their shield faces became a wall of red and gold along the hillside.

'They're forming for war,' Galronus said, breathlessly.

'Shit,' was all Fronto could find to say.

Behind him, calls went up for the troops to fall into their centuries, cohorts and legions.

'Do we still go to the general, or form up with our men,' Galronus asked quietly. They were expected to be part of Caesar's staff meeting in a quarter of an hour, but the call to formation probably superseded that. 'If Caesar wants us, he'll send runners. For now we return to our units.'

The two men jogged back to the equisio's compound, where Bucephalus and Eonna had been prepared for them. As they reached for their reins the two men clasped hands.

'Good luck.'

'You too. Fortuna watch over you.'

Galronus mounted and trotted away toward the assembling cavalry back along the valley. Fronto cantered around behind forming legionaries, back past the Ninth and toward the Eleventh, who were in position at the far end of the Caesarian line, where they had been last night.

As he rode, he watched the Pompeian army forming. Despite the deprivations and the desperation of each and every man on that hill, they were fully armoured and falling in to perfect formation. The legions moulded the front line, with the neat cohorts of auxilia behind, cavalry at the flanks, and they were moving at a sedate pace forward, down the slope, accompanied by the musicians' melodies.

Caesar's legions were forming fast in response, and by the time the Pompeian regulars were all down from the hill on the flat ground, Caesar's lines were advancing to meet them. A series of calls went up and Fronto recognised those for the Ninth and Eleventh to pull back to the main force and join the formation. This was no longer about stopping them getting water. This was going to be a fight to the finish.

Already the Ninth and Eleventh were moving, coming back toward Fronto, but he could see two cohorts at the far end remaining in position. As the legions moved to answer Caesar's summons, Fronto frowned and rode on toward the two cohorts who had not yet moved.

His gaze turned back over his shoulder and he could see the forming armies. His heart rose into his throat. The butcher's bill for this fight was going to be appalling. And they were all soldiers of the Republic or trusted allies. There were no enemies of Rome here. Just sons and brothers. The Pompeian forces had stopped now, all on the flat ground before the hill. Caesar's army had moved forward in order to achieve the room to form into legions. The result was that the two armies were close enough already that the front lines could probably smell each other's breath. When the first volleys of pila flew, hundreds upon hundreds would die on both sides.

Madness.

Trying not to ponder on the coming apocalypse, Fronto focused on the two units ahead. Still those cohorts hadn't moved. Fronto was closing on them now, waving an arm, trying to get the attention of any officer present. His heart sank as his irritation rose when he spotted a chestnut mare at the rear of the cohorts, standing riderless and held by a soldier. Salvius Cursor's horse. The man was there somewhere on foot.

Fronto began to work through his favourite choice phrases and blistering insults, trying to find something suitably acidic with which to lash his tribune when he found him. And when this was over, if the bloodthirsty runt was still alive, Fronto would deliver an ultimatum to Caesar. Either Salvius was transferred away or

Fronto would step down from command of the Eleventh. He simply couldn't work with the man any more.

His eyes bulged in furious shock as there were several whistle blasts and his cohorts suddenly burst into life, running at full pelt toward the hill.

What was the lunatic doing?

Almost seven hundred men ran across the turf, feet pounding, shields clonking, chain shirts hissing as they thundered toward an empty hill, for the army of Petreius and Afranius was now on the plain, facing Caesar.

He almost fell off Bucephalus in surprise when a small unit of swift, lightly armoured auxiliaries suddenly burst free from undergrowth near the hill, bellowing with rage and running forward to meet Salvius' cohorts.

Eyes wide and brain clicking things into place, Fronto angled toward the two groups of soldiers. Petreius' men had put on a good show, assembling like a parade ground formation and slowly descending the hill. They had drawn every eye in Caesar's camp and, in response, Caesar had called his army together, consolidating them to face the enemy. And it had been one big, glittering distraction, while another swift, small unit made a break for the river to fetch water. Every eye and ear in Caesar's camp had fallen for it. Except for one man. One man whose need for bloodshed and death was ascendant and paramount. Who could not be relied upon to follow orders. Who had almost come to blows with Fronto. Who had been trying to start a fight since the beginning. But who had not fallen for the ruse.

And now Salvius had got the fight he was looking for. It had been a clever move of Petreius', and it would fail, only because of Salvius. But there was every chance that this small skirmish might just kick off the full-scale thing on the other side of the hill.

Shit, shit, shit.

Fronto raced for the fight, even as the two units met head-on. There were seven hundred or so legionaries. They were tired. Salvius had had them working for Mamurra since before dawn. And there were perhaps a thousand of the Hispanic swordsmen serving Pompey. But they were thirsty and demoralised. The two forces hit one another at pace and the killing began. Initially the legionaries had the clear upper hand due to their equipment, but within ten heartbeats things began to even up, for the enemy were lithe and swift.

Fronto rode in, drawing his sword.

He hit the rear flank of the enemy infantry and brought his sword down at a wide angle, rolling his wrist so that the blade struck and then sliced along and free rather than jarring or sticking in the wound. The Pompeian soldier was wearing only a white wool tunic with a leather shirt over the top. The blade cut through leather, wool and flesh, incising deep enough to reveal the white of bone. The man fell forward, howling his pain, sword falling from his grip even as Fronto swept his blade up and over the neck of Bucephalus to cut down on his left, severing the tendon in a man's neck so that his head lolled horribly to the other side.

Hacking and chopping, Fronto pushed into the enemy, careful to try and turn any blade that came near Bucephalus. The big black mount gave a brief whinny of pain as a sword scored a pink line across his rump, but this was a trained cavalry horse, and no such small scratch would stop him.

Another man fell, his face a mashed pulp of horribleness.

Another. A cut to the arm almost taking off the limb.

And another.

Fronto blinked. Salvius was suddenly in front of him. As might be expected of the psychopath, he had waded into the enemy ahead of his men and was busy laying about himself with gladius and pugio, stabbing and tearing, hacking and slashing. He was already so covered in blood and gore that he might be mistaken for some dreadful monster made of opened meat and organs. And he was about to die.

Fronto saw it coming. One of the enemy soldiers Salvius had stabbed through the gut and then turned from to attack another was not dead. In fact, he was clearly not as incapable as the tribune believed. As Salvius thrust and hacked, bellowing curses that would make a gladiator blanche, Fronto watched the wounded soldier he had turned his back upon heft a dagger. He had it raised and positioned. One good downward stroke and it would plunge into Salvius' neck, ending the tribune's life mid-battle.

Fronto felt the world slow down.

Salvius Cursor was about to die. The bloodthirsty little bastard would be out of Fronto's hair forever. But he was a Roman, and a tribune, and one of Fronto's officers, for all he loathed the man to the core. And there was no denying his effectiveness in the correct situation – to whit: mindless slaughter. Fronto had prided himself always on his sense of honour. His sword came up a little. He could just stop it happening. He could probably reach the man and kill him before that blade entered Salvius' neck.

And yet his sword, slopped and slick with blood already, was not moving any higher. It was as though his arm had counted up the reasons to let the tribune live and found them lacking. Fronto couldn't believe it. Had he willingly chosen to let Salvius die?

His arm moved in response. In that odd slow-motion world, Fronto bit down on his anger at the man and started to move. Honour was too important to sacrifice for convenience.

Yet he was too late. His sword arm had paused, hadn't it? The delay had cost him precious moments, and he would not stop the blade in time. His bloodied sword was lancing out as the man's dagger descended, but the dagger would find its target first. Fronto felt horror at himself. His delay had cost the tribune his life!

Fronto's world spun and tilted. He watched the dagger fall, then stared, shocked, as it fell away. Some freak accident in the press had occurred. One of the native swordsmen had been shoved. He had lost his footing and fallen to one side. His own blade had just caught the dagger man in the side through sheer chance. Salvius turned at the pained cry, his expression one of confusion. He saw the dagger man falling away, blade still raised. Saw Fronto behind him with the gory sword still extended.

Nodded his thanks!

Fronto felt cold. He finished his part in the fight mechanically, cutting and trampling, and as soon as it was over, he left, riding back to Caesar's main force across the open grass with the most dreadful hollowness opening inside him.

He had consciously decided to let Salvius die. Only for a moment, but that had been enough. The man should by all rights be dead now, and it was Fronto's fault. And yet some beneficent – or possibly malicious – god had enfolded the man and saved him at the last moment. And somehow, despite everything, Salvius believed it was Fronto who'd saved him.

Sweating cold sweat and shaking uncontrollably, Fronto rode for somewhere – anywhere – where Salvius Cursor wasn't. If he survived this day, Fronto would get drunker than he had ever been. And he would owe a lifetime of offerings to the gods.

* * *

Petreius did not look pleased. In fact, had he been chewing on a wasp with his privates in a vice, it was unlikely his face could be more sour. Fronto sat silent and dour, his emotions still in turmoil and grateful for this welcome interruption. Yesterday he would have rejoiced and whooped at the very idea that the enemy wished to discuss terms. But what had happened earlier on the battlefield around the hill had shaken Fronto to the very core, and it was hard to become enthusiastic about anything.

Afranius looked tired by comparison with his fellow general, rather than angry. The senior officers with them, including Tribune Bucco and the younger Afranius, bore strange expressions that were a mix of defeat and hope. For while they had failed in the end, every man on that hill had to be looking forward to an end to hostilities.

'Had we managed to secure that water supply, this conference would be very different,' Petreius snapped at his companion.

'But we didn't. And the army can go no further.'

Petreius glowered and Afranius turned back to Caesar. 'I cannot repent of my loyalties, Proconsul, and I will not apologise for carrying out my duty to the best of my ability. We took our oath to Pompey Magnus and to have rolled over and shown our belly as you crossed into the province would have been to unman ourselves. I trust you can appreciate that?'

The general nodded. 'No man can be truly blamed for holding to his oath and doing his duty. Pompey himself is misguided and badly advised. It is my hope that I can bring him to battle with the minimum of casualties and reconcile, healing the republic. I am grateful that these two armies will not come to blows any further than has already befallen us. The damage would not be to you or I, but to Rome. I am, in fact, disappointed that the bloodshed has not been avoided entirely. I have done my best at every turn to avoid giving battle.'

The lines of the two armies remained less than a pilum throw apart, with the officers in the small space afforded between them.

There was no air of malice about either side, and a palpable sense of relief filled the valley.

'Pompey himself would have to concede that we have done the best a man could do and carried out our duty as far as possible,' Afranius added, as if trying to reassure himself. Petreius looked less than convinced, and Fronto could understand that. He could picture Pompey's reaction to hearing of their capitulation and it was not pretty.

'We throw ourselves and our men upon your clemency, Caesar, which is legendary.' Afranius sighed. 'I pray that it extends even to the legions of Pompey?'

Caesar sat silent for a moment. 'I offered terms,' he said finally, 'near Octogesa. To your son and your officers. I offered *very favourable* terms, in fact. They were not accepted. Indeed, they were not even rejected. My officers were cut down in cold blood and hounded out of your camp like criminals or wild animals.'

Afranius threw an unpleasant look at Petreius, whose lip curled nastily.

'I apportion the blame,' Caesar continued, 'for this continued campaign of discomfort and trouble squarely with the officers, barring those who sought peace or have come over to our standards. Men have died needlessly and the butcher's bill continued to grow even days after peace was offered, because those of you in senior command were unwilling to accept that you had lost.'

'I told you he would offer you nothing,' spat Petreius. 'There is still time to end this nobly, with sword points and the blast of cornua.'

Afranius turned angrily on his fellow general. 'The officers were unanimous in their support for seeking terms. You alone stand ready to fight. Even if you give the order now, no man will draw his blade for you willingly. It's over.

'I am willing to offer new terms,' Caesar said quietly. 'Different terms. The Ilerda legions can no longer be trusted. Despite my earlier offers, and the clear need to end matters as peacefully as possible, they fought on even when all was clearly hopeless. That mentality has its place, but I cannot have it at my back. The Ilerda legions will not be sent back to their garrisons.

The bulk of this army, auxilia included, were raised specifically to counter my legions in Gaul. They are not required for the expansion and maintenance of this province. At most *two* legions are required in Hispania Citerior. Thus all the Ilerda legions will be disbanded. Their men will receive appropriate recompense as though completing their term normally.'

Afranius nodded his understanding. Petreius seethed and picked at the stitching of his saddle.

'The legionary officers likewise will return to Rome or to their homes, where they will be forbidden from seeking an active part in military service until this crisis is over and the government of the republic is whole again.'

'And us, Caesar?' Afranius asked.

'The same. Yourself and Petreius. You are both loyal Romans with a solid record of service and it would diminish the republic to deny it the potential of your talents in the future.'

'Caesar, this is a mistake,' Antonius said, though the general held up a hand to quieten his friend.

'I have suffered betrayal for my clemency already this year. Ahenobarbus, whom I granted liberty immediately turned upon me and barred one of my most important cities against me. I would not have that happen again. You will both take an oath – you and every officer above centurion grade – not to side with the rebel army of Pompey against me. An oath on your name, that of your familia, on sacred Venus, on wise and war-like Minerva, and on Apollo the oath-keeper. No noble Roman would break that oath. You agree to take such an oath, and I will grant the clemency you seek.'

Afranius bowed his head in acceptance. Petreius continued to sit proud and angry, with just a curt nod.

'Then let it be known that hostilities are now ceased. All senior officers will present themselves before my staff to take the oath, and as soon as their word is given, water and supplies will be made available while my officers begin the task of dissolving the legions.'

* * *

Salvius Cursor had given himself a good scrub, but the signs were still there. At his hairline, in his ears, under his nails were the dark red remnants of his battlefield fury. He was hale and hearty. Every now and then he would glance across at Fronto, his expression unreadable. Fronto had not yet been able to meet his gaze.

'The question remains,' Caesar said to his officers, 'what our next move should be. I yearn to return to Massilia and thence to Italia to prepare against the return of Pompey, and the campaigning season marches on apace. Autumn is but a short ride away. Yet Hispania cannot be said to be even nearly settled. Until trustworthy men have been placed in all positions of power and influence here, and all Pompeian partisan sentiment suppressed, we cannot rule out a rising against us and so I cannot yet turn my back upon the peninsula.'

He gestured to Quintus Cassius, the commander of the Sixth Legion. 'Cassius here served as a quaestor in Hispania under Pompey a number of years ago, but has been a staunch supporter of our cause for some time. Cassius, I am appointing you governor of Hispania, with two legions at your disposal. You will settle the province and watch the borders carefully for any move from Varro in the west. I will convene a meeting at Corduba of all the citizen municipia townships in Hispania to confirm the loyalties of the province and make any appropriate changes to local governance.'

He straightened and rubbed a shoulder wearily. 'At such a juncture, we can be sure of Hispania Citerior and the southern cities. It should not be too much of a stretch then to deal with Varro and bring Hispania Ulterior under control. Once that is done, we can turn east once more, sure that the west is fully secure.'

'And what of the enemy legions, General?' Fabius asked.

The officers had presented themselves and given their oath on the field the previous afternoon and, once they had recovered, eaten and bathed, many had gathered their personal effects and taken their leave, heading in various directions for their homes or to take ship to family holdings. The Pompeian legions, however remained on the hill, recovering and awaiting instruction.

'I have already given orders that those soldiers with land or holdings in Hispania be dismissed to return to their homes. They will be departing this day. The rest – some two thirds of them by all estimates – will be given two options.'

He motioned to Quintus Fufius Calenus, who stepped forward. 'Caesar?'

'The remaining troops will be given the option of taking a new oath. Those who wish to do so will be filtered into our extant legions to bring our numbers back up to strength. They will not be concentrated in any grouping. For security they will be widely dispersed throughout all legions such that no two of them continue to share a tent. The rest of the men are your responsibility, Calenus.'

'Sir?'

'They must be removed from familiar territory and Pompeian influence. You will take one of our legions and escort those Pompeian troops who have not been added to our numbers east. They will be marched out of Hispania, across Narbo and the province there to the Varus River within Cisalpine Gaul. There they shall be settled as veterans in peace. Calenus, this is your task. Settle them somewhere safe and then return to Massilia with your legion.'

'And Massilia, General?' Fabius asked.

'Trebonius is a good man. We will have to trust that he has the situation in Massilia under control. I know Governor Varro of old. He is not a strong man, nor a particularly brave one. I cannot see him holding Hispania Ulterior against us, or not for long at least. He is no Petreius. By the end of autumn, I foresee Hispania being settled, and I will then bring all spare legions with me back to Massilia. If Trebonius has not taken the city by then, the increase in manpower should help draw matters to a close.'

Fufius Calenus cleared his throat. 'General, might Trebonius not benefit in his siege from the presence of Mamurra?'

The general nodded thoughtfully. 'I believe you are correct. And his talents would be wasted in political manoeuvring and threat in the south. Mamurra, return to Trebonius at Massilia and help him put an end to it.' Caesar turned, his eyes playing over the gathered officers. 'Fronto, you can take a cohort of the Eleventh and escort Mamurra east. I doubt I shall have use of your rather unique oratorical talents in Corduba. Take Salvius Cursor. He seems to have a knack for resolving dangerous problems.'

Fronto winced. It was precisely what he'd hoped for: a return to Massilia. He could stop by Tarraco and the family on the way and then try and resolve Balbus' little problem. But one thing he had hoped for above all else was to leave Salvius behind. His eyes rose to the tribune, who was looking directly at him, and deep-seated guilt suddenly flowed through every part of him once more.

'As you say, Caesar.'

Damn it.

Damn it, damn it, damn it.

Chapter Seventeen

2nd of Sextilis – Massilia

BRUTUS strode out of the building that served as his headquarters on the island, hurriedly pinning his cloak in place. It may still be summer at Massilia, but the sea could carry a cutting breeze nonetheless.

'What did it say, precisely?'

The sailor – one of a number of scouts he had put in position facing the city to keep him apprised of any activity – shrugged. 'I've been a long time out of that game, admiral. My knowledge is rusty at best, but there is definitely another fleet departing Massilia with immediate effect. The signals didn't carry the same warnings of direct danger, though. Whoever it is using the signal light was quite vague.'

'If he is risking everything to send us signals from the walls, we have to trust that he is doing the best he can. Perhaps the enemy are fleeing? Maybe Ahenobarbus is returning to his master? Whatever the case, we need to stop ships leaving every bit as much as entering Massilia. How's the fleet?'

'Ready to sail, sir.'

Brutus nodded and descended the stairs toward the wharf. In more peaceful times, this island and the small dock and structures on it had been used as something of a 'holding pen' for busy times in the port. When ships were backed up they could put in here to jetties and wait for their turn in Massilia, for the city was without doubt one of the busiest and most wealthy of all the ports on the Mare Nostrum. Now, it served as Brutus' base of operations and was perfect for the task, but for the fact that the jetties were not facing the city. In fact, the place was part of an archipelago of four islands, and the various rocks, combined with the shape and orientation of the islands, made this very location the most comfortable, sheltered harbour, but faced inconveniently away from the besieged city.

Eighteen ships sat at the jetties, almost filling the small port. Twelve he had built at Arelate, plus the six he'd captured during that ridiculous naval engagement over a month ago. They were now all well-supplied and decked out for war, and the crews had been augmented with every good sailor or brave soldier Brutus could lay his hands on. The Massiliots might still outnumber him, but his fleet was better and more prepared than ever.

Across the harbour, men were scurrying aboard ships and things being made ready. The ships were prepared to sail.

'Give the order,' Brutus shouted, waving to the musician at his balcony above the quayside. The man lifted his horn and blew a sequence of notes. The ships began to move, pulling away from the jetties almost immediately, and Brutus picked up the pace, making for his flagship, the *Superbia* – a wide and strong trireme taken from Ahenobarbus last month. There was something satisfying about using the enemy's best ship as his command vessel. He had renamed it the Superbia – the Pride – in acknowledgement of his family's descent from Tarquinius Superbia, the last king of Rome.

Barely had he slipped aboard than the ramp was drawn in and the ship began to depart, following much of the fleet, which was already making for open water. The south-east-north-west orientation of the harbour made for easy arrival and departure, the prevailing summer winds allowing ships to drift into port close-hauled on a port tack, with little need for rowing, and out in a similar fashion. The sailors used their oars to heave the vessel out away from the wooden jetty and then beat a short rhythm in the water to the piper's tune just to gain momentum. By the time Brutus was at the bow with the commander of his legionary marines, the sails had billowed free and then been set to broad reach on the starboard side. The oars were shipped and the wind carried the Superbia smoothly out of harbour and toward the Mare Nostrum.

No matter how many times he experienced it, this moment always thrilled Brutus. No grunting dip and thrust of oars, no fighting, ramming, desperate manoeuvring or shouting of orders. No worry about the enemy. Just the beautiful, peaceful, almost dream-like placidity of drifting out on the water with the practiced precision of a good sailor.

All too soon the peace was over. The Superbia rounded the first of the two rocky headlands and began to jostle into position at the heart of the fleet. As they approached the second bluff, a signal was given by the trierarch at the rear and the entire fleet fell into unified motion, the same tune playing on each vessel, its piper tapping the beat with his foot as hundreds and hundreds of oars rose, circled and dipped, tearing through the water and pushing the vessel onwards before breaking free in a burst of white foam and cycling to dip again. On each ship the sail was furled. There was little wind and it would only take a mis-set sheet to cause havoc with the fleet's disposition.

It was not as peaceful as the departure under calm sail, but there was something beautiful about such organised efficiency at sea, too. The mechanical precision of it all.

The trierarch prepared to turn, shouting the orders for the rowers and the aulete with his pipes but, as the first ships rounded the headland, the whole plan changed and orders were given to push dead ahead, with an increase in pace.

The Massiliot fleet had indeed put to sea again, and there were as many ships now as there had been on that previous occasion. Brutus strained to see the enemy, his eyes watering in the salty breeze. They had departed the harbour of Massilia, but rather than racing for the island as they had last time, they were running south along the coast toward the headland where the shoreline turned east. The same prevailing wind that had allowed Brutus' ships to drift out of the harbour under sail was filling the enemy's sails and driving them at speed.

They were fleeing.

They *had* to be.

At this distance – something around a mile and a half – the precise makeup of the ships in the fleet was rather difficult to determine, but the young Roman's sharp eyes and practiced seamanship picked out a few salient details. While there were as many ships as there had been on that previous occasion, they were this time of a much different makeup. Many were much smaller – fishing boats or minor traders that had obviously been hurriedly outfitted to bulk out the fleet. None of those would be of great use against the besieging fleet, many of whom were large, heavy military vessels.

331

But they were not coming for a fight. They were running along the coast. Perhaps they had hoped, with the many rocky headlands and coves combined with the impressive speed of the following wind, to clear the area before Brutus and his fleet got wind of their emergence?

'Beam reach,' Brutus shouted back at the trierarch.

'Sir?'

'Set full sail on the beam reach. We have to catch them.'

'Admiral, if there is just one mishap...'

'Order the ships to space out as best they can, but I want every oar in that water pushing us forward and we make use of every breath Zephyrus gives us. As soon as they round the second headland and break east, the wind will throw them ahead. Forget the risks... full sail and oars.'

The trierarch clearly disapproved, but the signal was given, regardless. Across the fleet, eighteen ships reacted with military efficiency, sails thumping free and booming as they caught the wind, while sailors hauled on ropes to secure them and set them in the beam reach position to make the best of conditions. Even as the sails caught and the ships were hurled onwards with sudden rapidity, the pipers on each vessel changed tune, the rhythmic melody changing to a jaunty, staccato refrain that had every oar rise and dip, rise and dip, rise and dip at a vastly increased pace.

Brutus leaned on the bow, his nerves jangling as he watched ships that had only a moment before been moving in perfect unison and at a uniform distance suddenly closing on one another dangerously. The sudden proximity forced others to veer slightly, in order to avoid a clash of oars that might prove disastrous to both. It was hazardous in tight formation to rely on both wind and muscle, but he could not let the enemy fleet get away.

They were running, and if they were running then there was a good reason. In all likelihood the ships carried something important, and the most important thing to the defending garrison was Domitius Ahenobarbus. It was hard to avoid a tiny thrill at the notion of catching the enemy commander at sea and putting an end to his defiance.

The Caesarian fleet was closing. The Massiliots were almost at the headland the locals called the Chair of Lug. Beyond that was the second, southernmost headland, Lug's Cross, and as soon as they rounded that one, it would all come down to whatever speed they could coax out of oar or canvas. Brutus' fleet was bearing down on the enemy at an oblique angle, making for the same turn. Each oar stroke brought them closer, and Brutus could see even now that it would not be enough to head them off, but they would be so close.

Every moment they were a little nearer. He could see the ships now, could see how many of the merchants and fishers that had been added to the fleet were near ruinous, but had been patched up with emergency measures and made sailable, if barely so. Why? Had Ahenobarbus put all his good Roman personnel on board and fled, leaving the city in the hands of the natives?

Simultaneously cursing and throwing pleas to Neptune and Mercury to close the gap, Brutus remained at the bow rail, watching his ships coming dangerously close to one another in a desperate attempt to catch the fleeing Massiliots.

As the first of the enemy ships rounded the high, white, rocky headland, Brutus clenched his teeth. His lead ships were gaining, but his own fleet had become of necessity somewhat spread out in an attempt to avoid collisions. The enemy were becoming similarly strung out, with two of the small, leaky native vessels being gradually left behind.

The two fleets rounded Lug's Chair and ploughed on south for the next main headland – Lug's Cross – which signified the point that the coastline turned east. The two small fishing vessels with the recently-fixed strakes and patched sails, which were clearly unable to keep up with the bulk of the Massiliot fleet, turned and made for a bay with a pleasant-looking sandy beach. Above the cove stood a small native village of the Albici where any fleeing native would find aid and shelter.

'Sir?' called the trierarch, gesturing to the two small boats.

'Forget them and stay on the fleet. All ships. Pass the word.'

There was a small amount of risk in that. Briefly, Brutus considered the possibility that Ahenobarbus had been clever and played the greatest of tricks, using his whole fleet as a decoy so that he could safely leave Massilia and put to shore just down the coast. But Brutus didn't think so. The man was clearly too arrogant for such a base ruse. Besides, he couldn't have known for certain that Brutus wouldn't send vessels in pursuit of the pair. He almost had.

'How far is Lug's Cross?' he shouted to the trierarch.

'From here about four miles, sir.'

Brutus fretted as he tried to judge the relative speeds. His fleet were gaining. It was fractional, but he was sure they were gaining. If so, they could afford to maintain the chase. If not he would have to try something new and dangerous... if he could think of anything, that was.

Chewing on his cheek, he held up his hand and put his thumb between his eye and the largest of the enemy ships at arm's length. Too big. He cycled through his other fingers until the fourth one matched perfectly the size of that ship. He then stood, silent, thoughtful, with his arm raised and that finger between him and the ship, one eye closed and squinting.

The deck beneath him thrummed with oar strokes, dipped and rose with the waves, yet he stood still, one hand on the rail for steadiness and the other raised. As they moved interminably forward and the jagged landscape south and east of Massilia slid by, gradually he saw the black of the enemy hull around his finger. Proof. They were getting closer, no matter how marginally so.

'We're gaining,' he shouted.

'But at this rate, sir, they might be in Greece with Pompey before we get there.'

Brutus ignored the comment and watched as the two fleets raced on, making for that high bluff that would signify the turning east. At that point they would be moving outside Massilia's sphere of influence and making toward Tauroentum along the coast, a small port town that happened to host one of Caesar's supply depots.

Gradually, the land slid by, each rock and cove marking perhaps a quarter of a mile along the chase. Then, faster than he had anticipated, the jagged bluffs of Lug's Cross were approaching. The Massiliot ships raced past beneath them and began to make preparations to turn, sails being shifted into the running position. Lug's Cross consisted not just of a rocky outcropping, but also of a barren, grey, craggy island separated from the mainland by a channel just fifty paces across.

Reaching the outer edge of the island, the first Massiliot ship turned and slid out of sight. Behind it, more and more ships did the same. Brutus eyed the narrow channel, just for a moment wondering whether a trireme with oars shipped might slip through it. Casting the idea aside as madness, he concentrated ahead. The Superbia had gradually moved toward the front of the fleet. Not quite the lead vessel, but among the front runners.

He watched ship after ship disappear around the rocky isle of Lug's Cross, and prayed as hard as he'd ever prayed that they would catch the enemy at the far side.

Three enemy ships.

Two.

One.

The last of the Massiliot fleet vanished around the outcropping, and the lead vessels of Brutus' fleet were but a whisper behind them. The first two ships of the fleet – the *Celeris* and the *Demeter* – turned the corner of the isle, their sails mimicking the enemy in their configuration as sailors hauled on ropes to take advantage of the strong wind.

Brutus clenched his teeth, spray rising in a fine mist around him, the dangerous rocks of Lug's Cross looming over the port bow, his knuckles clenched white on the rail.

The Superbia rounded the headland.

Brutus' breath caught in his throat.

This was no flight from Massilia at desperate speed. The defenders had lured him – lured his ships. In the wide sea beyond the point, a massive fleet awaited. Already those Massiliots who had been first around the headland were turning and forming up on the flank of a force of fresh Roman warships flying the eagle and lightning flag of Pompey.

Brutus ran a quick count in his head but quickly lost track. Of the newly-arrived Romans there were sixteen – all strong, veteran military vessels. Of the Massiliots, in excess of thirty. More than double Brutus' numbers, at least.

'Admiral?' shouted the trierarch.

'What?'

'The order to turn back, sir. While we can.'

Brutus' eyes narrowed as he peered at the enemy. There was a chance, depending on who these new arrivals were. He took a deep breath.

'Sound the order for full speed.'

* * *

The Caesarian fleet bore down on their enemy at speed, each ship now piping and hammering a pace like the pulse of a racing horse, oars ripping through the water like lion's claws, sails full and rounded, throwing them east.

The Massiliots were still trying to form themselves up. There was a certain feeling of panic about their sudden movements, while the newly-arrived Pompeian fleet sat in formation to one side. There was no homogeneity to the force arrayed before them. Had Brutus planned something like this, the two fleets would now be working in concert to destroy the Caesarians. In fact, the Pompeians sat with their oars still, very much separate from the Massiliot force that was turning desperately to face their pursuers.

'Sir, we can't take on that many ships,' the trierarch said in a hiss, having come forward urgently.

'Yes we can.'

'It's madness, sir.'

'Perhaps. But *calculated* madness. Look at the enemy closely.'

'Admiral?'

'What we face are two separate fleets. The new arrivals are not forming up with our friends. I think we're looking at two different strategies here. The Massiliots think they're leading us into a trap and that the Roman fleet are here to leap on us. And I think they expected us to flee at the sight. See how they panic and how desperately – and badly – they turn? And the Pompeian ships are not moving to take us. I think *they* expect the Massiliots to do the work. They are here to support and mop up. That ship is the Argo.'

He pointed to what appeared to be the Roman flagship. 'The Argo is the favoured vessel of Quintus Nasidius. I've met Nasidius and talked to him. He's a good sailor and a capable strategist, but he's a cautious man. Not one to force an action unless he's certain. I don't think he trusts the Massiliots. Possibly not Ahenobarbus either.'

'You don't think he'll attack us?'

Brutus shook his head. 'He will, but only if he thinks it will be an easy win. Until then he will happily let the Massiliots weaken us.'

'And they will. They alone outnumber us two to one.'

'Maybe, but they're scared, tired, disordered and didn't expect us to keep going. Have the orders passed around the fleet. No one is to make for Nasidius' ships and I don't want a single arrow sent their way. We leave them out of this entirely for as long as possible. Concentrate on the Massiliot vessels.'

The trierarch, still clearly less than convinced, saluted and ran off to the aft once more.

The Demeter, slightly ahead and to the right, responded well to the relayed orders. He had been making for the largest of the opposition, which was clearly the Argo, but immediately veered off to port once more, selecting as a new target one of the largest ships of the Massiliot fleet. The Celeris tacked across the front of Brutus' flagship, moving to the shoreward side to join in taking on the ramshackle fleet of the besieged city.

Brutus turned. The rest of his ships were spreading out, all of them now in sight, with the last rounding the headland, all heeding their orders and manoeuvring toward the left to take on their erstwhile enemies rather than the new Roman fleet. The rear vessels were even now moving to ramming speed in an effort to close the gap.

The Superbia was making for one of the larger triremes in the enemy fleet but Brutus, eyes still narrowed into the salty spray, waved an arm at the trierarch. 'Come to port a little. Make for the rounded trader with the green sail.'

'Sir?'

'Just do it. Ramming speed. Ship oars on approach and at the very last moment bring us to the right, alongside. Archers prepare to loose when you're close enough to see them pissing themselves.'

Uncomprehending, the ship's captain and crew did as ordered, shifting their focus from the big warship to the smaller trader. It was a gamble, but a good one. The sort Brutus liked, because it was gambling not on events controlled by luck or nature, but on

337

the spirits and cunning of men, and Brutus knew how to read an enemy.

It might help a little to take out one of the biggest enemy vessels first, but there would be a good chance they would be bogged down in close fighting then, no one would see what happened, and nothing would change. But with the trader…

The smaller vessel was slightly separated from the others. It was of very poor quality and had recently been badly repaired for this journey. Yet despite this, it had been decked out well above the rowers and housed two heavy bolt throwers of the sort that could deliver a critical blow to a ship's hull. Sometimes it was better to make a big show than to be quietly effective.

The Superbia bore down on the trader. Brutus could picture the captain's face. It would be a mask of panic, wondering what madman was bothering with him when there were bigger ships to take out.

The flagship tore ahead, every oarsman groaning with effort as it raced through the waves at ramming speed.

By now, he reckoned, the merchant captain was shitting himself, wondering how to get out of the way. He would be looking left and right, but the Massiliot fleet had lined up to face their pursuers, and he was neatly tucked between two larger vessels. Given the opportunity, he might have been able to move backwards, but there were other ships in the way there too. And forward was just into yet more danger, of course.

There was a barely-audible thud. The captain had at least decided on a useful plan of action. A heavy iron bolt from the artillery on board shot through the air and vanished beneath the waves some twenty paces in front of the Superbia. They would have time for one more shot, maybe two if they got both artillery pieces ready, and then it would be too late. He would have to hope this one wasn't a fluke and that they were just bad at range-finding in general.

'Ready?'

Thirty paces.

Twenty five.

Another shot. Efficient attempt, speedy loading. Bad aim. The second bolt missed the Superbia entirely by the height of a man, plunging off between the dipping oars and into the water.

Twenty paces.

There were now audible shouts of alarm from the merchant crew.

Fifteen paces.

Nothing was going to stop the collision now, at least in the minds of the trader's crew. Their ship was a rickety hulk that had been sitting in port pretty much derelict and had been hastily nailed, caulked and pitched back together, decked out and filled with a nervous crew. What they were facing in Brutus' command ship was a huge, strong military trireme in fully working order, commanded and crewed by hardened, enthusiastic warriors and bearing a bronze beak on the prow designed to tear through a ship's hull like a pilum through a summer tunic. The Superbia would rip through the trader and scatter its timbers and crew across the waves.

Ten paces.

But that would *also* tie down Brutus' flagship.

'Now.'

The Superbia suddenly dipped to the right and Brutus' knuckles strained to hold him at the rail as every oar on the ship rose sharply from the water and disappeared into the ship. The wind in the sails was enough to maintain the blood-chilling momentum of the Superbia and, with the talented helmsman at the rear steering oars, the ship immediately lurched left slightly again.

Five paces.

Brutus braced and dropped below rail level and every archer and marine did the same. Splinters could kill on board ship.

The Superbia soared alongside the small trader, their hulls mere feet apart, screams of panic on board the other ship. The great trireme smashed through the trader's oars like kindling, shards and pieces of jagged timber whirring through the air. Better still, because of the spacing of the ships, at the far side, Brutus could see a similar thing happening with an enemy warship. The Massiliot trireme had assumed Brutus was going to ram the trader and so had not shipped oars. Consequently, the Superbia was shearing the blades from their oars too as it ran between the ships.

Even as the archers risked the hell of flying splinters to rise and release their arrows, Brutus could see through the rail the dreadful effect of sailing through a line of oars. Every pole they had hit had been pivoted back at speed within the ship, crushing and smashing the men trying to row. Ribcages were flattened, men broken in two. Screams and blood flowed. It was horrifying.

The arrows finished the job. On his own authority the archers' commander had split his forces to face both sides. Arrows raked the merchant ship and the more distant trireme at once.

Brutus could almost feel the enthusiasm among the Massiliots melting away.

And suddenly they were out from between the ships and into the very heart of the Massiliot fleet. Behind them, dismay filled the air. The trader was little more than a blood-soaked dead hulk, most of its crew crushed or pinned with arrows, its sails torn and port side oars smashed. It drifted forward, out of the fight entirely. The parallel trireme had similar problems, having lost its starboard oars and suffered a cloud of arrows. It wheeled slightly as its trierarch and crew tried to regain control.

Battle had now been joined fully.

Brutus glanced back to see enemy ships engaged with his own fleet. Grapples flew through the air, trailing ropes, and found purchase, hauling ships close enough for their soldiers to cross and begin the wholesale violence for which they were trained. Arrow clouds formed above individual fights. Most of the grapples were from Caesarian ships, but Brutus knew with a lump in his throat that most of the arrows had been loosed from Massiliot ships. They were filled with the Albici, the majority of whom were competent archers.

Still, despite the fact that the Massiliots outnumbered them and were fighting back with strength and the courage born of those who know they have no other chance, he could see that his own fleet were gaining the upper hand.

'Admiral?'

He turned again at the shout and saw the helmsman pointing wildly ahead.

The Superbia had carried through the front rank of Massiliot ships and even now was passing through a second. This line, however, was wider spaced, and there was plenty of room for the Superbia to pass between vessels. His archers were loosing at longer range now, landing arrows on the ships to either side, and it had been Brutus' intention to burst from the rear of the enemy fleet and slew round with as much speed as they could muster to come up behind the remaining Massiliots.

His plans had just changed.

Two triremes, each a good sized and strong Massiliot ship, were bearing down on him. They had been the first two ships to pass the headland and had moved into position, forming the rear of the enemy fleet. And now they were coming for the Superbia.

'What do we do, admiral?' shouted the trierarch.

Brutus, his heart in his throat, looked left and right and quickly over his shoulder. They were distinctly short on options. Astern, the ruination of the trader and the destroyed oars of the trireme had caused them to drift closer together, blocking any hope of back-watering and extricating themselves, the way they had come. And the ships of the second line, though they were wider spaced, were still close enough to prevent the Superbia from veering left or right. Ahead lay the two vessels converging on him. The two fastest and most powerful ships in the Massiliot fleet, each with artillery and with bronze beaks of their own. They were trapped.

'What's faster than ramming speed?' he shouted to the trierarch.

'Nothing. There's nothing faster than ramming speed.'

'Then you need to invent it. Hold the straight course as fast as we can go. Don't deviate unless I shout.'

'Sir, we can't ram two ships.'

'Just sail. And fast.'

The trierarch's eyes were wild as he saluted. Brutus heard the aulete playing his fastest tune, then trying desperately to speed up even that. The men at the oars gasped in disbelief and effort as they bent to a pace that no ship's crew could maintain for more than a few heartbeats.

'Row, men,' Brutus shouted. 'It's row or die. But be ready. I'm going to give the command to ship oars shortly, and then to row once more. You have to be fast.'

They bore down on the two ships that were coming at them from oblique angles ahead-left and ahead-right. They had just cleared the second row of Massiliot ships. There was nowhere to go but straight between the two ships. And there almost certainly wasn't adequate time to do it.

'They're going to hole us from both sides at once, sir,' shouted one of the senior crew nearby where he clutched his sail-rope and stared, terrified, at the ships converging on them.

'Maybe,' admitted Brutus. 'But maybe not.'

Neptune, Zephyrus, Mercury and Fortuna, he said silently, *I will devote an altar to each of you if you see us through this, and I'll build a bloody temple over the top with my own money.*

The Superbia shot forward like an arrow from Neptune's own bow, carving a path through the waves the likes of which had never been seen. Brutus wanted to shout encouragement to his men, but found his voice silent, his throat dry, his skin prickling and ice cold.

The two triremes closed at a frightening pace. The Superbia was aimed slightly toward the one on the left. Brutus could now clearly see the crew of that ship preparing for a head-on collision. The other ship was preparing archers and artillery, expecting to hit the Superbia amidships.

Five.

'Two points to starboard,' yelled Brutus.

Four.

The Caesarian flagship turned very slightly, aiming now directly between the enemy vessels.

Three.

There were cries rising from both Massiliot ships now, a strange mix of triumphant euphoria and desperate panic. Some of them believed they were about to drive home the critical victory of the fight while others were seeing disaster looming. Entirely understandable, thought Brutus, since he felt much the same. It was all on a throw of the divine dice now.

Two.

'Ship oars!'

One.

Every oar aboard the Superbia rose within the ship, standing vertical.

Brutus closed his eyes as his vessel slipped between the two who were converging on it. He heard a number of dreadful noises and cries and, a moment later, opened them to see open blue water ahead. He had never sweated this much.

'Row, you bastards,' he shouted, exhilaration filling him. As the oars were run out to each side and the musician began his tune once more, Brutus turned and looked along the length of the ship across the stern.

The enemy vessels never stood a chance. They had gambled all on pinning Brutus with their rams, just as he had gambled all on the speed of his men. While the Superbia shot free like a bolt from a scorpion, the two Massiliot ships collided. Oars splintered and sheared, killing their rowers in droves. Neither was at enough of a side angle for the bronze beaks to tear open their hulls, but the metal rams caught, one being torn from the ship entirely, leaving a gaping hole at the prow. Both ships ground to a halt, scraping alongside, tearing timbers from each other and wrecking their hulls. Brutus heard a fatal cracking noise from one, and immediately its stern rose slightly in the water. Its spine had cracked. The two ships were mangled and tied together by their mutual wreckage.

They had done it.

Now they only had to win a battle against incredible odds.

* * *

The Superbia turned ponderously. The men, exhausted from their incredible labours, responded to a much lesser pace from the aulete, relying more on the sails to come about than the oars. Brutus was impatient to rejoin the fight, but he also knew it was a lot to ask of his men, taking into account what they had already given and what they had just been through.

Ahead, two more of Brutus' ships had pressed through the Massiliot fleet and were bearing down on the two damaged vessels to finish them off. Beyond that, the battle was hard fought.

'Bring us back into the action,' Brutus shouted to the trierarch, who simply nodded and distributed the commands. The flagship gradually righted and began to make once more for the Massiliot lines. Selecting one of the strongest looking of the enemy ships out on the flank, Brutus gestured toward it.

'That one. Ram it if you can.'

'Sir, that's dangerously close to the Pompeian fleet.'

Brutus nodded but waved the argument aside. It was. But that was part of it. The new ships – they had to be led by Nasidius, else they would surely have joined in by now – were still sitting silent and still, observing the as-yet inconclusive battle happening off their bows. If they were going to be swayed to attack by Brutus' own successes, he felt sure they would have done so by now. And if his victories were not pushing Nasidius into joining the fight, then perhaps…

The large Massiliot trireme on the flank was far from oblivious to the danger. Spotting the Superbia bearing down on their rear at increasing speed, they immediately began to move. Hemmed in to fore and starboard by their friends, they began to turn to port, toward the fleet of Nasidius. As their oars began to roll and dip and the ship picked up speed, the trierarch behind Brutus shouted for any change in orders.

'Make for where they were, but be prepared for last moment changes,' Brutus replied.

Familiar with his admiral's strange and uninformative style of command, the ship's trierarch nodded.

Brutus watched as they bore down on the position of the departing trireme. The fleeing ship was now making for the relative safety of the Pompeian galleys, while the vessel beyond was already locked in combat with another of Brutus' ships. Currently the battle against the Massiliots could still swing either way. The enemy had more vessels, even after the destruction Brutus had already wrought. And the Caesarian crews might be more tired, but they were better and stronger.

Time to change the odds to the tune of one…

'Ready…'

He watched the lines of warring Massiliot vessels as they closed, and marked off distances in his head. There was no point in attacking the vessel ahead, for they were busy with another Caesarian ship. Besides, the two were tied together with grapples and ropes and sinking them might just take an allied ship to the sea bed as collateral. And the ship to the left was even now picking up speed as it fled for the Pompeians.

'Three… two… one… hard to starboard!'

This time, the trierarch had anticipated the move. As the helmsman hauled on his steering oars, the commander bellowed 'ship oars!'

The Superbia veered suddenly to the right.

The crew of a liburnian that had been decked out and filled with archers suddenly burst into desperate activity, shouting warnings and panicking. Men who could see what was coming threw themselves into the water at the far side and began to swim as fast as they could, buffeted by the waves.

The Superbia hit the liburnian at tremendous speed, even having shipped their oars.

The bronze beak at the prow of the ship tore into the side of the enemy vessel just below the waterline. The bronze plates that had been attached to the prow from there up slammed into the timbers, cracking and splintering strakes, snapping oars as though they were toothpicks, killing oarsmen by the dozen.

Every man on the Superbia's deck was thrown forward with the collision. A few, like Brutus and the helmsman, maintained their grip on the timbers and staggered in place. Many fell to the deck. The enemy ship lurched, driven sideways through the water by the power of the collision, and rocked dangerously. Men screamed and fell into the water or were thrown around like a child's doll.

Even over the clamour and din of death and destruction, Brutus could hear the fatal sound of water gushing in through a holed hull. The liburnian was doomed, taking on water at sickening speed.

The Superbia's trierarch called out his orders and a dozen sailors rushed to the front, two men to an oar, lowering the great timber poles and using them to push against the ruined liburnian's hull. At the same time, the flagship's oars were run out and the crew began to backwater, extricating themselves from the sinking ship.

Brutus straightened as they came free and began to retreat into open water. The liburnian was listing badly now as the hull filled with ever more water. Those men below deck would be fighting the terrible force of the sea rushing into the space, while those atop the deck were throwing themselves out into the waves and desperately trying to swim clear.

The hole they had made was enormous, especially in comparison to the small hull of the liburnian and, with a tremendous crash, the broken ship slammed down sideways onto the surface, the mast snapping like a twig, and began to slowly disappear beneath the waves. The lucky men who had managed to swim clear might get picked up by any ship not currently involved in a fight, or they might continue to swim away from the battle. Good luck to them. They would have to swim half a mile against the sea's currents and waves to reach shore. Most would die before they even cleared the last fighting ship. Perhaps the ones who hadn't made it clear were the lucky ones, for as the liburnian finally disappeared under the water, the vacuum it created pulled a number of men after it into the depths, where they at least would drown quickly, rather than sinking under the surface after an exhausting quarter of a mile of fighting the waves.

Brutus hardened his heart. No man could fight a battle if he allowed his conscience to rule him.

There were distant calls and, along with every face on the ship, Brutus turned in response. Orders were being given throughout the Pompeian fleet.

The men of Brutus' ships held their breath.

The first great Pompeian trireme moved. It turned, slowly, ponderously, and began to sail away to the south. Another followed, and then another. The flagship – the Argo – went with them, bearing Nasidius away from the battle. Within moments, the entire Pompeian fleet of sixteen ships was sailing away, and the Massiliot who had fled toward them was tagging along with them desperately.

Brutus could almost taste the wave of dismay that washed over the remaining Massiliots. They had been abandoned by their saviours, and the same fleet under the same man who had crushed them a month ago outside the harbour of Massilia was doing exactly the same again further along the coast.

They had won. Brutus knew it. The fighting wasn't over yet, but the battle was won. In addition to the Pompeian fleet sailing away and putting ever more distance between them and the Caesarians with every heartbeat, he could see how everything had changed with the knowledge that the enemy had been abandoned. The two Massiliot ships that had collided were even now disappearing beneath the water while Brutus' vessels that had gone to finish them off were selecting new targets from among the enemy fleet. The liburnian was gone from sight, and two more ships of the Massiliot fleet were sinking, just masts and beaks jutting from the waves, sails bobbing loose on the water while men tried to climb onto them to save themselves. Other Massiliot ships were damaged or broken beyond repair, including the green-sailed merchant Brutus had hit first. Others were ruined. Two alone of all the Caesarian ships had suffered severe damage, but at a quick glance it looked likely that both could be saved with speedy work.

The enemy were running, now.

Brutus watched any free Massiliot ship turning and racing away. They simply could not get past the fight and the remaining ships of Brutus to follow Nasidius wherever he was going, so they turned tail and sailed away north around the headland, making for Massilia and home.

He let them go. Their return to the besieged city would add little strength to the place, and their tidings of defeat and abandonment would further damage the morale of the defenders.

Even as those ships disappeared from sight around the rocks, Brutus counted. One Massiliot escaped with the Pompeian fleet. Five sunk. Four currently tied to his own vessels with ropes and grapples, and which were now surrendering, realising they were lost. He had captured four more. Five, if he wanted the ruined trader he'd first hit. No. He would save the men from it and sink the thing. It was of no value. Even if one of his own damaged ships could not be saved, he had come into battle against three to one odds with eighteen ships under his command. Within the hour, he would be sailing back to the island base with twenty one ships and a stunning victory.

Was it possible to enjoy a triumph in a ship instead of a chariot, he wondered?

'Signal any free ships and tell them to return to port and harry the enemy as they go. I want those bastards running for their lives all the way to Massilia and panicking the populace when they get there.'

For the first time that morning, the trierarch of the Superbia grinned at him as he saluted.

Chapter Eighteen

26th of Sextilis – Massilia

FRONTO crested the hill and his heart sank. He had lived much of his young life in the villa at Puteoli, or in the town house at Rome. And he had spent many of his adult years stomping around one muddy fortress or another. In fact, he'd only spent a relatively short time in his estate at Massilia. But they had been some of the most important years of his life. They had been the years with Lucilia. With the twins. With his family. He hadn't realised quite how much he'd grown comfortable with the place until now, when he knew he would never be comfortable there again.

The carefully tended gardens were gone. Instead, the villa – and Balbus' too – were bedecked with various Roman military flags and banners, and the grounds were filled with hastily constructed timber buildings to house the many officers and civilians who were part of the necessary process of the siege. The paddock and the orchard were gone, making way for construction sites and work camps. The entire place had become a sea of mud and wholesale destruction, swarmed across by an ant-like army in silver and red.

Was this what it was like for the barbarian when Rome came calling?

It was clear in an instant that Massilia was no longer a home to him, and would almost certainly never be again. Of course, now he had Caesar's help, once the forces of Pompey had been subdued, he would have the Rome and Puteoli property again, as well as various other rural and urban estates.

And there was always Tarraco.

Leaving Ilerda, Fronto had made straight for the provincial capital and the seaside villa a few miles up the coast. He had, naturally, been worried that the effects of the war in Hispania might have reached the villa, but had been relieved to find all in good order. The family had been happy and comfortable. He had berated them for sending no word during all that time in Ilerda and immediately regretted it. Balbus had sent him two letters from the family, but between rebels and bandits and the endless troubles with the supply chain, they had simply never arrived. Had *Fronto* sent *them* a letter? Well, no, he had to admit.

But the fact remained that all were well. Fronto was welcomed home with open arms. Salvius Cursor had been greeted with politeness and had been the very soul of courtesy, which did little to help assuage the guilt that flowed through Fronto every time he looked at the man. Mamurra had been treated as an honoured guest. They had tarried at the villa for several days. Fronto kept finding excuses whenever Mamurra expressed the need to move on, but in truth it was simply that he was relishing peaceful time with his family. On the third day Titus Pullo, the senior centurion of the cohort accompanying them, came calling. The interim governor was beginning to make difficult noises about playing host to the visiting force at his expense while their officers 'lounged about at the seaside.' Fronto sent back a terse message, telling the man they would move on when they were ready.

It had been a good decision, in the end, to delay, for on the fourth day there came a knock at the villa door and, when opened, the figure of Galronus stood grinning in the doorway. The Remi had petitioned Caesar to join them, given the political nature of Caesar's coming duties and the lack of a role for active cavalry. He had been granted his petition, on the condition of carrying out various minor tasks and delivering a few messages for the proconsul.

In the end it had not been Mamurra, or Salvius, or even the encamped cohort, that had pushed Fronto into moving on. It had been his father-in-law. Balbus remained edgy over the existence of a number of dangerous letters that remained in Massilia and the lack of word from Catháin. They had left Tarraco and the villa on the tenth of the month, with a tearful Lucilia and two miserable looking boys watching them from the threshold. Fronto tried not to be disappointed when the twins waved at Salvius. He had caught the tribune more than once playing with them, teaching them sword moves with a stick from the garden. He had itched to tell the man to leave his family alone, but there was no reason other than his personal feelings, so he could hardly justify such a demand.

Fronto had argued on that last night that his family still needed protection. The war was far from over yet. But Masgava had been immovable. He was coming with Fronto, as were Arcadios and Aurelius. The villa had a full complement of capable staff who could look after the family. But Masgava was adamant that Fronto could not look after himself.

So on the morning of the tenth, Fronto had ridden out ahead of the cohort with a small complement of familiar companions: Mamurra, Salvius, Galronus and the three surviving members of his former singulares unit. Sixteen days of travel, limited by the speed of the infantry cohort accompanying them. And now, as the parched summer began to give way to the first thoughts of autumn, they had arrived.

Swallowing his dismay at the level of destruction, Fronto waved the party on, down toward his villa.

The walls of Massilia were still intact, though they showed numerous scars and blackened patches. The ground before them was a patchwork of burned grey and muddy, dry brown with barely a blade of grass to be seen. Huge piles of timber lay in stacks, and vast pens of animals were dotted about. Legions were camped in different places, with vexillations cut from them and positioned here and there as required. Massilia steamed gently. There was no sign of fighting, but figures were moving about on the walls.

The besieging force had numerous pieces of artillery constructed, vineae, wicker screens and shields and the like, but there was one grand edifice that drew the eye in the centre of it all. The twin aggers that had been constructed months ago when Fronto was last here were still in evidence, but the northern one, which marched from Trebonius' main camp to a central point on the walls, stopped some hundred paces from Massilia's defences. And where it ended, Trebonius seemed to have built a squat tower.

'What in Hades is that?' Fronto breathed, pointing at the tower as they moved toward the villa.

'Looks like Trebonius has constructed a sort of bridgehead defence,' Mamurra replied, deep in thought.

'Has to be thirty feet across and thirty feet tall. What's it made of? Brick?'

Mamurra nodded, and they rode on.

'It all speaks heavily of inactivity and unwillingness to commit, to me,' rumbled Salvius Cursor.

'What?'

'Two months. Almost three, in fact, and all they've done is char the defences a little. And instead of breaking the walls down, they're building their own. Makes me wonder whether Trebonius has the mentality of the besieged as much as his enemy.'

'Let's not start casting aspersions without knowing the facts,' snapped Fronto.

They reached the grounds of the villa swiftly and Fronto sent the cohort from the Eleventh off under Pullo to find an appropriate site to make camp, while he and the other officers rode through the gateway and dismounted, tying their horses to the hitching rail. The grounds were filled with men going about their tasks. Each one was appropriately deferential to the new officers in their midst, but it still felt like an unwelcome invasion to Fronto as he watched men erecting a tripod of timber on a spot where he used to roll around and play with the boys.

The guards on the door of his villa stood to either side and granted them instant entry. Half the new arrivals wore the uniforms of senior officers, and the others were clearly their guards.

Fronto's disappointment did not end at the door. His villa did not look like his villa any more. His furniture had all gone, his personal effects too. The mosaics were chipped and scuffed, the fountain seemingly broken, since it was dry and inactive. The wall paintings were all damaged where men had been careless in passing.

In the atrium, he gestured to Masgava, Arcadios and Aurelius. 'I'm perfectly safe here. You know the villa. Find part of it occupied by someone unimportant and turf them out. Set it up for us.'

The three men nodded and walked off to secure a place in the house, while Fronto led the other officers into his tabularium, which he assumed had been commandeered as the office of the senior commander. He was not surprised to find Trebonius at the desk, surrounded by maps and documents. Two clerks sat in the corner, scratching away at wax tablets.

'Gaius,' Fronto murmured as he passed into the room.

351

Trebonius looked up from his work, frowned for a moment, then broke into a weary smile. 'Marcus. Good to see you. And Mamurra. And Galronus and Salvius too. Is the general with you?'

'He still has matters to attend to in Hispania,' Fronto replied. 'But the main fight there, I would say, is over. Once Varro is leashed, the general will turn east again. In a few weeks, I suspect.'

Trebonius nodded. 'But he sent you?'

'It was suggested that you might be able to use Mamurra's talents. We escorted him with a cohort of the Eleventh. How do things lie?'

Trebonius gestured to the chairs opposite him. There were two. Fronto and Mamurra sank into one each, while Galronus loitered near the door and Salvius remained standing, arms crossed, a disapproving look on his face.

'Out,' the siege's commander said to his clerks, waving at the exit. 'And shut the door.'

Once they had gone, Salvius and Galronus took their chairs and pulled them up to the table.

'We've been at something of an impasse,' Trebonius sighed. 'The walls are thick, the defenders strong, the town well-stocked and their commander defiant. And there are methods I could use to bring down Massilia in short order, but they would cause widespread destruction in the city, which the general expressly forbade, so my hands are tied somewhat. We pick at them, and they laugh at us, and it goes on day after day. If it hadn't been for Brutus' rather impressive successes with the fleet, I'd say we were losing here, but he is managing to make them sweat blood any time they try to leave port. Eventually, of course, the city will start to starve, but that could be next spring, and the idea of waiting out a siege over winter is far from pleasant.'

'There are ways to take the place,' Salvius Cursor said quietly.

'But not without huge collateral damage for the civilians,' Trebonius said again. 'And that, Caesar does not want.'

'Tell me about your tower,' Mamurra mused.

'The problem was that we could hardly do anything close to the walls without coming into the effective range of archers, slingers and artillery. My lads couldn't do anything without getting hurt. And whenever we managed to get shields up there – the big wicker ones – they sallied out of a gate and destroyed them, then our men died again. Problem is, with the aggers, it's difficult to get enough men close to make an active push without just opening them up to arrows. So I had them build the fort. It's not particularly big, but it's enough to offer protection. Whenever I've made a push near the walls since then, our men can fall back into the fort for safety.'

Mamurra nodded. 'You've not thought about raising it?'

'What do you mean?'

'Making it into a proper tower, rather than a squat wall. It could be constructed, even within arrow shot of the enemy. I have experimented with ways for doing just that. Build a wooden framework inside the brick and use it to climb and protect as the walls increase in height. Straw mattresses lodged inside against the brickwork to help absorb the impact of artillery against it. Wetted hides to prevent fire arrows damaging the interior as you work. There are other angles to take and work on, but you can build the tower from the inside within range of the enemy.'

'But why would we do that?' Trebonius frowned.

'To give you the freedom to work. You say you are at the mercy of their missiles close to the walls, and this is what keeps you from success?'

'I didn't quite say *that*.'

'It is what you intimated,' Mamurra brushed the denial aside. 'Then if you wish to work properly, you have to render their missiles harmless. Move vineae into place along the agger so the whole causeway is a tunnel of safety, and build up the tower. I will draw you up the plans. It will need to be five – perhaps six – storeys.'

'That's insane.'

'That is required. It will bring you to an equal height with Massilia's walls. The walls of the tower will be strengthened. Five feet of thickness should be adequate to withstand any punishment, especially with the mattresses to back them. We will leave apertures at intervals to allow bolt throwers and archers to sight the walls and the area nearby. And the roof will project. Beneath the eaves there will be well-protected space enough for a whole unit of archers. Between the archers and artillery, they should be able to clear the Massilian walls of men and machines enough to work below in relative safety. You can then take whole cohorts forward to provide protection from sallies, while we work to...'

He reached out and grasped the map before Trebonius, hauling it round so that it faced him. 'This tower here. It is opposite your little tower. Once we have everything in place, we begin to undermine that tower to one side so that it falls safely away from our forces. Once they lose a tower and we have a breach, the day is yours, I think.'

Trebonius blinked.

'You think this is possible?'

'Of course.'

'Then I am grateful that Caesar sent you, Mamurra. I will have the word passed to my officers that the project of the tower is now in your hands. Do whatever you need to.' He looked up at Fronto. 'And your orders?'

Fronto shrugged. 'I presume we're seconded to you. I've a cohort of the Eleventh making camp. Salvius and I command them. Galronus is my adjutant, and I have three singulares with me. Make what use of us you wish, but I would request one consideration?'

Trebonius nodded. 'And what is that?'

'However you do it, when we get inside those walls, I want to be among the first men in.'

A suspicious face now. 'Why?'

'Because I have business interests and employees in Massilia. I know Caesar – and you – are all in favour of taking the place with the minimum of violence and destruction, but we all know that there will be at least some trouble. Legions will not besiege a town for months and then smile and drink with the defenders the day they get inside. There will be at least some killing and damage. I want to try and protect what is mine.'

Trebonius nodded. 'I had forgotten that you were now a man of Massilia, Marcus.'

'Should be damned hard to forget,' sighed Fronto, 'when you're sat in my villa planning your siege.'

* * *

14th of September

Fronto fretted. Somehow, though the siege of Massilia had drawn out over three months, it had never occurred to him that things would not suddenly resolve themselves quickly now he was here with Mamurra. Somewhere beyond those scarred, heavy walls, were Catháin, many of Fronto's worldly goods, and a few letters that might easily get his father-in-law a one way trip down the Gemonian Stairs, following his own head at some distance.

Everything he cared about that was not in the villa near Tarraco was behind those walls. And there was no way in. He had taken to walking the length of the defences, not really in the hope of seeing anything useful, but simply because it was less irritating than sitting in a room and waiting to hear news. How the officers who'd been here for three months were managing to maintain their spirits, he had no idea. Wine, he suspected, since the supply line from here to good wine country was short and efficient.

It had become a common enough sight now, that the soldiers no longer panicked when a small party of officers wandered among them apparently out for a stroll. Fronto and Galronus, accompanied by Masgava, Aurelius and Arcadios. On occasion, Brutus too. The young officer had come running to meet them when he heard the news that they had arrived. Though he spent all his time on the islands opposite the port, he made sure to drop by on a social visit from time to time, and the five of them had visited Brutus on his island once, too, enjoying a brief trip around the bay on a small liburnian to view the city from a side they would not otherwise see.

Not once, no matter how often he scanned the parapet, had Fronto seen a figure that could be Catháin. Today was no exception. Fronto and Galronus, with Masgava, Arcadios and Aurelius following on closely, strode along the south agger. The raised embankment crossed the muddy dip toward the city walls close to their southern end. Beyond, Fronto knew, was the harbour. He could see the point where the walls moved down to the water's edge at the inland end of the natural harbour and projected out into the water, terminating with a squat tower. Beyond the harbour, facing the city's wall-less front, was an area of marshland so treacherous that no army could cross it. So secure did it make the city that the Massiliots had never bothered to wall it in. Trebonius had snorted at the notion and set two centuries of men to finding a passage across the marshland that would bring them to the shore opposite the harbour. Thirty five men had vanished without trace before the idea was abandoned. The Massiliots had been right.

The south was therefore of little interest except to observe the city's interior from a distance, and scouts had been set to watch from there now, beyond the marsh at considerable distance. A seaborne assault was suicide. The natives were a rich port, and knew how to protect their assets. Crossing the marsh and then the harbour was suicide in a different way, as the marshes would be filled with Roman dead before even a man got as far as the water. Which left the walls.

It was easy to see how Trebonius had become bogged down here for months. Had he been able to use fire or otherwise endanger the place, it would have been easier, but Caesar wanted a city to occupy afterwards, and one with a grateful population. Not a charred columbarium full of corpse-ashes.

Still, things were finally moving on, now that Mamurra was at work. It was still slow, but at least it felt as though they would get there eventually. The tower had been complete for days, and had proved once again Mamurra's reputation to be well-earned. Artillery had been ferried from the camps to the tower under a great long roof that covered the northern agger. The weapons had been positioned carefully at high vantage points. Archers had been sent there one unit at a time in rotation.

The enemy had reacted swiftly, Ahenobarbus had sent out a sally straight away – a strong one. Almost a cohort of men, mostly Roman legionaries, with native Massiliot support. They learned immediately that the tower contained more than arrows. A cohort of legionaries had been assigned to the tower, a quarter of them based in the thing's lower levels and the rest under the cover of the vineae passage along the agger.

The numbers had been evenly matched, but as the city's defenders moved to strike at the legionaries in the tower and under the shelters they came under attack from the missiles in the tower and by the time they pulled back, desperately, to the walls and the small postern gate from which they'd issued, they left behind a landscape strewn with their dead.

The tower then began its work in earnest. Scorpions loosed huge iron-tipped bolts through the holes in the tower, while the archers released swarm after swarm of arrows at the wall top. The missile troops loosed with wild abandon, safe in the knowledge that they were in no danger of running low on ammunition, with vast reserves back in the camp and a good supply line constantly feeding the army. All day the first day, and all day the second, the bolts and arrows had flown.

At first the Massiliots had fought back in kind from their artillery positions or with bows from the towers and wall parapet. But it had been to no avail. The walls and towers of Massilia had their crenulations, but they were open to the air, and with the sheer quantity of missiles pouring at them they never stood a chance.

By comparison, Trebonius' men were safely ensconced in a covered tower, using only small apertures to loose their missiles, and the Massiliot replies rarely made their way through the armoured position. The result was a clear success. By the sunset of the second day, everyone concerned had found their maximum ranges. The defenders kept clear of the turret and the walls within reach of the siege tower. All fell eerily quiet.

Then, a few days ago, when everyone was beginning to feel deflated at the fact that things had settled once more into a waiting and watching game, Mamurra revealed the next phase of his design. In one of the lesser, more peripheral, work camps, he had been working on something else.

It was a vinea, or something like, but on an enormous scale. Mamurra called it the *Musculus*, and it would certainly require plenty of muscle to move it. Where the vinea were usually between fifteen and twenty feet in length and half that in width, following good Vitruvian principles, this beast was more than three times that size, formed not of good adzed branches, but of tree trunks two feet thick. Where vineae roofs were formed of light timber and dampened hides, this monster had a roof of tightly-packed brick on shingles of tile and clay. Damp hides were still pinned atop to add an extra layer of protection, preventing water from being cast down to sink into the clay and weaken the brick roof. And even atop the wooden frame, then the shingles, then the clay and the bricks and then the hides, a wicker net of raw vines stretched, preventing dropped stones from tearing the hides to allow in the water to crack the clay to move the bricks so that the enemy could put fire into the structure.

It was a monster.

This morning, the structure had been declared complete and had been moved to the north agger. In preparation, an entire legion was detailed to remove the vinea tunnel that had rested upon it for weeks. Then, moved in the same slow, ancient fashion more commonly used to portage ships, the Musculus was rolled atop perfectly shaped logs along the agger. Each time a log rolled free at the back, twenty legionaries carried it forward and dropped it in place in front of the structure. So, with a constant cycling of logs, the Musculus slowly closed on the walls of Massilia. Finally it reached the end of the ramp and, with only a minor drop back onto the grass, rumbled forward.

Fronto had been genuinely impressed. Not only was the new construction as hardy as the walls of a town, if not more so, but it was surprisingly portable and had been moved into position with relative ease. But the best part was Mamurra's planning. To Fronto's knowledge, the siege engineer had not even been to the walls of the city barring two quick runs to the tower to check on progress. And yet, the moment the Musculus was dropped into place and the logs rolled free, his perfect planning became clear. The Musculus was precisely the correct size to fit between the end of the agger and the wall of the city, butted up against the tower.

Even as the new machine stopped moving, already the legionaries were busy replacing the vineae along the agger once more.

The result was that by the end of that morning, a man could walk in relative safety from his bed right up to touch the wall of Massilia without once having to worry about an arrow. The Massiliots had braved the walls once more in an attempt to destroy the monster, casting down rocks, weapons, fire and then water, anything they could find. But quickly, the damage they had been taking from the Caesarian brick tower made their attempts too perilous, and they desisted. The postern gate opened briefly, but no sally came forth, perhaps on observing the fact that more than a legion of men now waited for them under the vineae, in the tower and beneath the Musculus.

And there, under that great roof, engineers moved into position and began work on undermining the tower.

That had been this morning. Fronto had watched it all. Now, while work was undertaken to bring the whole siege to an end at the northern agger, Fronto stood atop the southern one. He could see the tower, the arcade of vineae and the Musculus some way up the slope. He had stopped at the white-washed stones that marked the extreme limit of the enemy's missiles.

'What the shit is that?' Aurelius said suddenly, pointing up toward the northern agger. The others turned to look, and blinked. A great timber arm was moving inside the city, approaching the wall top and beginning to protrude.

'That,' Fronto answered, 'is a crane. Ahenobarbus is up to something. Come on. I think things are about to become unpleasant.'

* * *

By the time they had reached the north agger by a circuitous route that kept them out of the reach of enemy missiles from the walls, the crane was almost in position. Fronto could see the enormous 'A' shaped timber frame rising proud of the walls, the cable's terminus out of sight behind the ramparts. A second crane was being manoeuvred into position next to the first. Massive constructions, there was no chance they had been built at short notice by the men of Ahenobarbus' garrison. Besides, they were of a decidedly Greek design rather than a neater, more efficient Roman one.

'How did they get those monsters?' Aurelius breathed as they hurried along the tunnel of vineae on the agger.

'They had them in the port. I remember them a couple of years ago being used to move the stones when the new quay was put in place. They're for city construction. Could lift a trireme out of the water, too.'

They watched, breathless, as the first crane began to work, the unseen windlass turning with a creaking audible even outside the walls. The cable started to rise slowly. Fronto and his companions came to a halt at the junction where the agger ended. The brick tower rose next to them, loosing missile after missile harmlessly. The crane was being operated by men safely out of sight behind the walls, its positioning sighted by some unseen fellow at a narrow window in the tower. There were no figures for the archers and artillerists to aim for, so they targeted the timber 'A', though attempting to damage a massive industrial crane even with a scorpion bolt was futile.

Ahead, under the massive Musculus, Fronto could see the men of some unnamed cohort, ready to react to any sortie from the walls. And beyond them, though he couldn't see it, Mamurra's engineers were at work, cutting away and levering out the stones at the base of the tower.

There was an ominous groan and Fronto's eyes roved nervously. At first he thought it might be the tower ready to come down. Towers groaned when the weight upon damaged foundations became too much for them to bear. But the tower was still solid. The Musculus, perhaps? But no. There was no reason for a groan from that.

Fronto looked out from beneath the Musculus again, up at the walls, and his eyes widened. The crane's cable had crested the parapet and its load was now visible. Strapped to the cable was a stone block of the sort from which the port quay was constructed. A block that took a cart to move. A block that weighed more *than* a cart and its mule together. A block almost as big as him.

'Shit.'

'What is it?' called a lilting voice, and Fronto turned to see Mamurra exiting the brick tower and strolling toward him, rubbing his hands together.

'Massive stone blocks. They're going to drop them on us.'

The engineer frowned and crossed to the edge of the Musculus, peering up. 'Oh, yes.'

'Oh yes?'

'Yes, it's quite big, isn't it?'

'That thing would punch through the ground itself when dropped from a height, Marcus,' Fronto told the engineer.

'Not through *this*, though.'

Fronto's eyes rose once more to the heavy roof above them. 'I wish I had your confidence.'

He was not alone. News of the block hovering above them had spread through the cohort and now legionaries were murmuring nervously.

'Have faith, Fronto,' smiled Mamurra just as a call from the wall top to release came. There was a distant creak, a slithering of rope and then the oppressive silence of something very, very heavy dropping through the open air.

Fronto prayed to a pantheon of gods.

The rock struck with a sound like a Titan falling to the ground.

The Musculus gave a great, convulsive quake. There were a number of noises that Fronto thought sounded a little too much like shearing timbers, and the roof gave an unearthly screech. Fronto stared in astonishment as several pieces of vine and hide scattered from the eaves of the edifice like snow, and then a rock that could crush an ox flat slid off the roof and slammed into the earth where it buried itself into the turf by more than a foot.

'This thing would withstand the sky falling on her,' Mamurra announced proudly, as half a cohort of legionaries stared variously at the fallen stone and the ceiling where it had struck. Someone let out a long, slow, nervous fart, and several people sniggered and heaped insults upon the guilty backside.

The rock was not the only one. Over the next hour the two cranes worked repeatedly to lift giant stones to the wall top and then drop them on the Musculus. By the time the third one hit, the men beneath were becoming quite blasé about the whole thing, joking and jostling and jeering at the unseen enemy above. Fronto had to congratulate Mamurra. He'd not have thought it possible. Every time the rocks struck, he winced, expecting the roof to give and men to be crushed flat, yet it remained sturdy and intact.

Finally, the rocks stopped coming and the soldiers sent up a rousing cheer, hurling insults at the wall top.

'Is it over?' Masgava muttered.

'Hardly,' Fronto replied. 'They've paused because they see they're getting nowhere, but they'll just be rethinking their strategy.'

Sure enough, with another quarter hour passed, things began to happen once more. Trebonius had come out to check on the situation and had been lavish with his praise for Mamurra. Salvius Cursor had come too, presumably in the hope that the enemy could sortie and he could bathe in Pompeian blood once more. Fronto tried not to be too near him.

361

And then a strange smell began to permeate the air. It was clearly emanating from the city and settled like a cloud on the whole area.

'I know that smell,' Aurelius said, suspiciously.

Mamurra nodded. 'Pitch.'

'And pine resin too,' added Arcadios. 'Smells like the wine casks back home.'

'Prepare for fire,' Mamurra barked at the soldiers. 'Ready the buckets. Bring up extra water butts and have the poles to hand.'

More barrels of water were brought forward along the agger, each lifted with poles carried by two men at each side. Buckets were spaced out along the Musculus, and every ten feet a legionary made ready with a seven foot pole with a forked end.

There was another nervous silence and gradually the smell changed, becoming more pungent and greasy, then cloying and hot. Arrows began to fly once more from the brick tower, trying to stop the men atop the ramparts. Fronto could not see what was happening from his position within the Musculus, and he sure as shit was not going to poke his head out and look up right now, but he presumed the Massiliot defenders were raising pitch barrels to the wall top and there lighting them. It would be far too dangerous to ignite them within the city and then try to lift them. So men would be hiding as best they could on the wall top and lighting the lifted barrels there.

Distant screams suggested they could not hide very effectively from the archers in the brick tower. Still they were managing to succeed in their task, for there was a cheer from above and a moment later a bang on the roof of the Musculus. Fronto could immediately smell the burning pitch and resin, but the barrel, having spilled part of its contents across the roof, rolled clear of the eaves and dropped to the ground, where it cracked further, spilling more of its deadly contents.

The soldiers recoiled, But men threw buckets of water over it, while others used the long poles to push the barrel away down the slight slope and out into harmless open grass. Two more men paused momentarily to be sure nothing deadly was going to drip from the edge of the roof and then stepped out into the open just long enough to hurl a bucket of water up onto the Musculus roof and then duck back inside. Fronto, grimacing, stepped out to check the damage.

The roof was intact! The stones had torn bits of the outer covering away, but had done no real damage, and the fire had taken no hold on the materials, fizzling to a sizzling gloop before even the men had added their water to the mix.

'Good work,' he noted to Mamurra as he ducked back underneath just as a second barrel was ignited above. He gestured to the structure around them.

'I've been toying with ideas as to how to protect a vinea from above,' Mamurra smiled, 'though combining all my theories into one cover was new, I have to admit. I'm confident that it'll stand against anything they can throw.'

As if to punctuate his words, another barrel of burning pitch struck. Once again, the legionaries quickly extinguished the flames and pushed the wreckage carefully away.

Fronto remained in the safety of the Musculus for a short while longer, listening to the barrels landing on the roof, and then decided to achieve a better viewpoint. With his friends in tow, he entered the brick tower and climbed to the highest level, where he could see over the parapet of the Massiliot walls and right down to the roof of the Musculus, scarred and stained, yet intact.

With a nod of satisfaction that all was secure, despite his initial fears, Fronto turned to descend the tower once more when he stopped, suddenly alert.

'Did you hear that?'

'Hear what?' Galronus replied. But then they all heard it. A deep groaning noise, like the stirring of giants beneath the earth, accompanied by a vibration than made his teeth ache.

'What, in the name of...' Aurelius' voice trailed into silence.

Fronto rushed over to the northern side, pushing between two archers, and peered down. Though the men within the Musculus were almost entirely hidden beneath its great roof, he could make out the signs of men fleeing. A quick glance back toward the camp, and he could see legionaries pouring from the end of the vinea tunnel. Shouts of alarm below and a voice of command he thought must be Mamurra.

The Massiliot tower cracked.

Above where the engineers were removing blocks, there was a strange and terrifying noise of tearing stones, and a crack ran right the way up from beneath the Musculus to the tower's parapet. There were cries of alarm in both Greek and Latin, and the tower shuddered. Fronto stared. He had seen the results of undermining a few times in his life, but it never failed to impress him, and these were some of the strongest walls he had yet faced.

The front of the tower began to separate from the rear, the crack widening into a gaping hole that widened the closer it came to the top. Once again there was a sound like a rock-face being torn in two, and the upper two thirds of the tower strained slowly outwards, swaying with unstoppable slowness, ponderously leaning. For a moment Fronto wondered whether Mamurra had planned this all badly, for his Musculus seemed in direct line and even the siege beast he had created must surely be crushed by the weight of a collapsing tower. The fleeing legionaries certainly seemed to believe so.

But the old bugger knew what he was about. He had set his engineers to removing the stones from the north-east angle, especially the northern side, close to the wall. Just when it looked as though a large portion of the tower must fall straight on the Musculus, it swayed off toward the other side, leaning out almost parallel with the wall.

It fell.

It was not the whole tower, but probably a third of it, tumbling out and crashing down to the turf. Large fragments of it smashed loose and bounced off the Musculus roof, doing no more damage than had the blocks the Massiliots had dropped previously.

Fronto stared into the cloud of dust, waiting for the haze to clear. Gradually it did so, and he took in what had happened to the walls of Massilia. The tower's inner side remained intact to full height. Its outer face was solid up to perhaps twice the height of a man, and then opened up so that the attackers could see the remains of the interior rooms. Even as Fronto watched, he could see cracks still opening across the rest of it, and mortar trickling out from between stones. Even Fronto, with not a jot of engineering skill to his name, could see that it would not take a great deal more work to bring down the rest of the tower. Another day or two at most and they would have a breach in the wall wide enough to send in a cohort at a time.

They had done it. In fairness, *Mamurra* had done it.

In the silence, accompanied only by odd groans of settling rubble, a cheer rose from the legions back across the agger. Men once more rushed forward into their positions, desperate to take advantage of the damage. The engineers hurried to work on the stones, ready to bring the rest of the tower down and open the way into Massilia.

'Look,' called Galronus, and Fronto's gaze rose and focused where his friend was pointing.

His heart thumped. The gates along the wall had creaked open and a small group of figures had emerged. A man in officer's uniform on a horse, walking it at a sedate pace, accompanied by men in Greek garb – nobles and politicians.

'Come on.'

Hurrying, Fronto led his friends down the tower stairs and then jogged back along the agger, desirous of being present when the city capitulated, which now seemed inevitable.

* * *

Fronto sat astride Bucephalus, heaving breaths and trying not to look exhausted, though his cheeks were clearly flushed from hurrying across the siege works and the camp. Fortunately, he'd had time, as Trebonius had delayed, making sure he was fully attired in gleaming armour with his general's ribbon knotted around his middle.

Then, he and the other officers rode out to meet the city's embassy.

Lucius Domitius Ahenobarbus' only concession to defeat was that he rode out to parley with no weapons at his side. The members of the Massilia boule were in their rich himations with decorative cloth fillets bound around their hairlines. A man who had to be the commander of the city's native guard was in old-fashioned Greek armour, again with no weapons. But Ahenobarbus was no fool. A century of archers waited behind them at maximum range, ready to move to support their commander. Fronto eyed the enemy commander warily. Ahenobarbus had already held two towns against them and there was something about him that appeared still defiant.

The Massiliots to a man looked beaten and dejected. Their expressions were hopeless.

Ahenobarbus looked…

Fronto couldn't tell. He'd never seen a man with so little expression. He was a mask untouched by emotion. Fronto would hate to play dice against him.

Trebonius led them all forward and came to a halt some twenty paces from his opposite number. Ahenobarbus inclined his head, barely enough to offer respect, and Trebonius followed suit. Silence reigned. The legions had been temporarily withdrawn from the siege works, leaving just a guard at the tower and Musculus.

'You are willing to capitulate?' Trebonius said finally. 'To open Massilia to us and disarm your men?'

Ahenobarbus took some time to reply. Fronto could see a tiny tic at work below the man's left eye.

'I have terms to offer.'

Trebonius frowned. 'It is understood generally in warfare that the *victor* sets the terms.'

'You are not the victor yet,' Ahenobarbus growled. 'And unless you wish to spend the next two months watching your men suffer as they attempt to control Massilia street by street and house by house, you will curb your arrogance and hear my terms.'

Fronto saw Ahenobarbus straighten a little. He was getting angry.

The Massiliot nobleman closest to Ahenobarbus stepped to his side and murmured something too quiet to hear clearly. Ahenobarbus did not look happy at the words, but he nodded.

'I believe that you were left by your populist master with instructions not to destroy Massilia, but to capture it. Equally, the civilian masters of the town would prefer a peaceful end. However, I know little to nothing of you Gaius Trebonius, other than your record of war successes in Gaul. Given the wholesale destruction and widespread death of almost everyone the proconsul met in his campaigns, the Massiliots worry that similar fates lie ahead for them, regardless of Caesar's orders, and we cannot be certain that you can prevent your legions from running riot in the city.'

With every pronouncement of Trebonius' untrustworthiness and potential violence, the Caesarian commander was becoming angrier, trembling and barely restraining his temper.

'However,' Ahenobarbus went on, 'Caesar has forged a solid reputation as a merciful victor and a man of his word, and it is well known that he can control his legions like few other commanders. I propose a truce – no aggression to be committed by either force until your general arrives in Massilia. When Caesar stands before these gates, the city will agree terms with him and open to the proconsul. These are not my wishes, you understand, but even as senior of Pompey's officers here, I am forced to bow to the demands of the independent city.'

Fronto found he was holding his breath.

'My recent dispatches,' Trebonius said, his voice level and carefully controlled, 'suggest that Caesar has already dealt with your compatriots in Hispania. My latest intelligence puts him in Gades four days ago, accepting the capitulation of Varro and the last Hispanic legions. Your allies in the west are gone and Caesar now puts trustworthy men in power there. Any day now he will begin to travel east once more. Perhaps he already has.'

This was news to Fronto. He frowned at Trebonius, but the man was too intent on Ahenobarbus to notice.

'Given that, and the likelihood that the general will be here within a matter of weeks, I am inclined to grant the terms to the boule of Massilia.'

Ahenobarbus nodded.

'On the condition,' Trebonius continued darkly, 'that you personally step down as commander of Massilia and place yourself in our custody.'

'You think me a fool?' snorted Ahenobarbus.

'I think you a dangerous liar,' replied Trebonius coldly.

The Pompeian commander stiffened.

'You have the terms I have already agreed with the boule of Massilia, despite my wariness at them. There will be no other terms offered and no deviation from the ones already stated. I leave you to consider your decision. If you consent to a truce until the arrival of your general, you need only send a messenger and I will have our bows and artillery silenced and seal the gates against sorties. If you do not accept the terms, you will bring a great deal of dismay to the boule and the townsfolk, but you would delight me, Trebonius, for I wish nothing more than to fight you to the last nub of a sword, and, if you refuse us, I will make you pay in lakes of blood for every building you take.'

The two men glared at one another.

'I take my leave,' Ahenobarbus snarled, 'and await your response.'

And with that, he turned and rode back to the city, the Greeks hurrying along in his wake and the archers following him in slowly. The gates shut tight a few moments later and all was oddly peaceful.

'What,' Trebonius said finally, with a sigh, 'do you make of that?'

'That was a deal proposed by the boule,' Fronto answered. 'I know them of old. They are entirely concerned with their own safety and wealth. In that, I would suggest their offer is genuine. However, Ahenobarbus I would not trust as far as I could spit a cow. The fact that he clearly doesn't like it is another point in its favour.'

Mamurra shook his head. 'Two days at most and I will crack Massilia for you like an egg. Why accept their terms now when you can force your own upon them at sword point in a matter of days?'

The general scratched his neck.

'Because I am stuck between two pit traps. Caesar gave me very specific instructions to take Massilia with as little damage and violence as possible. Here, that is exactly what is being offered by the town's council. But if I refuse them, I'm certain Ahenobarbus was being quite serious when he warned me he would make us sweat blood for every house we take. It is within his power, and certainly within his will, to leave Massilia a smoking ruin of a charnel house and fill it with the dead of both armies. I cannot risk that.'

'You would *accept* his terms?'

The voice was incredulous. Fronto closed his eyes wearily. The voice was also all too familiar.

'To risk the alternative is unthinkable,' Trebonius sighed.

'Respectfully, General, I disagree,' Salvius Cursor said flatly.

'Oh?'

'It seems to me that Ahenobarbus and the boule of Massilia are at odds. There is a good chance that if you break the walls and enter the city under arms, the Massiliots will throw themselves upon your mercy, regardless of the Roman officers to whom they play host. They might even give you Ahenobarbus to save themselves.'

'I'm not sure I saw that level of division among them,' Trebonius replied.

Fronto nodded. 'And even if there is, they may still consider us more of a threat than him. Remember, Salvius, how we fought Petreius and Afranius at Ilerda. They were as divided as commanders can be, yet they managed to hold us off for months and even in the end surrendered together. The boule are selfish, but they are also obstinate. I have met them in person many times. Whatever Ahenobarbus threatens, I warn you that if you force the issue and enter Massilia under arms they will make you pay for it.'

Salvius Cursor threw a sour look at Fronto. 'General Trebonius, Caesar's legions are the most loyal in all the republic, but we all know why. It is not a love of their general that drives them, though they do seem to have it, nor is it the need of Rome that leads them on. It is what has always driven soldiers, no matter who they are or who they fight for: money. Many became quite wealthy through loot and slave sales after Gaul. The three legions on this hill know that those walls harbour one of the richest cities in the west. They hunger for plunder. You would do well to give it to them.'

Trebonius straightened. 'I most certainly will not disobey my commander's orders for the sake of supplying extra loot to the men, at the expense of a city with whose support we could very much do.'

Fronto frowned. Salvius was being his usual pushy, violent, irritating self. And yet he might well have just hit upon an unpleasant truth. Fronto could just imagine the talk around the campfires later when the legions, who knew they were days away from having the town laid open at their feet, were told they had to wait weeks for a peaceful, non-profitable solution. It would not go down well.

'The decision is made,' Trebonius announced. 'We shall accept the boule's terms. There will be a truce of non-violence until

369

Caesar arrives to personally accept their surrender. Send a courier to the gate with our confirmation. And I want dispatches sent to Tarraco, Corduba and Gades to locate the proconsul and pass on word of what has happened.'

A peaceful conclusion, Fronto sighed. It might yet be weeks away, but at least it had been offered and accepted. The security of his business and people, of Catháin, and of Balbus' letters seemed at last to be assured.

Chapter Nineteen

26th of September – Massilia

THE passage of time had become kinder. Knowing now that every idle hour brought Caesar closer to Massilia and a peaceful resolution more likely made the waiting so much more satisfying. And they *did* know he was getting closer, too, for a courier had arrived only this morning with news that Caesar was pausing on route at Tarraco to finalise matters there. And Tarraco was close. If the general came on without his legions, he could be here in days. Even with the legions, perhaps a fortnight.

Then Fronto would get into the city. He would secure his buildings – the warehouse and the office – would find Catháin, and would secure Balbus' stupid papers. And he would have to do it fast. The legions would be given strict instructions to be courteous and merciful to Massilia and its populace but no matter how much control Caesar had, there would be incidents. And Fronto wanted to make damn sure those incidents didn't involve his people or property. And even with the best will in the world there might well be legitimate ways those documents ended up in Caesar's hands. Routine searches, for instance. No, he would have to be in swiftly and secure everything.

But that was days away yet. His musings were interrupted by a snort. Galronus was fast asleep already, though the sun had been down less than an hour, five cups of watered wine combined with constant fresh sea air enough to send the Remi nobleman into slumber any day. As Fronto's friend lay rasping away like legionary work party sawing timber, Fronto sat straight and stretched, rubbing his face wearily.

It was almost over.

He sat still for a moment, wondering whether to try and sleep or whether to abandon hope for now until Galronus stopped sawing wood and went back to his own room. He could wake the Remi now, of course, and tell him to leave, but Fronto doubted he would sleep easily anyway. He was far from tired enough yet.

Settling on a stroll as the preferred course of action, Fronto rose, tightened his belt and tied his laces. He threw on his cloak and pinned it in place. It did not seem cold here, but the nights became chillier the closer you got to the sea. Moments later, he was strolling out of the headquarters building... his villa. Gods, but he'd even stopped thinking of it as his villa now, despite the fact that he'd managed to reacquire his own bedroom from some legate he'd never heard of, who was thoroughly apologetic when he found out. Crossing the atrium, he passed through the front door between two saluting legionaries.

'What's the camp watchword tonight?' he asked them.

'Calamitas, sir.'

A nod. *"Disaster"*. Great.

A quick wander through the ruined grounds of his villa took him past the camps of two legions and then down between the small fortifications that marked the line of siege investiture. A palisade ran between them across the land outside of Massilia, punctured by numerous gates, two of which led to the aggers.

For a moment, he paused. He contemplated sauntering down to the seafront away from the city and walking along the shore. But he was alone, and the further he got from the camp the less he would be able to rely on support should anything stupid happen. There were people in these hills who would resent the Roman presence, and, of course, there was always the ever-present threat of bandits. He could wake Masgava, he supposed. Certainly the Numidian would not think twice before rapping him hard on the head for wandering out of camp without a bodyguard.

No, staying close was the best answer. Maybe he could examine the latest damage to the enemy tower? Yes, that would be a good little walk to tire him for sleep. Though the besieging legions had left off their attack now for a week, the immense damage that had already been done to the tower had left it delicate and in danger. Every day a new piece fell off it and, every few days, the men said it leaned a little more, as though it were willing itself to fall and let them in.

They couldn't wait to get in. Salvius had been right about the mood among the men, as Fronto had confirmed while wandering among them. And that was why the legions were still happy to remain in the brick tower and guarding the Musculus, despite the lack of activity. Each man hoped for the tower's accidental collapse, leaving them with the opportunity to loot with impunity until an officer managed to call them back. They would be reprimanded, of course, but a man can deal with a reprimand when his purse is full of silver.

Fronto approached the gate to the north agger at a gentle stroll. The legionaries there, hardly averse to letting men *out* in normal circumstances, had become considerably more relaxed since the truce came into effect. Though they were well turned out and snapped to attention as Fronto approached, he could see them slouch back into a comfortable position as soon as he moved away. He smiled. Soldiers were soldiers, the world over.

Strolling down the agger for a few paces, something made him pause. He listened carefully. There it was again. Not loud, but definitely there, ahead: the distinctive sound of a lot of men in armour trying not to make noise. He turned around and jogged back to the men on the gate.

'There's a lot of movement up ahead. I'm concerned the enemy might be about to try something.'

One of the soldiers frowned. 'I think that will be the Seventeenth, sir.'

It was Fronto's turn to frown now. 'What do you mean? There's only supposed be a half a century of men up there on guard, and I'm sure it's the Eighteenth's rotation today.'

The soldier looked confused. 'Your tribune, sir.'

'What?'

'Tribune Salvius Cursor, sir. He went out at sunset with a cohort of the Seventeenth.'

Fronto suddenly felt very cold. 'Did you not report this?'

No, of course the man hadn't. Why *would* he? Why would *anyone* report a tribune and a cohort of men leaving the line of investiture and moving into the siege works? Tribunes had ample authority to pass check points with ease. Shit, what was the man up to now?

'I....'

'Never mind,' Fronto cut him off. 'Be alert. Something is about to happen. I don't know what, but whatever it is, it'll be trouble.

And send a runner to the headquarters. Find any officer and tell him that Legate Fronto says there's trouble at the tower.'

'And is there, sir?'

'I have a horrible feeling there is, yes. Get on it.'

The soldiers sprang into action, shouting over a compatriot and sending him to the headquarters while they positioned themselves ready for trouble. Fronto left them to it and began to walk along the agger. As he paced toward the walls, the feeling that something calamitous was afoot grew almost exponentially, and within ten heartbeats he was jogging.

His fears were clearly well founded. Fronto reached the end of the agger and found a full cohort of men geared for battle moving beneath the Musculus and the vineae. He could see siege ladders carried among them, too. It took him only a moment to spot the plume of a tribune among them.

'Salvius!'

The tribune turned at the sound of his name, and had the temerity to display a look of indignant irritation at the interruption.

'Salvius, get here. *Now.*'

'What is it?' snapped the tribune, moving men aside and traipsing toward him, impatiently.

'*What is it*? What are you doing?'

'What we should all have been doing a week ago. Taking Massilia.'

Fronto stood silent, staring for a moment. Of *course* that was what he was doing. Fronto could see that. What he'd really meant was *why* in the name of all the gods was he doing it?

'Look, Fronto, I know you have this thing about propriety, but the fact is that the legions want this. They're desperate to finish this. And Trebonius wants it, too, but his hands are tied by Caesar's orders. Someone has to take the lead and do the dirty work, and it sure as shit was never going to be you.'

'You'll get torn to pieces by the general for this. How stupid are you?'

Salvius Cursor snorted. 'We'll only be in trouble if we lose. If we win, the general will heap praise on us.'

'You cannot take these men into battle. They're not even your legion!'

Again, that arrogant snort. '*They* came to *me*, Fronto. This isn't me dragging a legion into my personal crusade. This is me answering a call to arms. Their own commanders wouldn't listen to sense, so they sought an officer who would.'

'Salvius, I am your superior and I am giving you a direct order, backed by the authority of both Trebonius and Caesar himself to back down and return to camp with these men.'

'Look, Fronto, just fuck off, will you? I've got work to do.'

Fronto's hands bunched into fists. He had no sword on him, though he was very, very tempted to punch the man. But Salvius was fully armoured, including helmet, and there was more chance of him breaking his knuckles than hurting the man. And disobedient psychopath he might be, but soft and cowardly he wasn't. Salvius would fight back, and hard.

'Last chance, Salvius. Bring these man back or I shall report this to both the general and their commanding officer.'

'Run along, Fronto.'

Fists still clenched, Fronto watched, furious and impotent as his tribune turned and marched off through the ranks of the Seventeenth. Madness. They had agreed a truce with Ahenobarbus. The siege was all-but over. They were just waiting for Caesar to come. And Salvius was going to jeopardise everything.

What could he do? How could he stop it?

A moment later, he was pushing his way through the ranks of legionaries, telling them to stand down and return to camp. Salvius paused, a space opening up around him as he turned. Fronto hurried forward and came to a halt in front of him.

'Stand down, Tribune, or I shall make you do so.'

'Don't be stupid, Fronto. You're unarmed. I'm not.'

Fronto turned to an uncomfortable looking centurion . 'Give me your sword.'

'Sir.' Polite and respectful, but his hands did not move.

'Fronto, if you make one wrong move, things could go very badly here. These men want Massilia. Everyone wants Massilia except you.'

Fronto stepped forward, so that he was just two feet from the tribune now. Where could he punch? How could he stop the man? Helmet with good cheek pieces, cuirass, greaves, pteruges. His disbelief at this whole situation hit a high as Salvius drew his sword, stepped back and raised it threateningly. Behind and beside him, Fronto heard the rasp of at least a dozen swords leaving their scabbards.

'Come on,' Salvius Cursor barked to his men, and the Seventeenth moved off.

Fronto, stunned and helpless, watched them go. Stepping out from the Musculus to either side, ladders were raised. The legionaries began to climb, and Salvius and his centurions were among the first. There was no fear or cowardice in them. How Fronto wished there was. Idiots.

He watched with a catch in his breath as the first few men clambered up onto the roof of the Musculus and, from there, hauled themselves up onto the ruined front of the tower, passing shields to each other as they climbed into the first open level. Pieces of masonry fell as they climbed, dust and mortar slithering out of the ruined stones and pouring like a white waterfall through the darkness. There were a few alarming creaks and thuds. One unfortunate man fell backwards into the open night, the stone block he'd been gripping as he climbed still clutched to his chest, the fresh hole in the wall testament to how weak the whole structure now was. The man landed with a crunch. Fronto didn't need to check to know he was dead.

Now, perhaps half a century were in the tower, with more entering all the time. There would be doors from there granting access to the walls, and possibly even the city itself. If the Massiliots were bright, they would have bricked them up by now. Certainly Ahenobarbus was clever enough to seal all the potential exits. That meant the men under Tribune Salvius would have to climb the entire crumbling tower to the height of the walls, which would be madness, unless they could break through a sealed doorway.

He doubted Salvius had thought that far ahead. The tribune had probably smelled blood and gone for it.

A cry of alarm from the tower drew his eyes. He half expected it to be one of the Massiliot guards sending out the warning about the interlopers, but the voice was coming from one of Salvius' men. He ran to the edge of the tower and bellowed for the others to back away and stop climbing.

There was a strange pause, and in response the men of the Seventeenth began to slide back down the ladders they were climbing, or let go of the stones and drop to the grass, others jumping down to the Musculus roof and running.

The soldier who had shouted the warning suddenly stiffened and toppled from the wall.

Then the arrows were flying like drops of rain. They were coming from every direction, from archers hidden in the walls and in the higher areas of wrecked tower. Ahenobarbus was no fool. He'd had men ready for just such an attempt as this. He clearly trusted Trebonius as much as the Caesarian officers trusted him.

Men were dying in droves in that tower. Tribune Salvius appeared suddenly amid the press, pushing a panicking soldier out into the air. He stood for a long moment at the edge of the ruined tower, arrows flying all around him, throwing his men to safety.

Fronto winced as the arrow hit the tribune. It struck him in the shoulder and the force sent the man hurtling out into the dark air.

The wounded men of the Seventeenth, along with a few of the still untouched ones, were fleeing now, trying to leave the ruined tower. Fronto heard the creak and the 'woof' noise and looked up, his stomach churning with horror.

The barrel of pitch tipped from the wall top into the ruined tower and where, a moment earlier, there had been black figures moving panicked in the darkness, suddenly there was an explosion of golden fire that illuminated the horror of burning men.

The barrel burst as it hit the tower floor, and the sticky fire sprayed out, even beyond the ruins, spattering those men who thought they had escaped to safety. Even in the darkness of the grassy slope below, men were dying as they fled the scene, arrows thudding into them.

Fronto heard the rhythmic thud of many boots behind him and glanced over his shoulder. A cohort or so of legionaries were pounding on toward him. It took a moment for him to realise it was Pullo and the men of the Eleventh.

'No closer!' he bellowed. 'There are archers everywhere.'

Pullo drew the column to a halt some distance back. Fronto's attention returned to the dying men of the Seventeenth in front of him. Many were still intact, running for the safety of the Musculus and then using its cover to hurry back to the agger. Fronto shouted to the first centurion he saw among them.

'Form your men up with mine.'

The officer, a snapped-off arrow shaft jutting from his left arm, nodded. As he turned and barked orders to his men, Fronto took in the burned cloak hanging from his shoulders and the angry red weals on the back of the man's legs where the fiery pitch had burned them.

Fronto was filled with a whole gamut of mixed emotions at the sight of Salvius Cursor limping between soldiers under the shelter of the great Musculus. One arm hung limp at his side, the arrow still jutting from the shoulder, and his leg was clearly damaged, but he looked intact otherwise. Angry, but intact. As he neared Fronto, he untied the thong on his cheek pieces and flung his helmet away.

'The bastards knew we were coming.'

'Of course they did,' Fronto snapped. 'If it had been me commanding those walls I'd have done exactly the same. And so would you, you idiot. And now you've broken the truce and unless we can put things right, we're back to war again and Caesar gets a ruined city of the dead when he gets here.'

'I don't think there's time to put things right, sir,' Pullo called, and Fronto turned to follow his pointing finger. The nearest gate in the walls had opened, and men were flooding out into the darkness, armed for war.

'Look what you've done,' bellowed Fronto at Salvius, and turned.

'Seventeenth Legion, get your wounded and get into the brick tower. Man the scorpions but not one shot unless you hear my order. Pullo, have the men form up on the agger. We can't deploy well, but if this comes to a fight, they won't be able to get to us easily.'

'*If* this comes to a fight?' demanded Salvius.

'Come with me,' snapped Fronto.

* * *

The force that had issued from the gate was formed of Roman defenders, Massiliot regulars, and Albici allies. Each moved independently with their own commanders, and the Massiliot and

Albici warriors moved out along the wall in the direction of the ruined tower. Once they reached the area, the native archers began to move around the grass gathering what arrows they could find that were still usable. In a siege situation, every missile reused was important.

The Roman contingent, three cohorts strong, marched toward the brick tower and the end of the agger, their officer out front but on foot. The man was wearing a tribune's uniform. At least it wasn't Ahenobarbus.

Fronto was striding out from the vineae into the open air, Salvius limping alongside, having trouble keeping up.

'We are walking into the range of their arrows,' the tribune warned.

'Yes.'

'Alone, toward three cohorts of the enemy.'

'Yes.'

'What are you going to do?'

'Anything I can to cease hostilities.'

The Pompeian tribune, a cadaverous man with a permanent sneer, called his men to a halt and stopped in front of them, folding his arms. Fronto and Salvius moved closer until they were perhaps ten paces away, and then stopped.

'Is this what a truce means to the insane proconsul of Gaul?' the tribune snarled.

Fronto inclined his head. 'This was a mistake wrought by a headstrong fool, counter to the orders of his general.'

The tribune took in the wounded man beside Fronto.

'This one?'

Fronto nodded. 'I hope this can be resolved with diplomacy. This man acted against orders and made an unsupported attack on the breach in your walls. As far as I can see no further damage has befallen Massilia, and I am unaware of any deaths they caused. Your men, conversely, have executed almost half a cohort. Hundreds of men at that tower, dead from arrows or burning pitch. I am not speaking in their defence, for they should not have been there, but I hope that the price they have paid is enough for you to consider the matter closed.'

The enemy tribune was silent for a moment.

'Lucius Domitius Ahenobarbus, commander of Massilia and Pompey's lieutenant, will not be satisfied with this.'

Fronto could feel Salvius emanating hate beside him. 'Perhaps I might point out,' Fronto said quietly, 'that while you have, as yet, launched no attack with your Romans, the very presence of three cohorts at the city gate suggests that Ahenobarbus was preparing for something.'

'We have a right to defend our walls.'

'You do. But three cohorts of legionaries exited that gate far too quickly to have been gathered from the walls or their barracks. They were waiting ready, armed and prepared. What was Ahenobarbus planning?'

'Stop trying to twist the situation to your advantage,' growled the tribune. 'You broke the truce, not us.'

'Yes, we beat you to it, didn't we?'

'An example must be made,' the tribune said in a dangerous tone. 'Give me the man responsible and I will take your offer of a further truce to the commander.'

'No.'

He could sense the surprise in Salvius. The man had clearly assumed that was why he was here.

'You seek for the cessation of hostilities to continue,' the Pompeian officer said. 'Give me the man who attacked our city for punishment. And do not press me, or I might think to extend it to his men.'

Fronto squared his shoulders. 'You will take no man from this field. You outnumber us here, but this entire truce was agreed as a courtesy to prevent unnecessary damage to the civilians of Massilia. Bear in mind how close we are to entering the city. If you do not agree to reinstating the truce, then you grant an open invitation to men like Salvius here to mob Massilia and do their worst.'

'Are you threatening me?' the tribune snapped.

'No. I am threatening the whole of Massilia. Accept the truce again right now, or I will not hold the men back next time they get a taste for blood.'

There was a sudden 'woof' of fire and a blaze of orange light from near the tower. Fronto turned, startled. The Musculus was ablaze. While it was impenetrable from external attack, the

Massiliots and Albici along the walls had set small jars of pitch among the timbers within it and lit them. The entire monstrous machine was instantly ablaze, flames licking the whole thing. Even as Fronto stared, he could see more of the natives tipping over the water barrels kept to prevent just such an occurrence.

There was no hope for the Musculus.

'*Now*, I will accept your truce,' snorted the tribune.

Fronto turned back toward the agger where the men of the Eleventh waited. Those legionaries in the tower were safe from fire behind five feet of brick, but the flames could very easily spread from the Musculus to the line of vineae along the agger.

'Pullo,' he bellowed. 'Tip the first two vineae from the agger. Make a fire break.'

In moments, the legionaries were pushing the timber shelters, hurling them to one side where they were in no danger of becoming part of the conflagration. The Pompeian tribune called to his men, and they turned, marching back toward the gate. Along the walls, the Albici and the Massiliots too were converging on the entrance. The officer lingered for a moment, a smug expression of victory nailed to his bony features,

'My compliments to General Trebonius. Tell him we will be less generous next time.'

And then he was gone, following his men back to the city.

'I am going to make him pay for that someday,' Fronto snarled. 'Ahenobarbus too.'

'You should have given me to him. It might have saved the Musculus.'

'Shut up, Salvius.'

* * *

'I should have you stripped of command and sent to Rome in disgrace,' Trebonius yelled, the force of his anger making Salvius Cursor lean back involuntarily. The tribune stood silent and at attention, the arrow still in his shoulder, his leg trembling as it tried to hold him up. 'Some might say,' Trebonius went on, 'that I do not have the authority to punish you. You serve in a legion Caesar still has with him in Hispania. But you are attached to my army, and that makes you my soldier. I am beyond words. What made you think this was acceptable?'

There was a pause. Salvius clearly thought it a rhetorical question.

'Well?' prompted Trebonius, shaking with rage.

'I prevented a mutiny, General.'

'What?'

'By accepting their terms and forcing the army to sit and wait while they know Massilia to be beaten and ripe for plucking, you have fomented unrest in your own legions. The men here were ready to ignore your orders and attack, sir. I did not take your men to fight. *They* took *me*. They needed an officer and they came to me.'

'That is not an excuse.'

'No, sir. But the loss of a couple of hundred men to death and injury has put everything in perspective for the rest of the legions. You will have no more unrest, I suspect.'

Trebonius took two steps toward him, narrow-eyed and trembling. 'Are you trying to tell me that you have done me a favour?'

Blessedly, Salvius kept his mouth shut.

'Thankfully, Fronto was there to keep the peace, though it cost us the Musculus.'

Fronto could see Mamurra seething at the back of the room.

'He's your man,' Trebonius said, suddenly, turning to Fronto. 'You deal with him.'

The legate closed his eyes. Fabulous. Just what he wanted. The guilt over his actions near Ilerda was still flowing strong in his veins. Would it help to assuage it if he was lenient? He'd taken the figurine of Nemesis he habitually wore on a thong around his neck and slipped it into a box in his kit since Ilerda. He wasn't sure he liked having the spirit of righteous vengeance touching him constantly when he had let Salvius face death unnecessarily. In honesty, he'd been feeling distinctly nervous about Nemesis ever since he'd made that whispered vow to Verginius in the quarry last autumn. He looked at Salvius Cursor. The man was a born fighter and a good soldier. He was even a good commander when he was set on a task with which he agreed. In a straight fight against an enemy the man would be an asset. He just couldn't be trusted.

'I'm removing you from active command for now,' Fronto said, aware of how pathetic it sounded. Many officers would have had the tribune beaten or even executed for what he'd done. 'You will continue to serve as my adjutant, where I can keep an eye on you, but you will have no command authority over any legionary. Now get to the medical tent and have that wound seen to.'

Salvius Cursor saluted to Fronto, then Trebonius, then turned and left the building without another word.

'Is that all?' Trebonius asked quietly, once the tribune was gone.

'The man is insufferable,' Fronto replied with a sigh. 'And potentially dangerous. But he's like a war dog. Keep him caged and then point him at the enemy and open it up. He's far too useful and effective to get rid of entirely.'

'If you say so, Marcus. I've not seen signs of that.'

'Because you've not seen him in the thick of battle. But I'm taking my lead from Caesar. Salvius has pissed off the general more times than I can count, yet Caesar still keeps him around. He must have a reason. Besides, Salvius used to serve Pompey and now he's the biggest anti-Pompeian of the lot. One day I'm going to find out why. Anyway, I'll keep him leashed for now. What will you do? Dispatches to Caesar?'

'Hardly,' snorted Trebonius. 'It's been just days since I told him all was good and that we had Massilia ready for plucking peacefully off the tree. I will try and keep knowledge of this little incident to a minimum.'

* * *

Fronto was sick of being woken in the middle of the night. He groggily pulled himself awake. 'What is it?'

His blurred eyes focused on the legionary and he was suddenly alert at the man's expression.

'The tower, sir.'

Now he was up, throwing on his tunic and cinching his belt. 'What's happened?'

'The brick tower is on fire, sir. Centurion Pullo said to come find you.'

Fronto was out of the room and running as soon as he'd put on his boots. By the time he'd rounded the headquarters and begun the descent to the agger, he could see it. The brick tower was ablaze, just as the soldier had said.

'Tell me it was empty.'

The soldier shook his head. 'Two centuries of the Seventeenth, sir.'

'Shit.' There were other officers hurrying along the agger now, and Fronto had to barge past tent parties of legionaries staring in shock.

He arrived at the end of the vineae moments later. The two shelters were still out of position, tipped to the side to maintain a fire break, which was fortunate. The Musculus was nothing but charred beams and embers now. But the brick tower was lost, he could see that immediately. The top blazed like a lighthouse, and flames roared from every window and aperture. Roiling black smoke poured into the sky.

'I can't hear screams,' he said hopefully.

'They stopped not long ago, sir,' replied bleak-faced Centurion Pullo. 'But there were plenty.'

'Why did they not leave?'

'The door seems to be thoroughly sealed from the inside, sir,' Pullo said. We tried to open it but couldn't. One of my lads took his dolabra to it and bashed a hole in the timber but all that did was let flames out.'

'I don't understand how it happened.'

Pullo shook his head. 'None of us do, sir. The wood inside and all the mattresses backing the walls would go up a treat, but it would take Apollo himself to get an arrow through those holes from the enemy walls. And how did they seal the door?'

'Whoever set fire to it, did it from the inside. Sacrificed himself. Insanity.' Fronto shook his head.

'But with the Musculus gone, sir, and now the tower, we're losing all our advantages. A week ago we were ready to crack Massilia like a nut. Now we've been set back months.'

'This is Ahenobarbus' doing.'

'Sir?'

'He didn't want this truce. The boule of Massilia forced it on him. Now he's finding ways to set us back so that he can persuade them to stand firm. Maybe he thinks he can hold on to Massilia until help comes?'

Fronto's gaze slid past the blazing tower to the ruined one in the walls of Massilia. Several figures stood within the ruins watching the tower burn, illuminated by the flames' golden light. They were Romans, and one was an officer with a red plume. He couldn't pick out much detail in this light, and at this distance, but somehow he knew it was the tribune who had faced him earlier.

'I'm coming for you, you sick bastard,' he muttered under his breath.

'What was that, sir?'

'Oh, nothing,' he said, turning to Pullo. 'There's nothing else we can do here. Pull everyone back to the palisade wall and have all these vineae brought back to camp too. If they stay here they might sprout flames overnight.'

Leaving Pullo, Fronto turned and stormed back along the agger. All the way, his thoughts churned. What sort of man burned soldiers alive just to get his way with a town council? He remembered how the three cohorts of the enemy had clearly been ready for something before Salvius launched his attack. Had they been coming out to burn the Musculus and the tower anyway, but the presence of Fronto and the cohort of the Eleventh halted them in their tracks? They'd still managed to burn the Musculus, but couldn't get to the tower at the time. But then, later on, when everything was settled and quiet again...

On the way back to his room, he made a visit to someone else's quarters. Salvius Cursor was awake, sitting on the edge of his bed and hissing as he tried to stretch his left arm, the wrappings of his wounded shoulder blossoming with red as he did.

'I don't like you, Salvius.'

'I know. It's mutual.'

'But there are people in this world I like even less. When we get into Massilia, whenever that is, and however it comes about, I am finding that bastard tribune we saw earlier and ending him. You want to make Pompeians bleed? You want to drown in their blood? There you go. I'm giving you him and Ahenobarbus. We find them both, and we end them both. Are you with me?'

He saw the light begin to shine in the tribune's eyes.

'I'm with you, Fronto.'

Nodding, Fronto returned to his own room, where he located the box and carefully unwrapped the figurine of Nemesis, kissed it and hung it around his neck once more.

Chapter Twenty

5th of October – Massilia

NINE days. An impressive achievement. Fronto had travelled the coast from Massilia to Tarraco and back more than once, and by his estimate it would usually take a legion, even at a forced march pace, ten or eleven days to cover the distance. Of course, Caesar had not brought his artillery and siege train, for that was already here. And he had little need for wagons, as he was following his own supply lines back from Hispania. Still, though, they had come faster than Fronto expected.

If anything was likely to finally tip the scales in Massilia it would be this sight. Fronto stood at the gate of what had once been his homely villa, now functional and drab, and watched the spectacle as the wind whipped and lashed at him, pulling at his cloak and tunic. Autumn had come to Massilia and it had brought storm winds to announce its arrival.

Under the grey slab of sky, Fronto peered at the column. Caesar was accompanied by three legions. The general and his staff rode to the fore in the grey, threatening air. Behind them came the Praetorian cavalry under Aulus Ingenuus, then the legions, one at a time, in perfect formation, impressive and gleaming despite the dullness of the day, with their own cavalry keeping pace, their standards aloft and powerful, their musicians cascading notes and the legions chanting one of their traditional marching cadences.

The moment the column had appeared over the hill some mile and a half away, the walls of Massilia had thronged with spectators. Fronto could see even now the subtle himations and chitons of the Massiliots of higher station, and the dull red and burnished bronze of the Roman garrison and, interspersed among them, the colourful tunics and trousers of the Albici tribesmen. Anyone of import or power was on the walls to watch the arrival of their enemy.

How many of those watching now regretted closing their gates to Caesar? He had seemed the poor choice to them. Denied by the senate of Rome. Challenged by the great Pompey. Trapped between an Italia and a Hispania both garrisoned against him. And yet now here he was: master of Rome and Italia, of Gaul, and of Hispania. The victor, undisputed.

The Massiliot predicament had just increased drastically. Their enemy had doubled in size, but had *quadrupled* in stature for, as Fronto was well aware, there was a weight carried just by the general's name that was worth a number of legions.

'They *have* to capitulate now,' Galronus said next to him.

Fronto nodded. 'The time has come. But nothing is ever quite that simple. Look.'

He gestured to the ramparts where the city gate stood facing the camp of Trebonius – the gate through which the enemy had sallied on several occasions, and through which their deputations had come. Rising to either side of that great portal were two heavy, square towers, and atop one of them some sort of disagreement had broken out between Massiliots and Romans, involving a great deal of clear gesticulation, even if the words were inaudible at this distance.

'Remind you of anyone?'

'Petreius and Afranius,' nodded Galronus. 'Two men sharing command is never a good idea, is it?'

'Three,' corrected Fronto, as the argument between the city's civilian council and the Roman commander was interrupted by a noble of the Albici waving his hands like a windmill in a storm. The argument raged on, with more men becoming involved as they watched.

'Ahenobarbus is trying to get them to fight, isn't he?' Aurelius mused, standing a few feet from them.

'And failing, I'd say, by the look of it.'

Now, only a quarter of a mile away across the open ground, Caesar and his companions drummed their heels on their mounts and rode out ahead of the column, bearing down on Trebonius' headquarters and the gate of Massilia. The senior officer gestured to his officers and strode out to meet the new arrivals. Fronto and Galronus joined them, leaving the three singulares at the villa's boundary wall.

The general reined in, Antonius and Varus alongside him, Plancus, Fabius and numerous others Fronto recognised behind. They looked bright and impressive, but Fronto had been through enough forced marches in his time to see the hidden signs of fatigue about their features. Caesar inclined his head to Trebonius.

'Massilia holds out still?'

Trebonius nodded in return. 'After a fashion, General. We have them by the throat. A truce of non-aggression is currently in effect. There was an unpleasant incident a week or so ago when they broke the truce and burned some of our siege works...'

Fronto caught the sudden sourness cross Mamurra's face off to the side of the gathering.

'...but it would seem that was the decision of the Roman commanders and not the boule of the city. The locals immediately pleaded to reinstate the truce. Ahenobarbus, as I understand it, was not happy.'

'Good. I do not wish the man the greatest of happiness. The terms of your truce?' Caesar asked.

'The Massiliots claim they are willing to capitulate and surrender their city, but only to yourself, General. It seems your reputation for magnanimity knows no bounds, at least compared to mine.'

Caesar smiled. 'It must have been difficult maintaining such a tense situation without mass violence erupting on both sides.'

Both Trebonius and Fronto turned to look at Salvius Cursor, who stood with the more junior officers to the rear. He failed even to flinch at their glances, his expression steady and alert. The tribune had not once apologised for his actions, and had maintained that it had been the right thing to do.

'There were a few *incidents*,' Trebonius rumbled, 'on *both* sides of the walls. But despite them the peace has been maintained and with the exception of one tower the city, as far as we are aware, remains intact.'

'Good work, Trebonius. And Mamurra and Fronto were of use to you?'

'Yes, General.'

'Good. Hispania is settled. I have left trusted men there in control, and two loyal legions now maintain the peace in the peninsula, the Pompeians disbanded and settled appropriately.

Once Massilia is dealt with, we can return to Rome for the winter and prepare to move on Pompey in the spring. All is coming together. First, though, we must deal with Massilia and its troublesome commander. Shall we?'

Trebonius nodded and called for his horse. The equisio and his staff hurried forward with the horses of the senior officers, who grasped their reins and pulled themselves up into the saddle, some requiring a little help in the process. Somewhere, a few miles off, a peal of thunder portended dire things ahead. Fronto noted that, alone of all the tribunes, Salvius Cursor seemed to assume he was invited and mounted his beast. Gesturing to Galronus, Fronto suggested that his companions mount up and keep pace with them, ready. Massilia was about to fall, and Fronto was determined to solve Balbus' little problem before others interfered.

A short while later the cream of the Caesarian officer corps descended into the dip before the great Arelate gate in the walls of Massilia. Hurrying alongside, Caesar's attendants moved to place a *curule* chair on a small dais for the general, but Caesar waved them aside and remained in his saddle. Fronto smiled as lictors rode forth on either side of the group, holding their fasces proudly, declaring the legitimacy and power of their master. Beyond them, forming an outer cordon, were Ingenuus' cavalry as always, and on the periphery: Galronus with Fronto's singulares. It had to be an impressive sight. As they sat waiting, Fronto noted the artillery on the towers above the gate disarming. They had to be just out of range here anyway, which had clearly been the general's design, but someone up there was taking no chances. The walls and towers here were now lined with just Massiliots and Albici. Fronto could see neither legionaries nor Roman officers up there. As he was contemplating the potential reasons for that, the gates of Massilia opened.

The boule of the city emerged on foot as if in procession, cool and stately, civilian and unarmed. They traipsed along the road from the gate to a position some thirty paces from the general, at which point Ingenuus' cavalrymen lifted their spears, preparing to defend their commander should anything untoward occur.

One man with saggy jowls and unruly hair despite the money he had clearly spent on attempting to style it, stepped forward, shivering in the winds that became more chilling and troublesome with every passing moment.

'Mighty Caesar, son of Venus and Proconsul of Gaul, I bring greetings from the city and boule of Massilia, for whom I am elected spokesman on this day.'

Caesar nodded – a slight incline, nothing more. There was an odd, uncomfortable silence.

'The honour of conveying our offer of surrender has been given to me,' the man went on.

Honour. Fronto rolled his eyes at politicians' need to embellish even their failures.

Still silence reigned.

'We...' he tried again, croaking into silence. 'I mean, the Roman governor...'

'Where is he?' Caesar interrupted.

'Proconsul?'

'Where is Lucius Domitius Ahenobarbus?'

'I cannot say, General. He would have no part in the capitulation of the city and departed our council in anger. The walls of Massilia are free of Roman personnel.'

'I can see that.' The general's voice was cold, business-like. 'This city closed its gates on me and took up Pompey's banner. I am, however, a man inclined toward peace and leniency. I may yet offer you generous terms. Those terms are, however, based in part upon the delivery of my enemies in the city. Bring me Domitius Ahenobarbus.'

The man looked distinctly uncomfortable now, sweating despite the cold.

'General, the commander... he has good veteran troops. I cannot say for certain where he has gone. It would take time to search the city for him, and then the city's garrison would have to extricate him. This will all take time.' He was blustering, floundering.

The general nodded. 'Trebonius? Can *you* bring me Ahenobarbus?'

His lieutenant straightened in his saddle. 'I have men champing at the bit, awaiting that very task, General.'

Caesar gestured to the boule's spokesman. 'In the absence of my enemy who has held your walls against me, I will accept the unconditional surrender of Massilia. There will be no terms requested by its council, military or population. Such conditions as are laid down in due course will be done so entirely at my discretion. Do you understand?'

The man nodded hurriedly, caught half way between panic and relief.

'On behalf of the boule, the garrison and the people of Massilia, I hereby surrender the city to Gaius Julius Caesar, Proconsul of Gaul.' His companions wore a number of different expressions, though not one made to counter his statement.

The general nodded again. 'All your men under arms will stand down and report to the largest open space in the city – the agora, I imagine. The boule will convene in their chamber one hour before sunset to hear my terms in full. All ships will be debarked and left empty. The population of civilian Massilia will return to their homes and remain there for the duration. This last is not a punishment, but a precaution. My legions have suffered their own privations during the siege and we are all, I'm sure, aware of the nature of victorious armies. Orders for peace and clemency will be given, and failures to adhere to those orders will be punished, but troubles are inevitable. Let us attempt to keep them to the minimum.'

The entire boule of the city bowed to the general.

'I shall now return to our camp and make preparations. You will go back to your city and see that my instructions are carried out. My legions will not move into the city until three hours before sundown, when I shall carry out my inspection of Massilia. Until then the city remains in your hands to prepare. Just one century of my men will be permitted to enter, however, with instructions to bring Ahenobarbus and his officers to me. You will accord them any aid they require in this task or you will forfeit any hope of clemency from me.'

Again, a bow from the boule.

'Good. See to your tasks, gentlemen.'

And with that, the general turned his back on the embassy, wheeling his horse and walking her toward the camp as the officers followed suit. The boule scurried back to the gates, rushing to prepare for the hand over of the city to the proconsul. There was another crack of thunder, distant, somewhere inland, perhaps near Aquae Sextiae over the hills.

Trebonius edged his horse toward Fronto and, once they were side by side and moving back toward the camp, the lieutenant cleared his throat.

'You wanted to be the first into Massilia? You heard the general: take one century of men and bring back Ahenobarbus.'

Fronto nodded and steered aside from the column, toward where Galronus and the others waited as Salvius Cursor emerged from the crowd and converged on them. Six men. Fronto looked at his companions. A prince of the Remi, a Greek archer, a Numidian gladiator, a superstitious former soldier and a tribune he despised. A stranger bunch of bedfellows he could hardly imagine.

'Where would Ahenobarbus go?' Salvius questioned as they moved off toward the camp of the Eleventh.

Fronto scratched his chin. 'He's trapped, as far as I can see. The city is besieged, and Brutus has managed to keep ships from going in or out for months with the help of someone in the city, so where can he go? And he has something of a bloody minded disposition, too, so I cannot imagine him walking up to us and laying down his sword willingly. He is the sort of man who would find a way out if there was one, but who would fight to the bloody end, if not. Right to the last man, like the Trojans at Priam's palace, tearing out bricks and throwing them at the Greeks.'

He sighed. 'The question is: where would he make his stand? He cannot maintain the city walls with the small Roman garrison he brought with him, for the Massiliots and the Albici won't aid him now. He has just under four cohorts as far as we know, so he will have to find somewhere very defensible. If he intends to hold anywhere against us, there are three sites separated from the houses and shops of the town, each on a prominence, he might consider. The temple of Athena is near the theatre and the agora. It's the smallest of the three and has no perimeter wall, but being compact – just a temple on a hill – that would be my choice to defend with just a small force. The sanctuary of Artemis is larger, surrounded by a perimeter wall and atop rocks on one side. But it has a large number of attendants and a few buildings to secure. And the sanctuary of Apollo is the biggest, with six or seven buildings and its own perimeter wall.'

393

'You think they'll be at this temple of Athena?'

'It's a good bet,' Fronto replied. 'The civilian population will be very compliant right now, hoping for the best terms from Caesar. Take Pullo and his century to the agora and make a few reasoned and calm enquiries of the men you find there. If Ahenobarbus and his legionaries have settled into the temple of Athena, they'll have been seen in the agora.'

'Caesar gave orders that the citizens return to their homes.'

'Yes,' Fronto sighed, 'but it will take hours for it all to happen fully. The agora will still be busy for a while, and Caesar also gave orders that the Massiliot defenders assemble there unarmed. And while you try and find out whether he is at the temple without storming a sacred site unnecessarily, I'll take my guards and Galronus and quickly check the other two sanctuaries then catch up with you. I used to live here, and I know the quick ways through the city.'

Salvius Cursor nodded and geed up his horse, heading for the camp of the Eleventh. As soon as he was out of earshot, Fronto turned to the others.

'Ahenobarbus will be at the port, the agora, or the temple of Athena, depending whether he's trying to run, negotiate or fight. But before we go there, I want to find Catháin. He's probably at the warehouse if he's still in Massilia. Come on.'

* * *

It was strange, entering Massilia that day. Fronto had used the same gate for years now, sauntering from his villa's grounds into the city and down through the streets to the warehouse or the agora or more often, he would have to admit, to the taverns. On occasion, he would use the main street that ran from this gate down to the port, but more often he would stray through the back streets, beneath the lofty heights of the two sanctuaries that stuck up like the vertebrae of Massilia.

He had never been the enemy. Well… strictly speaking he had never truly been a Massiliot either, and the city's government, traders and nobles had been uniformly difficult with him, but he had never felt more out of place than now.

The grey cloud had lowered noticeably, streaks of steel in the sky, topped by rolling white thunderheads. That they moved so ponderously from the hills over the city was impressive, given the ever-increasing speed of the chilly winds.

The people of Massilia disappeared from view at the sight of the five Romans striding purposefully down the street. Women swept babies from their path as though Fronto might hold the slightest interest in someone else's snotty offspring. The air was becoming close and unpleasant, though it remained cold, and the feeling of impending explosive doom was all around.

It did not take long to reach the warehouse, though, each of the four men with him familiar with the place. The main doors were shut tight, as was proper. Fronto approached them and drew a small ring of keys from his belt pouch, selected one and then reached out. He stopped.

'What is it?' Galronus asked.

'There are two locks. I only put one in.'

'Catháin has been busy, then.'

'Good man, he knows what a besieged city is like. Saving what he can and protecting everything from looters and opportunists.' Fronto gave the door an experimental push. 'Barred from the inside, too. Come on. Let's try the back way.'

Dipping into a side alley, Fronto led his friends to the rear of the warehouse and closed on the smaller, single door. 'Two locks again,' Galronus pointed.

'This one's *always* had two locks, and I have the keys.' A moment later, he snicked each lock open and, lifting the latch, gave the door a shove. It opened inwards with a noise like a tomb cover grating aside, and stuck slightly on the gritty floor. Inside, all was dark. Fronto glanced questioningly at his companions and Galronus nodded, drawing his sword, an action followed by the Masgava and Aurelius. Arcadios unslung his bow from his shoulder and fished an arrow from his quiver.

He stepped inside.

The same preternatural sense that had saved him a dozen times on the battlefield visited him again now. As the hairs rose on the back of his neck, Fronto suddenly ducked. The stout ash club hummed through the space above him, parting his hair before thudding into the door edge with a deep, ligneous thump. Had the blow landed, Fronto would probably now have been searching the floor for his brains. He continued with his ducking motion and turned it into a roll, somersaulting forward and coming up into a combat-ready stance, sword grating out of its sheath.

The door suddenly burst wide open as Galronus and Aurelius hit it simultaneously, and light flooded into the darkness.

Cathàin stood illuminated, blinking with one eye, club still in hand and still overextended. Fronto stared in shock. The strange northerner was disfigured. His mouth was swollen and lumpy. His left eye was a bulbous purple mass with a closed slit at the centre, and his nose was at a jaunty angle and surprisingly flat. A clump of hair was missing above one ear, with just raw flesh in its place. His left arm was tightly bound to his chest with a makeshift sling, the club in his right.

'What in Hades' own latrine happened?' Fronto whispered.

Cathàin shook slightly and made an odd purring noise. It took Fronto a moment to realise the man was laughing.

'Murff ee mugga lou.'

'What?' Galronus asked.

'He said "you should see the other fellow",' Fronto snorted, rolling his eyes. 'Who did this to you?'

'Armans.' Cathàin paused, breathed slowly through his wrecked nose. He dropped his club and crossed to a small stool, picking up a cup of wine and taking a careful sip through his cracked lips. He hissed at the pain.

'Hurts,' he said slowly. 'Talking. Hurts.'

'Keep it to a minimum,' Fronto said. 'Romans did this?'

Cathàin nodded. 'I... was sneaking onto walls. Signalling your navy. Caught me.'

'You're the one who's been signalling Brutus?' Fronto stared. 'You mad sod. That's about as dangerous a job you could ever choose. Ahenobarbus is not a forgiving man.'

'I know. They were... going to crucify me. But I got away.' He paused, wincing again and took another painful sip. 'Tribune hurt my face... broke my arm. Arsehole didn't bother with my legs, though. More fool him. I *know* how to run.'

He grinned and then whimpered as the motion brought fresh blood through the splits.

Fronto frowned, a suspicion creeping over him. 'A tribune? A tribune did this?'

A nod.

'Looks like a corpse? Sneers a lot?'

'Sounds like the one.'

'I am going to tear that bastard's spine out through his nose,' snarled Fronto. He suddenly remembered the reason they were both here. '*Balbus.* Balbus sent you to find some papers for him...'

'Burned,' Catháin sighed. 'Days ago. Couldn't get them out of the city. Once I'd been caught and escaped I knew the Romans would be looking for me. Couldn't let them find the papers, so I burned them all. Balbus' papers. Yours. All the business. Everything. Sorry.' He stopped and rested his sore mouth, wincing at the pain of continued conversation.

'Don't be sorry,' Fronto said, through a wave of relief. 'The business is probably done with now, anyway. We'll start it up again in Tarraco, but I think our time in Massilia's ended.'

Catháin nodded his emphatic agreement.

'What do you know about Ahenobarbus? Do you know where he is?'

Catháin sighed painfully, took another swig of wine, and braced himself for more soreness. 'Probably gone.'

'What?'

'He's had three ships in dock readied for more than a week now. The fastest ones in Massilia. He's known it's over for a while – that the boule would ignore his demands and seek peace. He's probably already gone. I went to warn Brutus about it, and that's when they caught me.'

Fronto realised he was trembling slightly. 'I saw Ahenobarbus on the walls this morning, arguing. If he's gone, he's only *just* left. Will you be alright?'

Catháin nodded painfully. 'Plenty of wine. Dulls pain.'

'Help yourself,' Fronto urged. 'And keep the door locked.'

Moments later, he was out of the warehouse again into the bitter wind of the grey afternoon and hurrying down the street followed by the others. 'The docks?' Masgava asked.

'The docks.'

This time, they were running. Salvius Cursor would be nearing the agora by now with a century of men. The port was close to the agora. If Ahenobarbus was fleeing Massilia, running back to Pompey, then he might still be there. They could still catch him. Feet pounding on dry, dusty cobbles they ran, slipping here and there with the inherent difficulty of hobnails on smooth stone.

Shops and bars hauntingly familiar to them whizzed past, and Fronto jinked around a couple of corners before his eyes locked on the tall masts he could see rising above the roofs against the grey, boiling sky. Breath coming in heaved gasps, the five men burst from a narrow side street out onto the port, peering off along the dock as the wind whipped makeshift covers from piles of goods.

They were too late.

The jetties of Massilia were more than half empty, and those ships that remained tied up were poor excuses for vessels, hastily patched and barely-seaworthy. The three good ships were busy pulling out of the harbour even now. The battering storm winds were troubling them a little, forcing them to carefully control the sails, but even as Fronto came to a stop, his chest rising and falling at speed, he could see the small flotilla already moving out through the arms of the harbour, past the ruined tower by the swamp and across the water.

Ahenobarbus had fled.

Impotent frustration tore through Fronto, and he could see similar in the eyes of his companions. All this, and the bastard had got away. Oh, they had secured Massilia but, just as he had at Corfinium, Ahenobarbus had escaped, whole and at liberty to seek his master, which he almost certainly would now do.

'Will Brutus be able to catch him?' Galronus asked quietly.

'Doubtful. These winds are coming from inland. They favour Ahenobarbus, but not Brutus. And Catháin said these were the fastest ships in Massilia. They're pretty swift. No, he knows exactly what he's doing. He'll be off and bound for Pompey and the east now.'

But even as he watched, something was happening. The lead ship had cleared the harbour and was making for open sea, but the second of the three had drifted oddly. There was a tiny, distant noise. They could hardly hear it over the general hum of the city, but it was a sound with which Fronto was thoroughly familiar. His eyes rose to the tower above the port entrance. The great bolt thrower atop it loosed again, the missile dropping and thudding into that second ship with the accuracy of a master artillerist who knew his weapon. Even as Fronto marvelled, tiny orange lights flared on the tower's parapet and then arced down at the ship.

Fire arrows.

There was no way Salvius had made it to that tower already. And his men wouldn't even know how to nock an arrow. That had to be the city garrison and the Albici. There would, he realised, be no love lost now between them and Ahenobarbus. The Roman had led them to naught but defeat and then fled in the face of the city's fall. Their best chance of good terms with Caesar was to hand over Ahenobarbus – the man now trying to leave the harbour.

That second ship was in trouble now, its sail on fire and men rushing around to put out various other small flames. The third ship was turning. Whether because of the threat from the tower, or perhaps the threat posed by the burning ship in the harbour entrance, the third trireme turned as sharply as it could, quite masterfully really, and began to plough its way through the water back toward the jetties.

'Pray that's Ahenobarbus,' Fronto shouted as he ran once more, moving to intercept the ship as it ploughed on toward the dock. The others pounded along behind him and, as the crowds dispersed rapidly in the face of potential fresh troubles, Fronto spotted legionaries jogging toward them. For a moment, he panicked that somehow the enemy had managed to outflank them, but he swiftly realised it was Pullo and Salvius with the men of the Eleventh.

The three groups were converging on the same jetty: Fronto and his friends, Salvius and his legionaries, the trireme and its fugitives. Beyond it, Fronto could see that the second trireme had now managed to put out the fires on its deck and had cut away the sail, turning and following its mate back toward the jetties. Two of the three ships had turned back.

Fronto quickly patted the figurines hanging around his neck – Fortuna and Nemesis, luck and vengeance. Perhaps both were at work right now.

'Three cohorts of legionaries at the agora,' Salvius Cursor shouted as they closed. 'All surrendering, but no sign of their commanders.'

Fronto nodded. 'One ship made it out. The others are coming back.'

'Centurion,' Salvius turned to the Pullo, 'take half the men and secure that intact trireme. The rest are with us.'

The centurion called off the names of five tent party leaders and forty men followed him along the jetty to the ship that was closing on it, while the rest followed Salvius Cursor in the wake of Fronto toward the next clear jetty. The ship that was limping back toward this one was scorched and missing its sail now, but was still largely intact and of good quality. Fronto cast up a quick prayer to Fortuna. A full trireme's crew would number around two hundred, and if they all turned out to be legionaries, confronting them belligerently might be the last mistake he and his small force made. But belligerent they were going to have to be. There was a one in three chance that the ship carried Lucius Domitius Ahenobarbus, and the man was 'required' by Caesar.

With three cohorts surrendering in the agora, there wouldn't be much more than a cohort left of legionaries. Four hundred or so men at most, split between three ships. They had to be using non-legionary crew for the oars. Still, if they were defiant and truly loyal to Ahenobarbus, Fronto and his forty five companions could be facing almost four-to-one odds.

'Follow my lead,' Fronto told the men on the jetty as they watched the fire-blackened trireme close on the jetty. Sailors threw looped ropes from the ship to the posts on the jetty, expertly lassoing them and hauling on them to pull the trireme up against the timbers. The ship came to a halt with a thud that shook the jetty and had every man on it staggering to retain his footing. No boarding ramp was run down from the rail that towered above head height.

The first pregnant drops of rain blatted against the wood by the Romans' feet. As Fronto looked up at the deep grey, leaden clouds, there was a staccato battering of rain on the wood. A sudden flash of white amid the clouds starkly illuminated the ships, and a boom tore the sky apart.

The storm had begun.

'We seek terms with the forces of the proconsul,' called a refined voice from the ship.

'The same terms will be offered to the cohorts as to the native garrison, provided their officers are willing to submit themselves to our prior judgement,' Fronto answered carefully.

'That is highly irregular,' announced the voice.

'That is my offer,' Fronto replied calmly, flatly, with finality.

A figure approached the edge of the ship and rose into view. He wore a sky blue tunic with dark purple edging, marking him as a man of rank. His cloak was of good quality wool, dyed dark blue. The trierarch of the ship, Fronto assumed.

'I will submit myself and the crew of the *Laocoon* to your mercies,' the man said in that same, clear voice. 'My passengers, I fear, will be reticent.'

Even as he spoke, the boarding ramp was run out and a number of burly, sun-bronzed men with numerous tattoos began to descend. Back across the ship several voices were raised in anger at the surrendering sailors. They were labelled cowards, women and deserters. Fronto gestured to his men, and the legionaries shuffled aside to make way for the sailors.

'You,' Fronto pointed at his optio – the ranking officer within this century. 'Take ten men and escort these sailors and their trierarch to the agora to join the rest of the surrendering forces.'

He watched as more than a hundred men disembarked and shuffled along the jetty to the port. Assuming the galley were fully crewed there would still be nearing a hundred Pompeians on board. Another quick plea to Fortuna, and he took a deep breath and marched to the boarding ramp, the others following on behind. Thirty six men, he had. Two to one odds at best, perhaps even three to one. And a fight now seemed inevitable, else the rest would have disembarked at the same time as the trierarch.

The ramp was already slippery with the rain and Fronto ascended carefully, rain blatting his armour in large heavy drops. He emerged onto the deck and cast his gaze about. The rest of the occupants – yes, seventy or so – were gathered near the steering oars at the stern, and along the twin decks at the sides toward the aft end. Even decked for war, the space for a fight was tight.

'Depart my ship and I will not have you skinned and used to patch the sail,' a voice called.

All thoughts of leniency evaporated at the sound of that voice. A voice Fronto had heard making insolent demands as his allies burned the Musculus. A voice whose owner had burned down a tower full of legionaries during a truce. A voice that had sneered as it beat the lifeblood out of Catháin. *No quarter.* Fronto found himself troubled as the rain continued to *dong* from his helmet and splat onto his clothes. Caesar needed to maintain his reputation and therefore the need for clemency with Massilia and its defenders. And though he had wanted Ahenobarbus brought to him, Fronto was fairly certain he would not harm the man. In the absence of the commander, who had probably fled on that first ship, Caesar would want the second in command delivered to him, and not just his head. But Fronto had vowed every night since the tower burned that he would end the man responsible. He cleared his throat.

'Any legionary, centurion, optio or sailor here who disembarks and makes his way to the agora will receive the same terms as the surrendering garrison. Your commander, however? No terms for you, Tribune.'

Legionaries parted at the rear of the ship and the tribune came into view at the end of the gap between decks. He did not look perturbed. Two huge guards stood beside him. His skeletal features regarded Fronto in the same manner that a cat regards a mouse.

'I remember you.'

'Good.'

'Last chance, Caesar's lapdog. Leave my ship or you will regret your decision.'

Fronto's confidence wavered for just a moment as more than seventy swords were drawn with a collective rasping hiss, but it returned with an answering scrape of iron on bronze behind him. As though the gods acknowledged the importance of what happened here, the storm chose that moment to break fully, the clouds opening and dropping swathes of water on them, which came down like watery pila, bouncing on the deck to knee height.

Fronto peered through the downpour. This could be ended with the tribune's death – he was sure of that. Their reason to resist would melt away. The enemy were gathered largely on the twin decks at the ship's sides and the small poop deck to the stern. His eyes dropped to the narrow sunken walkway between the two decks, some ten feet below and only five or six wide. It was the walkway along which water was delivered to the oarsmen beneath the decks, and where the aulete played his pipes. It led almost directly to the tribune at the rear, where the stairs rose to meet the stern deck. And it was empty. Of course it wouldn't be for long, and it would be incredibly dangerous to run along, open to pila and swords from above at either side.

'Two squads,' he barked over his shoulder. 'One on each deck. Remember you're the fighting Eleventh, heroes of the Nervii, Avaricum, Alesia and Ilerda. Make your blows count. There are two or three for each of you, so don't get greedy.'

Dark chuckles rippled behind him as the forty men split into two units, half of them heading over to the mast and using the bridge there to cross to the other deck. Two sets of hardened legionaries eyed one another.

'The pit?' Masgava rumbled under his breath.

'Yes. The tribune's the goal.'

'Last chance, legate,' called the Pompeian officer from the rear deck.

'Charge,' Fronto shouted as another dazzling flash of silver tore through the clouds and a deep boom rolled across Massilia. The water was hissing all around the ship now as the rain ripped into it. Shouts and the clang of iron on iron were just audible from the other vessel two jetties over, where clearly things were going just as well.

Chaos broke out. The legionaries in Fronto's party ran, brandishing weapons. The legate kept his hand up, holding his companions back. Let the chaos settle in first…

The two forces met on both decks with a noise like gods at war. Clangs and thuds and shouts and screams. The rain battering the wood of the ship with a constant drumming and the hiss of the water created a symphony that threatened to drown out all else. Fronto could barely see the tribune now through the torrents of falling water, the deep gloom of the storm and the shadows of the two melees aboard the side decks.

'Now.'

Without further pause, he dropped into the narrow walkway between the decks. Only as he landed and his knee reminded him that it would never be truly right again did he realise quite how far down ten feet was. He paused long enough to whimper, wipe the tear from the corner of his eye and test the strength of his leg, and then he was moving again. He had jarred it, but his knee would hold up. The thuds behind him announced the arrival in the walkway of Salvius, Galronus, Masgava and Aurelius.

Fronto was running. It was perhaps forty feet to the stairs and the poop deck where the tribune waited. A gauntlet to run. With his companions following on, the legate pounded along the timbers between the rows of oar benches toward his target at the rear. His nailed boots slipped and skidded across the sodden, slick timbers, but momentum kept him pressing forward. With a scream, a legionary fell into the narrow walkway, clutching a bloody rent in his chest, links of chain and gouts of blood falling through the air in his wake. The body hit the walkway and Fronto hurdled the thrashing shape without pause. Twenty feet...

With a defiant roar, a legionary dropped into the gap, shieldless but brandishing a sword and bracing himself. Fronto raised his own blade to try and remove the obstacle at speed, but the legionary suddenly sprouted an arrow from his face and fell backwards with a shriek and a gurgle. Arcadios had found his vantage point, then.

Moments later arrows were flying as though a whole unit of archers were present, the impressive speed of the little Greek putting shaft after shaft into the enemy. It was still not enough to clear the way. Ten feet from the stairs and the gauntlet had finally closed in. Here, the enemy legionaries to each side were from their rear ranks, not busy fighting Fronto's men and, as they became aware of the five men pounding along the walkway below them, they began to react.

Swords lashed out, swung downwards, mostly too high to hit home, but close enough to cause concern and make the runners duck instinctively. And men were starting to drop into the gap again. The first disappeared with a cry and an arrow in the throat, but there was already a snarling legionary immediately behind him. Fronto didn't stop. His sword lashed out. He missed, but barged the man aside and Salvius, savage that he was, stabbed the man twice in the gut before running on. The stairs were just a couple of paces away now.

A legionary hit the deck before Fronto and the legate feinted left. The man was still a little disoriented from the drop and fell for the slight jig, not watching Fronto's eyes or feet. The legate dodged right at the last moment, slammed the point of his gladius into the gap beneath the raised sword arm and felt it punch through flesh into the vital space inside. The man gurgled and fell aside. Fronto reached the first step and began to climb. For just the blink of an eye, he risked a look back.

Salvius and Galronus were with him. Aurelius and Masgava were snarled up in the walkway, cutting a bloody swathe through the ever-increasing mass of enemies there. Fronto turned back in time to see a big man with expensive mail and an elaborate helmet appear at the top of the stairs, roaring. Before Fronto could consciously react, the soldier was punched back with an arrow to the chest. Bless you, Arcadios.

Fronto slipped and slithered up the treacherous steps and emerged onto the deck with his two close companions hurrying to catch up.

The tribune stood facing him, his two bodyguards at his flanks. A fair proposal under most circumstances, but the rear ranks of the legionaries on either deck were now turning to face the threat to their commander. Any moment the three of them would be swamped by soldiers.

'How many can you kill?' Salvius shouted at him.

'Er... two?' hazarded Fronto.

'Good. Get to it.'

Even as Salvius spoke, he leapt forward. One of the bodyguards bellowed and stepped forward to meet him, but the young tribune was quick as a striking cobra. His sword seemed to whisper past the guard's head harmlessly, and then he was turning and racing back across the deck to hold off the tide of legionaries. Taking his cue from the blood-mad Salvius, Galronus dipped across to the other side and began to swing his long, Gallic blade, holding off the legionaries on that deck.

The side decks narrowed at the end to accommodate the stairs between them. As long as Salvius and Galronus were careful, they could hold the tide of humanity for the precious moments Fronto needed.

He faced the cadaverous tribune and his bodyguards.

Three. He'd said two, hadn't he?

Then, suddenly, as the right hand of the two guards turned his head slightly, the gash in his neck opened up and a jet of crimson burst from it across the deck. Salvius had far from missed, after all.

Horrified, the big bodyguard dropped his sword and clutched at the wound, the blood spraying out in fine jets between his fingers. He was out of the fight, and not long for the world.

The other bodyguard – a bulky man with an old-fashioned helmet and torcs and medals hanging all over him – stepped forward. His sword flickered out a few times, experimentally. Fronto stood still, facing him. A few months ago in Hispania, the goading bitter words of the young officer now fighting alongside him had driven Fronto into trying to prove himself, to prove he was still vital and strong. Realisation had come slowly, but it had come. He *was* vital and strong. He just wasn't young any more, and no amount of exercise and danger was going to solve that problem. But where he lacked the spry agility of the tribune and could no longer leap into the fray as Salvius had done, experience and wisdom filled the gaps left by youth.

He watched the bodyguard's blade.

Lance... lance... dance... twist... lance...

The blade moved left in the next part of this repetitive sequence and Fronto simply stepped inside the reach of it and slammed his blood-slick sword into the man's throat. As the bodyguard, astonished and in agony, staggered, his eyes wide and his sword falling away from desperate fingers, Fronto almost casually jerked his hilt first left and then right, then withdrew it, the ruination of the initial wound adequate to prevent sucking flesh fighting the pull. Gore and blood poured through the jagged hole and the man fell instantly, his legs thrashing and hammering on the timber.

Fronto stood silent, watching the tribune. Around him, the incessant downpour hammered the timber deck, washing the pools of blood into one great greasy pink lake across the whole ship. One thing to be grateful for with the storm was that the rain suppressed the stink of offal and bowel that accompanied any real fight. All he could smell was the salty air and the tinny overtone of the storm. A flash illuminated the tribune and made him look more skeletal than ever. Even as the crash of thunder rolled above them, Fronto found his conscience entirely clear. This wasn't a man. This was a spirit of the restless dead who had somehow found a body.

'I have information your general will want,' the tribune said quietly. He didn't look afraid. It was a reasoned negotiation, not desperation.

'No.' Fronto was not a force of reason right now.

'Then come, so I can kill you.'

The tribune drew his weapon finally. It was a nice sword – decorative hilt, but a proper soldier's blade. The way he held it suggested he knew well how to use it.

Fronto felt an odd chill run through him. He was facing a Roman, preparing to kill him. Not in the cause of war, but in a very personal way. The conditions could hardly be more different, yet it dragged him back momentarily to another time. A chilly day here, in the battering rain, on a ship. Last time it had been hot and dry and sunny, in a quarry. He had been sorely wounded last year, and still felt the effects of it. Last year he had allowed it to happen, in a way. Verginius had been a friend. This was not. The tribune was a vicious bastard who burned men to death. Oh, Fronto had done terrible things in the prosecution of a war, but this had been during a truce. The men who had died in that tower had been innocent and settled in for the night. This had been murder, pure and simple.

The tribune's blade sat still in his hand. No fancy plays. Nothing. Just ready to react.

There was something about the man's eyes, though. Fronto squinted through the rain and realised that the tribune was not looking at him, but over his shoulder. He turned sharply. The legionary's sword was already lashing out. It was the man with the arrow protruding from his torso, who had been at the top of the stairs, and there was no time for Fronto to bring his sword up in response.

He was going to die.

The legionary, teeth bared as he swung down for his kill, was suddenly thrown aside as a second arrow hit him, punching him left and sending him to the deck. Fronto stared. Right behind where the legionary had been about to kill him a moment earlier was Salvius Cursor with his sword lowered. The blood-soaked young tribune nodded.

'*Now* we're even.'

Fronto stared as Salvius swung his blade up to block an attack from another legionary. Masgava and Aurelius were emerging from the walkway now, the latter sporting a nasty wound to the upper arm. They filtered off to either side, Aurelius coming to support Salvius, and Masgava falling in beside Galronus, where the Remi prince was reminding the legions of Rome just how much reach a Gallic long sword had. A small pile of bodies was already mounting up before him.

Fronto turned back to the tribune.

The officer's blade came up ready. Fronto took a step forward. He reckoned, just from looking in the man's eyes, that they would be something of a match. The tribune was not young, but he was clearly a veteran who knew what he was doing. Fronto closed his eyes for a single heartbeat. This was now the work of the gods. He was not a legate of Caesar but a vessel for the wrath of Nemesis. He would have to trust to their care.

Another step forward. Careful. Slow.

The enemy sword came out sharply, in a sudden jerk. Fronto stepped forward, taking the blow and praying that Fortuna and Nemesis still favoured him. The sword was well-aimed. It struck just below the bronze edging at the bottom of his cuirass. A bowel-opening blow. The sword sliced through two of the hanging leather pteruges and struck the second layer of them below. The angle was just slightly oblique and, unless a blow hit pteruges dead-on, boiled leather can turn a point. The blade, instead of lancing deep into Fronto's gut as intended, sliced a long, angry line across the top of his hip and then slid off harmlessly to the side.

Fronto was not trying anything graceful. He was revenge now, pure and simple. His own sword slammed into the tribune's corpse-like face, hilt first, breaking teeth and nose. As the enemy officer staggered back in shock, Fronto dropped his sword. He turned and grabbed the man's extended sword arm, pulling it down as he brought up his knee and breaking it permanently at the elbow.

The tribune howled in agony through his broken teeth, lurching this way and that in the driving rain, his sword dropping. Fronto bent and swept up both the tribune's sword and his own discarded one. Blade in each hand, he approached the tribune.

'Ugh…' snarled the man, unable to form proper words with his crippled face. Fronto jabbed out with the swords. The tribune leaned back out of the way, but Fronto had not been attempting to wound with them. As he leaned, the tribune collided with one of the steering oars and fell. Fronto strode like the shadow of Nemesis herself over to the prone man, who was gagging and trying to rise with his non-shattered arm. Using a sword point, Fronto pushed him back down to the deck. Once the man was prone again, Fronto raised his foot. There was another flash of bright white and a crack of thunder that hid the dreadful sound as Fronto stamped his hobnailed boot down on the tribune's other elbow. The man screamed and rolled around, unable to stand without the aid of his two broken arms.

'Those are for Catháin and for the men in the tower.'

Straightening, he stamped once more, this time on the man's knee, which shattered with a horrible bony crack.

'That one's for Nemesis.'

And then the final joint. The other knee splintered with an unforgettable noise. The irreparably crippled tribune howled unintelligibly through his ruined face as he jerked, unable to do anything else.

'But the last one was for me, you piece of shit.'

He turned. The fight had gone out of the enemy. More than half were dead already, but the rest were dropping their weapons and raising their arms.

'You're a cold bastard, Fronto,' Salvius Cursor said, eying the broken tribune.

'From you, I'll consider that a compliment.'

Salvius gave him a horrible smile and then turned to address the soldiers. 'Get these captives to the agora with the others.' He turned back to Fronto. 'I'm going to see what happened on the other ship.'

Fronto nodded. He looked at Aurelius, who was bleeding well but seemed to be content and whole otherwise. 'Make sure this one doesn't die. I want him treated so that he'll live as a cripple and delivered to the general. He said he had information.'

Aurelius shook his head as he walked past to the ruined man. 'He's right, Fronto. You're a cold bastard.'

* * *

Marcus Falerius Fronto stood on the tower top above the harbour entrance with Salvius and Galronus. In the distance, Ahenobarbus' ship was little more than a dot now, white sail against a dark grey sky, periodically lit by the flashes of lightning that were now moving out to sea. Brutus' ships were pursuing, but there was clearly no chance of them ever catching the trireme, without the prior warning that Catháin had apparently been providing over the weeks. It seemed that Brutus had won two of the most unlikely sea victories in the history of the republic because he had been prepared in advance. Fronto doubted Catháin's name would make it into records, but the man deserved recognition from him, at least.

Leaving their jetty, Salvius had confirmed that the only senior officer on the other ship in port had been an auxiliary prefect who had surrendered with little trouble. Some of his men had put up a fight, but most had capitulated with their commander. Ahenobarbus had fled Massilia and slipped their grip, racing away to join his master, the lone Pompeian senior officer to make it out of Massilia.

But they had to savour the moment anyway, despite losing Ahenobarbus. Ten months ago, they had been in Ravenna, with Pompey in command of Rome, the man's legions in Hispania holding it for him, and Massilia treating with the senate in their favour. Now, as the season drew to a close, Italia, Gaul and Hispania were all settled in support of Caesar, with legions in position to maintain that situation. Pompey controlled the east with a massive army, but from being an outcast on the northern border with the enmity of the Roman aristocracy, Caesar was now the undisputed master of the west, legitimised by the senate.

And the unnamed tribune had claimed to have important information, so perhaps there was another victory yet to be savoured. The medicus had said it would be days before the man could be safely interrogated, but he was stable, and would live to talk to the general.

Victory.

'Will you stay in Massilia now?' Galronus asked quietly.

Fronto shook his head. 'Tarraco, I think. And one day back to Puteoli and Rome, but not while Pompey's shadow is still cast across Italia. In Hispania we are all as far away from the war as we can be. And you'll be coming presumably? For Faleria?'

'We'll stop now? Go home?' The Remi sounded surprised.

Fronto nodded. 'I've no stomach for fighting Romans. We were lucky this year. We took almost all our victories without mass slaughter. But that time is coming. When Caesar meets Pompey it will be brutal, and nothing will stop oceans of blood flowing.'

Galronus nodded, but Fronto could see Salvius regarding him sidelong.

'You disagree?'

Salvius Cursor shrugged. 'I will fight until I hold Pompey's still-beating heart in my hand.'

'What did he do to you?'

Salvius ignored the question and returned his gaze to the grey sea.

Epilogue.

15ᵗʰ of October - Massilia

'NO. I am going home. Back to my family.'

Caesar shook his head. 'I still need you, Fronto. This is not over yet.'

'I don't care, Caesar. I've done my time and more.'

'You forget, Fronto, that you owe me.'

'I've paid that debt.'

'You've paid that debt when I say you have, Fronto. You came to me an exile with nothing. I have rebuilt your life and saved your family. I will have at least another year for that. Curio took Sicilia but has run into numerous problems in Africa. Gaius Antonius struggles in Illyria with Pompey so close. We hold the west and Rome is safe, but the threat in the east grows each month.'

'My family need me.'

'They do, I'm sure. Winter with them in Tarraco. Or bring them to Rome for the cold season. All will be safe there now. And then, come tubilustrum in Martius, we turn east and take the war back to Pompey. I will be consul then and Rome will be behind me.'

The tired legate locked Caesar with a steely glance.

'Fronto, I have lost Labienus to the arms of the enemy. Only Marcus Antonius and you are a match for him in the field. I will not relinquish one of my greatest resources to the mundanities of retirement. You will march with us next spring. Do not press me on this. I would hate to have to revise my support of your situation.'

'You would threaten me?' Fronto said coldly.

'To save Rome and settle the republic, I would threaten my own family. Nothing must be valued higher than the republic, Marcus. You know that. You have always held to that, as have I.'

Fronto glared, still, but he had lost and he knew it. Because the general could ruin him and destroy his family. Because perhaps he *did* still owe Caesar. Because he could never support the animal Pompey. But mostly because Caesar was right. He could never sit quiet and bounce his son upon his knee while Rome was being torn apart around him.

'One more season,' he acquiesced with a sigh. 'We defeat Pompey, and then I am free. I owe you nothing.'

One more season...

* * *

Tribune Quintus Cassius Longinus lay in the darkness in indescribable pain. The medicus had been less than comforting and careful with his ministrations. The man had pronounced in a fairly offhand manner that not only would Cassius live, but he may well learn to walk again, though he would never be whole. He would always lurch and limp, dragging the one leg whose knee was irreparable. He would rely upon a crutch his whole life. Luckily the one arm that still worked was the one that would be needed for the crutch. Tremendous comfort.

The medicus had delivered all this information as though reeling off a list of supplies from a tablet. He was a military physician and would have seen this damage and much worse in his time. Soldiers who were crippled in the line of duty could be given *missio causaria* and be honourably discharged with part or full pension, but those who could not put their pension into a new career because of their wounds would inevitably end up begging on street corners.

That would not happen to Cassius, of course. His family were of ancient patrician blood and had money aplenty. His cousin Gaius was Tribune of the Plebs in Rome, and another cousin, Lucius, held a powerful post. He would never need to work and would be looked after well enough.

Quintus faced a choice. A life of twisted reliance upon others, and likely constant pain was not to be desired, but it would grant him the opportunity of revenge someday. But that would also mean he would be interrogated. He was under no illusions as to Caesar's willingness to press him for information, and he had plenty to give. No. He would go like a Roman and take his information to the grave. Caesar would be angry and would blame Fronto. And Gaius Cassius would blame Caesar and Fronto. Revenge would come one day, he knew. His cousin, the man who had survived Carrhae – the

413

battle that killed Crassus, would make Fronto and Caesar pay one day.

With no small amount of agony, he bent the elbow of his left arm and removed the two items he had carefully purloined over the days of his treatment. The coin he pushed between the jagged shards of his ruined teeth, sliding it under his tongue. With difficulty, as long moments passed, he manoeuvred the doctor's blade. It was not long – slightly longer than his index finger – but it was the best he'd been able to shuffle aside without being seen. The blade was lifted with the damaged arm, the other too broken to even move. He positioned it, feeling the tip scraping the skin where it dipped between the two ribs.

A defeated officer fell on his sword. It was the way.

Quintus Cassius Longinus rolled off the pallet and expired with a cruel but satisfied smile.

THE END

Historical Note

49 BC, the first year of Caesar's account of the Civil War, is a tough proposition for a Roman military novel. It is the biggest year of non-battles and non-sieges to be found in his accounts. Almost everything in this year was resolved with diplomacy and negotiation, despite a little to-ing and fro-ing of the legions to achieve it. Despite the constant threat of mass battle and dreadful sieges, there is surprisingly little bloodshed.

Caesar crosses the Rubicon (we all know that moment), and embarks upon a campaign across Italy in which almost every town falls without a fight. Sometimes, just to build up the tension for a non-event, Caesar describes for us days or weeks of constructing siege works and cutting off forage before the town simply surrenders and everyone moves on. Oh, and for the record I have gone with the phrase 'Let the die be cast' which is historically and linguistically far more accurate than the more common phrase bandied about.

Massilia is no different to the Italian non-sieges. It was the focus for a sizeable part of Caesar's army for most of the year but, when it all comes down to it, there was surprisingly little bloodshed once again. In the end the city surrendered and Caesar was lenient as usual – ever the damned politician, eh? Some of the most interesting and ingenious siege works ever created – no one knows whose idea they were, but Mamurra seems the likely culprit – and nothing much ever comes of them but their being burned by the enemy. The one real shining glory of Massilia, and I would say the one thing that stands out for me having written this book, is the victories of Brutus at sea (I'll come back briefly to those shortly.)

Then Ilerda... which I count among my least favourite battles to read, to be honest. It spans many weeks and involves a great deal of manoeuvring and minor disasters, but there is only really one big fight, for the middle hill top, and that is far from conclusive. Yet again, that huge campaign ended with negotiation. For the Romans these non-martial conclusions were all good, of course, and I hope to have got something of that over in the story. No Roman really wants to see fields of Roman dead. But from the point of view of a man writing a military novel, it is somewhat frustrating when every fight becomes an argument and then a handshake and everyone goes home to eat beans and talk about the old days.

Still, there is action to be found on smaller scales, and it was nice to put Fronto back in control, even if age is beginning to make him take a slightly less active role. And the chance to portray old friends was good, too.

I think you know most of the main characters. Ahenobarbus is new, but is a true historical character, as are Petreius and Afranius. Letting them all go free was probably not Caesar's wisest decision, for you've not seen the last of any of them. Salvius Cursor is my own invention, and I enjoyed writing him. The world of literature needs fewer goodies and baddies, and a lot more interesting grey characters, I feel. The bad guy, the unnamed Pompeian tribune, was also my own creation, and he was a later addition to the plot who became all the more central when it became clear that nearly everyone involved was neither hero nor villain.

I made a number of notes as I wrote which I wanted to address here, but several of them are pretty much the same thing, so I will give a blanket nod in their direction. More than once I took a series of passages, in Caesar's own version of the tale, and compressed them. There was an exchange of letters with Cicero, for instance. Brundisium dragged out for some time. The cavalry campaigns across the Sicoris went on interminably. But these are stretches of the same thing going on for many days, and would be rather tedious to read, so I took the liberty of editing them out.

Toward the start, when Caesar sends his men south in secret from Ravenna, Plutarch has them move under a man called Hortensius. I have unashamedly replaced him with Salvius Cursor. Mea Culpa. And I am unrepentant. In Ilerda, when there are so many conflicting calls within the enemy camp, I have extrapolated the division in command from a few small comments into something more major. There does, to my mind, have to be more to it than a series of arguments, else those two officers, who were both eminently qualified veterans, would have made Caesar fight for control of Hispania much harder.

I have given my own slant on the bridges and ford at Ilerda. There is plenty of description of these events in the sources, but precious little explanation. I have tried to take the descriptions of Ilerda's bridges and ford and make them make sense in terms of both strategy and topography. There is no physical evidence remaining of any of them. I have also shuffled the distances involved here and there between bridges and camps to make sense of a bewildering array of largely uninteresting information. Once more I hold up my hands. Mea Culpa. Better to write an interesting novel that includes much fact than a blow by blow account of the war that includes a yawn a minute. And I have never knowingly changed history beyond shuffling a few days or a few miles to make things more sensible.

In fact, when it comes to Ilerda, reading Caesar's account, there is little clear reason for much of what he does. It is, as I said before, somewhat bewildering. It all looks reasonable until you try and reconstruct the great man's words in the face of geography, at which point I tear out what little hair I have. This, to my mind, suggests that much or all of this source material was probably not written by Caesar but by one of his close colleagues – possibly Hirtius, who likely wrote the last book of the Gallic Wars. Caesar in his Gallic Wars tends to be much more revealing. The burning of the Ilerda granary is my own addition to the tale to add a little motivation to what follows. Again, I am unrepentant. I write novels, not textbooks.

I moved the second naval battle of Massilia by a few days in order not to ruin the flow of the story. In truth, the battle actually happened before the capitulation of the forces at Ilerda, but it fit the story much better to move it a couple of days and made no great historical difference. Oh, and I moved the centre of action for Brutus' second victory from the town of Tauroentum to somewhere closer to Massilia on the way because the idea of describing a forty mile sea chase before the battle makes me yawn, so there's not much hope for the reader. Similarly, Ahenobarbus had seemingly fled Massilia just before Caesar arrived (though the storm winds did happen and the two ships did turn back to port.) But I felt it would be robbing the reader of a satisfactory conclusion if the man had just gone without it being part of the tale.

For reference, at the siege of Massilia, the burning of the siege works is put forth by Caesar as the enemy being devious and untrustworthy and breaking the truce. Interestingly (and the basis for my attack at the tower with Salvius) Cassius Dio tells a different tale, making their attack a response to a push by the Caesarian forces. I liked this idea and went with it.

There is a wealth of scholarly material to peruse over this year, and all of Caesar's life. As always, I primarily used Caesar's campaign records, with additional comedy material by Plutarch and Cassius Dio. But there are more modern writings that deserve a mention. Adrian Goldsworthy. Pat Southern and Tom Holland form a core to my understanding, while Leonard Curchin's book on Roman Hispania and, perhaps surprisingly, the Les Voyages d'Alix book on Massalia/Massilia aided my understanding of the regions and towns involved. There are many others, of course, but these are the core.

I would like to take a moment to thank in particular the wonderful Jona Lendering who maintains Livius.org. Jona solved a problem I had with the timing and dates of the campaign and pointed me in the direction of further material.

Finally, before I sign off and consider moving to the 2nd century AD to pick up the story of young Rufinus in Praetorian 3, I would like to note that Fronto will be back in Marius' Mules XI next year. I am always faintly surprised when I read a review of the latest Marius' Mules book to see so many people being sad that the series has ended. It hasn't. I suspect when I conclude the series on book 15, people will review and tell me how much they're looking forward to the next one.

Heh heh heh.

Until then, Vale, my friends.

Simon Turney

23rd May 2017.

If you enjoyed Marius' Mules X, please do leave a review online, and also checkout another great book that was also released this month:

Legionary: Empire of Shades

By Gordon Doherty

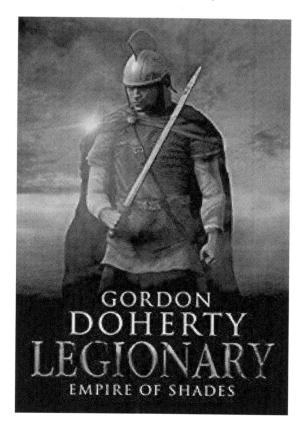

379 AD: Thracia has fallen to the Gothic horde... With the ashes of Adrianople still swirling in the air, the Eastern Roman Empire is in turmoil. The emperor is dead, the throne lies empty and the remaining fragments of the army are few and scattered. Numerius Vitellius Pavo, now Tribunus of the XI Claudia, tries to hold his patchwork ranks together amid the storm. One of the few legions to have survived the disaster at Adrianople, the Claudia do

what they can to keep alive the dying flame of hope. When word spreads of a new Eastern Emperor, those hopes rise. But the coming of this leader will stir the Gothic War to new heights. And it will cast Pavo headlong into the sights of the one responsible for the East's plight – a man mighty and seemingly untouchable, and one who will surely crush any who dares to challenge him. From the ashes of Adrianople, new heroes will rise... with dark ghosts in close pursuit.

Printed in Great Britain
by Amazon